REALM of THIEVES

TITLES BY KARINA HALLE

DARK FANTASY, GOTHIC & HORROR ROMANCE

Darkhouse (EIT #1)

Red Fox (EIT #2)

The Benson (EIT #2.5)

Dead Sky Morning (EIT #3)

Lying Season (EIT #4)

On Demon Wings (EIT #5)

Old Blood (EIT #5.5)

The Dex Files (EIT #5.7)

Into the Hollow (EIT #6)

And with Madness Comes the Light (EIT #6.5)

Come Alive (EIT #7)

Ashes to Ashes (EIT #8)

Dust to Dust (EIT #9)

Ghosted (EIT #9.5)

Came Back Haunted (EIT #10)

The Devil's Metal (The Devil's Duology #1)

The Devil's Reprise (The Devil's Duology #2)

Veiled (Ada Palomino #1)

Song for the Dead (Ada Palomino #2)

Black Sunshine (The Dark Eyes Duet Book #1)

The Blood Is Love (The Dark Eyes Duet Book #2)

Nightwolf

Blood Orange (The Dracula Duet #1)

Black Rose (The Dracula Duet #2)

A Ship of Bones and Teeth

Ocean of Sin and Starlight

Hollow (A Gothic Shade of Romance #1)

Legend (A Gothic Shade of Romance #2)

Grave Matter

Nocturne

Realm of Thieves (Thieves of Dragemor #1)

CONTEMPORARY ROMANCE

Love, in English/Love, in Spanish
Where Sea Meets Sky
Racing the Sun
The Pact
The Offer
The Play
Winter Wishes
The Lie
The Debt
Smut
Heat Wave
Before I Ever Met You
After All
Rocked Up
Wild Card (Night Ridge #1)
Maverick (Night Ridge #2)
Hot Shot (Night Ridge #3)
Bad at Love
The Swedish Prince (Nordic Royals #1)
The Wild Heir (Nordic Royals #2)
A Nordic King (Nordic Royals #3)
The Royal Rogue (Nordic Royals #4)
Nothing Personal
My Life in Shambles
The Forbidden Man
The One That Got Away
Lovewrecked
One Hot Italian Summer
All the Love in the World (Anthology)
The Royals Next Door
The Royals Upstairs

ROMANTIC SUSPENSE

Sins and Needles (The Artists Trilogy #1)
On Every Street (An Artists Trilogy
Novella #0.5)
Shooting Scars (The Artists Trilogy #2)
Bold Tricks (The Artists Trilogy #3)
Dirty Angels (Dirty Angels #1)
Dirty Deeds (Dirty Angels #2)
Dirty Promises (Dirty Angels #3)
Black Hearts (Sins Duet #1)
Dirty Souls (Sins Duet #2)
Discretion (Dumonts #1)
Disarm (Dumonts #2)
Disavow (Dumonts #3)

REALM of THIEVES

KARINA HALLE

ACE
NEW YORK

ACE
Published by Berkley
An imprint of Penguin Random House LLC
1745 Broadway, New York, NY 10019
penguinrandomhouse.com

Copyright © 2025 by Karina Halle
Penguin Random House values and supports copyright. Copyright fuels creativity, encourages diverse voices, promotes free speech, and creates a vibrant culture. Thank you for buying an authorized edition of this book and for complying with copyright laws by not reproducing, scanning, or distributing any part of it in any form without permission. You are supporting writers and allowing Penguin Random House to continue to publish books for every reader. Please note that no part of this book may be used or reproduced in any manner for the purpose of training artificial intelligence technologies or systems.

ACE is a registered trademark and the A colophon is a trademark of
Penguin Random House LLC.

Book design and title page illustration by Jenni Surasky
Interior art: Dragon Egg © A_Zys / Shutterstock
Map: © David Lindroth Inc.

Library of Congress Cataloging-in-Publication Data

Names: Halle, Karina, author.
Title: Realm of thieves / Karina Halle.
Description: First edition. | New York : Ace, 2025.
Identifiers: LCCN 2024045493 (print) | LCCN 2024045494 (ebook) |
ISBN 9780593819821 (trade paperback) | ISBN 9780593819838 (ebook)
Subjects: LCGFT: Fantasy fiction. | Romance fiction. | Novels.
Classification: LCC PR9199.4.H356239 R43 2025 (print) |
LCC PR9199.4.H356239 (ebook) | DDC 813/.6—dc23/eng/20241001
LC record available at https://lccn.loc.gov/2024045493
LC ebook record available at https://lccn.loc.gov/2024045494

First Edition: June 2025

Printed in the United States of America
1st Printing

The authorized representative in the EU for product safety and compliance is
Penguin Random House Ireland, Morrison Chambers, 32 Nassau Street,
Dublin D02 YH68, Ireland, https://eu-contact.penguin.ie.

For my mother, Tuuli

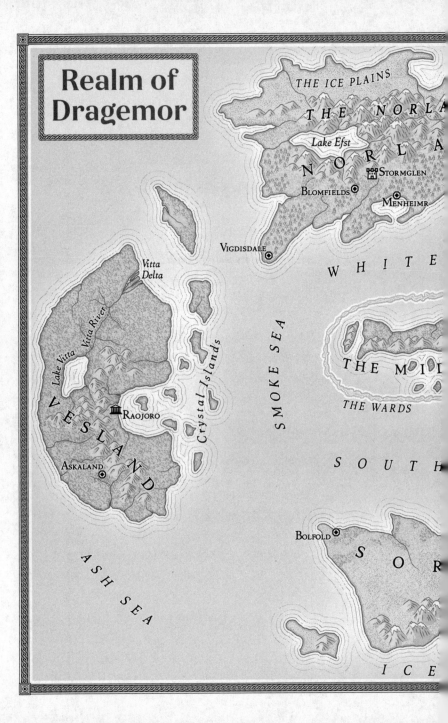

Glossary

<u>S</u>yndikat A cartel or mafia family

<u>S</u>jef Head of a specific Syndikat

<u>R</u>odegiver Third-in-command of a Syndikat; Master of Coin

<u>S</u>uen The magical substance inside the yolk of a dragon egg that gives humans (and some animals) special powers when ingested

<u>T</u>he <u>B</u>lack <u>G</u>uard The military of Esland

<u>T</u>he <u>F</u>reelanders Exiles from Esland who live in freedom in The Banished Land

<u>T</u>he <u>D</u>aughters of <u>S</u>ilence A convent

<u>T</u>he <u>R</u>eckoning of <u>F</u>lames The prophecy in which the world will return to the dragons

The Power Players

House Kolbeck of Norland Norland is a rainy, mountainous (Pacific Northwest–type) land and is divided into five relatively peaceful kingdoms, with House Kolbeck servicing each one in the dragon trade. Kolbeck is run by the powerful and cold Torsten Kolbeck, along with his shifty brother and his studious eldest son. The hero of *Realm of Thieves*—Andor Kolbeck—is the black sheep of the family. He desires more power within the syndikat but is constantly blocked by his disdaining uncle, while his own father sees Andor's hotheadedness and disorganized personality as a fatal flaw.

House Dalgaard of Sorland Bitter rivals of the Kolbecks. House Dalgaard is a vicious syndikat that is partially controlled by the Kingdom of Sorland, which is the oldest Kingdom in the world. Dalgaard is comprised of three brothers who run the syndikat—a set of twins and an older brother—and they aren't afraid to get violent to get what they want.

House Haugen of Vesland Though not as powerful as the other two syndikats, House Haugen has still amassed great power and controls the suen trade in the West. This family is controlled by women, and the land of Vesland itself is a fertile, tropical climate that supplies food to the other realms year-round.

The Saints of Fire The dragon-worshipping religious cult that controls the eastern realm of Esland. Followers believe that in the Reckoning of Flames the wards will fall and the dragons will spare them thanks to their sacrificial offerings (human and otherwise)—while incinerating the rest of humanity. They believe the Saints of

GLOSSARY

Fire will rule the world at the dragons' side. The derogatory term "Soffer" (Saints of Fire follower) is often used to refer to members.

THE DRAGONS Trapped on the Midlands, a narrow, volcanic island in the middle of the ocean, the dragons are contained by magical wards . . . for now. Their eggs imbue humans with magical powers, but only the most reckless—or desperate—dare to make the journey through the spooky, unforgivable terrain to steal eggs on behalf of the syndikats.

> **SYCLEDRAGE** Clever and cunning dragons, sycledrages have no wings and are similar in size to an ostrich, with sickle claws on their feet that can slice a human in half. They lay ostrich-egg sized eggs.
>
> **ELDERDRAGE** These are the second-largest dragons—about the size of a *T. rex* with a 30-foot wingspan. Their eggs are also large: at least 2–3 feet tall.
>
> **BLOODDRAGE** Fast and winged, these cat-sized dragons drink blood. Their eggs are not much larger than a chicken egg.
>
> **DEATHDRAGE** At 40 feet long, these are the largest type of dragon, with the largest eggs (3–4 feet tall). Deathdrages are very rare.
>
> **SLANGEDRAGE** Only rumored to exist, these 2-headed dragons measure up to 20 feet long, and are said to lay eggs similar in size to sycledrages'.

History of Dragemor and the Egg Trade

A LONG, LONG TIME AGO THE WORLD OF DRAGEMOR WAS A WORLD FOR dragons. Humans lived in the polar regions of ice and snow, their civilization restricted to the cold where dragons didn't tread. Over the centuries, however, people got tired of being subservient to these dragons, cowering in fear in the most inhospitable places on the planet. Slowly they began to infiltrate the rest of the world.

But the dragons were fierce beasts that could not be ignored or tamed. They preyed upon people, and when they weren't hunting them and eating them, they were roasting them alive (just for fun). It seemed impossible that people could ever thrive alongside the dragons. They were powerful beasts that would wipe out every human if they could.

But then a man disappeared into a dragon's lair—and resurfaced years later, armed with magic. He used his newfound powers to coax all the dragons to the remote, volcanic island of Midlands and put up magical wards around it, forever confining the dragons at the center of the world.

With the wards in place, civilization was finally able to thrive. Three continents—Sorland, Norland, and Vesland—were conquered by humans, while the dragons remained contained safely in the Midlands. Only the easterly realm of Esland remained uninhabited because of its harsh, unforgiving terrain and desert climate.

The dragon threat was neutralized (for the time being), and soon enough on Sorland, a passionate group of people assembled, calling themselves the Saints of Fire. Led by Cappus Zoreth, a man who saw himself as a messiah, the Saints of Fire believed that the dragons were gods and that it was wrong to imprison them. Zoreth had the gift of sight and saw a future where the dragons would eventually be set free under his own power. Zoreth believed that if they ensured the dragons were treated with dignity, worshipped, and revered, in the end the dragons would spare their lives. While this group got traction, fighting for the dragons' well-being and freedom, they were ultimately ostracized and banished to Esland, where they began sending sacrifices to the Midlands for the dragons.

Somewhere along the line, intrepid explorers from the other lands visited the Midlands hoping to capture a dragon to use for war purposes. They were unsuccessful and many died in these raids, but they did stumble upon a discovery that would shape the world. People realized that if you ate a dragon's egg, a component inside it called the *suen* would manifest in your body in various magical ways. Different types of eggs translated into different types of power and magic. There's even been talk of a dragon's egg that grants immortality, though those eggs have yet to be found (but *have* become the most desired bounty, since immortality may be the only way for civilization to ever survive if the wards come down). Although consuming dragons' eggs is illegal since the governments fear citizens ever coming into magic and power (especially since once you have acquired magic from suen, you're able to pass it down to your children), an extremely lucrative egg trade developed. Powerful families in each of the realms started their own *syndikats* and now control the egg supply and process the suen into potions.

Each syndikat has a different way of operating, but will either have one of their main family members going to the Midlands with a crew of egg stealers or completely hire out the task. Both methods are risky because the former puts the powerful families at direct risk, and the latter can and often does mean that the workers hired for the job may steal the eggs (or consume them) for their own gain. Not to mention, only the most reckless—or desperate—thieves are willing to risk the journey . . .

REALM of THIEVES

Prologue

They gave the girl a new name when they first brought her into the convent, discarding her old one like an oily rag that dirties more than it cleans. "Daughter of Pain," the ancient woman had christened her with a quick sweep of cataracted eyes. "I see it deep within you, even the pain you haven't yet faced."

The girl didn't give a damn what the woman saw. Pain? She felt only rage at that point, a living and breathing vessel of anger that had been simmering to toxic levels ever since her parents died. But that wasn't what the Harbringer saw as the girl was brought into the Great Hall of Zoreth on the first day of her initiation. She saw the physical pain in the girl's body. Not just the fury and the grief and frustration at a life being shattered to fragments—every Daughter of Silence was suffering, after all—but the pain that was deeper inside yet, waiting to come out when she became a woman. A pain that would debilitate the girl and lead her on a desperate quest for relief, a quest that would combine with vengeance.

But at that moment, as the girl was stripped of her old name and her clothes and put into the black cloak that covered every inch of her skin, her eyebrows and her head shaved, her lavender hair discarded in spools on the marble floor, the last proof of what she was, a girl born under the lavender moon, there was only that slithering, seething rage.

All the girl's life her parents had fought against this very institution. They fought against the cruelty of the convent, the hypocrisy of the religion itself, the dictatorship that ruled over the Saints of Fire and those who followed it. Indeed the people of Esland had no choice but to follow it. They told the girl that she could not help being born in Esland but that they would spend every living minute trying to change it for the better.

Her parents did their best to change it. But their best was not enough.

They should have known this would happen to me, the girl thought as the old woman took her roughly by the elbow and led her out of the cleansing room and back into the quiet halls. *They should have known that all their risks for a better tomorrow would land me here one day.*

The towering obsidian walls and ceilings around her gleamed from frequent polishing, making it look like the girl was being led into the dark belly of a dragon, which was no accident. The convent wanted to instill fear into these girls. They were here to be punished, not to be pious. Punishment was always the point of the Daughters of Silence, no matter how their public façade spun it.

The girl shut her eyes as the image of her father's last moments slammed into her head, as if that would prevent her from seeing it. Him standing on the gallows block. The defiant look in his emerald eyes, his long dark purple-streaked braid captured by the wind that held the decay of low tide that stretched outside the city walls of the capital. He was so proud even in those last moments, except for that very last moment when he looked to the girl and her mother, who had been captured by the Black Guard and forced to watch at the foot of

REALM of THIEVES 3

the gallows. In that split second the girl didn't see defiance or anger or even fear. Just sorrow. Like he was cloaked in the grief he knew would befall his two most beloved people after he took his last breath.

And she watched him take his last breath. Watched as the bottom dropped out from under his feet, as it dropped from beneath everything she held dear, and as that rope winched up and sliced into his throat and chin. Her father didn't cry out, didn't thrash, like he was willing his body to go as silently as possible. And while her mother wailed and buried her head in her hands, the girl kept watching, knowing that the twelve years she had with him in her life wouldn't be enough and to take every last glimpse of him, no matter how gruesome, even if the image would be burned in her head for years to come.

"You should be afraid," the Harbringer had whispered in her ear, her breath smelling foul, like the fermented herbs that the cloisters burned at all hours of the day. "You must fear the gods or you will live and die in vain."

The girl opened her eyes at that, feeling just a thread of the defiance that her father wore so well. She saw the statues of the dragons before her, their so-called gods. There were two carved of the smaller varieties, the sycledrages that were known to be as smart as a dune fox, with sickle claws on their monstrous feet. The woman thought her eyes were closed because of them, but it couldn't be further from the truth. The girl didn't fear dragons, not in the ways the Saints of Fire followers did. Her fear was healthy; their fear was not. Their fear would ruin all Esland one day, if not the world.

"We must stop them," her father had once said to her as they sat side by side on the edge of the docks, cleaning the kelp crabs he'd caught for dinner. He kept his voice low, knowing that there were few allies, even among the impoverished fishermen such as himself. "If we don't, I fear it will be the end of the world as we know it."

The girl remembered pondering that as her legs dangled above the clear blue water, her fingers green with the crabs' blood. To her there was no other world than Esland. She'd barely seen the land beyond the capital. Once, her father had taken her on the boat along the south coast to check out new fishing grounds, and she was able to take in as much of Esland as she ever could. It was dry, desolate, and inhospitable, but the girl found something so imaginative and dramatic about the sandstone cliffs above the bright blue water, the rolling hills that huddled behind the convent that she would later be imprisoned in and the sparse desert beneath, the far-off peak of the dormant volcano that pierced the cloudless sky, a symbol of the Banished Land to the south. The fact that there was a world beyond this one was hard to comprehend, especially when Eslanders weren't allowed to leave their continent to visit any of the other three realms, and outsiders were rarely let in.

"What will happen to the world?" the girl had asked. She'd often heard her parents talking about the end, but so did the followers. They were obsessed with it. The devout called it the Reckoning of Flames, and they believed that one day Zoreth would return to their world and release the dragons that were confined inside the magicked wards that surrounded the Midlands island in the center of the ocean. They believed that the centuries that they had been feeding the dragons with their supply of rockdeer (and the lowly human sacrifices) would mean the dragons would spare them but incinerate the rest of humanity, ensuring that the Saints of Fire would be the rulers of the world with dragons at their side.

But her father, and those in the rebellion, had a more horrifying vision of the future.

He had looked around at the other fishermen on the docks, wincing at the unrelenting sun, and once satisfied they weren't listening, he leaned in close to her. "The wards will collapse in my lifetime, if not yours," he whispered, never one to hold back the truth. "Not because of Zoreth. He's dead. He's not coming back. They'll collapse because this government will have enough magic to destroy those wards. But the people of Esland will not be spared like they think. Dragons aren't sentimental."

Strangely the girl didn't feel terrified then about the end, and she didn't feel terrified now, even as she was led toward her chambers in the depths of the convent. If anything she welcomed the dragons' return. Anything was better than living a life of silence, under rules she'd been taught to break, while both her parents were dead.

The old woman brought the girl to a stop outside a big black door and knocked on it with her bony hands, hard as stone. She waited a beat and then opened it.

Inside was a row of twelve beds, each one sparsely covered with a thin pillow and rough bedspread. At the foot of each bed was a preteen girl on the cusp of womanhood, each scalp shaved, body cloaked in black, head bowed and attention on the floor.

"Daughters of the Sixth Ward," the woman said. "I want you to meet the Daughter of Pain. She will be joining us for eternity."

The girl wouldn't have spoken even if she had been allowed to; still, she found it disconcertingly eerie how silent the room was. How unnatural all of this was. The Daughters didn't even take a vow of silence; it was an order thrust upon them. They weren't allowed to whisper to each other when alone, let alone cry, and the girl suddenly felt so stifled by it all that she longed to scream.

The old woman poked a long sharp nail into her side, anticipating this. "Behave yourself and you'll endure your pain with dignity. Rebel and the rest of your life will be a living damnation."

You don't know who my parents are, the girl thought bitterly, though the irony was that of course she did. That was why she was here. But the Harbringer didn't know how deep their rebellion lived in her veins.

So the girl would be silent for now. She would bite her tongue and plot and wait and find the perfect time to let it all loose. She would find one moment to gain her freedom or she would die trying.

That much she knew.

Chapter 1

Brynla

"This is as far as I'll take you," the man says. His voice is as gnarled and rough as his hands that grip the oars.

I stare at his pockmarked face for a moment, my stomach pinching with unease at the thought of this mission going even remotely wrong.

"This wasn't what we agreed upon," I say. Beside me Lemi shifts on his haunches, casting a wary eye at the boatsman.

"I said I'd take you to Fjallen Rock," the man says, and nods past me at the hazy shape of land shrouded by smoke in the distance, backlit by the orange glow of the Midland volcanoes. "That's it right there."

I give him a tight smile. I don't want to start arguing with my only ride back to Esland and a stranger at that. "You know I meant past the wards."

"You should have been more specific, then, girl," he says, eyes narrowing. "Because that's not what you said. There's no law against coming this far. There is a law against going through the wards and to the Midlands."

"The last boatsman—" I begin.

"Your last boatsman is no more," he says, flashing me a smile of missing teeth. "Otherwise you wouldn't be using me now, would ya?" His salt-crusted lips curl into a smirk.

I live more in each second of the day than you'll ever live in your lifetime, I think as I try not to scowl at him. It's hard for me to rein in my temper, but tonight I don't have the luxury of letting it loose. I'm about to be dropped off at the most dangerous place in the world and I'm counting on this asshole here to pick me up. If he doesn't, my dog and I are as good as dead.

"Also, most boatsmen wouldn't allow a hound on the vessel," he says, eyeing Lemi, who eyes him right back. "You're fortunate I'm such an animal lover."

I roll my eyes at that. On the two-hour boat journey he's done nothing but try to spear every turtle, dolphin, and whale that's come in passing distance.

I take in a deep breath to quell my mounting frustration, hoping I can reason with him. "But if you don't go through the wards and bring the boat to shore, how am I supposed to come back with the egg?"

"That sounds like a you problem, not a me problem," he huffs and sits back, crossing his arms until I get the point.

I sigh. It *is* my problem, and I don't have the luxury of trying to figure out a solution with him. My plan was to be dropped off at the rock and, if I was lucky, I'd find an elderdrage nest. If not I'd head farther in to the other islands. But elderdrage eggs are at least three feet tall and they weigh a ton. It's hard enough to carry them back across the rugged land and then swim them over to the boat, even with Lemi's help.

Which means that now I'll have to find either sycledrage or blooddrage eggs, and both are significantly smaller and harder to find in an unattended nest, let alone any nest at all.

But going back to the Banished Land empty-handed isn't an option either. I need to come back home with something or I might be paying for it with my own blood. I've been too sick over the last few moons to come to the Midlands, so I already owe Sorland's syndikat, and they aren't the types to let a few absences go. Not only that, but the faster I get my coin, the faster I can hire a healer so that my monthly pains don't continue to take me out of the game. I swear every month, every year, the pain gets worse, like it's some punishment for being both a woman and alive. Even surgery from the discredited doctors in the Dark City costs more than I have saved so far.

Lemi lets out a *whumpf* of air through his nose, bringing my focus back to him. Of course more money would pay for more food for him and for my aunt Ellestra.

Staying alive is infinitely expensive.

"Fine," I say to the boatsman, hating how right he is. My last boatsman disappeared while I'd been recuperating. People disappear all the time in Esland, especially those who have dealings with the Freelanders—the exiled such as myself—and the more likely you are to visit the Banished Land, the more likely it is that you are an unsavory character to begin with. My last boatsman might have been knifed during a card game gone wrong, or he might have been captured by the Black Guard and taken to the capital for execution. If it was the latter, they would know he'd been helping a Freelander steal dragon eggs to sell to House Dalgaard, Sorland's syndikat, which means they'd be looking for me.

But they've been looking for me for the last nine years, ever since I escaped the convent. And, somehow, I'm still here.

"Promise me you'll be here when I get back," I implore the new boatsman. It's awful having to put your trust in someone you don't even know.

"I'll have to be if I want my egg," he says casually, splaying his calloused hands.

I swallow hard, still unsure if I'm making the right choice. I'm always paid handsomely for the services I render, often based on what eggs I end up stealing. If I don't, I'll be left behind. Another reason I can't come back to the mainland empty-handed tonight.

"I don't know how long I'll be," I tell him, glancing up at the dark sky. It's the cycle of the pink moon, the crescent shape barely visible through the smoke from the volcanoes. Pink moon dragon eggs are mellower than the others, much like humans born under it, but beggars can't be choosers in this case. Some people prefer the softer side effects that come with consumption of pink moon eggs, though the Sjef, the head of the syndikat, Ruunon Dalgaard, would scoff at that. The syndikat is the opposite of soft.

"You bring me the finest and the strongest eggs," Ruunon had said to me the one and only time I'd met him. It had been a heavily guarded clandestine meeting on the blackened lava fields outside the Dark City. "You do this consistently, and we will have a fine partnership."

So much was implied with what he didn't say. That if I didn't, then he'd kill me, Lemi, my aunt, and anyone else I knew. That was the way the syndikats worked. I had never met any of the other houses from Vesland or Norland and their crime families, despite how regularly their hired thieves pilfered the Midlands, but I imagined they all operated in the same way. With ruthlessness and violence and aversion to mercy.

But at that moment, when Ruunon offered me the job, I felt the first taste of hope since my father had died. It was dangerous to work for such men, but the promise that came along with it, the promise of a better life, sealed the deal.

"I'll leave at dawn," the boatsman says gruffly. "I'll be here until then. You don't show, I'll assume you're dead and you'll be left in my wake. And no, I won't give the dog a ride back even if he makes it."

I try not to narrow my eyes at him. "I'll see you before dawn," I tell him before I say the wrong thing. Then I look to Lemi. "You okay with a night swim?" I ask him as I gather my empty bags and tie them to the holsters and straps around my leathered armor.

Lemi just wags his tail eagerly, knowing his fun is about to begin.

"Now don't go disappearing on me. You'll be towing me to shore," I warn my dog, adjusting my two swords on my back, thankful that they're made from ash glass forged in the depths of the Banished Land, weapons as light as they are strong.

Lemi seems to frown at that, his fluffy brows furrowing over his warm brown eyes.

I stand up, the boat rocking back and forth from my weight, and give the man one last glance, willing him to be here until dawn and not either chicken out or sell me out. Then I take a deep breath, preparing myself for the half-mile swim, and swan dive overboard.

Despite my armor and swords, I barely make a splash, the dark, frigid water engulfing me. I take in a harsh gasp of air as I surface, just as Lemi lands in the water beside me. Shivering already, I manage to swim over to him, grabbing ahold of his harness with stiff fingers. I hear the man on the boat chuckle behind me but I don't bother paying him any attention now. All I can do is hope he'll be there when I get back. Focus on getting the goods and getting back before the sun rises.

Lemi pulls me through the water with ease, though I can tell he just wants to shift himself onto the shore already. "Easy, boy," I warn him. He's shifted before while I've been holding on to him and it's most unpleasant. Even though I don't end up traveling with him, there is a bone-rattling shock as I'm left behind and he shifts elsewhere.

Thankfully the wards are close now. They're nearly invisible to the naked eye, save for the faint glimmer of rainbows when you look at them from your peripheral vision. In the dark they're harder to see but you still feel them, the faint hum and vibration of energy they give off, eons of magic condensed, a warning to those who may have strayed off path. A warning that would work on anyone else except for me and any other egg thieves.

The wards are magicked walls that extend to the bottom of the ocean and high into the farthest reaches of the sky. In the Old Text of Dragemor, the First Sorcerer—Magni—said it was akin to a dome, one that would prevent any dragon from escaping, whether they swam to the inky depths or tried to soar into the stars above.

The dragons can't get out, but *we* can go in.

And, with any luck, come back out again.

I instinctively hold my breath as Lemi swims through the wards. They're about as thick as a window pane and my skin prickles with heat as we push to the other side. The water is as warm as the air on this side of the barrier, the atmosphere heavy with smoke. There are three active volcanoes along the Red Rift that snakes across the belly of the Midlands like a gaping wound, and depending on which way the winds are blowing, your visibility can be close to zero. At the moment the wind is pushing the volcanic fumes my way, so as soon as we reach shore I'll have to wear a mask in order to breathe properly. Just another punishing feature of this forsaken land for those who dare to tread it.

The shore feels far away this time, the craggy features of the small island of Fjallen Rock hidden in the grimy haze. There are times I think the Midlands and its austere and terrifying geography can be quite beautiful, in the same way a dragon can be beautiful. But you're always aware of the danger. Of how feeble and useless you are in comparison. The Midlands and the beasts that fly above it dole out death without second thought.

But that's why I have Lemi. I couldn't do this without him. The other thieves who pilfer the Midlands have heightened abilities and powers thanks to their egg consumption, senses that may help them find the precious commodities and fight back against dragon attacks.

REALM of THIEVES

I have no powers except my dog and years of training with the best fighters of the Banished Land.

Now as we're getting close to shore, Lemi swims faster. While the eggs—and more specifically, the suen compound that's extracted from them—don't work on me for reasons I still don't understand, they do work on Lemi. He's stronger and faster than any dog ought to be, plus he has the ability to shift through time and space, as long as it's to a place he can see or a place he's already been to. The moment my boots reach the sharp rocks of the seafloor I let go of his harness and he immediately disappears in front of me. One moment he's here, the next he's vanished into thin air, with only a faint whiff of his warm doggy smell left behind.

He quickly reappears farther down the coast, his giant black body blending in with the lava-sculpted shoreline, his head down to the ground, sniffing for our prize. I let out a sigh of quiet relief and keep my eyes on him as I stagger out of the water and onto land. I should have stopped worrying about him years ago after he proved no dragon could catch him, but even so, I watch him like a hawk.

It's only for a little while, I tell myself, though I feel the bitterness on my tongue. All those *one more time*s and *soon I can stop*s and *almost there*s and *not long now*s have melted into chains of hope that keep me fastened to this trade.

The existence of tomorrow is more intoxicating than any drug.

I want to call out to Lemi so that he doesn't go too far, but now that I'm on land, I don't want to attract any attention to myself. Instead I pull up my mask from around my neck so that it covers my nose and mouth. It's wet but that makes it easier to breathe, and in no time I'll be completely dry, with the heat and the winds the way they are.

I start walking along the coast, the seawater squishing in my boots, keeping an eye on Lemi while minding my step among the sharp rocks. Occasionally a rock will move and charred legs will appear—a lava crab that scatters back into the dark sea. If I felt more optimistic about tonight's hunt, I'd spear the crab and take it back home with me because they're my aunt's favorite dish and she's been doing all the cooking as of late. But now that my plan has changed, the less I have to carry with me, the better.

Lemi is still visible, though he's getting farther and farther away. I've always had unnaturally good eyesight, and the constant eruptions from the distant volcanos of the Midlands illuminate the sky in an orange glow, but even so he's getting harder to spot.

An image of my mother flashes across my mind, as it always does whenever I step foot in these dragon lands. The scene is of the last time I saw her, at the front of the square ship, the lone person at the helm with five hundred rockdeer packed behind her. Though I grew up in the capital I had never seen what happened every moon at Sacrifice Bay on the outskirts of the city of Lerick. I always thought the deer would be bleating, terrified at being herded onto the long, wide boat, but what struck me was the silence. It's like they knew their only purpose in life was to end up as dragon food.

The silence extended to my mother. She had the same look in her eyes as the sacrificial deer, as if she always knew her purpose would come to this, to be used as a pawn for a religion of sycophants and hypocrites. She stared directly at me while the Black Guard held me in place at the front of the crowd, forced to watch, just as they forced me to watch my father's execution, and then with a lingering look that I still can't seem to decipher to this day, she turned around and steered the boat toward the very land I'm standing on now.

Both of my parents were so elegant and poised when facing their death. I fear that when my time comes, their composure will not have been passed on to me.

I sigh and shake my head, clearing the memory before my attention goes to Lemi again.

I freeze.

My heart thundering in my throat.

Lemi is gone.

And in his place is a dark-cloaked figure standing at the end of the shore.

I'm not alone here.

Chapter 2

Brynla

I blink just as the wind shifts and the haze clears a little, trying to make out the figure standing in the distance. I pull down my mask, as if that will help me concentrate better, and squint, while my other hand reaches over my shoulder and pulls out one of the swords, the ash glass sliding silently. There's no doubt the dark figure has seen me, but even so, I don't want any noise to attract the dragons and definitely not before I've found their nest.

Has to be another thief, I think, slowly walking forward toward them, wincing at the sound of my boots crunching on a dead crab and blackened barnacles. But the Norland and Vesland syndikats have their thieves landing on the north and west sides of the Midlands. I always come from the east. There's no chance that any of them could have traveled this way, at least not by land. So either this person is from another syndikat and has come by boat to the east side or . . .

Or perhaps Ruunon hired someone else while I've been out sick. Perhaps this person is my replacement. Perhaps I'm being watched to see how well I do.

To see if I fail.

The skin on my neck prickles. Whether this person is meant to replace me or whether they're part of an enemy cartel, I don't think they mean to let me live. Coming across them was no accident. They wanted me to see them.

This isn't good.

I stop just as movement comes from my right and Lemi suddenly appears out of the air, his tongue hanging out from the heat but otherwise looking unharmed. I quickly glance back to the mystery figure but they're gone.

Vanished.

There's no one there at all.

"What in damnation?" I whisper, looking around quickly for the missing intruder. "Lemi, did you see that?"

I know Lemi doesn't understand most English but that doesn't stop me from talking to him like he does.

Then another, even more terrible thought comes to me. Did that person see Lemi shift? Shifting dogs aren't normal as far as I know, and if any of the other syndikats find out that he's instrumental in finding dragon eggs, he'll end up the target, not just me.

I reach back and draw out another sword for good measure, gripping them tightly as I start walking toward where the figure was. I know I need to concentrate on finding the nests, but I'm not sure how I'm going to do that now with someone else here.

I glance out at the ocean, wishing the haze would clear. I can't see the boat past the wards, but I don't know if it's because of how far away it is or that the fog is obscuring it . . .

Or if it's gone. Maybe the bastard already up and left me. And if he didn't, I'm starting to think that maybe paying the guy and just getting a ride back to Esland without the eggs might be the best course of action for me. I'll figure out what to do with the Dalgaard syndikat later.

Lemi lets out a huff of air from his nose, his long floppy ears now pricked straight up in the air like a fox's. He's caught a scent.

"Lemi," I whisper to him, "Lemi, stay."

But Lemi doesn't listen once he's gotten the scent. At least he knows enough not to shift so that I can follow him, but even so, he's off and running away from the shore.

I sigh heavily, adjusting the swords in my hands. He's heading in across the middle of the rock, which is thankfully more level. I scramble up the sharp and craggy cliff until I'm on top and then take off after him. I keep looking around me as I go, trying to see where that person could have gone, not wanting any surprise attacks from behind me or from the sides. So far it looks like I'm alone but I can't trust that. How does someone just disappear like that? Is it possible he was a figment of my imagination? The world here does play tricks on you.

Fjallen Rock is the closest piece of land to the wards, with Esland just over the horizon, which is why I usually get the boats to drop me off here. It's built like a table, with a sharp and undulating coastline that leads up to a steppe. The surface of the steppe is volcanic and mostly flat with large pockets of scarred earth left behind from past explosions and lava flows, and it's in these craters and crevices that the dragons like to lay their eggs.

Usually it's the elderdrage that use this island as their nesting grounds, but occasionally the smaller sycledrages or blooddrages will nest in the craters, especially if some of the elderdrages have moved on. Because the only food the dragons have come in the form of the rockdeer herd that gets delivered once a moon, the larger dragons are known to eat the smaller ones when they're hungry. And those smaller dragons are the ones I need to find right now.

The farther we run across the steppe, the thicker the volcanic fog gets, and I have to pull up my mask in order to breathe, the potent air stinging my eyes and making them tear up. I can feel the sticky trails of the black salve I've applied around my eyes for protection melt into obsidian rivers down my cheeks, gathering in my mask. Sweat pools under my leathered armor and I wish I could take it off, but I have to wear it in case of a dragon attack. While the armor won't protect against the claws of a sycledrage (or a broadsword from an enemy), it is designed to withstand the blast of fire, which is a dragon's first line of defense.

Finally, Lemi stops running and goes totally still, his nose pointed toward the ground, which means he's found a nest. I pray to the universe that it's a nest of blooddrages, which are the smallest, not much larger than a chicken egg, and still pack quite a punch for their size. Also the blooddrages themselves are easier to deal with, as long as there's only a couple of them to fend off.

Suddenly a shadow passes over me and I instinctively drop flat on the ground, not moving an inch, not making a sound even as I land on the hard rock. I don't dare move my head to look but I know that Lemi is doing the same.

Wind from dragon wings blows strands of hair loose from my bun, and the thick air fills with their distinctive scent, the smell of sulfur mixed with something herbaceous that reminds me of the convent. I lie as still as I can. It's probably a dragon keeping an eye on the nest, and from the way it hasn't attacked me yet and the gusts from the wingbeats, I know it's large, probably an elderdrage. The bigger the beast, the easier it is to evade them, so long as you don't make any quick movements or sounds. Their sense of smell and eyesight aren't the best, thankfully.

When the steady *whump whump whump* of the wings fades away, I slowly raise my chin off the ground and crane my neck to see the dragon passing over Lemi, about one hundred feet in the air, continuing on a steady flight toward the Midlands, its extra-long tail trailing behind it like a whip. It lets out a high squawk, one that I now recognize as a warning. It hasn't spotted us but its instincts have it on high alert.

I wait until it disappears into the smoke, and then I quickly get to my feet and hurry over to Lemi, who is now on all fours, his focus on the nest again.

"Good boy," I tell him as I pat his silky head and peer down over into the shallow crater. There are two eggs nestled in the grass and seaweed that the dragons make their nests out of, both over three feet in height and at least a foot at the widest point. Their shells are covered in scales of a light pink color with dark magenta on the edges. They're beautiful, gleaming slightly with iridescence that shines even under such foul skies, which means they're unfertilized and ripe for the taking.

I exhale and wipe my brow with my gauntlet. I can feel time ticking away—the Midlands have a strange way of making it move faster altogether. Once I thought I had been gone an hour but it turned out to be a whole day. The weather behaves unnaturally too. Acidic rain falls up from the ground and into the sky. When the Great Sorcerer Magni first magicked the land to imprison the dragons, it was said the magic altered the way the environment behaved, and I've seen those effects firsthand.

Lemi whines impatiently and gives me a pointed stare, wondering why I'm not taking out my bag and putting an egg inside.

"How will we get it back to the boat?" I ask him, putting a hand on my hip. "You can't tow me with it, and I can't swim in all my gear without some help."

He tilts his head, his tongue lolling out to the side.

"I suppose you could tow me to the boat and then you could shift back for the egg," I muse, tapping a sword along my chin. "That way the boatsman will have to stay for your return."

He seems to nod, and I slide the swords into the sheaths on my back and then step down into the small crater. The bag I carry with me was made by my aunt and is constructed like a net, which means it's light to carry on its own but strong and expands to fit the largest eggs. She used twine enforced with threads of jormungander, a giant

REALM of THIEVES

water snake, scales pilfered from the rivers of Norland. Supposedly, anyway. Since I've never been there, there's no way to verify it, and the Dark City is rife with counterfeit items.

I lay the net flat in the crater and then place my hands on the top of the closest egg, rolling it back and forth carefully until it's in the bag. The shells are tough and leathery, but even so you need to be cautious. A broken egg can spell disaster if you aren't able to rescue the yolk before the air alters its chemistry. I keep a flask on me for just this reason, so I don't have to come back totally empty-handed if the worst happens.

Once the egg is nestled in the bag, I climb back out of the crater and do another quick survey of the barren landscape, looking for the stranger. He's still nowhere in sight. Satisfied that I'm safe for now, I reach down and carefully haul the net out of the crater like my father used to haul up salt trout from the ocean. My muscles strain from the effort, but I push through it and then squat down and up so that I'm carrying the egg on my back, clasping the bag over one shoulder.

Sweat stings my eyes again and I glance tiredly at Lemi. Some days my body is weaker than others, especially when I've had a bad bout of my ailments. This is one of those days. Nothing I can do but accept it and keep going.

"Shall we go?" I ask him.

He snuffs at that, protesting that he wants to hunt more, but I start walking, the bottom of the egg bouncing off my ass with each stride. I go carefully, taking one step at a time across the rugged terrain, ignoring the way my muscles are starting to ache, the way that my armor is sticking to my skin. Perhaps the boatsman is doing me a favor by making me swim all the way back to the boat. I'm burning up.

I'm about a hundred feet away from the nest when the dragon's roar fills the air, so loud that it reverberates in my bones, my heart rattling in its cage.

22   KARINA HALLE

I cry out in surprise, trying to freeze in place, but my toe stubs into the edge of a rock and I'm falling off-balance, twisting to the side, the weight of the egg pulling me backward.

I land on my back, crushing the egg beneath me with a devastating crack, the red yolk spilling out around me like blood, just as the wingbeats from the mother elderdrage fill the air, blowing back my hair and filling my nose with sulfur and spice.

I lift my chin just enough to see her soar down in front of me.

Fuck me.

She's terrifying.

She's glorious.

And she's looking right at me.

She lands just beyond my boots, her massive thirty-foot wingspan blotting out the glow of the volcanoes, her head lowered, showcasing the spiky scales that run from the tip of her flared nostrils over her expressive brows and down her neck and the length of her gigantic body. She takes a step forward on heavily clawed feet, thick muscles rippling under her pebbled skin, her movement shaking the ground, her ghostly silver eyes focused solely on me.

Lemi must have shifted the moment he heard her roar, but now he's back and doing what he always does, which is to be a distraction and save me from certain doom. Though he could easily take down a person or large animal, he is no match for a dragon of this size, so he'll get the dragon's attention off me enough to let me escape before he shifts to keep from being caught.

But the moment that Lemi shifts in front of the dragon, she has her sights on him.

She raises a clawed foot and brings it down on Lemi just as I scream at him to shift and get away, my cry breaking in the air.

But it's too late.

Lemi lets out a howl that shatters my heart, she pins him under her claws. Blood starts to seep out from under his motionless body, and I choke back a gasp, staring at the sight, willing it to be untrue. Willing time to start ticking backward. Willing all of this to be some awful dream.

But I've seen loved ones die in front of me before.

And they weren't dreams either.

A rattling sound comes out of my throat and I'm choking on fear and pain, the agony of a heart being pierced, and I have to force myself to look away. I don't want to look away; I feel I'm betraying Lemi if I stop staring at his unmoving body.

Oh fuck.

No. Please don't let this be happening.

But I must. I bring my attention back to the dragon's face and I don't dare move, I don't dare breathe, even though tears are running down my cheeks.

Lemi, Lemi, please not Lemi.

No matter how much I want to run over there, no matter how much I want to scream, to cry, I know if I don't try to stay still, I'll end up dead as well.

The dragon spears me with her gaze, her head coming closer and closer, until her nose is at the sole of my boots. She lets out a snuff.

I've never seen a dragon this close before. I'm not sure anyone has and lived to tell the tale. I'm shredded by the pain of losing Lemi and yet I'm so utterly enthralled by this creature, even though I know I'm about to die. It's like I'm trying to suck in every last detail of life that I can.

I don't really believe in any gods or goddesses, but if I had to it would be the one my father believed in. That god was fair and just and merciful. So I pray to him in vain, to let this be quick and let me be reunited with Lemi and my parents soon.

The dragon inhales, her nostrils flaring to the size of dinner plates, then blows her hot herbaceous breath on my body. Ever so slowly she runs her nose over my boots, over my calves, up my thighs, pausing and sniffing as she goes, her eyes pinned on me the entire time.

I'm practically squirming as I try to hold it together, try to keep myself from screaming, from running. My lungs are tight, my breath coming sharp and shallow, hot tears spilling from the sides of my eyes and to the ground. I lie as still as possible, locked in her gaze as she brings her mouth over my stomach, her scaled lips pressing against my belly.

Terror, terror, terror.

I feel the hard poke of ancient teeth against my armor, and then she continues to smell me, up, up, to my chest, to my chin.

Oh god.

Then she stops on a sharp inhale.

I stare at her wide-eyed.

Predator and prey.

This is it.

This is the end of everything.

I should close my eyes. I shouldn't watch my demise as it happens.

But I don't.

I suck in the last drops of life.

I had so believed in a better tomorrow.

But that tomorrow ends today.

I watch as her head tilts ever so slightly and her pupils contract into dark slivers before expanding into black holes that swallow all the silver pigment. It's like staring into a void. Then she pauses and her head tilts ever so slightly, enough to make me frown right back at her.

I swear she's looking at me like . . . like . . .

An arrow comes from nowhere and slams into her neck, piercing her thick hide with ease.

The elderdrage lets out a deafening bellow that blows out my eardrums, raising her giant head in surprise, her attention on her assailant.

My attention follows. I turn my head to see the stranger standing nearby, a bow at their side. They're cloaked and I can't see their eyes but they are standing still, their focus on the dragon. They should be running, for no arrow could ever do any significant damage to a dragon unless it went straight through their eye, but the person doesn't move at all.

They're merely watching and waiting.

Then the dragon gives another roar, which trails off into a low whimper, and the great beast starts to sway on its feet until it topples over to the ground in a heap just a few feet away, the impact creating cracks in the rock and shaking the earth.

What in damnation just happened? Did they kill the dragon?

How is that possible?

I'm staring at the dragon, waiting for it to get up and take its fury out on me, but it lies totally still, its eyes closed. The only sign that it's alive is the faint rising of its pebbled stomach.

I look back to the stranger now and they're crouched at Lemi's side. They run their gloved hands back and forth over my dog's body, muttering something under their breath.

Lemi!

"Get away from him," I manage to cry out, my words caught in my throat. I roll over and try to push myself up but keep slipping on the red yolk that coats my armor in crimson slime. A few minutes ago this substance was worth everything in the world and now, without my dog, it's worth nothing at all.

I manage to get to my knees, then stagger up to my feet, off-balance and hollowed out. The stranger still has their hands on Lemi, though something is different. I swear I see Lemi's tail twitch.

No.

Then it thumps in a lazy wag.

Once, twice . . .

"Lemi!" I yell, and start running toward him, hope rising inside me like a weed. I come to a stop beside the stranger and see Lemi's side rising and falling in steady breath. There's no longer blood around him and he looks completely unharmed, his shiny black coat untouched except by the stranger's hands.

I fall to my knees beside my dog as the stranger straightens up. I meet their eyes briefly, golden and disarmingly bright and framed by the same black salve I use around mine.

"What did you do?" I ask them just as Lemi lifts his head and gives my arm a lick. Tears trickle down my face again, this time from joy. He's alive!

How is he alive?

"He's a tough dog," the stranger says. A man. His voice is low but his tone light, as if we all weren't just in a life-and-death situation.

Lemi continues to lick my hand until he gets up and shakes his body out from head to toe, drool flying everywhere, landing on both of us in gooey strips.

The man chuckles and holds out his hand, and Lemi goes to him for a pet, which he gets around his ears. Usually he's wary with strangers but he isn't with this guy, probably because he just saved his life. Or did he? Perhaps that dragon never really hurt Lemi after all. I swear I saw blood, but maybe I only thought I did in my hysteria.

But he did save your life, I remind myself.

I get to my feet, wiping my hands on a patch of clean, dry armor.

"I guess I should be thanking you for saving my life," I tell him.

The man continues to pet Lemi, though his golden eyes are fixed steadily on me. With the cloak still over his head and a mask that covers the bottom half of his face, all I really see are black brows and those gleaming eyes. They aren't telling me much. If I could at least see his hair color I'd know what moon he was born under and get a hint of his personality.

"I'm sure you'd do the same for me," he says wryly, as if knowing that I wouldn't. "Lavender girl."

I ignore the nickname about my hair. "I would if I had an arrow that could bring down an elderdrage," I admit, twisting around to glance at the dragon that's still lying on her side. She's absolutely massive, seen from this angle, and a chill runs through me at the thought of how close to death I was, how close I was to losing Lemi.

I glance back at the stranger, frowning. "How did you do that, anyway? Is she sleeping?"

"She's sleeping for now," he explains warily. "She's been tranquilized. We have about ten minutes before she wakes up. We won't want to be here when she does."

Tranquilized? In all my time doing this I'd never heard of any sort of potion or formula that could make a dragon go to sleep. How much easier my job would be if I had that.

"Where are you from?" I ask him cautiously.

"A small town called Stormglen Creek," he says. "And you?"

Stormglen Creek. Creek. There are no creeks on Esland. The only source of water in our realm comes from two aquifers deep underground that are heavily controlled by the Saints of Fire. It's only with their "blessing" that they allow people in the Banished Land to access it, but even then our rations are tight—when it's not poisoned.

"It doesn't matter where I'm from," I answer, not wanting him to have any information about me, information he might be able to use.

His eyes flick over my face, squinting in amusement. "I see. Well, I'd say you're from Esland due to your dialect but you don't seem like a Soffer." He uses the derogatory term the Freelanders have for Saints of Fire followers—interesting to learn that they're known as that in the other lands as well.

Because I'm not a Soffer, I want to tell him, but I bite my tongue. If I do that he'll know that I'm from the Banished Land, though I guess that's already a given since I'm here stealing eggs.

He chuckles again and then reaches up and tugs his mask down around his neck so I can see a long straight nose and full lips that are twisted in a half smile. "I'm Andor Kolbeck," he says, extending his hand.

I stare at him, awestruck. It's not just that he has the most charming smile with dazzling white teeth, but that his name is Kolbeck.

"From House Kolbeck?" I exclaim quietly.

He stares down at his gauntlet-clad hand, the one I'm not shaking. He takes it back. "I suppose the greeting customs of your people are different."

"House Kolbeck? Of the Norland syndikat?" I repeat, ignoring that.

Something dark flickers in his gaze for a moment. "Yes. I take it you've heard of us."

Easy now, I tell myself. *Don't let it slip who you work for.*

"Everyone knows the houses," I explain.

He crosses his arms. "Is that so? See, I would have thought everyone would know the different kings and queens of the realms. Not the houses. The kingdoms are the ones thought to have true power. Unless you know exactly what power the houses have." He pauses, his tone growing unkind. "And I think you do."

I swallow, my mouth thick and dry, and give him a quick smile. I think it's time I make an exit.

"Hard to know what to think," I tell him, adjusting my holsters on my back. "I'm just a girl from Esland. Well. I better get on my way before the dragon wakes up."

Andor nods at the remaining egg in the crater. "You're not going to take that?"

"Best not to push my luck. You might not save me a second time."

He lets out a dry laugh and I glance at Lemi quickly.

"Come on, Lemi," I say as I turn around and start walking off. I expect to hear the gallop of his paws on the rock as he races after me, but I hear nothing at all.

REALM of THIEVES

"I'm afraid the dog is coming with me," the Kolbeck says, his voice turning cold and hard. A command, a sentence, another knot in my plan. It's enough to make my heart freeze. I stop and turn to look at Andor, wide-eyed.

His mouth lifts slightly, his eyes darkening. "And so are you."

Chapter 3

Andor

I DON'T EXPECT THE LAVENDER GIRL TO TAKE THE NEWS OF HER kidnapping well.

"I'm not going anywhere with you," she says, her brown eyes narrowing at me, ready to fight. "And neither is my dog. Lemi, come."

The big dog gives a little whine and reluctantly leaves my side. Loyal to a fault. If only it were so with humans.

The hound trots over to her and I watch them walk away for a beat before stealing a glance at the dragon. Time is ticking. The beast will wake soon, and I should collect that last egg while I can.

Then again, I can't let the lavender girl go either. I've been working on this plan for the last five moon cycles, and she's the whole reason I'm on this side of the Midlands. Her and her dog. My father will be thrilled to know we have a suen-sniffer. Might even tell me I did a good job, though I won't hold my breath.

I have to make a decision and fast. She won't get away, I made sure of that when I hired Tromson, but dealing with the egg will be too cumbersome, especially if she puts up a fight. Despite her reputation

REALM of THIEVES

in the Banished Land as a top thief, I have yet to see her fighting skills. I have a feeling she'll make me work for it.

I stride over to the crater and drop down into it, swiping the sharp hollow sapper out from my boot and plunging it into the bottom of the egg. By the time the slippery red suen starts to drip, I've got a container underneath, collecting the resource. I glance up at the dragon again and then the girl, who is just about to disappear over the horizon, half-swallowed by the billowing smoke. I wonder if her dog will sniff out another nest or if she's going to head back to Tromson at the boat. Seems such a fucking waste to leave the egg behind like this, especially when I'll only be able to tap a portion of it.

My uncle's recent words to my father ring in my head: *What's the point of sending Andor anymore when the raid always turns into a fool's errand?*

I swallow down the bitterness and force myself to focus just as the girl and her dog pass out of sight and the dragon begins to stir, moving its legs slowly, its long claws scratching loudly over the black aerated rock. I don't have enough of the poison left for another arrow—I need to leave. I quickly seal the container and remove the sapper from the egg. Then I climb out of the crater and run toward the shore after the girl.

The dragon growls and the ground trembles as I feel it get to its feet. I pick up the pace, with my cloak flowing behind me, glancing over my shoulder to see the beast shaking its wings out. In seconds it will be airborne. I wish the poison didn't leave the system so quickly.

I make a mental note for Steiner to adjust the formula and I keep pumping my legs until I see the girl again, this time in another crater, busy gathering smaller blooddrage eggs, the dog watching her work intently.

"Hide!" I holler at her, my speed increasing. "She's awake!"

32   KARINA HALLE

The lavender girl stares at me with her large dark eyes, unsure what to do for a moment, then yells at her dog. "Lemi! Go to the boat. To the boat!"

The dog looks reluctant until she yells "Go!" again.

And then he disappears into thin air.

Fucking fascinating. I've seen him shift before but never so close. There's no time to marvel over it, though.

In seconds I'm launching myself into the air until I'm pushing the girl to the ground, covering her with my cloak.

She lets out a whimper of pain from the impact, but her armor should protect her from the worst of it, as shoddy and threadbare as it is.

"Shhh," I whisper harshly into her ear as I press her down into the crater, hearing the sickly sound of eggs cracking beneath us as I do so. "Don't move. I won't be able to save you again."

"I never asked you to save me the first time," she grumbles.

I slip my hand under her face until it covers her mouth, making sure she really shuts up, just as the steady beat of dragon wings fills the air.

I am not getting paid enough for this, I can't help but think. Truth is, I'm not really getting paid at all. It's my duty as a Kolbeck, more than anything, and I'm the only one even remotely suited for these expeditions. Steiner would spend his time trying to catalog the flora and fauna of the islands, Solla would find a cave and never come out, Vidar would find someone else to do the dirty work, and my uncle Kjell would try to fight a dragon and fail miserably. Only my father would stand a chance at doing this job. He'd also be the first to throw me in the line of fire if it meant his escape.

The dragon lets out another cry, a breeze coming off the powerful wings, stirring up the fine black sand gathered in the crevices. I hear the sound of it expelling fire close by, feel the heat as the flames warm our back. It shouldn't see us, not with my cloak covering us both up.

It was designed by Steiner to mimic the surroundings, completely camouflaging us, as well as protecting us from any fire blasts.

I hold my breath and wait. I can feel Brynla's heartbeat through her back, the stiffness of her muscles as she keeps still.

The cloak works. The dragon keeps flying onward, then turns back to her nest again. With her back to us, we can make it over the ridge where we'll be hidden. She won't be a happy dragon when she discovers that both her eggs have been destroyed, but thankfully they weren't fertile anyway.

I stand and grab the girl's arm, yanking her up beside me.

"Ow!" She scowls at me, trying to get out of my grasp. Up close her features are an intriguing mix of youth and hardness. Her eyes hold a world of pain and anger in them, her mouth and jaw set in the same tense way. But her full pink cheeks and lips, her smooth sun-kissed skin, and the way her lavender hair is braided in coils at the back of her neck make her look youthful. She's tall and broad shouldered, strong in her stance, but has full breasts and wide hips, thick thighs and a round stomach. She looks healthy and strong.

She gives me another sharp look, this one telling me to stop staring at her.

"We need to get behind the ridge before the dragon looks back," I say, keeping my voice low. I keep ahold of her arm and haul her up and out of the crater like she weighs nothing at all. She grumbles the whole way, swearing under her breath.

"So what they say about you is true," she says.

"And what's that?"

"All the syndikats use suen." She says this derisively, as if she doesn't partake in the magic herself. "I hadn't seen a thief in action before."

"And suen doesn't do that for you?" I counter, pulling her forward until we're over the bony ridge and out of sight of the dragon. Everyone who ingests the suen from dragon eggs has their natural abilities amplified. I was born with a natural strength and agility, and suen in turn gives me preternatural strength. My youngest brother, who was nothing short of a genius as a child, now has a brain unlike anyone I know. Sometimes I hear of people who get brand-new abilities that come from nowhere, but those people are few and far between. Brynla, I would assume, also has natural strength that suen must magnify, even though she acts like she's above its usage.

She doesn't say anything, her fingers twitching at her sides. I know she wants to grab her swords. I'm half-inclined to let her. See what she's made of. See if she knows how to listen.

I come to a stop, forcing her to halt too, my grip a vise around her elbow.

"Now that I've saved your life for a second time," I tell her, leaning in, "perhaps you can do me the honor of listening to what I have to say."

Her gaze goes over the wild shore where waves lap against the rock. The illumination from the volcanoes doesn't extend as far here, and the dark horizon is swallowed by low charcoal clouds. Somewhere beyond that is Tromson on his boat and hopefully the dog.

"What do you want?" she asks stiffly, not looking at me.

"I need your help," I tell her. "Most importantly, House Kolbeck needs your help. Your expertise."

She frowns at me, her guard dropping for a moment. "Me? Who am I to you?"

"You're Brynla Aihr," I say, watching as her pupils shrink in surprise. "Daughter of rebel leaders Branne and Sonja Aihr, now deceased. You reside with your aunt Ellestra Doon in the Dark City, living as a fugitive from the Black Guard and the Daughters of Silence, from which you escaped nearly a decade ago. And you're one of the best thieves in the business." I pause. "Only problem is, you're working for the wrong side."

REALM of THIEVES

Her throat bobs as she swallows. "How . . . how do you know all that?"

"I've been watching you," I admit. "Ever since the blue moon."

She calculates how long that's been. "That's half a year," she whispers, licking her lips. Then she gives her head a shake. "I don't understand."

"Yes, you do," I say, taking my hand off her arm. "You and your dog are worth a lot of money, which is why the Sjef of House Dalgaard hired you. Don't play dumb, I know your dog is what helps you find the eggs." She opens her mouth to say something, and I continue. "I said I was watching you, didn't I? House Kolbeck is no different than House Dalgaard in that aspect. We have spies everywhere."

I might be exaggerating, just a little. Our spies consist of a white raven that Steiner knows how to communicate with, and Dagruna Bjarr, a woman with shape-shifting abilities who works for the king of Norland.

Brynla's gaze turns hard as she meets my eyes. I can sense her muscles twitching, her fight-or-flight instincts rising. "What do you want?"

"I want you to work for House Kolbeck. We'll pay you handsomely."

She thinks that over for a moment. "You do know what would happen to me if I switched sides. Sjef Ruunon wouldn't let me go easily, and if he learned I was working for House Kolbeck . . ."

"He'd kill you and your dog and your aunt," I supply. "Or possibly keep your dog and kill the rest of you. I'm aware."

"So then you understand why I won't be working for you."

I breathe in sharply, my adrenaline spiking in anticipation of what's to come. I had prepared for this, but despite the chaos that seems to follow me wherever I go, I prefer it when things go smoothly.

"You're declining?"

"I'm saying no," she says with a raise of her chin.

"Then I have to insist." I can't help but smile at her defiance. "After all, you owe me for saving your life, twice now, and for saving the life of your dog."

Brynla stiffens at that. "I owe you something in return, yes, but not this."

"What is *this*?"

"My freedom," she says, her tone hard and final.

"Then I'm afraid you leave me no choice," I tell her. I reach into my cloak and pull out a syclesaw, the polished dragon claw reflecting the dull light.

Her movements are fast. Both of the swords from her back are drawn and she's in a warrior's pose, her jaw set as sharp as the blades, her gaze focused.

"I am a Freelander," she says boldly. "I will always have a choice."

"And I'm a Norlander," I tell her, moving the syclesaw over to my other hand and back again, rubbing the smooth claw under my thumb as I do. "We also have a choice, as does Sorland, and Vesland, the rest of the wide world. All the more reason to get out of your goddess-forsaken realm. See how everyone else survives for a change. See how we live. Are you afraid you'll like it?"

She doesn't move, her gaze continuing to hold me. Her eyes are so dark and determined. I know I'll win, but I might not walk away unscathed.

"Or are you afraid you're not worthy of a better life?" I add.

There. Something shifts in her eyes, just for a moment.

I hit a nerve.

I decide to switch tactics. "You really think your shoddy armor will last you over time? You think ash glass can stab through the hide of a deathdrage? I've been watching you, Brynla Aihr. You're one of the best, but you're also the luckiest person I've ever come across. I've never even seen a dragon get close to you until today, but look where that got you. Had I not been there, you and your magic dog would be dead." I pause. "People say you're a force to be reckoned with, that you can fight your fellow man, but after today, I'm not sure how you measure up against the dragons."

"I do just fine," she practically growls, her grip on the swords' hilts tightening. "I'm still here, aren't I?"

"Because of luck. But tonight, your luck has officially run out. Two botched raids and you almost died twice. If you come with me, we can give you your luck back. We can take your thieving to another level entirely. You'll be unstoppable. Perhaps one day finally get your revenge against the Soffers. Isn't that what all Freelanders want?"

I let that last sentence dangle in the volcanic air.

She hesitates for a moment.

"I don't know you," she eventually says. "And I sure as fuck don't trust you."

"Nor should you," I admit, my brow rising at her language. "I don't trust my family either. But I'll repeat what I said earlier: you don't have a choice."

I put the syclesaw back in my other hand and her eyes go to it, taking in the sight. I know she's never seen a weapon like this either, crafted from the ten-inch curved claws of the sycledrage. "If you don't come with me tonight, you'll be delivered right into the arms of the Black Guard and your own execution."

Her nostrils flare, fear finally sparking in her eyes. Just what I wanted to see.

"And so what?" she says, starting to slowly move around me in a circle, swords still drawn. "If the Dalgaards find out I went with you, it will be the same fate for me."

"Except we can protect both you and your aunt," I tell her. "We can get her out of the Dark City. So either you come with me right now and join our side, or you die the same way your father did, hanging from the gallows."

38 KARINA HALLE

She gives her head a small shake, eyes narrowing into something so cold I feel it in my chest. She's a marvel, this one.

"There's a third option that you've forgotten about," she says quietly.

"And what's that?"

"That I kill you."

She grins. Sweet and deadly.

Then she's at me faster than I can blink.

Chapter 4

Brynla

 I'm not going anywhere with this Syndikat thief.

I do my best to catch him off guard. I launch myself low, knowing to kick him out beneath his center of gravity.

It works too, for a moment. My boots strike his shins at enough of an angle that his knees buckle, and I have both my swords raised, ready to pin him down to the ground.

But instead of collapsing, he rolls over the craggy volcanic rock, his armor protecting him from the jagged ground. He gets up on his feet just as I'm coming over him and he quickly twists at the waist and raises his fist, knocking my arm off-balance. My hands instinctively grip my swords, unwilling to drop them, though the impact makes my bones vibrate.

I quickly spin and move out of the way, trying to regain my footing, expecting the sharp claw of the sycledrage that he so flagrantly showed off to slice into me. But he's sliding his weapons away into the inner folds of his cloak, as if he knows he doesn't need them.

He thinks I'm some backward Freelander, I think as I hold out my swords. That my skills are so lacking he barely needs to fight. He's trying to prove something.

My wounded pride becomes my fuel.

I fake a stab to his left shoulder before I drop to the ground, the rocks digging into my palms as I pivot on my upper body, swinging around and kicking at his ankles. It's enough that this time he does fall back and I dive over him just as he makes impact with the terrain.

My shins press down on his thighs as I hold one sword against his throat, the other at the soft leather along his side, a weakness in the armor.

"I should kill you right now," I tell him, pressing the sharp edge of the ash glass up into the crook of his chin. My voice is eerily calm, though inside I feel as if I'm caught in a whirlwind.

His amber eyes stare at mine for a moment and I think I see a shred of fear in them. Then he blinks. "My gods, you're a stubborn little thief, aren't you?"

I narrow my gaze. "You should be begging for your life."

"On the contrary," he says. His mouth curls up. The bastard is smirking at me. "You should be begging for yours."

"You're the one with two blades ready to end you."

"And you're the one I'll be delivering to the Black Guard for your very public execution."

I don't want to kill this man, this arrogant product of House Kolbeck. I've never killed anyone before and I don't want to start now.

But if it means saving my own life, I'll have no choice but to slit his throat.

He grins at me, egging me on, and before I can react he moves with a sudden burst of energy that knocks me backward.

I go flying onto the hard ground, stunned, the air knocked clear from my lungs, and I'm trying to take in a breath just as he comes around me and puts his forearm across my windpipe, yanking me upward and into his lap, the back of my head against his chest.

"You can't fight me and win, Brynla," he says gruffly, my throat burning. "Now what will it be? Your execution? Or your servitude?"

REALM of THIEVES   41

I make a move for my swords, which fell when he sprang up from under me, but he holds me even tighter, the strong muscles of his forearm flexing against my throat.

"You're not going to make this easy, are you?" he says in my ear, his breath tickling me, and I feel myself growing weaker with lack of oxygen, the glow of the volcano seeming to become blotted out at the corners of my vision.

I'm losing consciousness.

Slowly but surely the darkness seeps across my eyes, into my brain, my heart, and everything goes black.

———

I wake up to hear the sloshing of water by my head, the creak of timber.

I'm lying on cold wooden planks in the fetal position, my limbs heavy as stone. The world spins. I try to move, to open my eyes, but the pain in my throat is immediate and my head feels full of soft cloth, making it hard to think.

But I have to think.

Where am I?

What happened?

Last thing I remember was . . .

Oh fuck. I was on Fjallen Rock, fighting someone, some man from House Kolbeck. He strangled me, I . . .

My eyes fly open into a darkened room, my vision foggy for a moment before daylight starts to seep in.

"Lemi!" I manage to cry out though pain ravages my throat, as if I can still feel the man's arm against it. I sit up and the room whirls enough to make me list to the side, my head in my hands, nausea rolling through me. A dry chuckle fills the air that smells of seawater and brine.

"You should take it easy. You've been out cold."

I look to the corner of the room where that man—Andor—is sitting on a barrel, elbows on his thighs as he peers at me with a half smile.

"And your dog is fine," he adds. "Before you start worrying."

I growl at him and immediately regret it, my eyes pinching shut in a wince as the sound burns me from the inside.

"Sorry about that," he says, sounding reluctant as he gestures quickly to my neck. "I needed to take you alive. I had no choice."

No choice?

I let out a pained cough. "You could have let me be."

"I couldn't do that. You had to come with me one way or another."

"You nearly killed me," I whisper hoarsely.

"I know what I'm doing," he says as he straightens up. "And it's become very apparent that you, lavender girl, do not."

If only I had the strength to wipe that smirk off his face. I'm still dizzy, though the more the seconds tick by the more I realize that the room is actually moving in addition to what my head is doing.

We're on a boat, in some sort of storage room belowdecks. Faint light creeps in through a porthole window that's so scoured by salt that I can't see anything outside.

"Where are you taking me?" I manage to ask, adjusting my seat. I may be on the floor but at least he's put sheepskins underneath me. I spot a copper canteen beside me, swirling carvings of delicate foliage engraved on the surface giving it a feeling of opulence in this dirty cabin.

"It's fresh water," he says, following my gaze. "You must be thirsty."

"Where are you taking me?" I repeat.

"That depends on if you feel like being a good girl or not," he says.

I'm really glaring at him now. He's dressed in the same armor as before except the black salve has been mostly wiped away from his eyes, making them look rimmed in coal, the golden amber of them glowing in contrast. His hair is thick and dark, pushed off his face in waves. I would have called him handsome, if only he hadn't kidnapped me.

"I've never been a good girl and I'm not about to start with you," I tell him.

He laughs, though there's an edge to it. "I'm afraid I'm starting to already regret this plan of mine." He gets to his feet and walks over. Instinctively I press until my back is against a wooden barrel.

He peers down, looming over me. "I asked you to make a choice, but you never gave me the answer I wanted. We're a quarter of the way across the White Sea, heading into the port of Menheimr. We'll be there in another two days, as long as the wind holds up and the waves obey. But I can make the captain turn this ship around to Esland. Sail right into the capital. Drop you off with the Black Guard. You and your dog."

I don't say anything for a moment, and I drop my gaze from the smug gleam in his golden eyes that tells me I'm screwed no matter which choice I take.

And obviously I want to take the choice that lets me live. I just want to do it on my terms.

I stare down at my armor and suddenly feel overwhelmed by the tight, damp leather, like I've been ensnared in it. Trapped. I flex my fingers.

"How long was I out for?" I ask.

"Enough for me to get you onboard. Maybe a couple of hours."

"And Lemi? Where is he?"

He jerks his chin up. "On deck. Having a great time with all the fish the crew is pulling up. Haven't seen him disappear once."

At least there's that, I think.

"Tell you what," Andor says, crouching down in front of me. "You can continue to be stubborn, or you can take a chance, makes no difference to me. I just need to know if you're choosing me . . . or death."

"I'll take my chances with death, thank you," I tell him.

Then slam my boot forward right into his groin.

He lets out a yelp and topples over to the side, and then I'm up on my feet and running past him. I push past barrels and mounds of knotted rope and run up to the next deck, which is filled with cabins and the galley. I hear Andor yelling something from below and I know I don't have enough time. I run into the galley and grab the closest knife, then scamper up the rest of the stairs to the top deck.

Outside the wind is sharp and cold, stinging my face, and a low fog is building in the distance, hovering above the dusky blue surf. The ship is probably a hundred and fifty feet long with clean, empty decks, and there are two large masts, the mainsails fluttering in the wind, and a handful of crew members. One is at the helm, one at the bow (whom I recognize as the lying son of a bitch who gave me the boat ride to the Midlands, though there's no time to dwell on the betrayal yet), and two at the side of the ship, fishing overboard. At their feet lies Lemi, who hops up when he sees me and lets out a bark, tongue lolling to the side.

"Lemi!" I cry out happily as he bounds toward me, though now I've attracted the attention of the crew.

"Andor let you loose already?" the man at the wheel, an older, chubby fellow with pale skin and ruddy cheeks, says to me from up on the aft deck.

"No." Andor's voice rings out. I pat Lemi with one hand while my other brandishes the stolen knife, just as Andor comes up from the deck below, still looking pained. Good. I hope he can never use his dick again. "She escaped."

Andor looks at me, eyes sparking as he pauses at the top of the stairs. "And here I thought my temper was bad. That was a cheap shot."

"You deserved that and worse," I snap at him. "You're the one who nearly strangled me to death."

"Well, you forced my hand, sweetheart. I didn't have many options."

"Yes, you do. Let us go," I say. "Now." I hold out the knife and watch as the other men stare at me with interest.

"Hey, that's my knife," a man with a scarred face growls. I'm guessing he's the cook.

But he doesn't move. None of the crew seems like they're about to advance on me, but I can't drop my guard. It's obvious Andor isn't about to let me go, and there's five of them and one of me. I'm honestly not sure how I'm going to get out of this. I can't see any land nearby, and Andor said we were a quarter of the way across the White Sea. I have no idea what the geography is like in this part of the world. There might be islands just out of sight, close enough that Lemi would tow me there. I could steal their rowboat . . .

"I wouldn't do it," Andor says, eyeing the knife. "There's nowhere for you to go."

"Even if there were, you'd only lie about it to keep me here," I point out, backing up slowly toward the railing with Lemi inching along with me, his ears perked up, wondering what's happening.

"Are you questioning Andor's honesty?" the boatswain asks, leaning casually against the wheel, the wind whipping back his patchy hair. "You won't find a more honest man out there. He tells the truth like it's an affliction, until you wish he was lying," he adds with a chuckle.

"I'll take my chances," I tell him, looking back to Andor. "I would rather face death on the high seas than be forced to help you or your house."

"Such a pity," he muses as I peer over the edge of the boat. The sea is rough and looks terribly cold.

"What is?" I say, quickly looking back at him. No one has moved toward me.

"That you are so obstinate you would rather die than save your aunt's life."

I freeze. "What are you talking about?"

"I told you earlier," he says calmly, splaying his hands. "You work for us, we get your aunt out of the Banished Land. She'll be free to go to wherever she likes in the world, and we'll give her the means to do so. And when you're done working for us, you can do the same."

I stare at him for a moment, then shake my head. He's lying. He's a rotten member of a syndikat, no different from Dalgaard or anyone else in this world. I want a better life but I know a devil's bargain when I hear it. Everything comes with a catch.

"What do you mean *when* I'm done?" I ask. "Since when is there a time limit to this favor?"

Andor shrugs, a strand of dark hair blowing across his eyes. "It's not a favor. It's an opportunity. A favor implies that you would be helping me from the goodness of your heart and getting nothing in return. An opportunity means you get something too. Bigger than your wildest dreams." He pauses, meeting my eyes and holding them there. "We haven't yet discussed our terms because you keep trying to kill me. But it's possible that you only work for us for a year, enough for us to get a leg up on Dalgaard. All you'll be doing is stealing eggs, same as before." He pauses and smiles with white teeth. "It's all negotiable, darling."

I hate that for a moment I'm intrigued enough to ask more questions. But I quell that feeling and bristle instead. "My aunt is a survivor. She'll be just fine without any rescue. She's built for the Banished Land, a place that would eat you alive."

His gaze remains steady. "Are you sure about that? Willing to bet her life on it?"

"More than I'm willing to bet my life on you," I tell him.

And then before he can say anything, I lean back against the railing and fall overboard, flipping backward into the sea.

Chapter 5

Andor

 I honestly didn't think she'd do it, but that's the second time I underestimated Brynla Aihr, daughter of rebels, before she did something rash. I suppose she's more like her lineage than I thought.

I watch as she flips over the railing, her dog Lemi leaping clear over it in a frantic pursuit after her, and then I'm running across the deck to look over the side. "Slow the ship, bring her around!" I yell at Toombs, our boatswain.

Down in the surf Brynla and her dog try to swim away from the ship but are pummeled by the waves and smashed against the hull. She can barely keep her head above the water, perhaps not fully recovered from when I made her unconscious. I know how to do it so that it disables the person and doesn't hurt them, even if they're buzzing with suen magic, but she should still be resting, not swimming in the frigid White Sea.

I sigh heavily, weighing my options as she struggles in the water below. I know what my father would do. He would let her swim, let her drown, it would make no difference to him. And part of me wants to let her go. After all, she's made some fairly stupid decisions so far and is turning out to be more trouble than she's worth.

But that's my fault really. I assumed that whatever I offered her would be better than the life she had in the Banished Land. I've never been there myself but from the stories I've heard, it's a cruel and rough life without any mercy. I thought she would be begging me to leave.

I didn't account for her tenacity, spite, and pride, or that she would react without thinking, like she's doing now. The more I push and corner her, the more she tries to run, even if it hurts her. Even if it kills her.

"Pass me that rope," I say to Kirney, my right-hand man. "I'm going in after her."

"You're daft," Toombs says as Kirney grabs the nearest rope and I tell him to fasten it around the cleat before I tie the rest around my waist.

I ignore Toombs, climb up on the railing, and jump overboard just as a large wave smashes into the front of the boat, the seas picking up now as if the sorceresses wanted to create an extra challenge for me.

I hit the surface like a net of stones, sinking deep before a wave twists me upside down, the rope tangling in my legs, water going up my nose until it burns. But I find my strength and kick to the surface as another wave breaks over me, the salt stinging my eyes.

The ship has slowed but Brynla and Lemi are still a ways off. I start swimming toward them in time to see Brynla's lavender hair disappear beneath the waves. Her dog sticks its head under, grasping the collar of her shirt with its teeth and pulling her up through the waves, but even with the dog's strength, I can see he's struggling in the surf.

I reach Brynla and grasp her by the collar, then grab the thick roll of fur at Lemi's neck, making sure both of them stay above the surface.

"I've got them! Pull us up!" I yell up at the crew, tugging at the

50   KARINA HALLE

rope around my waist just as another wave smashes against the side of the ship.

Slowly, they begin pulling us up the side of the boat. I hold on to both Brynla and Lemi with all my strength. Brynla spits out water, stirring in my grasp as she dangles above the waves. She glances up at me and for a moment I think she's going to do something foolish again and cause me to let go, but thankfully she goes limp.

"Almost got ye," Kirney says from above, and with a few more grunts and heave-hos we're hoisted up to the railing, where the boys pull the three of us over the edge and into a sodden lump on the deck.

Lemi gives his body a thorough shake, drenching the crew with drool and seawater as a result, then comes over to Brynla, licking her face until she sits upright, breathing hard. For a second I'm jealous of both the dog and Brynla, wondering what it would be like to have someone—human or beast—care that much about you.

"Aye," Toombs says with a gruff chuckle as he wipes away the drool from his face. "They say it's bad luck for a woman and a hound to be onboard." His expression then turns dark. "Maybe next time I don't stop the ship."

Despite being an old sea captain who's worked for my father for many years, Toombs is probably the most moral member of the Kolbeck crew. So when he's ready to toss someone overboard, I have to wonder if I've made some sort of mistake by rescuing the girl.

She hasn't said anything. She's sitting with her back against the railing, still catching her breath while her dog lies down beside her, his giant head in her lap. She avoids my eyes and I'm not about to crouch down again. My dick still aches, and not in a good way.

I nod at Toombs. "Get underway again. We're going straight home."

"Aye," Toombs says, heading back to the helm while the rest disperse to help with the sails.

I glance back down at Brynla, watching her for a moment, her

REALM of THIEVES

chest rising, her focus on her dog. It's curious that she's still struggling to catch her breath. I know suen gives the user a wide variety of magic and powers and it's hard to predict what magic will come through for each person, but one thing that seems common in all who consume it is an increase in strength and fitness. Why is she so weak?

Maybe Steiner's raven, Moon, or my informant got their information wrong. She's a good fighter, I'll give her that, and she seems adept at stealing eggs, at least with Lemi's help. But I'm starting to wonder what her actual magic is, because I'm not seeing it.

That doesn't mean I should underestimate her again, though.

I reach into my boot and pull out a foot-long knife. Both Brynla's and Lemi's eyes automatically focus on it. The hilt is carved from bonewood, dotted with various gems, with a silver sword emblem to signify the Kolbecks. The blade itself is made from semitranslucent water crystal, which, when dry, can cut through anything, even stone. It doesn't appear dangerous with its iridescent ridges. Looks like it's carved from ice more than anything. I shake the water off, then blow on it while undoing the rope around my waist.

"What is that?" Brynla asks quietly, and I can see her curiosity overpowering her. So she likes weapons—duly noted.

"This is Dagger," I tell her, flipping the blade over and over in my hand now.

She coughs. "You named your dagger Dagger?" she asks, deadpan.

"A knife can be your best friend," I tell her. "Doesn't your best friend deserve a name?"

Satisfied it's dry, I bring the dagger down across the rope, cutting it in two like a hot knife slicing through butter, and then before Brynla can ask what's happening and fight back, I grab her wrists and tie the rope around them tight.

I step back just as Lemi starts to growl at me, showing large, sharp canines.

Shit. I didn't want the dog to turn on me but I suppose tying up its owner will do that.

I quickly bring out a small vial of tranquilizer I had tucked inside my armor and hold it out for Brynla to see.

"This brought down a dragon; it can bring down your dog. I don't want to hurt him—and I won't—but I have no problems putting him to sleep."

I could add a few more threats in there, but frankly I'd be lying. The only animal I'd ever hurt is a dragon and even then it would be in self-defense, like what happened last night.

Lemi continues to growl, even getting up and stepping toward me. I quickly calculate if I can get the serum in his mouth without losing an arm.

"Lemi," Brynla warns him with a sigh. "Sit."

Lemi's growls disappear and he sits back on his haunches, his tongue hanging out the side, going from a monstrous killer to a giant puppy in seconds.

Then Brynla lifts her hands. "Was it really necessary to tie me up?"

"I'm afraid you've taken me by surprise one too many times," I tell her.

A satisfied smile flashes across her face.

"All right." She clears her throat and leans back against the railing. "So now what?"

"You're just going to gloss over the fact that I saved your life a third time?"

"I never asked you to," she replies. "Not my fault you aren't able to lose gracefully."

I blink at her. "Lose gracefully?"

She shrugs. "You weren't saving me because you wanted to. You saved me because if I died it would have meant you lost."

"Lost at what?" I frown.

"Whatever game you think you're playing. The one you're so desperately trying to make me a part of."

I suck on my lower lip for a moment. On the one hand, I don't like how perceptive she is, even if she's not entirely correct. On the other hand, she's impressing me.

"I'm not playing a game," I tell her, sliding the knife back into my boot. "Not with you, anyway. The only game I'm playing is the one we're all playing."

"Us against dragons," she says, her voice going low.

"Us against House Dalgaard," I tell her. "And in the end, they're the ones who will lose. As for everything transpiring between you and me, well, that's a deal. A negotiation that hopefully leads to a partnership."

She snorts. "This isn't a negotiation. You're kidnapping and blackmailing me into working for you. Which will be your biggest mistake. As long as I'm in your care, you're going to be looking over your shoulder, waiting for me to betray you. After all, if I work for you, I'm betraying House Dalgaard. What makes you so sure I won't do the same to House Kolbeck? Highest bidder always wins for thieves like me, don't they?"

Finally, something I can work with.

"Because I'll make it worth your while."

Chapter 6

Brynla

 Two days later, land appears on the horizon. At first I just see the low bank of fog blanketing the water until it clears and mountainous shapes appear, piercing the sky from below like a row of serrated teeth.

"There she is!" yells Toombs from the helm. "Our fair Norland."

I'm sitting on a crate of oranges, Lemi lying on the deck at my feet. He was napping but now his head is up at the sound of Toombs's bellow, sniffing the air. To me, it smells like sea spray and the damp wood of the ship, which I've gotten used to over the last forty-eight hours, but I have no doubt that Lemi's picking up the scent of distant lands.

He's probably picking up on my energy as well. I'm sitting up straighter as my nerves prickle, looking down the length of the ship to the waves and the world behind in an anxious kind of wonder.

Norland.

I've heard about this place my whole life. Of course, I've only heard bad things. The government of Esland always made every other realm seem worse than the one we were imprisoned in. Norland was supposed to be a place where monsters lurked in the rivers and lakes, making the water poisonous and dangerous to drink. Where the east part of the land had fractured into a separate territory called Altus Dugrell and the two lands were constantly warring with each other. Legend said the entire north was covered in snow and ice so cold that nothing could grow there while bloodthirsty trolls lurked in the glacier caves, and the south was nothing but a blanket of constant rain and fog, enough that it drove people to slowly lose their minds. We were taught that Norlanders themselves were duplicitous people who would stab you in the back the first chance they got—if they hadn't already drowned themselves in the sea or under a barrel of pine alcohol.

Despite what I've been told, I've gotten to know the crew a little, and everyone seems fairly well-adjusted. For a bunch of thieves, anyway. Still, I have no idea what to expect from Norland or its citizens.

Toombs is by far the most jovial and easy to talk to, and he seems to have taken a shine to me, giving me candy from his seemingly bottomless pockets every chance he gets. There's calm and collected Kirney, who appears to be Andor's confidant; Rolph, a diminutive but spirited boy of sixteen with bright orange hair who can scale a mast in mere seconds; and a rotund sailor with a bald head who doesn't speak much and goes by the name of Feet (his feet seem ordinary, so I'm not sure what the name is all about).

Considering I'm their hostage, I've been treated quite well. At least better than I had expected from House Kolbeck. At first I was kept in the cabin with my wrists bound together. Andor only untied me so that I could use the ship's latrine and the small barrel they have onboard for bathing. At least the water was warm and fresh. But today I've been given the freedom of the cabin. It's small but private. The porthole is too small to fit through (I tried, but my rear acted like a cork), and they've stationed guards outside my door.

Usually it's Andor, joined by Kirney or Feet. I suppose they aren't so worried that I'll jump overboard again—I doubt any of them would rescue me a second time—more that I'll try to kill one of them and force the boat back to Esland.

Honestly, it has crossed my mind. The blade that Andor used to slice through the ropes looked like it would put my ash glass to shame. If I could get my hands on that . . .

Now it's too late. As the continent of Norland comes into full view beneath the towering clouds and beyond the fingers of fog, I know Lemi and I could jump off the ship and swim for it. I feel much stronger now than I did when I made my first futile (and frankly embarrassing) attempt, thanks to the simple but protein-rich meals of fish I'd been served in my cabin, and I don't doubt I'd make it to land.

But then what? The crew may have treated me with some modicum of respect, but that doesn't mean the rest of the Norlanders will. What if all I was taught about them is true? What if I stand out like a sore thumb here? Andor keeps remarking on my purple hair—is it possible that this is a color only found with Eslanders? From the derisive way he said *Soffer*, I'm going to assume that they aren't well tolerated. Without any weapons I might not survive very long in Norland on my own.

I bristle at the idea of having to rely on someone else for protection.

"You're looking a little green," Andor says as he strides over to me, having come up from the lower deck.

I glance up at him, my features bending into a scowl. "I guess I'm thinking about stepping foot in Norland for the first time."

He stares at me for a moment, those watchful golden eyes taking me in, the corner of his lips slightly curled. He always looks like he's on the cusp of telling a joke, like he finds this whole kidnapping-and-blackmailing-me thing to be most amusing.

"You were thinking about swimming for shore," he says, dropping down into a crouch to scratch behind Lemi's ears, and I feel my scowl

REALM of THIEVES

deepen. Aside from Tromson, Lemi seems to like everyone here, and it would be a lot easier if he didn't like Andor.

Andor looks up at me. "I'd tell you it's a bad idea except I know that would only make you do it."

"You say that as if you know me," I tell him, unable to keep the venom out of my voice.

He straightens up, towering over me. I thought that without his armor Andor would look less imposing, but that hasn't been the case. Now that he's dressed in only charcoal-colored pants, a dark brown leather vest, and a black shirt with sleeves that go to his elbows, I realize the armor didn't add much to his muscles—he's just as strong and defined without it.

Well, he's had suen, I remind myself, trying not to notice how his clothes cling to him. *That's what gives him the power and strength.*

Although most people I've met who've taken the substance don't look like him.

"Oh, I would never profess to know you," Andor says, scratching at the stubble on his jaw. "Not yet."

"Keep it that way," I mutter under my breath, averting my eyes from the intensity of his gaze and looking back to the horizon. The fog bank in the distance starts to split down the middle, letting rays of sunlight through, reflecting off the sea like burning mirrors.

"It's the goddesses," he says, following my gaze. "They're welcoming us home."

"Goddesses?"

He stretches his arm out, pointing at the horizon. "See those tall curving shapes in the distance, in front of the mountains? Those are the Goddess Gates that protect the harbor of Menheimr, the jeweled city."

I squint at the shimmering light and look past to where two points form close together. At first I thought they were two mountain peaks but the closer we get, the more I can see the outline of two

58   KARINA HALLE

women with their faces pressed together. It's hard to tell from here but the statues have to be hundreds of feet high, putting our dragon statues outside the convent and around the capital of Esland to shame.

"Who are the goddesses?" I ask as I glance back at him.

"Technically they are the sorceresses, Vigdis and Valdis," he explains. He cocks his head at me. "I assumed you knew about them, but I forgot the Saints of Fire have their own gods."

"I don't follow the Saints of Fire," I remind him sharply. He continues watching me and I let out a pained sigh. "I don't know much about the other realms and their gods."

"Did it hurt to admit that?" he asks with a chuckle. I eye his boots, hoping he has his dagger in there so I can whip it out and hold it to his throat. His laugh deepens, as if he knows what I'm thinking. "Vigdis and Valdis are the descendants of Magni, the First Sorcerer. Others consider them to be part of the Grand Sorcerers, but here in Norland they are also gods."

"I thought there was one sorcerer for each realm?" I ask, vaguely remembering what my parents had told me.

"So you do know something," he remarks, folding his arms. I look down at Lemi instead of the veiny muscles of his sun-warmed forearms. I don't need that distraction. "Well, Vigdis and Valdis are sometimes considered to be one. She's a twin of herself. So Norland gets two. Which is just as well since we share a border with Altus Dugrell—they can share our gods too. Vesland gets the sorcerer Verdantus, Sorland gets Vandill. Even though the Midlands contains only dragons, Voldansa is considered the goddess of that realm, though no one knows anything about her. And Esland gets . . ." He eyes me expectantly.

"Vellus," I answer. "But no one in Esland believes in Vellus; at least they don't worship her like a god. They know that Magni existed as the First Sorcerer, and his daughters that followed had the same magic as he did. But it was a sin to worship anyone but the dragons themselves. The dragons came first; they are the beings of the original creation. They are the first and last gods to the Eslanders."

"So what do you believe?" he asks. He sounds genuinely curious, but I can't tell if he's trying to glean information off me to use against me later.

I shrug and raise my chin. "I have no god."

His brows rise. "You don't believe in anything?"

"I wouldn't say that," I say carefully. "I just don't believe in what a government tells me to. And I'll certainly never believe any sort of religion that uses its faith like a weapon."

He frowns at that and nods. "That I can understand. I'm sure you'll find Norlanders to be deeply tied to their goddesses—when it suits them." He finishes with a smile that shows off a crooked canine. If I believed in the goddesses I'd thank them for that. I was starting to think he was too perfect.

"Seems like we'll have fair seas heading into the harbor!" Toombs yells from the aft deck. "Bring in the foresail!"

The crew start running around the deck as we near shore, and I find myself getting to my feet and walking down the length of the ship until I'm at the bow. Lemi follows beside me, standing up on two legs and leaning his paws against the railing to take it all in, nose raised to the wind.

With the breeze blowing back my hair, now I can finally smell what Lemi has been smelling this whole time.

It brings tears to my eyes.

The air smells like dreams, like things I've only imagined. I smell something that's similar to the herbs burned at the convent and yet much fresher and deeper. It invigorates me from the inside out, like it's filling a well in the desert, like there are seeds inside me taking root and growing.

"What is that?" I whisper aloud.

I feel Andor's presence behind me. He's got a peculiar sense of energy about him, something that I would again chalk up to suen, but I don't think that's it. It's like he's full of barely contained fire, like the lava smoldering in the depths of a mountain.

"Norland," he says, a hint of pride in his voice. "But what you're really picking up on are the umberwoods. They're a type of cedar found only in Norland. They've been growing since the dawn of dragons; some are as high as four hundred feet tall. People say they're the only trees that could withstand living among the deathdrages." He comes around and stands at the rail beside me, his arm brushing mine, enough for a faint spark. Enough for me to move my arm away an inch. "Even though I've seen my fair share of dragons in the Midlands, it's hard to imagine them ever existing here."

Lemi lets out a *whumpf* through his nose and then rubs his head against me, his tail wagging. I can tell he's excited to get off the ship and explore new lands. I wish I could say the same, but I won't let all this awe and novelty wipe my mind of the fact that I'm here against my will. All it took was a new smell, of all things, and suddenly it's as if I *want* to be here.

"So how should we do this?" Andor says, looking down at me. "Should I bind you again or can I trust you enough to let you walk freely?"

I wiggle the tension from my jaw. "You can trust me."

"Hmmm. I want to, I really do," he muses. "If you run, you won't get far. We have eyes all over Menheimr. You won't get past the city gates without a sword in your back. And not everyone here will appreciate a magic dog."

At that he turns away and strides back down the deck, barking orders at the crew, the boat tilting slightly as it turns toward the entrance to the harbor.

That sense of wonder is back again. It's impossible to shake.

Tall cliffs the color of white ash rise straight up from the blue-green sea on either side of us. Colonies of birds rest in the cracks and

REALM of THIEVES

61

crevices along the vertical drop, some of them swirling around like white blossoms falling slowly from trees. The top is lined with a stand of tall trees, perhaps not as tall as the umberwoods I'm apparently smelling, but still a thick forest that undulates along the ridge.

The cliffs come close together at a narrow opening where the sea passes through into the harbor beyond like the nexus of an hourglass. The goddesses stand across from each other at each end of those cliffs. They look the same, rising hundreds of feet into the air, sculpted hair flowing behind them, dressed in gowns that look stunningly lifelike, identical blades in their hands not too dissimilar from the one in Andor's boot. Vigdis's and Valdis's faces meet in a kiss above the water, creating a bridge at the top, and I swear I see the tiny figures of men. Watchmen?

It would make sense because down below at the base of the statues' feet are sparse-looking buildings that are also lined with people, making me think of army barracks. The harbor is as heavily defended as the government buildings in Lerick, Esland's capital.

But when we follow the line of ships to sail between the narrow passage, we don't pass through any checkpoints. I suppose all the boats here, including Andor's, are already known to the soldiers at the barracks.

"Look at that, Lemi," I whisper as I crane my head up while we pass underneath the goddesses. High above, swirls of white birds spin and dance, and beyond them the stone faces, and I have to look away before I get too dizzy. The size and grandeur of everything is too much, and even Lemi drops down to his haunches.

And then my attention is stolen by the harbor itself, which opens into a half moon. Modest, whitewashed buildings dot the shoreline, growing in size and density until they seem stacked at the bottom of the crescent. Here the buildings have colorful roofs—teal, magenta, yellow, green—that glitter in the sun like jewels. Behind them are forested mountains and then distant white peaks.

Snow.

I've never seen snow before in my life; I've only heard about it.

But that's what that must be on those craggy mountaintops.

Suffice to say my mouth was hanging open the entire journey into the harbor and by the time the ship pulls into the ship docks beside a long, busy pier, I'm stunned into silence.

"Well," Andor says to me as he approaches. I can barely take my eyes off the people milling below on the docks, who stare up at the ship with vague interest before carrying on their way. Some of the men are hauling up nets from their boats; others are trading fish with people, women mostly, who have come to haggle for the catch of the day, handing over shiny gold coins. It reminds me of the docks of Lerick, where I used to sit with my father as he took in his haul, except the people here are dressed differently, more opulent and layered, warmer, I suppose, and instead of a sand-blasted city that's been baking under a hot sun, Menheimr's jeweled houses sparkle under a bright sky, the air fresh and sharp, with the rich green of the forested hills rising beyond the shimmering roofs.

"Welcome to the north," Andor says with a flourish of his arm.

I give my head a shake, trying to knock some sense back into myself. I won't get very far if I'm gawking like an idiot. I need to stay sharp. I don't *want* to be here.

I look down at Lemi to ground me.

And it's at that moment that Lemi disappears.

Chapter 7

Brynla

"Lemi!" I cry out, looking wildly around the ship for my dog.

"Ah shit," Andor says, nodding at the pier. "He's taking himself on a walk."

I look to see Lemi walking along the wooden wharf, people parting in fear as he saunters past, sniffing the air.

So much for keeping a giant magic dog unnoticed.

"Lemi, get back here right now!" I cup my hands around my mouth and yell at him.

His ears prick up and in an instant he disappears, reappearing beside Andor on the deck with a sheepish look on his face.

"Well, I was hoping we would arrive in Menheimr without too much fanfare," Andor comments with a sigh, giving Lemi a quick pat. "I have a feeling Lemi will be the talk of the town for several moons."

I almost find myself apologizing before I swallow it down and stop myself. Why should I apologize? Andor's the one who kidnapped the both of us. If I didn't feel it would risk Lemi's safety, I'd encourage him to shift all over the city and terrorize the citizens.

64 KARINA HALLE

But I have to play nice. I'm in strange new territory. As pretty as it is, and as normal as the people seem so far, I can't let my guard down, not even for a second. Especially not when Lemi has become the center of attention.

"All right, let's go." Andor grabs me by the elbow and I immediately try to shrug out of his grasp, but his grip is strong and he *tsks* me under his breath, like I'm some ornery horse. He takes me down the deck and Kirney hands him a metal box, which Andor tucks under his arm. I assume the box contains the suen he must have pilfered from the dragon eggs. The suen that should be *mine*.

Then he leads me down the gangplank and off the ship, Lemi thankfully staying close to us, with everyone else keeping a safe distance as we pass. Still, even though the city folk eye me and Lemi with a mix of fear and disdain, they all smile warmly at Andor, many of them greeting him as "Lieutenant Kolbeck" or "Handlangere," a word I don't recognize. He nods politely at everyone as he goes, occasionally greeting someone by name.

Turns out my kidnapper is well respected in town. I suppose this shouldn't be a big surprise since those who come from the syndikat houses have a lot of power.

And yet they don't seem to fear Andor. They seem to admire him. I see it in the men who tip their hats at him and in the eyes of the women as they pass in their wide, fancy skirts and lace-trimmed necklines. It's only then that I realize what I must look like in comparison. I had taken a bath on the ship, but I'm still in my dirty armor and my hair is pulled back in a messy, tangled bun. Compared to these women with their dark hair in ornate updos and perfumed skin and traces of rouge on their lips and cheeks, I must look like a street rat. I've gotten used to the Dark City, where everyone is living on crumbs and just scraping by.

I've never felt so out of place before. It makes me feel off-balance, as if I'm floating through the world, and not really here.

REALM of THIEVES   65

Andor seems to notice this because he leans in slightly and murmurs, "You're doing great."

That makes things worse. It's like he's feeling sorry for me.

"Great for what? For someone being forced against her will?" I say to him.

"Yes," he says, and his grip on my elbow relaxes slightly.

"Do you normally kidnap women?"

"Only if they deserve it."

Then he grins and takes me down a cobblestone street where a carriage awaits, emblazoned with the words HOUSE KOLBECK on the side. It's made of sleek dark wood, and four large black-and-white horses are at the front, snorting impatiently. The sharply dressed driver sitting on the coach seat above gives us both a nod and then hops down to the ground.

"I can't remember the last time I've been in a carriage," I say as we approach, though I meant to keep that thought in my head.

"Is that so?" Andor asks. "That's probably a good thing; this coach has seen better days."

The driver opens the door for us. "Good to see you back, Lord Kolbeck," he says, his gray bushy mustache moving as he speaks. "Ah, and you have a guest."

"Nice to be back on land, Gudwale. This is Ms. Aihr," he tells the driver. "And her hound, Lemi. Hopefully there isn't too much mud on the roads."

"It's drying in some places," Gudwale says as we step into the carriage. "Had a storm pass through the day before last, left some lightning hail, which your brother made quick work of."

I take a seat facing the forward direction, once again looking out of place with my dirty leathers against the plush green velvet seats. Lemi stands by Gudwale on the street, looking as suspicious as a dog can look, but once I pat the seat next to me he comes bounding inside, the carriage rocking on its wheels from his weight. Gudwale wiggles his mustache as he watches Lemi sit beside me on the seat. For a moment I think he's going to yell at me about having a dog on the upholstery, but he doesn't.

"He's a fine hound, my lady," Gudwale says with a quick, kind smile before he shuts the carriage door.

Andor takes a seat across from me and the carriage starts to pull away.

"What about Toombs and the men from the ship?" I ask, craning my head out the window to watch the harbor disappear behind the buildings.

"They live in the city," Andor says.

"Even Kirney? He seemed like your right-hand man."

He nods. "Even Kirney. Stormglen is heavily guarded and not everyone is welcome, even my best man and the captain of my ship."

"And yet I am?" I ask, pursing my lips as I glance at him.

He holds my gaze for a moment, then flashes me a smile. "Let's hope."

I frown at him, wondering what that means, until the carriage wheels bump over a large cobblestone and I'm jostled in my seat.

I turn my attention out the window, watching as the city of Menheimr rolls past. It feels like noon, at least from the way my stomach is growling, but all the shops are full of patrons, the streets bustling with carriages and pedestrians. Rows of pastel-green doves line the eaves above the streets, their feathers iridescent in the sharp sunlight. Every now and then between the shops and residences I spot a secluded courtyard surrounded by lush foliage, or a neat square with a flowing fountain at the center, populated with people lounging on green-speckled stone benches. Back in Lerick everything shuts down midday. People hide inside from the heat of the relentless sun. The fact that there are fountains here with water flowing freely— *wastefully*—makes my head spin.

Andor makes an amused sound and I glance at him, my eyes nar-

REALM of THIEVES 67

rowed automatically. He's watching me with large pupils, a smile tugging his lips.

"What?" I snap.

"Nothing," he says after a moment, then turns his attention back out the window.

I do the same, though I can tell he's staring at me again. I probably should act a little more blasé about everything. I feel my shell harden.

Still, the fresh scent of water, umberwoods, and blooming flowers that flows in through the carriage windows makes me breathe in deeply, and I feel as if something inside me is growing, invisible shoots sprouting from within. I'm not sure how I feel about it.

We leave the town, the buildings becoming farther apart, turning into red-timbered houses with grass growing on the roofs and large plots of fertile fields dotted with fuzzy, long-horned cows the size of horses and plump white sheep sprinkled here and there like dollops of cream. Beyond the fields thick with grazing animals, past the fruitful orchards with rows of gnarled trees bending toward one another like bowing men, and the rows of gilded wheat that wave delicately in the breeze are forest-covered slopes that reach up and up, interspersed by the occasional waterfall. I've never seen a waterfall before, though I've heard of them, and to see the water flowing so freely, so powerfully, stirs up something deep inside me.

I don't want to be here. And yet . . .

I stare out the window in wonder, deciding it's not worth the effort to keep pretending that none of this is impressing me.

The road becomes rougher with muddy patches as the wheels churn in the ruts, and then I remember the last time I was in a carriage.

It was the only time I was in a carriage.

Moments after my mother sailed off for the Midlands.

I was ripped away from my aunt, Ellestra, by the Black Guard. I remember the large metal gauntlets digging painfully into my shoulders, the way my aunt screamed as she tried to hang on to me. I was dragged to a waiting carriage and they threw me inside, locking the door. I couldn't escape and through the windows I saw the ship that had my mother disappearing into the night, heading toward her fate, her doom. I watched as the carriage pulled away from the only place I'd ever known and along a dark road into a long night that would culminate with my arrival at the convent.

The place where I ceased to have a name.

Where I ceased to have a voice.

Where I swore I would have my vengeance.

And yet I thought I *had* my vengeance. I thought that stealing the precious eggs they revere so much and working for House Dalgaard was somehow sticking a dagger into the sides of the Soffers. But it hasn't been more than a pinprick. I've barely made a dent.

"Worried about meeting the rest of the Kolbecks?" Andor asks me.

I blink and bring my gaze to his. For a moment I had forgotten where I was. Who knows what expression took over my face, what truth he tried to glean?

"I'm worried about my aunt," I hedge. It's not a lie—but I'm not about to tell him some sad memory from my past.

He nods and pulls out a necklace that was hiding beneath his shirt, its pendant grasped in his hand as he twirls it over and over again.

It's a tooth.

A dragon's tooth. Must have belonged to a sycledrage, perhaps the same one he got the claw from.

"We'll get her safe, you'll see," Andor says.

"How am I supposed to believe that?" I tell him. "Thanks to Lemi, everyone in Menheimr is going to know I'm here. You said so yourself. Word will travel. Someone is probably sending a raven to Dalgaard as we speak."

Lemi huffs at that, perhaps an apology, then lays his head in my

REALM of THIEVES   69

lap. Andor continues to twirl the tooth around the chain. "And if that happens, they will also report that you were here against your will, under armed escort."

"And then my aunt will get word of that and worry. It might kill her. Who knows what she will do?" The last thing I want is for her to go off on some sort of rescue mission.

He stops moving the tooth for a moment and stares at me thoughtfully. A wash of something soft comes over his face, like longing, but not quite.

I'm about to ask him what he's staring at, when he starts moving the tooth again, sliding it up and down the chain of the necklace, making a whirring sound that seems to fill the cabin.

"Steiner's raven will deliver her a message that you are in good hands and that you'll see her soon," he says.

I ignore the very untrue comment about being in "good hands." I clear my throat. "And how do you expect this bird to reach her? You don't even know where she lives."

"Moon is very adept at seeking people out. She can fly faster than any ship can sail. She'll find your aunt and relay the message."

"And if the message falls off?" I say, thinking of the passenger doves we have back in Esland that will fly to certain areas with tiny scrolls attached to their legs. Not to mention the difficulties a bird would have flying in the underground caverns.

He looks at me with bright eyes. "It can't fall off. Moon speaks her message."

"You have a talking bird?"

"You have a shifting dog," he counters.

"So is it like a parrot?"

Andor shrugs and keeps the tooth whirring back and forth on the chain. "Something like that."

The sound of the pendant is starting to grate on me. I frown at him. "What are *you* so worried about?"

"Me? Nothing."

"You keep fidgeting with your necklace."

His hand immediately drops away, his palms splayed on top of his knees. He looks out the window at the passing trees and then his leg starts bouncing. Now *I'm* starting to get anxious.

The rest of the journey takes us through rolling fields and deep forests, the red-barked trees with the trunks the size of this carriage reaching high into the canopy above, and Andor is strangely silent the whole time, save for his fidgeting. By the time the coach turns off the main road, the late-afternoon sun is hidden away by the towering trees and far-off mountains, and we haven't spoken another word to each other.

The road we're on now is different from the mud and ruts of the main one. It's paved with tiny pebbles, with a neatly trimmed strip of grass between the wheel tracks. On either side the land has been cleared into a meadow, making it easy to watch the curve of the road as it heads through iron gates and climbs up a small hill to a castle at the top, half-hidden among umberwoods and other trees.

"Welcome to Stormglen," Andor says as the carriage rolls underneath the arch above the gates that boasts the name of the estate in ornate cursive.

"I thought you said it was heavily guarded," I say, looking around the rolling fields and seeing nothing in sight except small yellow flowers. Even the woods seem far away now.

"Just trust me," he says. "There's a reason everything is so open around Stormglen. We can see the enemy coming from a mile away."

"And do you have many enemies attacking you?"

"We did at one time. My father believes that time has come again. Everything is a cycle in this world." His expression grows serious for a moment, his lips set in a hard line, his black brows furrowed together. "Don't you feel it? Don't you feel like everything in this world is moving toward some sort of new end?"

REALM of THIEVES   71

"I don't worry about things like that," I tell him, leaning forward as the carriage pitches up the hill. "I'm too busy trying to survive. Must be nice to be able to sit back in your heavily guarded castle and worry about the end of the world."

He takes my comments in stride, running a hand through his hair. "Fair point. But if all you care about is surviving, then the end of the world concerns you too."

I shrug and turn my attention back to the window, though I have to admit I'm curious.

Soon the carriage plateaus on the top of the hill, rumbling through a path of sculpted trees until it comes to a stop. Gudwale opens the coach doors for us and puts out his arm for me to take. I glance at Andor, who gestures for me to go forward.

I hesitantly take Gudwale's arm and step out of the carriage, my boots echoing on the stone ground. And that's when I'm glad I'm holding on to him, because the sight before me nearly makes my knees buckle.

Stormglen sits around us like a lion, a sprawling estate of a castle as long as it is tall, seeming to swallow up the entire hill. We're standing in front of massive wooden doors that are closed, an iron grille of portcullises above them, with stone garrisons that rise up on either side of the gates. There looks to be space behind it, perhaps a courtyard, before it rises up three stories with two semicircular bastions on either side of the gates. The castle itself is made from some sort of iridescent black stone that shimmers silver in the waning sun, and trails of green vines climb up the walls in places, making it look less austere. The windows are arched with gilded frames, and there are stained-glass windows covering the arrow slits along the bastions and parts of the tower, as if the place is torn between being a castle and a fortress.

Lemi sniffs my hand and I can feel him wanting to run forward and explore, perhaps pee on many of the various potted trees that line up around the outside of the walls, but I make a motion with my fingers for him to stay still.

Just as the large wooden doors swing open and a tall, stocky man with a thick neck and long dark hair steps out, a scowl on his face, a large mug of what looks like ale in his hand.

He fixes his black eyes on me. Looks me up and down, wrinkles his nose, and says, "Who in damnation is this?"

Chapter 8

Andor

  I HAD HOPED THAT WHEN WE ARRIVED AT STORMGLEN, MY uncle would not be the one to greet us. Though "greeting" usually conveys niceties. There are no such things with my Uncle Kjell, especially when he's had a few drinks.

"Uncle," I say, pasting a smile on my face. I do it more to piss him off since he always says I'm grinning like a fool. "This is Brynla Aihr," I tell him. "And her dog, Lemi."

It's only now that my gawking uncle pulls his eyes off Brynla and notices the giant black hound sitting patiently beside her. His grimace deepens and he looks to me.

"Am I supposed to know who the fuck Brynla Aihr is?" he grumbles. "Other than the fact that she's a foreigner. A purple-haired one at that. Sunburnt skin. Fucking hell, she's a bloody Eslander, isn't she?"

I expect Brynla to bite back but she remains silent, though I can feel the negative energy roiling up inside her.

"She's an Eslander," I say. "One of the Freelanders. From the Banished Land. And she is now a prisoner of Stormglen."

Brynla flinches and looks at me as if I've betrayed her. Perhaps the word *prisoner* was a bit too harsh, even if it's technically true.

"A prisoner?" Uncle Kjell takes a step forward to her, looking her over again. "She's not bound."

"We have an agreement," I tell him.

"An agreement, eh?" he says, narrowing his eyes at me. "And does your father know about this?"

I square my shoulders, breathing out sharply through my nose so I can focus and stay calm. "No."

"No?" Brynla says, pivoting to face me, her dark eyes blazing. "You mean they don't know about your plan?"

I give her a stiff smile, mentally willing her to keep quiet. "I'm sure I've mentioned it in passing to my father before. He'll think it's a good idea."

"Is that so?" Kjell says. "Taking an Eslander prisoner. A Freelander at that. Knowing you and your schemes, it's about as useless and harebrained as the last one. Tell me, nephew, what is this agreement you have?"

"Nothing I'm willing to discuss with you," I say to him, and grab Brynla's arm, pulling her around him and through the doors into the courtyard, Lemi staying close to her heels. "The goods are in the carriage," I call to him over my shoulder.

"You kidnapped me for nothing," Brynla seethes under her breath as I lead her between the fountains in the middle of the yard and Solla's rose garden.

"What little faith you have in me," I tell her with a grin.

"I have zero faith in you," she says.

My smile shakes slightly.

"I'll just have to prove you wrong," I say.

Just like I have to prove everyone wrong, all the time.

It's fucking exhausting.

We enter the main doors and step inside the hall, the smells of dinner cooking coming from the kitchen. I spot my sister, Solla, heading toward the great chamber, a book in her hand.

REALM of THIEVES

75

"Solla," I whisper to her, hurrying Brynla along the obsidian floors, Lemi's nails clicking on the surface as he trots behind us.

Solla stops and stares at us, blue eyes bright and wide. "You're back early," she says in her quiet voice, clutching her book tighter to her chest. "Who is this?" she asks, trying to sound polite, but I can see she can't make heads or tails of Brynla and Lemi. I've certainly never brought a girl home—I'd never subject a woman to this place— and most definitely not a hound.

"A prisoner," Brynla says dryly as I loosen my grip on her arm.

"Is the dog prisoner too?" Solla asks, brushing her bangs out of her eyes with her free hand.

"Yes," I tell her. "Listen, I need you to do me a favor."

Even under her hair I can see her thick brows knit together. "What?" she asks, ever hesitant.

"Can you take Brynla to her quarters? Put her in the yellow room. The dog can go with her too."

"Oh, she has a name?" Solla asks.

I wince. "I'm sorry, I forgot my manners."

"When don't you?" Solla mutters under her breath.

"*Solla*," I say, "this is Brynla and her hound, Lemi. Brynla, this is my one and only sister, Solla. She's the sweet one in the family, don't worry."

"And you want the sweet Kolbeck in charge of the prisoner?" Brynla asks, raising a brow at me.

"I can bite if I need to," Solla says, completely deadpan. I'm not worried about my sister. Even if Brynla tries something, she won't get far. Kjell will have put the guards on high alert already. Besides, Solla knows how to take care of herself when she needs to. Her gifts are impressive.

"You certainly can," I say. Then I sniff the air because I know it will get a rise out of Brynla. "And draw her a bath and fetch her some new clothes. She needs it."

Brynla glares at me but then self-consciously sniffs her shoulder. Honestly we all smell the same after being on the ship, just an overall sense of fish, brine, and oil.

I let go of Brynla's arm and Solla beckons for her to follow her down the hall to the east stairs. Brynla and Lemi reluctantly trail along, with Brynla glancing at me over her shoulder with a wary look.

I give her a reassuring smile that I'm sure she doesn't find reassuring at all, considering how the scowl on her face deepens, and then I quickly duck down the wing to my father's study and knock on the door.

"Come in." I hear his gruff voice through the door.

I open it and step inside.

My father is sitting at his desk, leaning back in his chair with one leg crossed, holding a glass of amber liquid. From the way the leather chair across from him has been pushed back and the telltale ring of condensation on his walnut desk, I know Kjell must have been with him right before he came out to the yard.

"One of the guards spotted your carriage coming up the road," my father says. "I was surprised it was you. You never come back from your voyages early. I take it you had a fruitful mission this time? Or am I just getting my hopes up?"

"Very fruitful," I say, sitting down in the chair. "In fact, I brought back more than you bargained for."

He gives me a tepid look, a gray brow arched. "Is that so?"

"I have suen from an elderdrage, as well as from a blooddrage," I say, leaning back in my chair, my left foot bouncing. "And I have a thief."

He frowns as he takes a sip from the glass. "What do you mean, you have a thief?"

"She's upstairs. Solla has her."

My father pauses, then slowly puts the drink down. "Andor," he says sharply. "Stop wasting my time like you always do and come out with it. What do you mean Solla has her?"

"Look," I say, leaning forward with my elbows on my knees, needing my father to take me seriously for once. "You know I've been working on a way to secure our position in the egg trade."

"You have been doing no such thing. It's Kjell that's been putting in the legwork."

I try to bury my frustration. "And where has it gotten us? Nowhere. We haven't advanced at all. The Dalgaards still control the trade."

"They only control the south," he counters dismissively.

"They're moving into Vesland, you know that's their plan. To control their trade and then take over the entire realm."

"And you know that we have fail-safes to prevent that from happening. The same fail-safes that will prevent another war with Altus Dugrell." He narrows his eyes. "Or have you forgotten your duties?"

I ignore that. "But the more suen that those Dalgaards obtain, the closer the kingdom of Sorland will get to building an invincible army," I try to explain. "Can't you see that's their end goal?"

"We all know that's their end goal," he says, eyeing me with disdain as he takes another sip of his drink. "But that's a goal they are decades off from achieving. You know what Sae Balek has shown me. I have seen the future. I know what the goddesses have planned for us. We continue what we're doing, which is working for the king while keeping our own interests. You, Vidar, Steiner, Solla—you'll all do what you must to keep our fingers in every pie possible. The rest will fall into place."

"You're not being proactive enough."

My father slams down the glass, hard enough that it nearly breaks. "Not proactive enough?" he bellows. "I'm sorry we can't all be as reckless, impulsive, and foolish as you, Andor Kolbeck. What has your so-called proactiveness gotten us over the years?" He gets to his feet and my heart starts to beat wildly. "Let's see." He ticks off a finger with dramatic flair as he comes around the desk. "You stole my ship on a last-minute journey to the White Islands . . ."

"Borrowed, actually. I was going to bring it right back."

"Because you had heard that the volcano was going to blow."

"Actually that was Steiner's idea," I cut in.

"And it did erupt and it sank my ship. You were lucky to get out of there alive. I still owe those pirates for saving you. There isn't a damn day I don't regret it."

"Technically those pirates are employed by me now."

He ticks off another finger. "Then you had the idea to go into the center of the Midlands in an attempt to find a mythical fucking dragon that doesn't exist anymore. You lost two good men to that pointless endeavor, may they rest in peace."

I do feel guilt over that. A lot of guilt. But I want to point out that my father is the one who assigned those men to come with me, and they weren't exactly reliable. It was their attempt to screw me over mid-raid of a deathdrage's nest that got them chomped in half to begin with, but of course my father refuses to believe me when I tell him what really happened there.

"And then," he goes on, louder now, and I know what's coming, "the day you were supposed to be married off to Princess Odelle, they caught you in bed in with her handmaiden! Do you know how badly you damaged the bond between our houses? That it's a miracle that Anahera is even willing to talk about marrying Princess Liva to our Vidar?"

"Does Vidar know about this?" I ask, my interest suddenly piqued. After I properly fucked it up with House Haugen, I'm surprised they want anything to do with our family. I know Vidar won't be too happy about being married off, even though that's part and parcel of being a Kolbeck.

"It doesn't matter what Vidar does and doesn't know," my father says with a dismissive wave of his hand as he half sits on the edge of his desk. The movement is stiff and makes the corners of his eyes twitch, which I know is his way of hiding pain. He sees me noticing

REALM of THIEVES

this too, a warning coming across his brow, telling me not to remark on it, even though we both know I could help him. He's never even let me try.

All because he's seen me try once before.

And he's seen me fail.

A failure heard around the world, a failure that follows me to this day, a slinking shadow of death and shame.

I brought a dog back to life, I want to tell him, but he wouldn't believe me anyway.

But the thought of Lemi reminds me of my prisoner.

"So I take it you don't want to hear my plan," I say to my father, smacking my hands on my thighs as I get up. "That's fine."

He frowns. "What plan?"

"The one that involves the thief I have upstairs."

He blinks. "You were serious about that?" he asks, eyes widening.

"You know I always am," I say, my jaw flexing. Why does everyone think everything I say and do is a joke?

"You're kidnapping people now?" He shakes his head, looking aghast.

"You're taking the moral road now?" I say, stepping around my chair. "Do you know how many people you've kidnapped? That you've held below in our prisons? That you've tortured? Murdered?"

"All in the name of the king!"

"So for once we're doing it in the name of Kolbeck. And I'm not torturing her. Her name is Brynla Aihr and I've been watching her a long time now. Through the raven, through Dagruna Bjarr, I've learned that she's one of the best." I decide not to mention Lemi for the time being. "She just needs help and training, something I can provide to get her to the next level."

He makes a noise of disgust. "If you need more help on your raids, you go down to the docks and you pay for them."

"You don't understand. She isn't like those thieves. She's in a class of her own. That's why she's been working for House Dalgaard for years. That's why they have the leg up."

His mouth drops. "You stole Dalgaard's thief?"

I swallow hard, finding my conviction. "Does that scare you?"

"You're a damn fool!" he shouts, his eyes blazing. "You've brought a Sorland spy into our very house!"

"She's not from Sorland. She's from the Banished Land. She's a Freelander."

"That's even worse!" He looks up to the ceiling and shakes his head. "Valdis, Vigdis, forgive my fool of a son, for he does not know what he does."

"I know very well what I'm doing," I snap. "I captured Brynla so she can work for our side. In exchange I will get her aunt out of the Dark City."

"Andor," he barks as he walks toward me. I hold my ground. He presses his finger into my chest, hard. "You had no right to bring a Freelander into this house. You know what kind of people they are."

"Actually, I don't," I say. "At least I didn't before I started dealing with them. But she's not like you think. Everything we've been told about them is a lie."

"Oh, is that so? She's a thief working for Dalgaard. Doesn't show much strength of character there."

"She's a survivor doing what she's had to do to survive. How can you not admire that?"

"Don't try to appeal to my sympathy, because I have none. There's a reason her people are banished, why no other realms have taken them in."

"Because they have no means to leave. And the ones that do won't be welcome on anyone's shores because of the lies that the Eslanders spread about them. How can you side with all the rubbish that comes from the Soffers in Lerick? You know they're as erratic as a ghost bat."

REALM of THIEVES 81

"Fuck, Andor," he mutters under his breath, going back around his desk. "You really messed up this time."

"I can't possibly mess up if I haven't been given time to prove myself," I point out.

"I want her gone, Andor," he says tiredly, plopping down in his chair. "This will only complicate things, especially with Altus Dugrell. Don't forget your promise to the princess."

A promise I never made, I think. *None of us ever do.*

"You don't need to worry about that," I tell him. "The thief hates me."

"Then make sure you keep it that way," he grumbles. "I would suggest you put her on your ship and take her back to wherever you got her from immediately, but now that she's been in our keep, I can't risk that." He pauses, eyes narrowing. "You do realize what you've done, don't you? You have to keep her here forever. You won't be able to let her out of your sight. You won't be able to let her go. She'll be a prisoner of House Kolbeck until the day she dies. Death is the only way I'll let that thief walk out of this house and right back to the Dalgaards."

I swallow hard. I almost play my other hand, the only card I have left, but now isn't the time.

"Then I better go make sure she hasn't tried to kill Solla," I tell him.

My father stiffens and drinks the remains of his glass.

Chapter 9

Brynla

Andor was right. Solla Kolbeck seems sweet, but now I know I can't underestimate her.

After he passed me and Lemi off into her hands, I focused on surveying the castle, looking for my exit. The odds of escape were low, but I hadn't seen a single guard since we pulled up to the castle. In fact, I'd seen no one except his uncle and Solla.

As we climbed the stairs, Solla behind me, we passed by a window that was open enough for me to squeeze through. I could get away and Lemi could shift back to the road, then come find me.

But before I could back-kick Solla down the stairs, the window slammed shut as if by an invisible hand. Lemi ran past me up the stairs and I felt a force at my back, as if that same invisible hand was pushing me along. I moved my feet fast to avoid tripping.

I got to the second floor and whirled around to look at Solla, but she only had a quiet smile for me. "You must be exhausted from the journey," she said as she took me down a wide hall, past tapestries and paintings of forests and waterfalls on the walls. "As much as you'd like to run away, I think you'd feel a lot better with a warm bath, a change of clothes, and something to eat, don't you think?"

REALM of THIEVES

And even though I yearned to run away, the idea of a hot bath was too indulgent to resist. Besides, even if I had made it out the window, where would Lemi and I have gone? We're in a new realm, in a new climate, with untold dangers that I have no experience with. Even if I could find my way back to the docks, which was doubtful, then what? Smuggle myself onto a ship and hope it's going to Esland or the Midlands, where no one ever goes?

So I let her lead me into a large bathroom, where she gestured to a flush toilet in the corner and a large copper bathtub in the middle. "We have indoor plumbing, thanks to my younger brother," she said. "If you turn the tap with the *C*, cold water comes out. If you turn the tap with the *H*, hot water comes out. There are bath salts and herbs and different soaps to choose from. Take your time. I'll give you privacy and lay out some clothes for you in the room across the hall. They'll be my clothes—I don't think anyone would be too happy about you wearing my mother's—and they'll be too big on you but I'm sure you'll make do."

Then she looked at Lemi. "Would you like me to feed him? I assume beef would suffice?"

I told her he'd love that but I wanted him to stay with me. He wouldn't go off with a stranger anyway, no matter how kind she was being.

And now she's left, closing the door behind her. I quickly go after it and lock it to make sure no one will walk in on me in the nude. Then I lean against it and survey the room.

I let out a loud breath. My knees start to shake. The adrenaline of the journey is starting to wear off, like I've been holding on to a cliff for too long and my hands have finally let go. Part of me thinks I should just curl up in the bathtub as is and take a nap— it's certainly big enough. But I remind myself that it can wait. I need to get through the rest of the day before I figure out what my options are.

"Well, Lemi," I say to him, and his tail thumps against the rose quartz floor in response. "How about I take a bath, then you'll take your turn?"

I swear his warm brown eyes narrow at me. He is not a fan of baths but he needs the Midlands volcanic stink and itchy salt of the voyage off him, not to mention the dried suen that's been sun-baked into his coat.

I slowly walk around the room, taking it all in. I'm sure to the Kolbecks it's just a bathroom, with the toilet in the corner half-hidden by a gauzy partition, the tub in the middle with wooden steps leading up to it, and a shelf that houses a bunch of glass jars filled with salts and herbs and liquids. But I'm also seeing the polished pink finish of the floors and the energy that flows through them, the copper-tiled ceiling that matches the bath, a long marble sink below curved mirrors lined with dragon eggshells, the gilded arches above a stained-glass window.

I peer through the blue stained glass—a motif of stars in a daytime sky—and open it a crack, the gold hinges creaking. Cool air flows inside and I breathe in deeply. That scent of the umberwoods and clear, fresh running water fill the room. The sun is gone now, hidden from this side of the keep, and the scenery looks surreal. All those tall green trees, the flowering fields, the rushing waterfalls, and the craggy snow-capped mountains in the distance look as if someone enchanted painted them, a world that I could have never even imagined. Even when teachers at school would talk briefly about the other realms, the idea of a forest when all we had in Esland were prickly shrubs, scrawny nut trees, and the occasional palm that dotted the capitol buildings, was beyond anything I could have dreamed.

Lemi whines from behind me and I when I look back at him he's gesturing to the tub with his muzzle.

"All right, I get it, I stink," I tell him. I walk over and turn on the taps and then while the bath takes time to fill, I try to decide on what to put in it. Solla had mentioned salts, and I remember my father used to put salts from the mines outside Lerick in his bathwater after he had a long day fishing. Said it helped the muscles. Would probably be nice when my womb is having a flare-up, though it seems to be behaving for now.

I dump in a fistful of salt from one of the glass jars on the shelf, some dried flowers with fragrant yellow and dusk-blue blooms, watching them swirl on the surface, until I think the water is high enough. Then I disrobe, discarding my dirty armor on the floor. I'll need to wash that too, after.

Gingerly I climb up the steps and then balance as I dip my toe in the water. It's hot but not scalding, and the combination of the rising steam with the cool air coming in through the window makes me quickly sink into the water.

It's heaven. Or some version of it, anyway. I can't remember the last time I had a proper bath. Of course we bathe, even in the Dark City, but water is scarce, sacred even. Occasionally we'll have a warm bath, but more often than not, Ellestra will meet me at the shore after I've returned home from a raid, and we'll dip into the ocean, using bars of fat soap to get clean—even though the salt only makes you itchier after. But it's better than nothing.

At the thought of her, my heart squeezes as if my chest has grown too small. She's in the caverns of the city right now. She'll be worried, she'll be asking around if anyone has seen me, dangerous questions that might attract the wrong people. Then what will she do? Make peace that her niece is gone, the last connection to her brother, my father? Will she seek vengeance? She's a fiery one, not unlike me. She might do something stupid. In some ways I hope she just forgets me. But I know that won't be the case, not when she went through so much trouble to sneak me out of the convent.

And if Ruunon notices my absence and finds her? Then what will happen?

It's enough that it feels like I can't get air in my chest. I close my eyes and sink deeper into the water, breathe in and out through my nose until I feel remotely in control again. I used to have these moments of panic right after I escaped the convent, and it was my aunt who taught me how to calm myself down, even though she never used this technique on herself.

There's no point thinking about these things right now when I can't do anything. I have to do what Andor says, whether I like it or not—at least until the next ship leaves and we can get to Esland, like he promised. I will hold him to that promise. By any means necessary. I don't care if I have to kill him to get my way.

After I finish washing my hair with the peppery-smelling liquids in the jars, the water is no longer so hot. I get out of the bath and then coax Lemi in. He does so reluctantly, though he seems to relax a little once I start rubbing the liquid soap on his coat. By the time we're both done with the bath, it's black from dirt.

I wrap a large fluffy bath towel around me, my hair wet and loose around my shoulders, while Lemi shakes, water flying across the room. I suppose we have left it a bit of a mess.

When I'm walking over to the wooden rack to grab more towels, there's a knock at the door.

I freeze, hoping it's not the creepy uncle as I hold the towel tighter around my chest. "What?"

Silence for a moment. I suppose I'm not acting with the best manners.

"It's Andor," he says. "Are you decent? Can I come in?"

I glance down. There's not much showing except my arms, legs, and cleavage.

"Yeah, I'm decent," I say. *On the outside, anyway.*

I warily move over and unlock the door and open it.

His eyes immediately go to my chest and widen.

"You said you were decent," he stammers, and I swear I see a flush of color above the stubble on his jaw.

I shrug. "Good enough. Can I help you?"

"I can come back," he says quickly.

I roll my eyes and open the door wider. "Just come in, then."

He hesitates, then strides inside the bathroom. I close the door behind him. If I'm supposed to feel some sort of shame or wariness about being around him while practically naked, I don't feel it. For some reason, I can't imagine him hurting a woman in that way.

At any rate, Lemi would be on him in a second.

"Now that you're here, does your sister have the ability to, say, move things with her mind?" I ask.

He gives me a crooked smile. "That's putting it mildly."

Fascinating. "Do all you Kolbecks have special powers?" Then I pause, realizing. "Oh, but of course you do. You're in the suen business." Of course, there are some people in this world who are said to have magic passed down through their blood, even though that magic originally came from their ancestors' ingestion of suen. Usually mages and witches. But I highly doubt that this applies to the Kolbecks.

"As are you. So what is your power, Brynla Aihr?"

"I seduce men and rob them," I answer sweetly, batting my eyelashes. It's a half-truth.

For the life of me I can't read the expression on his face, but his eyes are darting everywhere except my chest. I clear my throat. "So what's so important that you couldn't wait until after my bath to talk to me?"

"Oh," he says, scratching at his jaw as he takes a couple of steps closer. "Nothing really. Just wanted to tell you something before I forgot."

"What?"

"Dinner is in an hour. You'll be expected to be there."

"Do all your prisoners have dinner with you?"

"You would be the first." He pauses as if he's about to say something else, then shuts his mouth. "I suppose I should, uh, warn you about my father."

"Is he anything like your uncle?"

"Worse," he says with a sour smile, and my stomach sinks a little. "He's not all that enthused about my plan."

"Ah, at least I'm not the only one. I'll be sure to tell him that too."

He stiffens slightly. "I wouldn't do that if I were you."

There's an edge to his voice that I don't like.

I swallow uneasily and try to ignore it. "Well, at least I don't stink anymore," I say, throwing my arms out.

A chain reaction is unleashed.

Andor suddenly leans in and brushes his nose to my shoulder and inhales.

The feeling of his breath against my bare skin makes my eyes roll back in head.

Sends a shiver rolling through my body.

Which then causes my towel to suddenly unravel, leaving me completely naked, the towel pooled at my feet.

I shriek.

Andor pulls back and meets my eyes, an apologetic twist to his lips.

But then in an instant his eyes drop to my chest. To my stomach. To *below*.

"Gods!" he swears, quickly spinning around to face away from me while Lemi starts barking, perhaps confused at the panicked way I ungracefully bend over and pick up the towel, holding it to my chest and letting it drape in front of me.

"All right, anyway, dinner in an hour. I'll send Solla or one of the handmaidens up to get you," Andor says, talking a mile a minute as he strides over to the door. This is the first time I've seen him flustered.

"You smell nice, by the way," he says before he closes the door.

I look down at Lemi, who is watching me with a tilt of his head. And I smile.

Chapter 10

Brynla

After the bath incident with Andor, Lemi and I quickly sneak across the hallway. The door is wide open and the wallpaper is yellow floral, so I assume it's the "yellow room."

Like the bathroom, it's grand. Too grand for me. It has the same gilded arches over the windows, though they aren't stained glass, and a burgundy velvet curtain frames two glass doors that open out onto a stone balcony that overlooks the courtyard below. I decide to look *after* I have clothes on, just in case I end up flashing some of the Kolbecks or their help.

I focus on getting dressed. On the sprawling bed—the largest I've ever seen—are three outfits laid out. Dresses in various shades of pink. I don't think I've ever had anything pink in my whole life. The colors we wear in Esland are dusty grays and browns and olive greens, the better to match the desert scenery. The hooded robes we wore at the convent were heavy and black. Anything with bright or pleasing colors would be seen as an affront to the dragons, as if we were trying to compete with their beauty. Not that I've ever seen a pink dragon before.

Solla is roughly my size—neither of us is particularly thin—but I am quite a bit taller than her, so when I slip on the undershirt, the

REALM of THIEVES   91

dress sleeves come halfway up my forearm, and the skirt hem hits at the ankle instead of the floor. The neckline is somewhat low with lacy pink ruffles, and the velvet accents on the gown make me feel as if I'm wearing fancy upholstery. I feel silly but it fits well enough.

Then I glance in the mirror and nearly jump. Yes, I definitely look strange with my hair down and the fancy dress, like I'm a child trying on my mother's clothes, as if my mother was some rich Norlander and not a rebel always scraping by on the outskirts of Lerick.

I start gathering my damp hair and braiding it down my back, looping it around a few times until it's in a loose bun. There. Now I look a tiny bit more refined.

"What do you think, Lemi?" I ask him.

He tilts his head, pondering. I don't want to hear his answer.

Knock knock.

"Who is it?" I ask, creeping toward the door.

I hear a muffled reply. "It's Solla. Do you need any help with your dress?"

My first instinct is to say no, I'm fine. I've never needed help getting dressed before, not as an adult anyway. All my outfits are simple tunics and pants I can slip on. The corset ties up at the front, and even my armor snaps together with buckles I can reach.

But I haven't worn a gown since I was a child, and I can't reach the laces at the back.

"You may come in," I reluctantly say.

The door opens and Solla pokes her head inside. I didn't really notice it before—I suppose I was too busy trying to plot my escape—but I see the resemblance to Andor. Though her eyes are blue, not amber, and her forehead is hidden by her thick, dark bangs, I can tell her brow works overtime with her expressions, just like her brother's. She's a really pretty girl, maybe a few years younger than me, petite with soft curvy lines and pale, smooth skin that point to a life of wealth and good, healthy food and having all your needs catered to.

And yet, even though she looks different from the wiry people of the Dark City, I wouldn't underestimate this girl. Not only because of her ability to move things with her mind, but because I sense a darkness behind the quiet posture, a strength in her diminutive height. The same darkness I've glimpsed in Andor when he's let his jovial mask slip for a moment.

"It's not too big?" Solla asks, coming inside the room and closing the door after her.

I turn around and gesture to my back. "I guess I need some help with the laces. I'm afraid you have a bigger chest than me."

She snorts. "I have a bigger chest than most women," she says, coming around and grabbing the laces at the back. "I'll tell you a secret with these dresses. Put the top on backward and then lace them up that way. Twist them around when you're done. You won't need anyone."

She gives the laces a sharp tug that nearly squeezes the breath out of me.

"Sorry, is that too tight?" she asks sweetly.

"No," I say with a gasp. "Who needs lungs anyway?"

She laughs softly at that and thankfully loosens the laces enough for me to breathe. If it were my time of the month and I was feeling poorly, I wouldn't be able to have any constriction around my middle at all. "Sorry. My handmaid used to lace me up so tightly that I often fainted just roaming around the halls. It was my father's idea, you know. To try to make some kind of point."

"And what point is that?"

"His attempt at making me lose weight—or make me look like I had," she says. "But I got the last laugh. I dismissed my handmaiden."

So he's not only a dick to Andor but to Solla as well. If that's how he treats his children, then how will he treat a prisoner?

"Besides, I've never wanted to depend on anyone," she goes on. I can agree with that.

"And your mother?" I ask. "Where is she?"

There's a pause in her lacing. Then she clears her throat and resumes. "She's dead."

I know her pain too well.

"I'm so sorry," I whisper.

"Happened a long time ago," she says. "I was only eight. And you?"

"And me what?"

"When did you lose your mother?" she asks, coming around the front of me, her eyes gentle. "Grief can always recognize grief. The loss of a mother runs deep. Steiner believes that if we could look at the brain, we'd see the damage of when we experienced loss. Like a black blight on a potato. His words, not mine."

As much as I appreciate the kind words and conversation, I don't want to get personal.

"I was old enough," I say, giving her a look to drop the subject.

She stares at me for a moment, reminding me of Andor. Then she nods slightly. "Why are you here anyway? It's been a long time since we've had a prisoner."

"Andor has a plan," I say with a sigh.

"Andor always has a plan."

"Do those plans ever work out?"

"More often than not," she admits. "He just has an unconventional way of getting things done. Leaps before he looks. Usually lands on his feet. So what plan are you?"

I shrug. "Why don't you ask him at dinner? I would love to know if this is another case of leaping before looking."

"Oh, I'm sure there will be many more questions, coming from all directions," she says. Then she looks down at Lemi, who has been watching this whole interaction with patient confusion. "Is he okay with other dogs? Vidar's dog, Feral, often lies by the hearth when we dine. He's not as wild as his name suggests. And sometimes Steiner's cat, Woo-woo, will drop by."

I can't help but laugh. "Lemi should be fine with Feral. I'll do what I can with Woo-woo. It's not that Lemi likes to chase cats, more that he likes to be an instigator and get the cats to chase him. Either way, I'll make sure it doesn't happen around the dinner table. Otherwise, I can keep him here in the room."

Or I can try. The chances that Lemi won't shift after me are low.

"What about shoes?" she asks me, glancing at my bare feet. "Do you need new ones?"

"I have the feet of a giant," I tell her. "Yours won't fit. I'll just wear my boots."

I grab the stockings she had laid out for me and slip them on, then pull on my boots that go up to my knees. Her nose wrinkles at first at the sight of something so dirty and utilitarian with her soft dresses. But then once I stand up she shrugs.

"Actually, I rather like the combination. Pretty yet rugged." She gives me a soft smile and then eyes the grandfather clock in the room. "We should make our way down."

"Come, Lemi," I say to him. "Stay by my side like a good boy."

We exit the room and step into the hall. I'm about to shut the door behind me, when the door shuts for me.

"Must be a drafty castle," I comment wryly.

Solla doesn't say anything to that. I want to ask about her mind-bending abilities but figure there's enough time for that later. I have a feeling I'll be spending all dinner fending off questions, not asking them.

We walk down the hall to the stairs and this time I'm able to sneak a peek down another wide corridor, one side lined with tall windows, the other with large doors spaced wide apart. I'm going to guess the chambers of the family.

Once we're down on the main floor my nerves start to kick in. Lemi notices this and nuzzles my hand as we walk. Either that or he wants dinner.

It's then that I smell it. The rich, hearty scent of spices and stewed meat wafting out from down the hall, making my stomach lurch in hunger. I haven't eaten since this morning on the ship, and that was only a few dried pieces of salted cod.

Solla takes me through two open doors and into a massive dining hall with shining stone walls the same silver sheen as the exterior. There is one large table in the middle to seat a dozen or so people, and there are two more tables at either end, enough to hold a banquet or a feast or whatever rich people in castles do. Along the opposite wall are large windows framed by thick curtains that give a view into an orchard grove. The outer castle wall rises behind it, the landscape grainy in the dusky light. Some built-in seating is underneath the windows, the backs of the booths lined with draped furs, and a great fireplace with crackling flames in the center. Above are several chandeliers lit with thick flaming candles that cast an additional glow into the room.

"Solla, dear, you're early," a woman says as she bustles into the room holding a tray of stacked dishes. She's short and round with a crooked nose and lively eyes, her dark hair pulled back under a bonnet. She looks both old and young, an age that's hard to place.

She pauses slightly when she sees me, then Lemi, but then continues setting the places around the table. "I was told we had a guest tonight but I wasn't expecting a hound, too."

"I hope that's not a bother," I say to the woman.

She glances up at me in surprise as she finishes putting down the plates. "No bother to me, but even if it were, I'm only the help." She exchanges a quizzical look with Solla, as if to wonder what corner of the world I've been dragged out of. I suppose I should get used to that look.

Once the woman has put down cloth napkins and silverware, she leaves the room and Solla pulls out a chair for me near the end of the table. "Here, you can sit across from me and next to Andor. Also farthest from my father and uncle, which you'll soon appreciate."

I sit down on the tall wood chair, taking in the ornate carvings of dragon tails wrapped around cedar trunks. Even though Norlanders don't worship dragons, their images are throughout the house.

Lemi comes beside me, his head on the table, until I tell him to go sit by the fire, which he does reluctantly, never taking his eyes off me.

Solla takes the seat across from me while the woman comes out again, this time bringing along an older balding gentleman with graying blue hair at the temples. They bring out glass jugs, gold carafes, and various crystalware and place them on the table along with a giant bowl of fresh-baked bread in the middle of the spread with a platter of melting butter. At first I think the butter has gone bad because of the dark flecks in it, but then the woman notices the expression on my face and tells me it's herbed butter.

Not only do I feel stupid, but I also feel ridiculous being served by these people. The fact that I'm technically a prisoner and yet they're the ones bringing me food doesn't feel right.

"What are your names?" I suddenly blurt out as the man places a goblet in front of me. "If you don't mind sharing." Both the man and the woman pause and look at each other. "I'm Brynla," I say quickly. "That's my dog, Lemi."

The man clears his throat. "I'm Belon," he says in a voice, his accent unplaceable.

"You can call me Margarelle," the woman says with a quick smile. "I hope your stay here will be a comfortable one, for however long it may be."

"Hopefully not too long," I blurt out before I realize what I've said.

Belon snorts lightly in amusement just as Andor appears in the doorway.

I have to admit, the sight of him doesn't annoy me for once. Not that I mind Solla's company, but in a strange way I feel I can be more myself in front of Andor than I can be with his sister. That is, until I remember that he's the one who's blackmailing me.

Andor stands there staring at me in disbelief, as if he doesn't recognize me. I suppose the color pink makes me look like someone else.

Then he gives me a flash of a smile, a dimple appearing in his stubble, and walks on over, pulling out the chair.

"You'll have to forgive me," he says, sitting down. "I didn't recognize you with a proper dress on."

"Yes, it's almost as if I were a lady or something," I say.

"Almost had me fooled," he says, reaching for a goblet made of onyx.

"Let's see if I can fool the rest of your family," I mutter under my breath.

"Oh, please don't," Andor says, giving me another playful smile. "It's the real you that's valuable to House Kolbeck."

If they find any value in me at all, I think. Judging by his uncle's reaction, I should prepare for the worst.

And with that thought, I feel my palms grow clammy. I shouldn't want to impress these people and yet somehow I do.

"Here," he says, snapping his fingers at Belon, who hurries over with a cask of wine. "Have some wine. We have our own winery on the slopes at the back of the keep. We get our reds imported from Vesland but our white grapes have done all right, thanks to Steiner's tinkering. He's got an evergreen thumb."

Belon pours some white wine into my goblet just as another man appears in the archway. He pauses briefly to look at me, a dark, arched brow raised in such a way that I know without a doubt he's Andor's older brother. They have the same square jaw, the long nose, the deep-set eyes and dark hair, though his hair is cut short and his eyes are green. He's as tall as Andor, maybe taller, and though he doesn't have the same bulk of muscles, he's still lean and powerful looking.

98   KARINA HALLE

He walks with controlled, languid grace, like a giant cat that can't decide if it's going to flop down and take a nap or pounce on you.

I find myself sucking in my breath, too wary to take a sip of my wine, my eyes never leaving his as he sits beside Solla.

"Who is this?" he asks, his voice even and rich as he looks me over with a measured gaze.

"This is Brynla," Andor says. "She's our guest."

"Prisoner," Solla speaks up, hiding a small smile behind her glass.

"Prisoner-slash-guest," Andor clarifies. He gives me a flash of a smile. "Brynla, this is my brother Vidar, otherwise known as the golden boy and heir to the Kolbeck dynasty. I'd tell you he's not as grumpy as he looks, but that would be a lie."

I can see that. Vidar seems to have a face carved from stone. Handsome but coldly so, his face dark and impassive. Not a person you'd want on your bad side, that much I can glean.

Vidar doesn't say anything to Andor; instead he focuses on me. "I'm not sure if I'm supposed to be greeting a prisoner, but if you're staying for dinner, then formalities take precedent. Welcome to Stormglen. I trust your stay here will be . . . tolerable."

"Thank you," I tell him. "I was hoping I would meet your dog."

There's a tiny flare of surprise in his eyes. "Feral? He'll be down once he smells the food being served."

"I thought he might get along well with Lemi," I say, gesturing over my shoulder.

Vidar looks around my chair, brows rising once he spots Lemi by the hearth. "I see. The prisoner-guest has a dog."

"I'm the prisoner, my dog is the guest," I tell him, allowing myself a sip of wine.

I swear he nearly smiles at that. Must be a trick of the eyes.

"And what do you think of the wine?" Andor asks me, leaning in slightly. I catch a whiff of his scent, like a mixture of warm amber and the umberwoods. I close my eyes for a moment, his smell making my stomach flip. Must be the nerves.

"It's good," I manage to say. "Though I don't have a lot of experience with wine. We don't normally drink it." And by that I mean, I think I've had it once, stolen from my aunt's canteen when she wasn't looking. It tasted like poison.

"What do you normally drink in the Dark City?" he asks.

"Did you just say the Dark City?" Vidar says sharply.

"Yes," I say, straightening up in my chair and meeting his eye. "That's where I've come from."

"I don't think we've ever had someone from Esland at Stormglen," Vidar remarks in a low voice. "I don't think I've even met anyone from Esland."

"And for good reason," another voice, louder and sharper still, booms across the room.

The Sjef of House Kolbeck has arrived for dinner.

Chapter 11

Brynla

The man who could only be Torsten Kolbeck appears, followed by his scowling brother, Kjell. Torsten stands behind Vidar's chair and eyes me with quiet disdain, his chin raised. He's older than I expected, taller too, and lanky, with thick white hair and golden eyes like Andor. His clothes are black and tailored to him; the decorative pads at his shoulders made of leather dragonscale give him the look of someone about to go to war *and* someone who commands the war.

I feel Andor's foot press against mine under the table and I know he's warning me to behave myself. I push my foot back against his, letting him know that I read him loud and clear.

And I'm not going to say anything if I can help it. I can see that Torsten is a man who would toss me in the dungeon without a second thought, and I'm not sure anyone in here would come to my aid. Above all else, I don't want to put Lemi in harm's way.

"So this is your prized thief," Torsten says, glancing briefly at Andor with the same disdain he seems to give me. "I'm not sure what I pictured."

"She didn't look like that when she was brought in," the uncle

REALM of THIEVES   101

says; his lip wrinkles as he goes to sit at one end of the table and Torsten takes his seat at the other end.

"Well, then," Torsten says gruffly, unfolding a napkin and placing it over his lap just as Belon comes over with the wine cask. "Now that we've gotten the pleasantries out of the way, we can eat. Where is Steiner?"

"Right here, sir," says a young man who quickly strides into the room. Tall and skinny, the youngest Kolbeck has a distinctive jaw; thick, wavy black hair and bright blue eyes that light up briefly when he sees me. But he's a slip of a man, bordering on a boy, and his presence is so slight and quiet that he nearly disappears in front of my eyes. "Sorry," he mumbles as he sits down beside Solla. "I was—"

"Yes, yes, we know," Torsten says, picking up his goblet. "Studying plants or the mind or the minds of plants."

"Well, actually—" Steiner begins, but he is silenced by a sharp look from his father.

"Let us be mindful that we have *company* dining with us," Torsten says, fixing his cold gaze on me now, reminding me of the water hawks that used to perch at the end of the docks in Lerick, searching the sea for fish. They never hurried, they always took their time, and they always caught their prey. "I'm sure our guest wants to listen to neither your science nor your magic."

"Why is she here, boy?" the uncle says to Andor, slurping loudly from his goblet. I try to hide the disgust on my face. "If she's your prisoner, she should be in the dungeon. In chains. With only scraps to eat. Not sitting here like the rest of us."

"Now, now, Kjell," Torsten says, his tone mocking. "Andor has promised us he has a plan for her. Well, thief, has Andor filled you in on this plan, or has he failed to run that past you?"

"Brynla is—" Andor begins.

"I wasn't asking you," his father interrupts. "I was asking her. Well? Does the girl speak or do you do all the speaking for her?"

I clear my throat. "I prefer to speak for myself."

"Good," Torsten says. "Then we can agree on something to start. Tell me, Brynla"—he pauses, measuring me with his eyes—"what the blazes are you doing at my dining table?"

Andor sucks in his breath and I feel his eyes on me but I don't dare look away from his father.

"Your son captured me while I was collecting eggs on the Midlands," I tell him.

"Captured you, you say." He arches a gray brow. "I would love to hear how my son would capture anyone. Poor boy can't even catch a fish."

His uncle snickers at the end of the table. No one else laughs.

"First he made me an offer, which I refused."

"And the offer was?"

"That I stop stealing eggs for House Dalgaard and steal them for House Kolbeck instead."

"And why did you refuse?"

I glance at Andor, his eyes intently focused on me, much like everyone else around the table.

"Because I don't know Andor. Because I don't know House Kolbeck."

"Because you're part of House Dalgaard."

"No. I am not part of their house," I say, unable to keep the sharpness off my tongue. I know what he's trying to get at. He wants to paint me as the enemy. He wants an excuse to kill me here and now. "My skills are for hire. Dalgaard happens to be the highest bidder. I have no connection to them otherwise, no allegiance."

"And yet you said no to House Kolbeck."

"As I said, I don't know Andor. Better to trust the evil you know than the evil you don't."

Torsten's smile is wry. "You're taking a large risk trusting it either way."

REALM of THIEVES

"Like I said," I remind him, "I didn't choose to come here. I was taken by force. I might be at your dining table, wearing your daughter's clothes and drinking your estate's wine, but I keep being reminded that I am a prisoner in this house and that as nicely as I'm treated, there is no escape for me."

"Or your dog," Kjell says snidely.

"Ah yes, my brother filled me in on our other guest," Torsten says, leaning back in his chair slightly to eye Lemi by the fire. "Andor neglected to tell me you had a hound. I suppose it was his bleeding heart that let you take him."

Andor clears his throat. "The dog is partly why Brynla is so successful." Then his gaze narrows on me thoughtfully. "Perhaps the dog is the whole reason why Brynla is so good at what she does."

I stiffen, the hairs rising at the back of my head. I manage to hold Andor's gaze. "Lemi helps me. I help Lemi. He will never work without me, no matter how hard you try. He will shift to a place that you have never seen and he will never come back, not without me."

In other words, *Don't you fucking* dare *try to take my dog away from me.*

"So you take her dog away, and then what do you have?" Kjell says, putting his goblet down with a loud *thunk*. "Just a purple-haired whore, with a stink you'll never be able to wash off, no matter how much soap you use."

Andor erupts from his seat and moves fast, so fast that he's a blur until he appears behind his uncle, a sharp knife in his hand, the shining blade pressed against Kjell's throat.

"Andor!" Torsten chides him.

"Prisoner or not, you will treat Ms. Aihr with the respect a lady deserves," Andor says into his uncle's ear, his voice seething. "Do you understand?"

His uncle scoffs, seemingly not concerned, until Andor presses the knife in harder, enough to draw a thin drop of blood.

"Andor!" Torsten says, getting to his feet. "Control yourself, for the sake of the gods!"

"Andor," I whisper to him. "Please."

My nonexistent honor is not worth it.

Andor doesn't move for a moment, just breathes heavily, his face frozen in a sneer. Then he grunts and straightens up, releasing Kjell. He walks around the table and back to his chair beside me, avoiding my gaze.

Bloody blazes, is this what dinner at the Kolbecks' is usually like?

"All right, sorry for the delay." Margarelle's voice rings out, interrupting the silent tension in the room. She bustles inside with Belon, both of them holding platters of steaming-hot food. My stomach immediately growls but as the food is being dished out, I can't stop thinking about what Andor did. He can't care that much about how I'm treated—it must come down to his volatile relationship with his uncle.

Belon spoons a stew of chicken and beans onto my plate, and the urge to eat is overwhelming. It smells delightful, the chicken browned and crisped at the edges of the skin, the beans and tomatoes rich in color and seeming perfectly spiced, making my mouth water despite the current circumstances.

"Don't be shy," Torsten says to me in his dry tone. "We haven't poisoned yours."

Though he doesn't say it, the word *yet* is implied.

And everyone at the table is staring at me, as if daring me to try it. Solla's eyes are bright and inquisitive, Vidar's cold and calculating, Steiner's perplexed, Kjell's angry as he presses a cloth to his neck, Torsten's full of haughtiness and disdain, and Andor, well, I suppose he's still trying not to look in my direction. Even Margarelle and Belon have paused by the door, watching me intently.

Fuck it. If I'm going to die by poisoned food, at least it will have been a good meal.

I have a bite. As expected, it tastes delicious.

"And?" Torsten goads. "Is it good enough for an Eslander? I can't imagine the lot of you surviving on anything more than desert bugs."

I paste on a smile and nod at Margarelle. "Compliments to the chef. It's very good."

Margarelle beams at me and leaves the room. At least someone here seems happy.

"You're from Esland?" Steiner asks between mouthfuls. "I must have missed the memo about an Eslander coming to visit."

"We all missed the memo," Vidar comments under his breath.

"I've heard that the Eslanders don't let anyone leave the continent," Steiner goes on, talking fast now that he doesn't have food in his mouth. "Were you smuggled out? Did Andor smuggle you out?"

"No," I tell him, having a sip of my wine and feeling it bolster my confidence. "I live in the Banished Land. The Dark City. I am free to go where I choose."

Steiner's brow crinkles, his mouth dropping slightly before it curves into a grin. "You're a Freelander? That's even better."

"What did you do to get yourself banished?" Vidar asks.

"I escaped the Daughters of Silence," I tell him.

"Impossible," Kjell says, slapping his blood-soaked cloth on the table. "No one who enters the Daughters ever leaves."

"Well, I'm sure you must know more than I," I tell him, wondering if he's perceptive enough to pick up on the sarcasm.

"So then what did you do to get yourself in the Daughters of Silence?" Vidar asks over his goblet, cold green eyes observing me with discernment now.

"I didn't *do* anything," I tell him. "I merely existed and paid for the sins of my parents. They're both dead, before you ask. They were rebels against the Saints of Fire."

"Doesn't explain how you escaped the convent," Kjell says gruffly before having another slobbering sip of his wine.

"No, it doesn't," I say, leaving it at that while taking another bite of the stew.

Torsten sniffs. "A Daughter of Silence, a daughter of rebels, and a thief for House Dalgaard. Seems a likely path in life."

"Thief for House Kolbeck." Andor finally speaks up. Torsten eyes him and a silent exchange passes between them, loaded with meaning that I can't decipher.

Suddenly I hear growling from behind me.

I turn around in my chair to see Lemi on his feet, tail wagging, as a shaggy-looking wolf dog comes from around the table and approaches him, teeth exposed in a low growl.

"Feral," Vidar warns him. "Behave."

I'm not too worried. Lemi is big, even compared to the wolf dog, and a lot of alphas see his size and think they can take him on to prove something. But Lemi has a trick up his sleeve that the rest of them don't.

Feral barks, ignoring his master, his hair on end, and Lemi bounces on his front legs, ears up and tail wagging, wanting to play.

And play in his own unique way.

Feral lunges for Lemi just as Vidar shouts at him to stop, but Lemi simply disappears into thin air, leaving Feral extremely confused.

And he's not the only one.

"What in bloody blazes was that?" Steiner yelps as everyone else— aside from me and Andor—lets out gasps of shock.

Suddenly Lemi appears again behind Feral. The wolf dog whips around and Lemi goes low into a play crouch. By now Feral is a little nervous, even taking a step backward.

REALM of THIEVES

107

Lemi barks, loud, the kind of bark where I'd normally tell him to be quiet, but I decide to do no such thing here. Let the Kolbecks be disturbed.

"How did he do that?" Kjell demands, but I pay him no attention.

"Lemi, leave Feral alone," I warn him. "He doesn't want to play."

Lemi ignores me and tries to get closer to Feral, but the dog ends up running out of the room with his tail between his legs.

Lemi is about to follow, but I tell him to stay put. "I'm sorry, boy, he doesn't want to play with you for now. I'm sure he'll come around later."

Lemi looks at me and barks, his tail still wagging.

I sigh and put my napkin on the table, looking at Andor. "I think I should probably take him outside. He might be like this for the rest of dinner."

"A ploy to escape," Kjell grumbles.

"Mmmmm," Torsten agrees. "Andor, you're going with her. Shame you'll be missing dessert."

Andor doesn't look bothered in the slightest. He gives me a nod, relief on his brow, and we get to our feet. We quickly leave the room and Lemi trots right beside me. I barely had enough to eat, but I feel bad that Lemi hasn't even had anything. Hopefully Margarelle will have scraps from the kitchen.

"But, seriously, how did he do that?" Steiner asks me, mouth still agape at Lemi's disappearing act.

Andor gives his younger brother a look that says he'll explain it all later and then leads me down the hall, past the kitchen, bakehouse, and storeroom, to the very end where there's a large wooden door beside a staircase. He pushes it open and we step outside, and I'm immediately engulfed by cool, fresh air and nightfall. I stop on the gravel path outside the door and breathe in deeply through my nose, not realizing how shallow my breaths were before, how hot I was getting in the dining hall. I feel like I can actually think.

Andor grabs a torch from the wall beside the door and stands beside me as Lemi trots off.

"Lemi," I call after him as his black body disappears into the shadows beyond the flame.

"He'll be all right," Andor says. "There's a fortress wall around the back here. This is where we have the vines, the orchard, and apparently where the cook's future vegetable garden will be since Steiner has taken over the current one."

"He's a curious fellow," I comment.

"You can say that again," he says. "But don't let his youth fool you; he's the brains of this family, of the whole syndikat, and I'd argue the monarchy as well."

I walk toward the faint shapes of trees. I can only just make out their shadows in the dark, but as I step closer I see round fruit hanging from their limbs. I reach up and touch them gently, feeling their weight.

"Apples," Andor says, bringing the torch closer so that I can see better. "You can't see in the dark, can you?"

I shake my head, noting how the fruit shines in the light. "Apples were one of the few fruits the higher classes had in Lerick. I never stopped to question where they got them from. All this time there was trade between Esland and Norland."

"They trade with our neighbors, the territory of Altus Dugrell," Andor says. "Many of the inhabitants there worship the dragons instead of the goddesses. One of the many reasons why they split with Norland." He pauses, seeming to think that over for a moment before he says, "I should apologize for my family this evening. They're . . . suspicious of outsiders."

I laugh. "I can relate. I don't think your father would have gotten

REALM of THIEVES

109

very far in life if he wasn't." I give him a sidelong glance. His high cheekbones look carved from stone in the shadowed light. "Besides, I am still your prisoner. I should be grateful that I'm treated as fairly as I have been."

"*Should* be grateful?" he asks with a quirk of his brow.

I give him a quick smile. "I would much rather go back home," I say plainly, hoping that perhaps he'll take pity on me and call the whole thing off.

He swallows, the sound audible above the faint chirps of nearby crickets. "You know you can't leave. I can't let you go."

"You almost seem regretful," I comment, taking my fingers away from the apple.

He reaches over and plucks it off the tree, placing it in my hands. "I'm not a man without regrets," he says.

"Like pulling a knife on your uncle." I turn the fruit over in my hands.

His smile is as sharp as that blade. "I only regret not killing him there and then."

I'm unsure of how Andor fits in with his bloodline—his lenient attitude sets him apart from the Kolbeck dynasty—but every now and then I see the danger in him, the bloodlust beneath the cocky grin. I have no doubt that Andor would kill his uncle if he could.

"And I don't want to regret bringing you here to work for us," he goes on. "I think I—we—could give you a better life."

I glare at him and toss the apple back into the air, making him catch it. "You know nothing of the life I had," I tell him, walking back to the door and making a clicking noise for Lemi to return.

"But when we get your aunt," he ventures, his footsteps sounding on gravel behind me, "then you won't want for anything."

I stop and face him, anger flaring inside me. "Stop acting like you're doing me a favor. You just want to use me to get a leg up on the other houses."

"Then *let me* use you and it will be easier," he says, a pleading tone to his command. "For both of us. For all of us. There are more things at stake here than just you and me."

I hate the idea of being used, a trait passed down through my blood. My parents were very vocal about how the Soffers used the citizens as pawns in their game of religious manipulation.

"Lemi," I call out, ignoring Andor. "Come here."

Finally Lemi appears, walking slowly through the rows of orchard trees. He stops and puts his head up, sniffing the air.

"It's going to rain," Andor says, heading for the door. "We better get inside."

My heart leaps. "Wait? Rain? Here and now?"

He pauses and stares at me, his brows coming together. "Yes?"

"Please," I tell him, unable to keep the whine out of my voice. "Let me see it. Let me experience it. I don't want to go in yet."

"Experience rain?" he says, looking up at the clouds. "You've never . . . ?"

I shake my head. "I saw acid rain once in the Midlands and took shelter just in time. That was it. I've never experienced real rain, not the pure water that falls from the sky."

He stares at me for a moment, probably thinking I'm backward and crazy. He shrugs. "Then you've come to the right place." He puts the torch back in its holder and leans against the castle wall, watching me curiously for a moment before he looks up at the sky again.

Then I feel it.

A splash of water on the back of my neck.

I look up to see a drop falling from the dark, cloudy sky, and in one slowed-down moment I see the flames from the torch reflected in it, right before it lands on my forehead with a wet splash.

REALM of THIEVES

I gasp, unable to keep the awe from my voice, and look at Andor with wide eyes.

"Lonely drops always lead to a deluge," he tells me, then nods at the sky. "Here she comes."

And suddenly it's like the sky tips a barrel of water over, rain streaming from the clouds and engulfing us in seconds. It hits hard, bouncing off my skin, soaking my hair, my dress, and Lemi starts running around in circles, happily snapping his jaws at the air, trying to catch each drop.

I giggle, a high, shrill sound that I haven't heard come from my own lips since I was a child. Then before I can stop myself from regressing, I throw my arms out, put my head back to the sky, and start spinning in circles with my eyes closed. The rain falls and falls and I feel like it's cleansing me of everything I've ever done and everything I have yet to do. Perhaps this is why the Kolbecks seem at peace with their nature—the constant rain here is always wiping their souls and slates clean. The Soffers always believe people were purified by dragon fire, but this way seems so much better.

Finally, once I'm thoroughly soaked, I stop spinning. Or at least I try to, but the world seems to go on anyway and I find myself listing over, off-balance and dizzy. Suddenly Andor is there, at my side, his arms around me and holding me up, solid and strong.

I allow myself to keep the joy alive for one more second than I should, and I lean into him. He stiffens, sucking in a breath, but he doesn't move. His grasp is wet and warm and he doesn't let up, doesn't let go of me until I know I need to push him away.

You're not supposed to enjoy the company of your blackmailer's arms.

I straighten up and step out of his embrace and see a strange darkness in his eyes, one that both makes me uneasy and intrigues me at the same time.

"Well, I'm thoroughly wet now," I say, and the way his gaze ig-

112   KARINA HALLE

nites, along with a lift of his brow, I know he's thinking of euphemisms now. "From the rain," I say, clearing my throat. "Shall we go inside?"

He nods, his lips curving into a ghost of a smile before he turns and heads to the door.

Chapter 12

Brynla

 I wake up to Lemi licking my hand.

"Go outside," I tell him with a groan, rolling over and pulling the covers over my head. "Go pee outside," I mumble again.

He whines and I hear him sit on his haunches, his nails scratching on the floor.

I could sleep forever, sinking deeper into a dreamless cocoon. To become aware is to feel my body, and my body doesn't feel right. My mouth is dry and tastes like wine, and my head feels like my skull has thickened on the inside. It's not just the alcohol, it's some sort of strange pressure in the air.

I dreamed it was raining, the feeling of water dropping on my chilled arms, as I looked up to a cloudy sky, as Andor watched me with amusement and held me in his arms.

But no, none of that was a dream, was it?

I push back the covers from my face and open my eyes, staring at the ceiling. Wooden reliefs of stags in a forest scene are carved into beams that cross pale gold paint. My bedspread itself is composed of the softest sheets beneath a plush golden velvet blanket with amber tassels at the ends, the same jeweled tone of Andor's eyes.

I roll my head to the side and look at Lemi. He's attentive, his head cocked to the side, watching me and waiting for something.

"You know how to travel outside," I say to him. "I'm sure you can appear down in the courtyard or the orchard and then come right back here."

It's then that I realize his paws are muddy. He's already done that. Now he wants something else. Breakfast, I suppose.

And there it is, the scent of fried salt pork wafting in from somewhere. I had left the door to the balcony open a smidge, just to feel the refreshing night air as I slept, though from a security point of view, I suppose that wasn't very wise. I left that dinner with the distinct impression that Torsten and Kjell Kolbeck want me dead.

But there would be other ways to do that rather than sneaking in a balcony door.

I sigh and throw the rest of the covers back, pivoting until I'm sitting on the side of the bed. Solla lent me a nightgown too, loose, comfortable, and modest. I wonder how long I'll go on wearing her clothes. I wonder how long I'll be here.

Last night I asked Andor to let me go.

He said no.

If he doesn't let me go willingly, I don't have a chance of escape. Not here, not with Torsten or Kjell, or even Vidar, not in a land that is so foreign to me that even rain feels like a religious experience.

If I want to get out of this, if I want to make it back to my aunt in one piece, then I have to play by the rules. I have to play the game, be the person that Andor and the Kolbecks need me to be. I've seen the darkness in Andor's eyes, seen how quick he is to hold a blade to his blood, and part of me thinks that he might be promising things like my aunt, like freedom, that he never intends to give. The captain of his ship said he's honest, but of course he would say that.

As much as I want to, I can't trust Andor. He's going out of his way to treat me well because he wants to lure me into a false sense of security, have me become beholden to the Kolbecks' side, at least until I'm no longer useful.

I have to find my own escape, at the first opportunity.

The Midlands.

The next egg raid.

I know that place better than I know this one. I'll do what I can to put Andor down, hopefully without killing him, and escape with Lemi. If I play my cards right, if I prepare with enough food and water, perhaps I can steal one of the rowboats and take it to the Banished Land. It's a long shot, but freedom might be worth that price.

My father taught me that freedom is worth *every* price.

With that thought, I get up and start getting ready. I use the bathroom across the hall, the rest of the castle quiet in the morning. After we came in from the rain last night, Andor took me to the kitchen, where I met the cook Nels and was able to feed Lemi some leftovers, which he happily scarfed down. I managed to sneak a bread roll with that herbed butter and bring it back up to the room to eat later. Andor escorted me but I have a feeling it was because he was avoiding going back to dinner. I have to admit, our goodbyes at the door were strangely awkward, perhaps because both of us suddenly remembered the last time we were in this area—he was smelling me and I was totally nude.

I change into one of Solla's dresses, this one light blue with velvet trim along a V-shaped collar that goes off the shoulder blades, bringing out the warm tones in my skin, then put on the backless slippers Solla had placed under the bed, the toe beds pinching and my heels hanging off, but they're wearable for being inside the castle.

If I'm going to stand a chance at escaping Andor, I'm going to need to figure out how he and the whole suen operation works. I'm going to need to talk to the brains of the family, Steiner.

I gather my hair into a loose bun and then step outside my room with Lemi at my side. I walk down the hall, taking my time to peer inside some of the open doors. They all seem to be guest rooms like mine, in various colors and themes, their beds all neatly made. I wonder if the Kolbecks often entertain people from out of town, if they throw lavish parties and dinners, if perhaps the royal family of Norland even comes to visit. They seem so guarded, I have a hard time imagining them at a ball or entertaining people, though I suppose I can't base everything on the dinner last night.

I make my way down to where the hall meets a wider corridor, where the main chambers seem to be, their doors all closed, the air humming with silence. Perhaps the Kolbecks sleep in. Then I go down the stairs to the ground level, just as a door below slowly opens across from the staircase with a low creak.

Incense wafts out into the hall in a cloud of light smoke, and through the half-open door I see many candles lit, flames flickering against red velvet tapestries. Both Lemi and I have come to a halt at the foot of the stairs, waiting for someone to step out.

A man does, though at first I think it's a woman because of the grace of his movements and his slight build. He's dressed in a gray robe, his hair red and waving to his shoulders, eyes deep-set, bright gold and piercing.

"Brynla Aihr," the man says to me in a rough, whispered voice, his mouth slightly crooked. "We finally meet."

He doesn't have any of the dark and brooding features of the Kolbecks, so I'm not sure who this man is. He has a smooth, high forehead, his skin pale with shadows under his eyes and cheekbones, and his age is hard to place, like he could be in his fifties, or he could be in his thirties.

"Who are you?" I manage to say.

"Ah," he says, with a slow nod. "I often forget that others don't know of me like I know of them. I am Sae Belak. The Truthmaster for House Kolbeck."

"The what?"

"Truthmaster," he says patiently, his lips tugging up in a crooked manner.

"I don't know what a Truthmaster is."

He lifts his chin lightly. "Hmmm. No, I suppose you don't. We are used by Harbringers at the convent and even by the government deep within the walls of Lerick's crypts. You've heard of Cappus Zoreth, the one with the sight?"

I scoff. Cappus Zoreth, the one who started the Saints of Fire, has been drilled into every Eslander's psyche at a young age, particularly at the convent. "I'm aware."

"Of course you are. It was the Truthmasters who gave him that sight."

Interesting. That is something I have never heard before. Regardless, this man and his robes and his way are giving me flashbacks to the Daughters of Silence, and I don't like it. Still, he's here and talking.

"So you give the Kolbecks sight, you help them see into future?"

He nods. "Only those who want to communicate with the goddesses directly. Most people don't. So far only Torsten and Vidar take part. The others remain . . . wary."

I frown. "You help people communicate with the goddesses? But the Soffers in Esland don't worship any goddesses. They worship the dragons alone."

"Maybe they are all one and the same thing," he says, his eyes shifting colors in a strange way, like there are literal sparks in his eyes. "Come, let me walk to you Master Steiner's lab."

I stiffen with unease. "How did you know I was looking for Steiner?"

A patient smile appears on his smooth face. "The goddesses told me. That's why I stepped out of the chapel to greet you."

I look down at Lemi. My dog is paying the Truthmaster close attention, his ears pricked up, but he doesn't seem to be nervous. Then again, he likes people more than I do.

"Come this way," Sae Balek says, and when he turns to face the light that's coming out of the stained-glass windows that look out into the courtyard, his eyes begin to change further, like the gold irises are starting to bleed into the whites, and the color is becoming metallic.

"You're noticing my eyes," he says as he keeps walking, facing directly ahead. "Do not be alarmed. This is them in their natural state. I use tricks of the light to make them seem normal, so that I don't scare people when I first meet them."

The man doesn't need gold eyes to scare people, but I keep that comment to myself.

"You're not curious as to why they're gold?" he prods.

"I assumed if it was important you'd tell me," I say truthfully.

His lopsided mouth curves into a smile. "You would be right. I have the sight—I do not need eyes to see. They have been taken out and replaced by the gold of the goddesses. Do you know about that material?"

I shake my head, more interested in the fact that he had his eyes taken out than the material itself. Why would anyone do such a gruesome thing? Even the extremist Soffers didn't go to such lengths—although they do come close.

"I'm sure Steiner will fill you in," he says, pausing outside an iron door that's across from the one Andor and I exited last night into the back orchard. He knocks lightly on the door and gives me yet another patient smile, though it's hard to read his face as anything but menacing with those two gold orbs staring at me, seeing but not seeing.

The door opens and a bleary-eyed Steiner is on the other side, a mug of something hot and steaming in his hand, the aroma rich and foreign.

"I have Lady Aihr to see you," Sae Belak says in his whispery voice. "And her loyal hound. Do you have any findings on the new growth?"

Steiner rubs his chin and yawns. "Not yet. Perhaps tomorrow. I'll find you when I do."

"That would be appreciated," Sae Belak says with a slight bow before leaving back down the hall, his robes fluttering behind him.

I look back to Steiner. "Good morning," I say to him, suddenly feeling awkward. "I'm not sure how that gold-eyed man knew I wanted to meet with you this morning, but he insisted he bring me here."

"Sae Belak? He knows a lot," Steiner says mildly, and then steps back, gesturing for me to come inside. Unlike the more tailored garments he was wearing at dinner last night, he's now dressed in a black smock that covers him to his knees, burgundy red pants beneath. "Andor mentioned last night after dinner that he wanted to bring you by the lab. I'm surprised he's not here."

"I haven't seen him," I say, stepping inside the room. "Sleeping, perhaps? Everything is so quiet out there."

Steiner smiles knowingly. "More like hiding. My father is grouchy if he's woken up before a certain time. He's a night owl. We all take our breakfasts in our rooms so as not to disturb him." He looks down at Lemi. "And how is your dog with cats?"

"It depends on the cat," I admit, lightly scratching my nails over Lemi's head in a comforting manner. "Do you want him to stay outside? I wouldn't want him to run around your lab and knock stuff over. He's not used to being in delicate spaces." I can barely see the lab myself, it's so dark inside this room, but I have a feeling everything that's stocked on the shelves and laid along the tables is of high importance.

"It's probably better for him to be in here, where you can watch him and where he's safe," he says pointedly, and I know he's concerned about his uncle or father doing something. "Woo-woo is outside harassing the chickens in the yard anyway. Woo-woo is my cat."

I nod and he strolls behind me and closes the door. For a moment I feel a flicker of fear about being shut in here in near darkness, but Steiner himself doesn't seem like he could do me much harm.

"Do you always work in the dark?" I ask, nodding at the single small candle that's halfway across the room.

"Sorry, I forget that not everyone can see in the dark," he says, going over to a long, low desk and lighting a couple of candles that sit in a brass holder emblazoned with a stag. "So, while I've got you here, do you mind answering some questions for me? I'm fascinated by Eslanders, Freelanders even more so."

"Sure," I say, folding my arms. "But we aren't that interesting."

"Ha!" he says, sitting down at his desk and pulling out a bound book with blank pages. "I suppose we're so used to ourselves that we don't know what it's like to view ourselves from the outside. You're interesting. Your dog is interesting. And Andor's plans for you are very, very interesting."

"He's told you about them?"

"Not particularly," he says, opening a drawer and searching with delicate movements. "But it's Andor, and he's always thinking outside the box—even when the world outside the box can get you killed. Ah! I think purple ink would be best for this. Purple, like your hair." He pulls out a vial of purple ink and a feather pen. "Might as well start with my first question. Your hair. Does it mean anything? Were you born with it?"

"I take it that my hair color isn't very common here," I say.

"Not really. The lighter hair colors, the brighter hair colors, those are more of a Sorland trait. It's been a thousand years since the first clans left Sorland and came to this continent. Over many generations

REALM of THIEVES

we grew taller, our skin grew paler, our hair darker. Occasionally you'll see someone with blue hair, or green. But they tend to be dark in color. I'm just curious if your hair was like that at birth or if the suen gave it to you."

I frown at that. "I've had it since birth. Suen can change people's hair color?"

"Sometimes," he says. "I've been studying suen since I was twelve, since the day I first took it, and I'm still discovering new things. No one is really sure how it works."

"Because it's magic . . ."

"Some say it's magic," he says with a shrug, writing in long elaborate strokes, his writing an art form in itself. "Some say it's science. I say it's both. Whichever one explains it is the one I will follow."

"So it's equal science and magic?" I ask, curious as anything since the subject of suen ingestion was considered blasphemy in Esland, and the Freelanders didn't seem to talk about it often. Probably because no one could afford to buy it. I could have made a killing selling it myself instead of to House Dalgaard, but I would have ended up dead very quickly. The syndikats hate competition.

"Until my experiments prove otherwise. Why, what are your thoughts on it? How do your powers feel to you?"

"I don't have any powers," I tell him, hesitating to finally speak the truth. "Suen has no effect on me."

"That's not possible," he says just as there's a knock at the door. "Come in!" he yells.

The door opens and Andor steps in. He's dressed in a dark, long-sleeved tunic with a V-neck that shows off a dusting of chest hair and his dragon-tooth necklace, half of the shirt casually tucked into his straight-leg pants, tall boots on his feet. His beard is groomed, his wavy hair pushed back off his forehead, and when he sees me, his eyes light up in a way that makes my stomach flip.

I probably just need breakfast.

"The Truthmaster said you would be in here," Andor says, and I manage to tear my eyes away from his body to notice he's holding two stone mugs in his hand, the steam and smell similar to the drink that Steiner has been having. "I brought you some coffee. Have you had it before?"

"No," I tell him as he shuts the door with his heel and strides over to me, holding out the mug. I take it from him and peer down into a light, milky brown drink, feeling strangely shy suddenly. A feeling I can do without.

"It's grown all over Vesland. We get it imported," Andor says, sounding rather proud. "I put milk and sugar in yours since that's how most people drink it."

"Not Andor, though," Steiner says with a laugh. "He thinks drinking it straight makes him more of a man."

"Perhaps it does," Andor teases. "You should try it. You could use a little hair on your chest."

Steiner waves that comment away with his hand. "Some other time. You didn't tell me that your thief here is untouched by suen."

Andor frowns as he has a sip of his drink. I'm still holding mine, waiting for it to cool down. We don't drink a lot of hot drinks in the Dark City; everything is already so hot as it is.

"What do you mean, untouched?" he asks.

"It doesn't work on me," I explain. It feels good to finally tell him this, like I've been harboring a grave secret.

"But that's not possible," Andor says.

"And I'm telling you it is."

"No," Steiner says, getting to his feet. "How have you survived getting dragon eggs all this time? You couldn't."

"Every thief we've ever used for our operations that has come back alive has had suen in their blood," Andor says. "We tried it the first few times with the unmagicked, but they died. Horribly. You need speed and strength and other suen-given abilities to do this job and make it out with your life intact."

I shrug. "Well, last night at dinner you insinuated that all my success is because of Lemi."

"That doesn't explain how you're still here, how you haven't been blasted with fire or eaten yet," Andor says. "What do you mean it's never worked on you? Have you properly taken it?"

"Yes," I say testily. "Don't you think my aunt gave me some before I started the job? Suen works for her but it doesn't work for me."

"Maybe you didn't have enough," Steiner says, getting to his feet. "We can fix that."

"Go right ahead, but I've had it several times."

"How old were you? It doesn't work if you're younger than twelve or thirteen."

"I was seventeen," I tell him. "Eight years ago."

Blazes, how time flies by.

"But how did you take it?" Steiner says as he starts rummaging through a shelf.

"In a shot glass," I say, still remembering the horrid taste, how slimy it felt on the way down. I can almost taste it. I take a sip of the coffee drink instead. It's sweet and bitter and feels good on the tongue, washing away the memory.

"That's a lot," Andor says. "You should have felt the first effects right away."

"Yes, those would have been your dominant traits," Steiner says, turning to face me with something short and silver in his hand. "They kick in minutes after first ingestion. Any extra suen after that won't be as powerful."

"Well, I didn't have any traits, dominant or otherwise. I've taken it about four times. I kept on trying."

"So you're just . . . a commoner," Andor says.

I glare at him. "I think I'd rather be called unmagicked."

"And all your fighting . . ." he goes on.

"I was trained."

"I can see that. And we'll have to train you even better. Steiner, you're going to need to get her better armor. All the upgrades."

"First we'll see what this does," Steiner says, holding out the silver stick in front of me, my face contorted in the reflection on the rounded surface.

I jerk my head back. "What is that?"

"It's the suen in a syringe," he says. "Only a drop under your tongue will do the trick. Open your mouth."

I swear I see Andor smirk at that. I do what Steiner says and feel the cold metal against my bottom teeth. He depresses the needle and frigid liquid fills my mouth. I swallow it down, the cool sensation following, making my tongue numb, but surprisingly there's no taste at all.

"How were you able to do that?" I ask him, smacking my lips together to get rid of the frozen feeling. "It has no taste."

"I was able to separate the special molecules, or elements, from the yolk using a centrifugalator I made. It's the molecules that hold the compound. This way you only need a little bit, and it's easier for the army to distribute among themselves." He tilts his head, peering at me closely with blue eyes. "How do you feel?"

I look down at my hands, as if they will tell me something, then up at Andor and Steiner. "I don't know. The same."

"Give it time," Andor says. "The dominant traits always come through quick, but the later doses trigger a smaller and slower response."

"I told you," I say, giving him a level look, "I've taken plenty before. And the real versions, not this lab-altered stuff. Red egg yolk straight back from a glass. This isn't going to do anything."

There's no use getting my hopes up at this point. Though I might look down on the substance from time to time, it's only out of jealousy. I want to gain some kind of advantage, some way to make me

REALM of THIEVES

feel less weak. But I've made peace with it. I've learned to rely on my-self and only myself, without anything extra.

Steiner continues to look at me in disbelief, and I have another sip of my drink while he stares. "It should be doing *something*. My intelli-gence expanded right away. In an hour, I was as smart as I'll ever be. Everything after that was just icing on the cake. Heightened senses, speed, though not strength. Not yet. I'll see how much time has passed before I dare take more."

I want to ask him what happens if you take too much, but instead I look to Andor. "And what was your dominant trait?"

"Nothing too useful," he says, his words blunt, his expression turning dark.

"He can heal," Steiner says. "With his hands." Now his brows come together, his eyes guarded as he looks away. "Wounds, ailments, things like that," Steiner adds quickly.

Tension seems to fill the air suddenly, an odd dynamic between brothers taking center stage. All I can think about is that he can heal. His hands heal. Is that what I saw him do with Lemi? That was more than just healing, that was bringing him back to life.

"Can you heal . . ." I begin, licking my lips, my heart feeling sus-pended as I work toward an answer. "Can you heal a disease? An af-fliction? Something that causes someone great pain?"

He frowns and his face seems to pale. He gives his head a small shake. "I'm not sure. I wouldn't count on it."

"But I saw . . ." I begin.

But his nostrils flare, his eyes sharpening as if they were a blade threatening me to stay quiet.

"Saw what?" Steiner asks curiously, looking between the both of us.

"Nothing," I tell him. "I saw nothing." I make a note to talk to Andor about this in private. Is this why my path crossed with his?

126 KARINA HALLE

Could he possibly be the solution to my problems? I don't dare get my hopes up.

I change the subject. "So what traits does the rest of your family have?"

"Solla can move things with her mind," Steiner says. "She's only had one dose of suen, though. She has no interest in taking more. I suppose she won the jackpot with hers, so why need to? As for our uncle, you'd be surprised—or disappointed—to know he's hard to kill. Meanwhile our father is a master of alchemy and transmutation, with some precognition, and Vidar is good at mind control."

Mind control. Fuck. Remind me to be on even higher alert around him.

"Are you sure you're not feeling anything?" Steiner asks, looking me over. "Maybe it's something useless or subtle. Maybe you can see beyond the colorscope or smell things that others can't?"

"I'm feeling annoyed by your badgering, does that count?"

"Your parents must have taken it," Steiner ventures. "Your immunity can't be genetic."

"My parents?" I almost laugh. They really don't know what it's like to be an Eslander, do they? "They never took it. They never even had the option. Is it really as widespread as you make it seem to be? Does every Norlander take it?"

"No," says Andor firmly. "It's reserved for the royals, for the houses, and for the armies. Those are the only people we will sell the suen to. Some people are able to buy it on the black market—a market even more discreet than the one we deal with—but it's very expensive and most commoners can't afford it. Besides, the king has declared it illegal, and people are thoroughly punished when they're caught taking it. That doesn't just go for Norland, but also in Altus Dugrell and Vesland."

"How are they punished?" I ask, thinking of how Eslanders deal with everything—by sentencing people to either death or the Daughters of Silence.

"Their punishment is joining the army," Steiner says. "Men, women, anyone. The king won't waste a drop of the power. The person will have to use it to fight for Norland."

"My father has often floated the idea of selling some of the excess suen, if there ever were any, to other markets," Andor remarks, "but the king would shut us all down and find another house to supply them."

"Probably House Vilette," Steiner says. "They *hate* us."

"And luckily the royal family isn't fond of them either," Andor points out. "But they will pivot if we deviate. We sell only to the king and that's it. He can't afford to have his population gain magic and powers, the very things they could use to rebel against him and the army. There could easily be an uprising."

He's making a good point, though I think it would be better if every commoner did have the power to rise up and fight. "Is the king not doing a good job?"

"He's never done a great job," Andor says, sitting on the corner of Steiner's desk. "But kings don't need to do a great job, do they? It's not as if the people have a choice."

"But they could have a choice if suen was dispersed throughout the population," I muse, tapping my fingers along my chin.

"Aha," Andor says with a smile. "I see the daughter of rebels has emerged. I would be inclined to agree with you too, if it were any other time in history."

"What's so important about this time in history?" I ask.

The two brothers exchange a look that says *Where do I start?*

Andor sighs as he looks at me, as if he's forced to play the role of tutor. "There's a lot of history to cover first. First, let's go make sure you and Lemi have some breakfast." He looks to Steiner. "Since Brynla is obviously immune to the suen, we need to give her as much advantage as we can—better armor, better weapons, whatever little devices you can create."

Andor motions for me to follow him to the door. I finish the rest of my coffee and walk across the room, Lemi trailing behind. Andor opens the door and pauses, looking at me with a torn expression before he glances back at Steiner.

"Oh, I need you to send Moon on another mission," Andor says to his brother. "I need the raven to visit Brynla's aunt Ellestra Doon in the Dark City. Tell her that Brynla is safe and will be coming to take her out of the Banished Land and that she should be prepared to leave in a month."

A whole moon cycle?

How on earth will I wait that long?

Chapter 13

ANDOR

"She certainly knows how to fight," Solla remarks as she leans against the stone table beside me, watching as Steiner and Brynla battle it out with wooden swords in the middle of the courtyard. It's morning, a clear crisp day, the sun just starting to dry the overnight rain from the foliage, and Brynla's daily training session is nearly halfway through.

"She certainly does," I say. My eyes are locked on Brynla's form, not just the fluidity of her movements, the way she seems to anticipate Steiner's next move, but on her actual body. The leather armor that Steiner engineered and had our seamstress create, crafted from none other than dragonscale, hugs every supple curve, from her firm ass to her breasts, even the soft roundness of her stomach. I shouldn't be watching her in this way—I should be paying attention to her strikes and her footwork and figuring out what she needs to work on—but I can't help it.

"Though she is fighting against Steiner," I add as Brynla knocks Steiner's sword from his hand. "Even you would win against Steiner."

"Hey," Solla says in annoyance, and then wipes her hands—caked with dirt from her garden—on my sleeve.

I flick the dirt off. "Using your mind powers doesn't count. You can't use telekinesis on a dragon."

"How do you know?" she asks smartly. "Have you ever tried?"

"No. And you'll never get to try either."

"What if I want to become an egg thief too?"

I give my sister a dry look. "I wouldn't allow it. Your place is here, at Stormglen. Someone has to be the lady of the house and Margarelle isn't going to be around forever."

"As long as Brynla's here, there will be two women of the house," she says. I don't like the teasing look in her eyes, the way she's smiling.

"Brynla is a—"

"Prisoner, I know." She lets out a long sigh and then rests her head against my shoulder. "I've just never seen a prisoner treated so well. She wears my dresses, sleeps in the nicest guest quarters, is allowed to eat dinner with us, has the seamstress making her custom attire, has a dog that's treated better than Grandfather when he comes to visit. She's only been here ten days and it feels like she's here to stay. Not to mention the way you look at her."

I shrug her off my shoulder. "What do you mean, how I look at her?"

"It's disgusting," she says, curling her lip for emphasis.

"You're wearing the fool's crown," I tell her, pressing my hand against her face and pushing her away. "Go back to your garden and busy yourself. I think you're running out of pastimes."

She feigns fighting back, rubbing her dirty fingers on my face until I push her far enough away. Then she runs off to her garden that runs along the walls of the courtyard, giggling.

Laughing, I wipe the dirt off my beard. I bring my attention back to Brynla only to catch her staring at me with a look on her face that I rarely see. There's a wrinkle across her forehead, a strange longing in her gaze. It only lasts a second before Steiner takes advantage of her distraction and slaps her on her armored shoulder with the sword.

REALM of THIEVES 131

"You'd be dead," Steiner says. "Pay attention."

Brynla shakes her head, looking slightly chagrined, then suddenly drops to her hands in a push-up position and kicks out at Steiner's ankles behind her, leveling my younger brother to the ground in a heap.

"No, *you'd* be dead," she says, towering over him and dusting her hands off.

Then she reaches out for his hand and pulls him to his feet, even though I know my brother doesn't need the help. We've spent every moment over the last ten days testing Brynla to see if any of the suen has taken a late hold, but she doesn't seem different, just as naturally strong as before.

"Go again?" Brynla asks him, brandishing her wooden sword as if it could slice him in two.

Steiner shakes his head, rubbing at his ass where he fell down. "I think I need a break. Andor, you want to take over?" he asks me.

"I'm not wearing armor," I tell him, holding my arms out, but I'm walking toward them anyway. "I'm not sure I trust her not to stab me."

"You'll have to take your chances," she says sweetly as Steiner tosses me his sword.

I catch it in midair, not even having to look at it. Okay, perhaps I'm showing off a little.

"You know I like to take chances," I tell her.

"Good luck," Steiner mutters under his breath as he walks away, the gravel crunching under his boots. "I'm going to see if Moon has come back to roost."

At the mention of his white raven, Brynla's face falls.

I take advantage and lunge, tapping her other shoulder with my blade. "There, you just died again."

She gives me a pained yet annoyed look.

"Hey," I say to her, trying to keep her focused. "Moon will be back any day now. It takes four days to fly from here to the Banished Land.

There's probably a day trying to find your aunt in the underground city, then four days back."

"That's nine days."

"And it's day ten. Give the bird a break." I reach out to tap her again, but this time she's quick. She swiftly raises her sword and almost knocks mine out of my grasp.

"Ah!" I cry out, grinning at her. "There we go. Give it to me."

"You don't want me to give it to you," she says with a smirk, and I strike again. She grunts, twisting at the waist, her footwork smooth, keeping her just out of my reach. Then she slices down at my sword, preventing me from cutting her the other way.

"You don't think I can handle a little blood drawn?" I say, stepping back and keeping my eyes locked on her warm brown ones so that she can't follow my next move. An easy mistake is to let your eyes betray your plan.

"I suppose you can simply heal yourself, can't you?" she asks.

"Actually no," I say, ducking as she strikes with a wide swipe. "It doesn't work that way."

"So how does it work?" she asks, trying to slice at my neck. I block her sword just in time.

"You're so curious about the healing," I say. She's been asking me about it here and there but I haven't been very forthcoming. I'm sure she'll find out one day. I'm surprised my uncle hasn't trotted out my failure at the dinner table.

"Maybe I have an ulterior motive," she says in a low voice, blocking a jab.

"Like what?"

She stares at me for a moment, opens her mouth like she wants to say something. There's a war being waged behind her eyes and it isn't one fought with swords. Then she shakes her head and with a growl attacks me, nearly plunging her sword right into my heart, pulling back at the very last second.

I suck in my breath, feeling the sharp point of the sword penetrate my shirt, poking the skin. Even though it's carved from wood, I have no doubt she would have killed me if she had driven it in at full strength.

She swallows hard, eyes wide as she takes in the sight. "Sorry." She abruptly withdraws the sword and turns her back to me, her head going side to side in a stretch, her hands on her hips.

"Don't be," I call after her as she walks a few steps away. I look over to Solla, who is in her garden, head poking around an elderberry shrub and watching us intently. She shrugs. Meanwhile Lemi, who has been dozing in the sun at the foot of the fountain, lifts up his head and watches Brynla with concern.

I walk after her. "Are you all right?" I ask, keeping my voice low and soft. I want to reach out and put my hand on her shoulder but I'm afraid she would lash out.

"I'm fine," she says, slowly turning around to face me. She winces as she runs the back of her arm over her forehead. "Just tired."

Right. It's not that. Still, I tell her, "Perhaps we've been working you too hard. You need some rest. I forget that you're not . . ."

"One of you?" she says bluntly.

I take a step toward her, fighting the urge to reach out and hold her hand, even for a moment. "Believe me, I think it's a blessing that you're not one of us."

She has that look in her eyes again, the one that wants to tell me something. Why can't she come out and say it? I'd go crazy if I had to keep my feelings inside.

"The other day," she says in a low voice, her eyes darting over to Solla, who has put her head back down, pruning a small tree, "when you said you weren't sure if you could fix ailments? Have you ever tried? Has anyone in your family come to you with a sore back, or a headache from too much wine?"

My throat thickens and I struggle to swallow down the shame. "No. They haven't."

"Really?" she asks, a sheen of hope in her eyes. I don't like that look.

"Really," I tell her. *For good reason.*

"Then how do you know you can't?" she asks, her gaze imploring and intense. "Listen, I saw what you did to Lemi. I don't know if he was truly dead when that dragon pinned him down, but I saw you heal him. I just didn't know it at the time. If you can do that—"

"He's just a dog."

Her stare turns acidic. "He's not *just* a dog."

"You know what I mean. He's not a human. On top of that, he has suen abilities. That makes us harder to kill regardless."

"You healed him," she says. There's a gravity to her voice that pulls at something inside me, something soft, something hidden. "So maybe you can heal me."

I blink at her in surprise, then look her up and down, as if I'll see some obvious wounds. "Did you hurt yourself or—?"

"You know what, forget it," she says quickly, turning and walking away.

This time I do reach out and grab her by the forearm, forcing her to face me. I pull her close to me, enough that she lets out a small gasp, but I don't let go and I don't care if I'm being pushy.

"Tell me what's wrong with you," I say, my voice coming out gruff and impatient. "What needs healing?"

Indignation sparks in her eyes. "Unhand me," she practically growls at me, writhing in my grasp.

I sigh and decide to release her. I expect her to walk off again but she stays where she is, only a foot between us. The air smells like basil and sun-baked stone, but there's something else too, sweet like honey, that seems to radiate off her. For some reason I have a hard time taking in a breath.

"This is . . . personal," she begins, squinting at me warily.

"You can tell me. I won't tell a soul."

She doesn't look like she believes me.

"I promise," I go on. "I would never. I keep my promises."

"It's sort of embarrassing," she says, her eyes flicking over to Lemi at the fountain, though I have a feeling she's just avoiding my gaze. I stare at her anyway, coaxing her to continue.

She sighs and rubs at her forehead with the heel of her palm. "I get pains every month. In my lower abdomen. Sometimes it lasts for a few days, sometimes it can last a week. Sometimes it comes in the middle of the moon cycle for no reason, to kick me when I'm down. I haven't had any while I've been here but . . . I know it's coming. It always comes."

I frown. "Have you been to a doctor?"

Her face twists into a wry expression. "What do you think? Yes. I've been to a few doctors. But doctors are expensive to visit, even in the Banished Land, and they can't help me. Only one doctor suggested surgery, but so far we've been unable to find a surgeon to do it for a price that I can afford, let alone one that will actually take it seriously. They dismiss it as a woman's problem. If you know what I mean."

I nod. "Is it something to do with the way you bleed once a month?"

Her head jerks back, as if I've said something scandalous.

"What?" I go on. "It happens. I know about it. I've even been with a woman when she . . ."

Her eyes widen and her cheeks bloom with color.

I clear my throat. She doesn't need to hear about the women I've slept with. "Regardless, I know. Sure, it's not talked about often, but I know. So the pain is associated with it."

She nods, rubbing her lips together anxiously. "I guarantee what I suffer through is far worse than what other women must." She swallows and looks away. "We shouldn't be having this conversation."

"Why not?" I frown, folding my arms.

"Because, as I said, it's personal, and I know ladies' issues aren't usually discussed with men."

"Ah, but you're a thief, Brynla, not a lady." She gives me a faint smile and I go on, gravity coming through in my tone. "Either way, I need to know. You asked for my help in healing you, and I'll do what I can. Perhaps I can't make it stop for good, but I might be able to take the pain away. Though I do think we should discuss this with Steiner. He has poppy resin that should help. He might even have some sort of elixir to, uh, stop those cycles from happening."

"I'll try," she says, exhaling loudly. "But I've had poppy resin before. I have to take so much to get rid of the pain that it will put me asleep for a week. I can't afford that, not in my line of work. And I've been taking a doctor's tea for years now, every month, and every month it keeps the bleeding at bay. So that's one less hassle to deal with. But it doesn't take away the pain. When we go back to get Ellestra, I'll have to get more of it."

"If you tell Steiner what's in it, I'm sure he can re-create it. You've seen the greenhouses he has at the side of the house, just outside his lab. He has everything and he loves a challenge."

"I'm not sure how comfortable I am telling your younger brother all of this."

"You're comfortable telling me this," I point out. "What's the difference?"

She studies me for a moment, her gaze flicking over my mouth, my nose, then my eyes. "I don't know," she says slowly.

"Could it be that you trust me?" I ask, trying to keep my tone playful and nonchalant, trying to hide the true hope in my voice.

Her expression falls, a hardness coming over her eyes. "No. I don't think I'll ever trust you."

Then she brushes past me, her shoulder knocking into mine, and walks away, leaving the scent of honey in her wake.

REALM of THIEVES

—

After dinner I decide to pay my younger brother a visit. The door to Steiner's lab is slightly ajar and I poke my head in to see that the back door that leads out into the raven's roost, greenhouses, and garden is wide open, the cool breeze of the evening coming in.

"Hello?" I call out, walking across the lab until I see Steiner appear halfway in the back door, an excited look on his face.

He steps in farther and I see Moon perched on his arm, her feathery form stark white against Steiner's black clothing. Brynla's lavender head pops up behind them, though she looks more anxious than not.

"Moon returned." I point out the obvious. "Hopefully with good news."

Steiner nods and looks at the bird. "Tell him, Moon."

I met with Ellestra Doon, the bird says, her formidable beak staying partially open, though Moon's voice appears inside my head as it always does. *I gave her the message. She tried to beat me with a broom first. Eventually I got her to listen. She says she'll be expecting you in a few weeks.*

"Thank you," I tell the raven.

She makes a rolling sound with her tongue, then hops up onto Steiner's shoulder and flies out the door, Brynla ducking her head just in time as she soars into the night to roost.

"I told you Moon would come back," Steiner says to her with a satisfied raise of his brow.

Still, Brynla doesn't look too convinced.

"So how does Moon talk like that?" she asks as Steiner shuts the door.

"Ravens are highly intelligent," he says. "More than you'd think."

"Yes, but the whole speaking inside your brain part." She pauses. "You gave the bird suen."

He shakes his head. "I haven't, though I suspect she might have had some before I found her. She had fallen from a nest, not old enough to be a fledgling. It's possible her parents brought some to the nest somehow. But other than Lemi, I've never seen cases of suen working in animals, so it's possible that the bird is just . . . magic. Somehow."

"So you didn't teach her," she says, adjusting the neckline of her dress, her breasts jostling on display. I try not to stare.

Steiner laughs, oblivious to her cleavage. "Oh, I've taught Moon everything I know. She absorbs knowledge like a sponge. But I'm a scientist. I'm not a sorcerer."

"I don't know," I tell him. "Sometimes they seem like one and the same."

He shrugs and heads over to his desk.

"By the way, Father is asking for you both to join the rest of us in the great chamber," I tell them.

Both Steiner and Brynla let out a tired sigh in unison.

"Hey, I don't want to be there either," I tell them. "But you know how he gets after a day of hunting. Wants to drink and make sure we all know to worship at his feet."

"I made it through a dinner filled with barbs from your father, your uncle, and occasionally Vidar," Brynla says. "I'd rather not be subjected to more if I can help it."

"I know. I'm sorry," I tell her. "One drink and then I'll sneak you out at the first opportunity."

"What about me?" Steiner asks.

"You're on your own, brother," I tell him. Then I reach out and press my fingertips at the back of Brynla's yellow dress. This is one that our seamstress had custom made for her, along with her armor and other things. The neckline at the back and the front are low and the material is thin and delicate, enough that I can feel the heat of her body through the fabric.

It would be so easy to rip this dress right off her, I think.

Then I'm hit with a pang of want, so sharp and violent that I feel my fingernails dig slightly into her, enough that she tries to step out of the way.

I swallow audibly and press my hand there again. "Come on," I say to her, heat flaring inside my cock, getting absolutely turned on for no good reason. She glances at me over her shoulder with a bewildered expression, as if sensing the change.

She lets me guide her out into the hall before I finally let my hand fall, my heart going fast against my ribs.

"Oh, by the way," I whisper as we walk past the kitchen. This is where Lemi pokes his head out. He's taken to spending a lot of time with the cook before and after dinner, and he stays put, having no interest in joining us. "If my father brings up the plans for the next raid, don't mention your aunt."

She looks back at me in surprise. "Why not?"

"He doesn't know."

Chapter 14

Brynla

 I stare at Andor as we walk toward the great chamber. Though his fingers are no longer pressed against the small of my back, I can still feel them there, like a ghost.

I bring my attention back to the more important matter at hand.

"What do you mean your father doesn't know?" I whisper, shocked at what Andor is telling me.

He opens his mouth, about to tell me something that will further aggravate me, I'm sure.

But before he can answer, Torsten's voice booms into the hall.

"There you are," Torsten says. He waves his glass of alcohol at us and gestures to the door to the great chamber. "I was thinking you were avoiding me."

"You're a hard man to avoid," Andor says, resentment flattening his voice.

I give Torsten a quick smile as we enter the room, enough that he sees I'm not here to be a problem, but not so much so that he thinks I'm someone he can take advantage of—even though by holding me captive, he's doing just that.

Just hang on a few more weeks, I remind myself. *Then you'll find your chance for escape. Then it won't matter what Torsten knows or doesn't know about Andor's plan to get Ellestra—I'll be long gone and he'll be headed back home empty-handed, save for maybe some dragon eggs. And that's all they really want, isn't it?*

The great chamber shares a fireplace with the dining hall, a circular feature that allows you to sneak a glance at the other room through the flames. But unlike the sparseness and grandeur of the dining room, the great chamber is cozy and small. There are thick rugs, both embroidered with tassels and ones made from animal furs, and several armchairs and couches are in a semicircle facing the fire, the rest of the family scattered among them, with side tables made from wide umberwood trunks.

The focal point isn't the fireplace itself, though. It's what's hanging above the fireplace: a dragon's skull, large enough to be an elderdrage. I'm suddenly reminded of my last encounter with one, the dragon I thought killed Lemi. The way I was able to stare into its eyes, so close that I could make out the vivid patterns around its pupil, the way that very pupil seemed to see me and *know* me.

But it was Andor's arrow that saved my life. Otherwise I would have either gone up in flames or been torn to pieces—or both.

"Impressive, isn't it?" Torsten says, coming beside me and staring up at the skull with reverence. "My father killed that one. He was a young lad at the time, younger than Steiner. On the very first day he went to the Midlands, he managed to slay an elderdrage. Instead of only taking the eggs, he and the crew dragged the entire body onto the boat. Nearly sank the damn thing but it would have been quite the sight to see, his ship coming under the Goddess Gates with a dead dragon on deck. The Kolbecks were always a family to be feared, but at that moment they became the house to be respected."

142   KARINA HALLE

He swirls the liquid around in his glass. "How times have changed," he adds, his low voice brimming with contempt. I have a feeling a lot of that contempt is reserved for Andor.

"Your father sounds like quite the man," I say politely.

He scoffs. "Unfortunately, he's still alive."

I look at Andor for guidance and he gestures to an emerald velvet couch across from where Solla and Vidar are sitting. I notice that Kjell isn't here, and I breathe a quiet sigh of relief.

I sit down beside Andor, the couch small for his large frame, and my thighs are pressed against his. I try to move over as much as I can, but he makes no such attempt and stays right where he is. If anything I swear he's pressing himself against me on purpose.

I give him a dirty look, but he just stares at me with a wicked gleam in his eyes, his mouth twisted in a smug smile. He's enjoying this. There's a small, ignored part of me that enjoys this close proximity too.

Meanwhile Torsten saunters over to me with a glass of alcohol, his movements as graceful as Vidar's. "Here," he says begrudgingly. "It would be bad luck if you were the only one not toasting House Kolbeck."

I grip the glass and watch Torsten intently. He's the type of man you never want to take your eyes off. When you encounter a predator, you have to watch them closely so you can be prepared for when they strike.

Meanwhile Andor has started to fidget with his dragon-tooth necklace.

"To House Kolbeck," Torsten says, raising his glass to his family before doing so to the dragon skull. "And to our enemies, for they only make us stronger."

"Hear, hear," everyone but me says, though Andor mumbles it under his breath.

I take a sip of the liquor, the strength feeling like it's singeing my

REALM of THIEVES 143

eyelashes, though I must say the finish is smooth and smoky. It tastes expensive, nothing like the stuff that's sold at the Dark City markets.

Torsten is watching me carefully as I swallow the drink down.

"And what do you think?" he asks me. "Have you had peat alcohol before?"

"I don't even know what peat is," I say, to which Solla laughs. I think she's making fun of me but it's hard to tell with her.

Torsten gives me a smile that doesn't reach his eyes. "Of course not. I suppose you don't have peat in your world. Then again, I'm sure there are things that are grown and enjoyed in Esland that we can't even imagine."

I don't know if he's being condescending or not but it doesn't matter. "There are certain things, such as alcohol from a cactus grown outside the convent, and nuts harvested from certain shrubs, but we don't get any of that in the Banished Land, especially not when the Soffers control our water," I say.

"Ah," Torsten says. "Your punishment for believing in the wrong gods."

"Our punishment for questioning the government," I say. "Which I suppose is the same thing."

"Mmmm. Did you know the Kolbecks were one of the first families who left Sorland once the dragons were confined?" Torsten asks me, his heavy-lidded, golden gaze steady on mine.

"I figured as much," I say. "Though I never learned much about the other realms. The schools in Esland are quick to censor the truth."

"We went to Esland first," he goes on. "Found it too inhospitable. Nothing but sand and rock and death. Then we moved on across the Drage Passage to what is now Altus Dugrell. We found a land of wealth and prosperity. But you Eslanders, instead of following in our footsteps, you went to Esland and stayed there, perhaps because it's the closest port to the Midlands. Your false beliefs stifled you."

"Not *her* beliefs, remember?" Andor says.

"Semantics," Torsten says. "She was raised in those beliefs. As much as we like to say that we're in charge of our destiny, where you're from, who raised you . . . all of that is imprinted deeply. It's hard to escape from your birthright."

I raise my brow at his statement. I want to point out that I did escape from my birthright and I am in charge of my own destiny. But seeing that I'm currently in the grasp of the Kolbecks, I don't have a leg to stand on, and Torsten seems the type to form an opinion about you that's set in stone, immovable no matter what you say.

So I decide to bring the conversation back to him and make it personal. The way he brushed away questions about his own father gives me something to work with.

"If what you say is true," I say to Torsten after a small sip of my drink, "then I'm extra curious as to what happened with your father."

He gives me a hard stare, trying to intimidate me. I stare right back, though I can tell that the eyes of the rest of the Kolbecks are volleying between us.

The standoff ends when he taps the side of his glass with his nail. "My father lives on property," he says. "A house at the end of the Blomfields where he's taken care of. He isn't . . . well in his head."

"He must be quite old," I surmise. Torsten has to be in his sixties or seventies, which would put his father at eighty or ninety, at least.

"You wouldn't know it by looking at him," he says under his breath, his gaze going back to the dragon skull. If I didn't know any better, I'd say he looks sentimental.

"Our grandfather Ollie is a reminder of the perils of suen," Andor

REALM of THIEVES 145

speaks up, which brings a glare of reproachment from his father. "He took too much of it over the years. Back then, before Steiner had a chance to modify it, it was a lot for people's systems to handle. Some even grew addicted to it without knowing about the long-term effects."

Torsten grunts. "They were the pioneers," he says gruffly. "People like my father risked their health to push the limits of the human body."

So now you keep him tucked away from you and out of sight? I can't help but think. Some reward for being the pioneer of the family.

"The dragon egg trade hasn't been going on all that long in the grand scheme of things," Torsten continues. "It was my own grandfather who had started using it when the effects were becoming known to the realm, and when thieves first started braving the Midlands. Before him, it was just used by witches and sorcerers."

"And so now you're not worried about ending up like your father?" I ask, knowing I'm flying too close to the sun with this one. "If the suen wasn't refined until Steiner got his hands on it, then that means only the suen over the last, what, five, ten years has had no ill effects. What about all the usage before that?"

That brings a sharp glare from him, like I thought it would. "I have seen what my father has become. I know how to exhibit control."

Still, there's a chance that he'll end up exactly like his father. And I can tell that's something he fears. He seems like a man who will hold on to the reins of his family until the bitter end, even if he ends up going mad.

He'll steer them all into madness.

But that's none of your concern, I remind myself. *You won't be here to see the demise of the Kolbecks, because unless he dies or there's some sort of interfamily coup, he'll be the one to run them into the ground, not the Dalgaards, not the Soffers. Just him and his own ego. And all of this will just be a bad dream.*

I glance at Andor at that thought, only to find him staring right at me, enough that I feel a flush of heat in my veins.

Well, I suppose even the worst nightmares can have their bright spots sometimes.

Chapter 15

Brynla

"Land ho!"

Above the sound of the choppy water smashing the sides of the ship and the groan of the timber as it rolls in the waves, Toombs's voice calls out, faint and faraway.

I know that being down in my cabin is making me feel worse—my stomach churns with nausea, my skin is clammy to touch—but I don't dare go on deck, not now. It's not just that the closer we've gotten to the Midlands, the more the weather has turned, sending lashings of rain and huge swells over the last twenty-four hours, which make being on deck a miserable experience, but that I'm in pain.

I don't want Andor to know I'm suffering. I know I'm the one who asked him for his healing help, but I don't want to seem any more vulnerable than I already do. At least Steiner was able to tinker around in his lab and find the right blend of special herbs and leaves to take the place of the tea I'd been drinking to ward off the monthly bleeding. That would be another complication to deal with, and the last thing I want is some dragons finding us first on the hunt because they could pick up on the scent of my blood.

Steiner also gave me some poppy resin to consume in case the pain

148   KARINA HALLE

gets too bad, but I've been cautious with it. The flower clouds the mind and makes you tired, and I need as much energy and clarity as I can muster, especially since I don't know if we're going to be heading out on a raid right away.

Fuck, I think, as another wallop of pain slams into me, gritting my teeth as I curl up into a ball on the bed. *This one is bad.*

Lemi lets out a sympathetic whine and rests his head on my legs. I keep my eyes pinched shut, swallowed by the pain as it ravages me, my womb feeling both heavy as stone and like it's being stabbed repeatedly by a hot knife.

He whines again, moving his muzzle under my hand, until I start petting him, the motions over his smooth, soft fur making the pain easier to handle. I don't know if it's because Lemi has suen in him or if this is our bond, but there's always some kind of energy exchange between us, particularly when I'm in agony or stressed, like he takes all the bad and gives me his good, and never asks for anything in return, other than a good butt scratch every now and then.

A knock at my cabin door makes us both jolt.

I sit up, trying to seem normal.

"Yes?"

"Can I come in?" Andor asks through the door.

I reach over to the tiny table and take out a nugget of poppy resin from the pouch, placing it between my teeth and my cheek, like Steiner told me to do. It won't be enough to get rid of the pain, but at least it will stunt it and I won't lose any function.

"Come in," I tell him.

The door opens and Andor pokes his head in. His hair is wet, making it look jet-black and long as it sticks to his forehead and neck. A water droplet runs over his jawline and down his throat where it disappears into his soaked collar, and I get the strangest sensation of wanting to lick that water off his neck.

Must be the poppy resin kicking in already, I think.

REALM of THIEVES

"How are you feeling?" he asks, looking me over. "You seem a little green."

I nod grimly. "A trade-off for staying dry," I say, wincing slightly as the cramps come again. At least I can blame my reactions on being seasick.

"Well, you won't be dry for long," he says, his eyes sparking in excitement, something I usually find so infectious, but not right now. "We spotted the wards. Toombs is going to bring the ship through them. Looks like it might be raining on the other side too, though hopefully not acid rain."

My stomach twists with nerves now, on top of everything else. "Hopefully not. So what's our plan of attack?"

He leans against the doorway in a casual manner, folding his arms across his chest, and I practice great restraint in keeping my eyes focused on his amber ones and not at the way his wet shirt is clinging to every taut muscle in his upper body. You'd think the pain would be distracting enough for me, but I guess not.

"Because we'll be heading to see your aunt after this, I stuck to the eastern portion of the Midlands. You know the valley that's shaped like a tooth and has that high bank of caves along one side of it? Last time I was there I noticed the blooddrages had started making nests inside the cracks in the middle. There were a lot of them. With the three of us, we might be able to get as many as we can at once. I'll collect the suen using the extractor, while the two of you distract them or fight them off. Shouldn't take much time at all. Then we'll head right back to the ship. Might not even have to stay the night."

My eye twitches at another wave of pain.

"You don't approve?" he asks.

"Actually," I say, clearing my throat, "I'm a little concerned."

"Why? You've been training, your armor is better than ever."

"I've been training against you and Steiner, not against dragons," I point out.

KARINA HALLE

"Well, if you needed a bigger creature, I'm sure we could have brought out one of the horses. Vidar's mount is a nasty piece of work."

I give him a wry look. "Blooddrages might be small, but they're vicious and can easily overwhelm you. Even if Lemi and I are distracting them while you collect the eggs, it won't be easy to fend them off, especially not several hordes of them. I dare say that you have the easier job with the egg extraction, though I suppose I'd probably do it wrong if we were to switch. I don't know how to use that syringe. In addition, I know the valley you're talking about. Because of the way it funnels air between the volcanoes and the sea, it's known for fire tornadoes."

"But would blooddrages choose to build their nests where the fire tornadoes could get them?"

"Since fire doesn't hurt their eggs, they might take their chances," I tell him. "That also means that if we happen upon a change in the weather, we need to get out of there quick. Those dragons will return to their nests and sit on their eggs to protect them from being relocated by the tornadoes."

He gives me a warm smile, tilting his head. "Sounds like I have you onboard."

I let out a shaking exhale, wishing the pain would just fuck right off for a moment. The resin is barely helping. "You're the one in charge of this operation, remember? I'm just the hired help. Oh wait, you actually haven't paid me for this. Oh right, that's because I'm your hostage and you're blackmailing me."

His smile twists. "Remember, I told you I would make it worth your while. We can talk payment after we get the eggs."

Then he straightens up and looks around my cabin, his expression becoming more stern. "You should probably get changed into your armor and be ready to go in about ten minutes. Once we get through the wards, the ship will drop us off as close to the shore as possible. I know Toombs doesn't want to anchor the boat within the wards—

REALM of THIEVES

he's paranoid about dragons roasting the mast and setting the ship on fire."

I hadn't even thought about that.

Andor leaves the cabin and it's only when he's shut the door that I let out a whimper and curl up into a ball on the berth again. I let myself deal with the pain and breathe through it for a few minutes, using breathing techniques Ellestra taught me, and try to stay focused on the real task at hand, which is getting back to her.

Even if Andor keeps his word, I can't rely on that. From what I've learned about him over the last month, I don't think he means me any harm, nor would he purposely let any harm come to me. But that doesn't mean he wouldn't use me for his own endeavors. His father has a strong hold on him, whether Andor knows it or not, and I'm just some girl he took to give his family a better hold on the black market. He's driven, despite his nonchalant attitude, and I think he will do everything he can to succeed.

So I have to think about this egg raid in entirely different terms. I'll help Andor get his eggs. But then Lemi and I will need to escape. Somehow. Maybe I can get my hands on the tranquilizing serum that Steiner made for the dragons. It saved us the last time. I just have to figure out how much to inject Andor with so that it either knocks him out or makes him easier to manipulate, and to do it somewhere where I'm not putting his life in danger. I want to be free, but if I can avoid killing him, I will.

Or . . . I could just leave him to the blooddrages. I'm sure he'd be able to fight them off eventually. We could use the opportunity to escape. Head back to the rowboat and start rowing along the coast. If the weather cooperates we could stay hidden in the volcanic fog, shielded from the sight of the dragons inside the wards *and* the ship outside the wards.

That's as good a plan as any.

I get dressed in my armor—a formerly tedious process made much more efficient by all the hidden straps, ties, and buttons engineered by Steiner—then start strapping on the sheaths that go on my back. I braid my hair back tightly and knot it at the nape of my neck, then grab my ash-glass swords and slide them there. Then finally I pull on my leather breeches and boots. I know I should feel more powerful than I do in my new armor, but I don't. If anything I'm slightly self-conscious over how my stomach is accentuated at the moment thanks to the war going on inside my womb, and the pain still throbs in the forefront, no matter how hard I try to ignore it.

Lemi looks at me, ears askew, and I attempt a smile.

"Silly things to be worried about," I tell him. "I'll be okay. I just need to be strong. I've done this before."

At that I stand up, grab my overnight pack, and start taking what I might need for the journey back to the Dark City. I eye the dresses that the Kolbecks' seamstress made for me and wish I could take them along, but I would stand out like a sore thumb in them. The high life was just a temporary world. All I really need is what I'm wearing, the poppy resin, and some food.

I leave my cabin and head into the galley without managing to see anyone. I go through the pantry, taking the lightest but most nutrient-rich food: almonds, dried sliced beef and strips of salted cod, and dried apples, and fill my canteen with water from the jug. Then I grab some fresh fish that was left on the counter and toss it to Lemi for good measure. He wolfs it down in seconds flat, leaving no evidence except fishy dog breath.

By the time I head up the stairs to the deck, we're just passing through the wards, the familiar prickling sensation making the hair at the back of my neck stand on end. My mouth goes dry as adrenaline surges through me, my pulse quickening, my stomach doing flips. Even Lemi gives an impatient whine, his tail wagging at the prospect of doing his job again.

It's hard to tell the time because of the glow from the volcanoes perpetually lighting up the sky while the fog and ash smoke darkens it. I know it should be the late afternoon but it could be the middle of the night for all I see. Though I've been to this part of the Midlands a few times before, it seems foreign this time. Probably because I'm not alone.

While Toombs is back at the helm, the rest of the crew are all gathered at the bow as we head into the harbor, with Kirney at the base of the ship's bolt thrower. The giant crossbow was crafted specially to defend against incoming dragon attacks, with spears and arrows big enough to take down a flying beast. It's an intimidating weapon and one that will safeguard the ship until we get ashore. For the first time, I feel like House Kolbeck knows what they're doing.

"She's a beauty, isn't she?" Andor says, patting the gigantic crossbow with affection as he walks over to me. With the breeze blowing his dark hair back and the sparks and embers in the air behind him, he looks like he's in his element, like he was born here on in this wild, inhospitable land and somehow survived—and thrived.

Just like earlier, a strange fluttering sensation happens in my chest, like I've forgotten to breathe for a moment.

I swallow it down and force a smile.

"She's very dangerous looking," I tell him. "I hope you won't have to use it."

After hearing Torsten blather on and on about the house and their history of dragon hunting, I know that killing the beasts is in Andor's nature, even if it's just out of survival, but there's always been something about it that rubs me the wrong way. I fear dragons. I've escaped death many times. And yet all those times I did what I could to not kill them. Killing them out of anything but absolute necessity feels wrong, like killing a dog.

"Me too," he says. He looks down at Lemi, and then his eye pauses at the pack I have on my shoulder. Something dark comes over his

154   KARINA HALLE

gaze for a moment, then vanishes before he looks back to me, his eyes seeming to glow in the firelight. "Are we ready?"

"As I'll ever be."

He nods and yells for the boys to get the rowboat ready.

They work fast and in no time, Andor, Lemi, and I and our gear are lowered to the sea. The waves are still rolling in, but at least we're far enough from the shore that they're not breaking over us.

Then we're set loose from the ship and Andor starts rowing us to shore.

"Are you nervous?" he asks.

"I always get nervous before a raid," I tell him. "Don't you?"

"Every time. But then again, there's nothing else quite like it. Nothing else that makes you feel so damn alive." He pauses, his mouth curving up. "Other than sex, of course."

He's joking, so I laugh and ignore the heat flooding my cheeks. I blame it on the wind that's blowing the fires off the distant volcanoes. "Other than that," I tell him, staring at the artistic way that the lava flows have sculpted the shoreline and not at the heat in his own eyes. The last thing I need right now on top of everything I'm feeling and everything I have planned is to start thinking about sex. And especially not sex with Andor, someone I hopefully won't see again after tonight.

I cough and pull up the extra fabric that's sewn into the neck of my armor, having forgotten what it's like to breathe the Midlands air. "So," I say, my voice muffled by the cloth. "I suppose House Dalgaard has one of those bolt throwers too. And what about House Haugen?"

"House Haugen has their own ways of defense. They also have their own area. They take the west of the Midlands, we take the north. It's the agreement between our houses. As for House Dalgaard? You should know better than anyone."

"I've only done what they've told me, and on my own. I've never seen them in action, never met with them on any of my raids."

"Well, while you're on your raids, they're out here with crews of their own, larger than mine. They seem to pick clean the entire southern coast every moon cycle. They work with great haste, something that doesn't seem to bother anyone but me."

I shrug. "Collect water while it rains, I guess."

"No," he says, almost to himself. "And, honestly, and I mean this with the greatest of respect for you, Brynla Aihr, but I don't understand why they've gone out of their way to bother with you."

I blink at him, feeling surprisingly dejected, just as the hull of the boat scrapes against the rough stones of the shore and Lemi shifts himself so he appears on the land, already chasing a bunch of black lava crabs.

"What do you mean?" I say as Andor hops out of the boat and starts pulling it ashore with me still in it, like the boat weighs nothing in and of itself. I scramble out of it, leaping off the bow and onto the rock. "You're the one who blackmailed me into working for House Kolbeck. Did you ever believe in me, or was this some sort of pissing contest between the houses?"

He gives me a placating smile and raises a palm in surrender before he pulls the boat the rest of the way. "I wanted to see what the big deal was," he says. "And I still stand by you being a great benefit to us. To me. Without any suen in your blood, what you do . . . is remarkable. But I don't know why House Dalgaard in particular needs you. A magic dog is a great asset, and so is a skilled thief. But they have many skilled thieves, Brynla. They have armies of people trained to sacrifice themselves for their house."

"If they have to sacrifice themselves, that doesn't sound like skill to me," I grumble, looking back over the dark seas to where the ship starts to pull away, the sails flapping in the hot wind.

"No, it doesn't, but they're expendable down there. The Sorlanders have started to worship suen the same way the Soffers worship the dragons themselves. They say the king has already gone mad on it, crazier than Grandpa Ollie. Anyway, the point of my meandering thoughts is this: why you? Why add you to their endless supply of thieves? What do you and your dog bring to the table that no one else does?"

I scoff, shaking my head. "Why are you asking this now? Why didn't you ask this before you fucking kidnapped me?"

He doesn't seem at all bothered by my indignation. "Because I wanted to see if I could find the answer. Even Steiner doesn't understand it, and he's been observing you around the clock since you arrived. But there's something there, Brynla. There's some reason. And it's not your dog, as crucial a component as he is. It's you. And I am determined to find out what." He reaches into his leather pouch that attaches with a belt around the waist. It's where he's storing the suen extractor needle, the tranquilizer serum, as well as the empty, protected vials for the suen.

"Regardless, tonight will be the first test," he finishes, coming over to me with a short black stick between his fingers. "It's salve. Ring your eyes with it."

I'm about to tell him I have salve, but it's back in the Dark City. And I'm sure this is Steiner's formula, which probably has some added properties to it. Laced with suen, the Steiner Kolbeck special.

I run the stick around my eyes and then Andor takes it back from me, doing the same. The way the amber gold of his eyes stands out against the black reminds me of some sort of viper.

"Shall we get going?" he asks casually as he slips the stick back in his pouch, as if he didn't just try to undermine his whole reason for kidnapping me.

I stare at him for a moment and then exhale, shaking my head. "Lead the way."

He starts walking toward the highest point of the shore, and I call Lemi away from the crabs so that he's at our side.

Well, it's a good thing you're planning to leave him to the dragons since he doesn't seem to believe in you much anyway, I tell myself as I walk behind Andor up the rocky slope, black pumice and pebbles spilling out from under my boots.

Yet I know I've often thought the same thing. I didn't realize how many thieves Dalgaard had working for them, but I did wonder why Sjef Ruunon sought me out. Having an egg-sniffing, shifting dog is a great advantage if you don't have any other advantages, if you're down to bare-bones tactics like House Kolbeck. But if you're already stocked and armed . . . why me?

I can't help but keep thinking that over as we walk for a couple of miles over the undulating rock, keeping our eyes peeled for dragons. Occasionally one will fly by in the distance and all three of us will freeze, holding our breath until it passes out of sight.

So far Lemi hasn't sniffed anything out and it's actually Andor who pulls me to a stop and whispers, "There."

My gaze goes to where he's pointing. We've been walking along a plateau composed of sand and rock, the winds getting stronger with each step, blowing from behind us and smelling of the sea, and blowing from in front of us and smelling like sulfur. In front of us the plateau seems to part, leading down to a rift in the earth that widens the farther along it goes.

"That's the start of the valley," he says, and starts running off toward it.

I take off after him, Lemi keeping pace, and scramble down the sides where the plateau slopes off. Once we turn the corner, the whole valley opens up. It's as Andor described and as I remembered. The valley is narrow where we're standing, the wind whistling past in both directions, creating whorls in the sand, then gets wider heading inland toward a ridge of volcanoes, lava spilling out the sides, too far away to be a threat to us. All along one upper ridge of the valley is a row of caves, some of which I remember being home to sycledrages at some point.

But they aren't the eggs Andor brought me here for.

Right along one of the cracks that runs through the middle of the valley are blooddrage nests sprinkled here and there, like a little breeding farm.

"There has to be a dozen of them, at least," he whispers to me as we lean against the rock wall. "And I only see two sets of parents on their nests. The rest have left them to hunt." He glances at me, his eyes dancing. "Looks like there are no fire tornadoes in the forecast."

Lemi whines, his head low to the ground and sniffing, giving me the signal that he wants to shift to the nearest batch of eggs. I put my hand on his head to warn him to stay in place for now. We have to figure out the best way to do this without attracting the attention of the blooddrages that are on their nests. From my experience, even if you're disturbing another nest that doesn't belong to them, they'll react and protect it, much like a bee protecting a sand hive.

Andor reaches back and grabs one of his arrows from his quiver, then his bow.

"I can't make the shot from here, but if we get closer I might be able to take them out."

"How many arrows do you have?" I ask, eyeing the quiver, along with his sword on his back. I know in his boot he has his opal-glass dagger. "Maybe you should give the bow and arrow to me. That way I can protect you so you can concentrate on the eggs."

He squints at me. "Only the arrows with the green end have been dosed with the serum. Have you even tried archery before?"

"Actually yes," I tell him with a raise of my chin. "My father taught me target practice. We'd do so with the Soffers' dragon figurines that he'd stolen, all lined up along the wall around our house."

"And how old were you then?"

That was before we moved into the city. "Six," I admit. "But I bet it's like riding a horse."

"And have you ridden a horse?"

REALM of THIEVES

I don't say anything to that.

"Let me handle this," he says, starting to creep forward. "You and Lemi concentrate on being a distraction. And if any dragons come for me when I'm not looking, you take them down. I don't care how cute they are."

That's the thing about blooddrages. It's easy to think they're cute and harmless because they're the size of a cat. But they're quick and they're vicious and they have a taste for blood. I'm not certain what they usually hunt here—I'm sure Steiner could have filled me in on their habits—but it's the blood of something since your bare skin is the first thing they'll go for. They have sharp claws and long, hollow teeth that will pierce your skin and suck you dry if given the chance. I've never personally been bitten, but I have been swarmed until they decided I wasn't worth the trouble.

"All right," Andor says. "Follow my lead and stay behind me. When I stop, you stop. Think Lemi understands that?"

"You just let me worry about Lemi," I tell him, gesturing for him to go forward while I reach back and pull both ash-glass swords out of my sheath. "Let's go."

Andor heads straight out into the valley and I follow, keeping slightly to the side, otherwise I wouldn't be able to see around his tall frame. The moment we step away from the relative shelter of the rift walls, the heat and wind seem to intensify, more of it blowing from the volcanic range. I pull up my neck scarf higher around my mouth and see Andor do the same, breathing becoming more hazardous with the flying dust and sand.

I trust Andor to keep focused on the blooddrages, so I scan the skies looking for anything that might be in flight, plus the fact that a sycledrage might poke its head out of one of the caves at any moment.

We're about a hundred yards out from the row of nests when suddenly Lemi goes still.

160   KARINA HALLE

"Andor, stop," I whisper.

He stops in front of me and we slowly turn around.

The heavy *thwump-thwump* of wings comes from behind us. They sound heavier than an elderdrage . . .

"Lie down flat, quickly," Andor commands, and the two of us drop down to the ground, Lemi copying us, just as the light seems to be eclipsed, a dark dragon-shaped shadow passing over us.

I don't dare move, don't dare look up.

It's a deathdrage.

The largest and most formidable dragon to have ever existed, one that I have only seen from far away.

And right now, it's flying over us.

Sand and dust get churned up as its massive wings beat overhead, and I hold my breath, praying it doesn't see us here. It's too late for Andor to pull out his camouflaging blanket, so we're sitting ducks.

"Fuck," I whisper, unable to keep the awe from my voice.

It's so beautiful.

And unbelievably terrifying. The wingspan alone seems to take up the entire valley, its head the size of a horse-drawn carriage, moving back and forth as it spans the land.

"Watch for the tail!" Andor cries out, and before I can act, he's reaching for me and pulling me over to him, then rolling us over just as the heavy, whiplike end of the deathdrage's tail slams into the ground. Lemi shifts just in time and I feel him appear behind us, safely.

"That was close," Andor says into my ear. He's on top of me, his arms holding me in a tight embrace.

I nod, the wind slightly knocked out of me, momentarily enjoying the feeling of his weight on top of mine. He's holding back a little and if he totally relaxed, I'm pretty sure he would crush me.

He pulls back and stares down at me, our noses brushing against each other, our breathing labored, and I feel myself pulled into the depths of his eyes, noticing the way black and brown lines seem to radiate outward into the amber, like the rays of a black sun.

Is he going to kiss me? The thought flits across my mind.

It scares me.

Because I think I might want him to.

Then he looks away, in the direction of the dragon's flight, breaking the spell.

And thank the gods, because the last thing I need to be thinking about right now is the fullness of Andor's lips. I need to be thinking about the gigantic dragon that just flew overhead, nearly taking us out with his tail, and the fact that we can't do anything until that dragon moves on. It's a death wish otherwise.

"Shit," Andor says quietly, and I follow his gaze. The deathdrage is heading right for the nests. "We might have competition."

The both of us watch as it lets out a roar and the blooddrages that were sitting on their nests suddenly take flight, looking incredibly tiny compared to the beast. One of them isn't so lucky and the deathdrage snaps it up in its jaws, its throat bobbing as it swallows it in one go.

The deathdrage lets out another loud roar and for a moment I fear that it might turn and come back around, potentially spotting us this time. But it flies on forward with great beats of its wings until it gets smaller and smaller.

We stay motionless, watching until the dragon disappears from our sight, swallowed up by the dark haze.

"We need to move fast," he says, looking back down at me. His gaze flits over my face, focusing on my lips for a moment, his nostrils flaring. Then he suddenly pushes himself off me and gets to his feet in one smooth motion, pulling me up along with him. "The blooddrages are gone from the nests. Who knows how much time we have before they return."

He starts running toward them, his bow and arrow out, and I

follow, Lemi loping beside us. The nests are all wide open and I'm not sure where the bloodsuckers would have flown to, but I don't think they would have gone far.

We approach the first nest, just a bunch of dried twigs and seaweed that's been lined along the bottom of one of the cracks in the ground. This batch has five eggs lined up in a row, their shells gleaming in green and purple iridescence.

"Take those," he says, running ahead to the next nest. "Might as well take advantage of the peace," he adds over his shoulder.

I don't have a suen extractor like he does, but blooddrage eggs are about the size of a chicken egg. I grab the ones I see, slipping them into my pouch while scanning the horizon for new intruders. My pain seems to have taken a back seat at the moment, the adrenaline making it dull while the rest of my senses are on full alert.

But perhaps the resin has dulled things more than I thought because suddenly Lemi barks just as I'm putting the last egg in, and two blooddrages appear from over the top of the cave cliffs.

"Andor!" I yell. "On your left!"

He looks up to watch them approach, swooping down like lizard hawks. Thank the gods these ones don't breathe fire or we would be literal toast.

I make a run for them, swords out, Lemi at my side and barking. The blooddrages don't seem all that interested in me, but Lemi shifts, appearing right behind them. He leaps up and snatches one of them by the tail, whipping the dragon around to the ground. The other one goes to attack him, but then Lemi shifts and appears beside me.

Now the blooddrage is coming right for me and I have my swords ready to swing. I'll chop its head off if I have to. It cries out, needle teeth bared, and I'm staring it dead in its beady red eyes as it gets closer and closer.

Then it inhales and gives a loud squawk and shoots upward, out of my reach. It goes up high and then starts diving toward Andor.

REALM of THIEVES 163

"Coming at you!" I yell at Andor as I start running toward him, hoping I can put myself between him and the blooddrage in time.

He looks up from his crouched position and drops the extractor, grabbing his opal-glass dagger from his boot and throwing it at the dragon. I watch as the knife spins in several tight successions before it strikes the dragon right in the chest.

The dragon screams and drops to the ground, writhing in the dust, and the other dragon that Lemi threw to the ground is struggling to its feet, crying out for them while tossing around a broken tail.

Andor quickly picks up his bow and arrow and shoots the dragon through the top of the head, ending its suffering instantly. Then he gives me a dark look.

"You can't be afraid to kill them," he says gruffly.

I wasn't afraid, I want to say. But what was I?

"I've never killed one before," I tell him, looking back at their two lifeless bodies.

His brows rise and he gets to his feet, walking over to the dragons to yank out his dagger and his arrow. "How is it that you've never killed a dragon before?" he says incredulously.

"I haven't had the need to," I tell him.

He frowns at me and then looks around. "We better hurry. There's still at least one more blooddrage out there."

Grabbing his gear, he moves on to the next nest, and I start scanning the horizon again just in time to see another small black form appear in the distance.

"There she is," I say. "Dead ahead."

I start running ahead of Andor to the next nest, hoping that this time I'll be able to take the blooddrage down before it comes for him. So far Lemi is proving to be more of a diversion than I am.

The blooddrage lets out a squawk, flying right for me, just as the other one did.

But as it gets closer, Lemi leaps up, trying to bite it in midair before he shifts, leaving the dragon confused and spiraling to the ground where it lands. It looks up at me, but it's like it doesn't see me at all. It only moves when Lemi reappears beside it, barking until it takes flight.

"Brynla!" I hear Andor yell from behind me, the panic in his voice making my blood run cold.

I whirl around to see a swarm of blooddrages, at least six of them, flying toward Andor from the direction we came in, only feet away.

I barely have time to act before all of them are on him, snapping jaws, flapping wings, and scratching claws.

And I know that the chance of escape I had been waiting for has finally arrived.

Chapter 16

Andor

One minute I think that Brynla is going to leave me to a grisly fate.

I see her standing there, watching me in both horror and confliction, and I can almost see her being pulled in the opposite direction. Lemi, bless that hound, is barking, running toward me and the blooddrages as they scratch and claw at me, trying to bite at any exposed skin.

But a different fear strikes in my heart, greater than the fear of being maimed or even death.

The fear that she's going to leave me here without a second thought.

And that she'll never think of me again.

Then she starts running for me, full speed, swords out, and just seeing her coming for me gives me enough strength to straighten up. With a roar, I shake off as many of the dragons as I can, though one has thoroughly attached itself to my head. I grind my teeth against the pain of his claws as he scratches at my cheek, dangerously close to my eye, his mouth trying to bite my neck.

But then Lemi leaps up, grabbing the blooddrage by the tail and pulling him back off my head, which unfortunately makes the dragon dig his claws in deeper until warm blood flows down my cheeks.

I growl, whipping my dagger backward, hoping to stab him and the one that's crawling up my chest, just as I see Brynla wave her swords around. She doesn't seem so hesitant to kill them now and starts hacking away at the ones closest to her, her eyes fierce and her jaw set in grim determination.

The other dragons suddenly release me and fly off, as if Brynla has terrified them, leaving the three of us with a couple of dead blood-drages at our feet.

"You're bleeding," she says to me, her chest heaving from exertion.

"I'll live," I tell her, wiping away the blood. "We should start heading back. I don't know what you did to make those dragons fly away, but they might come back with even more reinforcements next time."

She nods and opens her pouch, peering inside. "So far none of them have cracked. I can grab a couple more."

She goes to the next nest and starts grabbing the shiny eggs and popping them into her pouch. I look around to see the damage. Most of my eggs are broken but I can at least extract the suen.

I crouch down and take out the extractor, making quick work of the mess.

"Uh, Andor," Brynla says. "We have a problem."

Fuck, what now?

I get up, the wind buffeting me in the face, smelling of sulfur. Toward the volcanoes where the valley opens up, fire starts to lick around the ground, swirling up and up toward the sky.

"Fire tornadoes," I say gruffly.

She eyes me over her shoulder, and though she looks worried, there's also a hint of *I told you so* in her gaze.

"We should start running," she says, snapping her pouch shut and putting her swords back in the sheaths at her back. Though I

REALM of THIEVES   167

shouldn't, though there are far more pressing things to think about, the sight of her standing in Kolbeck-crested armor, with the wind whipping her lavender hair free from her bun, and the fire tornado burning and spinning in the background, I feel momentarily dumbstruck. Awed. Like I'm seeing an actual goddess come to life, and my first instinct is to get down and kneel.

"Andor," she says, her voice sharp now, bringing me out of my momentary lapse in reality as she runs to me and tugs at my arm. "Now!"

I nod, feeling strangely dizzy, and I turn, running quickly along the valley floor toward the narrow entrance that feels more far away than I remember. I hold back enough to keep pace with Brynla, not wanting to leave her behind in the dust if I apply my full speed.

We're only a few yards from the exit out of the valley when suddenly the air pressure changes and the sky rumbles with thunder, shaking the ground beneath us, enough that Brynla nearly falls and I grab her arm to hold her up.

Flames ten feet high appear at our only way out, making us skid to a stop. From above, the dark, ashy clouds reach down like a spiraling hand, and I watch in a mix of dread and fascination as the spiral and the fire connect.

In seconds the fire roars, whipping up high and fast, racing up to the sky, the heat blasting my face.

"Fuck!" I cry out, grabbing Brynla's hand to make sure I don't lose her and whirling around to see that the fire tornado that we were originally running from has spread into three, swirling across the valley floor to greet us. I look up the sides of the rift to see which one will be easiest to climb, only to notice the mass of dust, miles high and wide, coming from the east, lightning flashing sporadically.

"Sandstorm," Brynla says grimly.

There isn't much time to think.

"The caves," I tell her. "We have to run for the caves!"

Brynla's fear-widened eyes look over to them. They seem so far away right now. I don't know how we're going to outrun fire tornadoes coming from either direction, or a massive sandstorm, but we're going to have to try.

"Lemi!" Brynla shouts at him. "Go back to the ship. Shift back to the ship and stay there. Wait for us to return."

Lemi barks but Brynla yells back. "Go, Lemi! To the ship. Now!"

His ears flatten, a sad look on his face, and then he disappears into thin air.

Still holding on to her arm, I start running as fast as she can keep up, pulling her along. The heat from the tornadoes is coming from both sides of us now, the wind whipping us into each other as we run. The roar is getting louder, covering up the sound of the pumice rock crunching underfoot, the harsh sound of our breathing.

I dare to look behind me and all I see is flames.

I glance at Brynla and she holds my gaze for a moment.

"You can make it if you let me go," she manages to say, her voice barely heard above the din.

I just shake my head.

Never.

We keep running until we hit the slope that leads up to the ridge of caves. I have to let go of her, needing both my hands to climb up the loose scree and sand, sliding backward a few times until I finally reach the hard ridge and get to my feet, reaching down and pulling Brynla up the rest of the way.

The fire tornadoes meet each other below us, combining into a supersize one, just as the sandstorm is almost upon them. One would hope the storm would put the fire out, but before it does it's going to push a wall of flames out of the valley floor and right into us.

I pull Brynla along and into the nearest cave, the opening narrow, barely wide enough for us to fit through. I guide her in first, then

REALM of THIEVES   169

come after and push her down to the ground, my body going over hers just as flames surge outside, shooting inside the cave above our heads.

Brynla screams and I keep her covered, the flames licking inside, though we're both protected by our fire-resistant armor. I hold her tight; I don't even think that I'm breathing, I'm just praying to the goddesses and waiting to survive.

But then the heat withdraws and in its place comes sand.

I get off Brynla and crawl forward, trying to seek more shelter. The cave opens up a little and hooks around the corner. I know there's a chance that sycledrages could be nesting in here, but they would have attacked us by now.

"This way!" I yell at her, trying not to get a mouthful of sand. I wait until she crawls beside me, then pull her over to the side so we're both sitting against the wall, out of the wind and sand that blow past, swirling and gathering in the unseen depths of the cave.

"Are you all right?" I ask her, keeping my voice loud enough to be heard against the infernal roar of the sandstorm.

She nods. "Yeah. Just a little sore but I'm okay. I think the eggs are crushed."

"Better them than you," I tell her. "I'll see what I can salvage when this storm dies down."

"How long do they usually last? I've never been through one."

"Can take days," I tell her.

The light in the cave is dim and I can barely make out the furrow between her brows.

But you've packed enough for that, haven't you? I think. I keep that observation to myself, for now.

"I'm sure it won't last long," I tell her. "I just wish you had the same ability as your dog, so both of you could have been sent to safety."

"I wouldn't leave you," she says.

I don't say anything to that.

Instead I look around the corner, shielding my eyes from the incoming sand. There's faint flickering at the mouth of the cave, and I get on my knees and crawl over to it, keeping my head down. There are a few fragments of burning branches tossed in by the storm, threatening to go out. I snatch one up and crawl back over to Brynla.

"What are you doing?" she asks, pulling her knees to her chest.

"Never know when a fire will come in handy," I tell her. "One that you can control, of course."

I reach into my pack and bring out a small piece of fireflame bark that comes from trees grown in Vesland. I stick the piece into a hole in the porous cave floor and light it with the fire, then toss the branch to the side, where it's immediately blown away and put out by the wind. But the fireflame stays lit, a steady glow that gives off a lot of heat considering how small the flames are.

Satisfied that it won't go out—that small piece of bark should stay lit for days—I look back at Brynla.

But her face is contorted in pain.

"What's wrong?" I ask, moving closer to her, placing my hand on her knee.

She twitches her knee out of my grasp and I notice the way she's clutching her stomach.

"Is it your pains?" I ask. "Did you bring any of the poppy resin?" I grab my pack and start rummaging through it. I know I should have brought some with me.

She lets out a gasp and nods. "I did," she says, her words coming out staccato. "But it's not helping. If I take too much, I'll be unconscious."

I put the bag down, wanting to help, needing to help.

"When did it start? Just now?"

Her eyes are pinched closed as she shakes her head. "No. On the ship."

REALM of THIEVES

171

My chest stings, hurt and a little angry. "Why didn't you tell me? I wouldn't have made you come."

"That's why I didn't tell you," she admits, fixing me with a pained yet hardened stare. "I didn't want you to worry and I didn't want to be made to stay behind. Even though you can't figure out why you need me."

I rub my lips together, reaching for her again. She flinches at my touch but I hold her knee.

"But I need you," she says softly.

I swallow hard, knowing what she's asking.

"Brynla," I begin.

"Why?" she says angrily. "If you have this power from the suen to heal, why won't you use it on me? What happened to you? What's scaring you?"

For a moment I feel myself freeze up, like everything inside me has seized.

And then it all comes out in a bitter rush.

"My mother," I tell her, the memories coming over me like a blackened cloak. They want to smother me until there's only darkness. I feel like I'm trying to stay above water, so I talk fast, too afraid to dwell in it. "My mother was dying. It came one evening, we don't know what it was. It was as if her body started to shut down. The pain she was in . . . she lost her voice from screaming. Her eyes started to bleed, her skin turned . . . like she was one big bruise. She couldn't walk or eat or do anything but die. She could only just die, painfully and slowly."

The heat of tears prickles behind my eyes but I ignore them. They can fall if they want. Brynla is looking at me with quiet horror, though I can't tell if it's from my confession or from her own pain.

"Everyone knew of my gift," I tell her. "I was only thirteen; I'd barely had time to understand what I could and couldn't do. I was able to fix a broken bird's wing. I could heal cuts that our horses got after a rough day's foxhunting. I was able to cure Vidar's terrible headaches, at least for a little while. And suddenly my father told me to heal my mother. And I knew I couldn't." I shake my head, a tear spilling down and stinging the fresh cuts on my cheek. "I just knew that I couldn't. Is that what doomed me? That I didn't believe in myself?"

"What did you do?" she whispers.

"What I had to. I would have done anything for my mother, anything. My father never had to make me do anything. I stayed by her side, I put my hands everywhere I could, her heart, her lungs, her head, and I felt her pain, this sickness, this dark disease. Death. I knew it was death. And then I felt my energy leave my body and go into hers and I had a hope and a prayer. I stayed with her a whole day and a whole night and then when the morning broke, she was dead."

Her eyes widen, then twitch, shifting through pain and sympathy. "I'm so sorry."

I swallow the lump in my throat, the sheer panic of sorrow clawing in my chest, like a ravenous beast that's waiting to be set loose and destroy me. I don't let the beast out often. It needs my grief to survive. "Not as sorry as I was. Not as sorry as my father was, who blamed me for my failure. What use was this power if I couldn't use it to save the woman he loved? What use was I?"

"But it wasn't your fault," she says, shaking her head. "Clearly, she was very ill. You did what you could."

"I did and it wasn't enough to save her. What good is the power to get rid of a headache and heal a cut if I can't save my own mother, my own flesh and blood?"

She lets out a shaking breath and leans against the cave wall. "I'm sorry you couldn't save her. But you can save others." She closes her eyes, her head dipping down as her hands go to her stomach, her breath coming in sharp.

I hate watching her like this.

REALM of THIEVES

"You saved Lemi," she says. "You can heal; it's your gift to use." She lifts her head and meets my gaze, her eyes watering. "Please use it on me."

I should be nodding. I should be at her side, doing all I can to help. But I just hear my father's voice.

Hear him calling me a disappointment. That I'll never amount to anything because I failed my first test. My final test.

"Please," she asks again, the desperation in her voice nearly choking her. Her brow is crumpled, anguished, pleading, and I want nothing more than to make her pain go away, to bring her relief.

But it's my own pain, the fear of it, that's stopping me.

"If I fail . . ." I whisper.

"Then you fail," she says, her eyes squeezing shut as she lets out a low cry. "You can't hurt me more than the pain I'm already in." She manages to look at me, her gaze piercing. "You owe me this."

She's right. I do owe her this. I owe her a lot of things, considering what I've done to her life.

I nod, feeling resolve, and before I can change my mind, I look through my pack again. I take out the blanket, laying it down on the softest surface of the cave, a mix of airy pumice and fine sand beside the fire.

"Lie down," I tell her, my voice coming out shallow. "On your side."

She staggers over to the blanket and collapses on her hands and knees before going into the fetal position. The pain is palpable. I wonder if I'll feel hers like I did with my mother. A different kind of agony, but an agony all the same.

I carefully walk around her so I'm at her back, and then I get down behind her so that I'm lying right behind her, trying not to get too close so I don't make her feel uncomfortable. I take in a deep breath and put my arm over her side, moving slow. She still startles under my touch.

174   KARINA HALLE

"I'm just putting my arm over you," I say, making sure she knows exactly what I'm doing. "I'm going to put my hand where the pain is. You just tell me where."

She swallows, her breath quickening.

I place my palm on her stomach and she takes my hand in hers, moving it farther down.

I swallow thickly, trying to concentrate on the task at hand and not where my dirty thoughts want to go. I pay attention to the feel of her lower belly, the way it's still soft and curving even under the leather armor.

"This might work better if I could touch your bare skin," I say, my mouth at her ear so that she can hear me over the ever-present roar of the sandstorm outside the cave.

She nods, letting out a whimper of pain.

I reach up and separate where her armored tunic meets her leather breeches. She immediately sucks in her stomach and I'm aware of how hard I'm breathing, of how controlled every movement I make is.

My fingers press against her bare skin, so soft, radiating so much heat that I feel it go up my arm.

She lets out a gasp.

"Am I hurting you?" I ask her, my voice gruff and ragged.

"No," she says. She sucks in her breath. "Just a little ticklish."

I grin to myself and then slowly glide my hand down over her stomach, to where she had guided me before. Her skin is even softer here, the swell of her stomach like a place I could rest for days and catch my breath. I want nothing more than to have my hand go down even farther, find that spot between her legs and make her forget this pain ever existed. It wouldn't heal her, but it would be more fun for the both of us.

But I'm not about to take advantage of a girl in pain.

I'm going to do what I can to rid her of it.

"Is this the spot?" I whisper into her ear.

"Yes," she says, her breath hitching.

"You might feel a strange sensation," I warn her. "Hopefully not too ticklish. Just something warm. So I've been told."

Her response is a groan of pain.

I get to work.

I close my eyes and concentrate on whatever reserves I have inside me, someplace so deep down that I'm not even sure that it can come from my own body. Possibly another world. Maybe this one, where dragons are born.

Then I feel the warmth rising up from that place, flowing through my arms, my veins feeling as if they're made of molten gold and sky lightning, and it leaves through my fingertips and the palm of my hand, passing into her.

She gasps, breathless, moving her stomach away from me at first, and then she moves it back so that my palm is flush against her skin. I keep my eyes closed, waiting for her pain to transfer back into me, anticipating the shock.

It comes with a bang, like someone has literally punched me in the gut.

I swallow a cry, not wanting her to think I'm suffering enough to stop, and grind my teeth together as the pain envelops me. It doesn't last for long, but by the time it runs through my whole body, I've broken a sweat and my pulse is galloping against my neck.

"Oh gods," she says through a soft gasp, and her head goes back against me. "It's working."

"Are you sure?" I ask, too afraid to get my hopes up.

"Yes," she breathes out. "It's leaving."

The smile on my face might just break it in two. Hope feels impossible to keep at bay now.

"I don't know if this will keep going after I stop," I caution her. "It might just work right now while I'm touching you."

"Then don't stop. Keep touching me, Andor," she says through a groan. "Please don't stop."

176 KARINA HALLE

Well, fuck me. Now I'm both incredibly proud that I've been able to take her pain away and incredibly turned on.

She lets out another breathless whimper and then moves her ass back until it presses against my half-hard dick.

I bite back a moan but with my mouth at her ear, I don't think there's any hiding it.

She moves herself harder against me, practically writhing, her gyrations making me harder than rock and causing my palm to slip farther down, my fingertips brushing over the lace edge of her undergarments.

My breath catches in my throat, my hand paused, torn between doing what I want to do, what I think she wants me to do, and doing what we both agreed on.

I manage to stay the course, pressing my fingers against her skin to anchor myself.

"Andor," she whispers, her voice sounding thick with either relief or lust or maybe both. "Don't take your hand away."

I don't particularly want to. "I'm going to try to shut off the healing and see if your pain is still at bay."

She nods, her head still back, her neck exposed to my lips, and I suck in another breath, closing my eyes and reaching back inside me now to the golden source of it all. I turn it off like you would a tap, the energy dissipating.

And still Brynla pushes back against my cock, rubbing it with slow, torturous movements.

"Are you in any pain?" I whisper, my lips moving against the sweet-smelling skin of her neck.

"No," she says. "It's still gone. It's gone." Then she slumps against the blanket. "It's gone," she says, her voice fading.

I peer down at her face.

Her eyes are closed, her features relaxed and soft, a small smile on her lips.

In seconds she's sleeping, breathing out deeply in slumber brought on by acute relief, her body finally letting go.

Finally finding peace.

And I brought her that peace.

Slowly, carefully, I remove my hand from her breeches. Then I keep it hovering above her stomach as I relax beside her, my arm holding her against me. I don't know how I'll sleep with her so close to me like this, feeling her heart beating through her back, the sweet smell of her hair making my blood run hot.

But, somehow, mercifully, I do.

Chapter 17

Brynla

 I WAKE UP SLOWLY, MY BODY TAKING ITS TIME IN RELAYING information.

The din of the sandstorm is gone.

Silence buzzes in my ears instead.

My side aches from sleeping in one position on hard ground all night.

But the pain? The pain is gone.

My eyes open to the dimness of the cave, lit only by a sputtering fire in the center, and I'm suddenly aware that the man who took the pain from me is flush against my back, his arm draped loosely over the dip in my side. His breathing behind me is steady; perhaps he's still asleep.

I take a moment to stare at the lava rock wall of the cave.

I take a moment to just . . . be.

When was the last time someone held me like this? When was the last time I fell asleep in someone else's arms?

In the Dark City, I never let myself get close to anyone other than my aunt; it was too dangerous to either become attached or let my guard down. But that didn't mean I didn't have my fair share of suit-

REALM of THIEVES 179

ors. I have sexual appetites just like any other woman my age, and men in the Banished Land were always more than willing to have a tryst here and there. When you're already living outside society's standards, no one judges you for what you do, and sexually promiscuous women aren't looked down upon. But the sexual encounters never became anything more than what they were—a chance to forget one's trouble for an evening and blow off some steam, hopefully in the form of an orgasm. Sex was common but intimacy, that was rare.

I close my eyes and relax back into Andor, holding on to this moment, whatever it is and wants to be. Last night he took my pain away. He touched me with his bare hands and I felt warmth and raw power coming from him that seeped directly into me. I felt it in my soul, like I was being brought to life, filled with strength and resilience and then . . . relief. Relief so overwhelming and acute that my body started to confuse it for something else. I wanted him, I wanted his hands to dip lower, I wanted to know what it would feel like to have those healing hands between my legs. For the first time I wasn't ignoring the physical attraction that I've felt for Andor—I was encouraging it. I was craving more.

But then I fell asleep before anything more could happen. I suppose it might have been wishful thinking that anything *would* have. Yet as I writhed in pleasure at the totality of that relief, I felt how hard he was, how much I was turning him on. Andor's always been a difficult person to read in some ways. He seems to feel everything all at once. And he's always been flirtatious and tactile with me, so I've never taken that to mean anything. Why should I read into that? I'm his fucking prisoner.

And now? Now what?

He gave me peace and suddenly the cage I'm in doesn't seem so bad anymore.

I don't know if that means I'm weak.

Or that I'm getting stronger.

"Good morning," he says, his voice thick with sleep and near my ear, causing an internal shiver to roll through me.

"Good morning," I manage to say. My mouth is so dry, the air even more so. I've gotten so used to being in the fresh, moisture-rich air of Norland that every part of me feels parched. Doesn't help that we've been sandblasted for hours.

I move my head slightly, looking up to see him staring down at me, his thick hair in a mess, his eyes half-lidded, his mouth curved in a small, amused smile.

I don't think I've ever wanted him more.

"How are you feeling?" he asks. "How is the pain?"

He's trying to sound easy but I catch the look in his eyes, the one that says my answer could change the world for him.

Luckily, I only have to tell him the truth. "I have no pain."

His face lights up as if shooting stars were passing overhead, a wide, breathtaking smile stretching across his handsome face, and my own heart leaps in response. "Are you sure?" he asks.

I nod and even though I don't want to leave the warmth and comfort of his body, I shift over slightly and sit up. "I'm a bit numb from sleeping like this all night, but no, there's no pain. In fact, I can't remember the last time I felt so energized. Especially in the morning. You know I'm not a morning person."

"It's hard to tell if that's you naturally or just part of staying at Stormglen," he says softly, sitting up and moving so that he's beside me. "Being with the Kolbecks has rubbed off on you."

There's only one Kolbeck I want rubbing off on me, I think.

"And how's your face?" I ask, peering at the ragged cuts over his cheekbones. Before I can stop myself, I reach out and gingerly touch his cheek beside the wounds.

His eyes flutter closed for a second as he leans into my touch, and I have the strangest sensation of my chest being bound with thread and that he's slowly unraveling it, maybe the first person to ever do so.

REALM of THIEVES   181

"I'll live," he says, meeting my eyes with such intensity that it makes my breath hitch.

The implications are subtly terrifying.

I drop my hand and look away before I make things too awkward. "Too bad your healing hands don't work on yourself," I tell him.

"As long as they work on you," he says, getting to his feet. He reaches down and pulls me up beside him. He's close, our chests nearly pressed against each other, and I have to tilt my head back to meet his eyes. He's still holding on to my arms, keeping me in place. My belly warms with the flutter of butterfly wings, wanting him closer still.

God, what is happening?

"I never got a chance to thank you for saving me yesterday," he says, his voice low and gravelly. "You could have left me under the blooddrages but you didn't. I owe you."

"You did just heal me," I point out softly, but his words are bringing forth a shadow, the one that's been lingering over me all this time.

"That's not enough," he says. "Your pain might come back. I might have just healed you for now." He swallows hard and lets go of my arm, putting his hand at the back of my head.

Suddenly I can't breathe. Wind from outside the cave whips its way inside, hot and sulfurous, making our hair dance.

I know what I can ask him.

How he can repay me.

Days ago I wouldn't have hesitated.

But now, now I'm too scared to say it.

Because I no longer know if that's what I want.

"I can let you go," he says, gravity in his voice and gaze. "I can take you to the Dark City and leave you there."

His answer feels like a rug being pulled out from under me.

It's what I wanted.

What I came here planning for, why I have extra provisions in my pack.

182 KARINA HALLE

What I was suddenly too afraid to ask for.

"You would do that?" I ask, shaking my head in disbelief. "Why?"

He runs his hand down to the back of my neck and grips me there gently. It's possessive. It's the opposite of freedom and yet I like the idea of him being possessive over me.

I don't want him to let go.

Not now, perhaps not ever.

"Because I know it's what you want," he says, rubbing his thumb over the side of my neck, making my heart flutter. "I might act like a fool most of the time, lavender girl, but I see more than you think. I saw what you packed, more than enough for a night. I knew that the first opportunity you had you would try to best me and make for the Banished Land. Maybe even leave me for dead. So imagine my surprise when you didn't. When you actually saved me. No suen in your blood to help you, you just marched back and charged those blood-drages head on. You scared them off, Brynla. That's how formidable you are. And that's how I know I don't have the right to keep you, to blackmail you, to make you become something you're not."

I hate the way I feel my face crumble. "How are you making me into something I'm not?"

"I forced you to work for House Kolbeck. You have no allegiance to us, not to me. You only have allegiance to yourself. You worked hard for your freedom and I stripped it away from you." He swallows, giving his head a tiny shake. "I don't want to do that anymore. You're free to go."

I don't want to go.

It's not just that he healed me—for the time being or not—but that something has flipped between us. Something has changed. And maybe it's only the fact that he's deciding to let me go, but . . .

I think I trust him.

"Then all of this will have been for nothing," I say to him.

REALM of THIEVES

"No," he says, looking surprised. "Not for nothing. I've had you in my life from one moon to the next. That wasn't for nothing."

Oh, blazes. My chest clenches at that, like the breath has been knocked out of me.

My throat feels too thick to speak properly. "I didn't think you'd let me go so easily," I manage to say.

He gives me a tight smile. "Nothing about this is easy. I want you here. But you knew that from the beginning. What do *you* want?"

"I want to see my aunt," I tell him. "I want to bring her out of the Dark City. To Norland, somewhere. I want a better life. I want a better tomorrow. That's all I've ever wanted."

His grip tightens on my neck, his gaze dropping to my mouth where it burns. "Then, if you let me, I want to give you a better tomorrow." The muscle in his jaw tics, his eyes looking anguished for a moment. "I can't give many people many things, but I think I can give you that. I can at least try."

Pride ripples through me, the urge to step out of his grip, the well-honed instinct to tell him that I don't need him to give me anything, that I don't need anything from anyone. For a moment I feel torn, like my vanity is about to rip me in two.

But I close my eyes and let myself give in.

I nod, about to tell him that's exactly what I want, but as soon as I open my mouth, Lemi's bark comes from outside the cave.

Andor releases me and steps back as Lemi comes bounding toward us, tongue lolling, tail wagging.

"What are you doing here?" I ask him, crouching down to his level as he slobbers all over me. "I told you to stay on the ship!"

He makes a bow and then barks again. He obviously wants us to get going.

I get to my feet, smiling as I ruffle up his ears with a vigorous head rub, then look over at Andor. "I guess this a sign to head back to the ship."

He nods and starts gathering up the blanket and the rest of our stuff. "I figured as much. Storms seem to have stopped, so hopefully it will be a quick journey back."

While he continues to pack up I excuse myself to venture farther into the cave to relieve myself out of sight. Lemi follows me, of course. Can't ever do my business without him there. When I'm done, feeling a little better, and still elated that my cramps are gone, Andor is packed up and ready to go. He hands me my pack and I sling it over my shoulder, and then I pick up my swords and slide them into the sheaths at my back.

He straps on his leather pouch around his waist, checking to make sure the vials of suen are all right, then nods. "Okay. I think we're ready. Just remember, we're still in the blooddrage territory. You saved me once but we can't depend on that happening again. I don't want to put you at risk like that. So let's move quickly and quietly."

I nod, though if he thinks that I'm just going to leave him to get eaten by dragons, he's got another think coming.

Chapter 18

Andor

"Where's Brynla?" Feet, my crewman, says to me as he passes me a mug of something. "We're about to start our card game. Always helps to have an even number of players."

"I think she's on deck," I say, sniffing the drink. I make a face. "Oh, did Toombs make his grog again?"

"It's rum," Toombs announces, slapping me on the back, making the drink spill over, the acidic molasses smell filling the air.

"It's grog," I correct him. He holds out his mug and I sigh reluctantly, tipping my vessel against his. "Down the hatch, I guess."

I drink back the awful stuff while everyone else chants, "Down the hatch, down the hatch!"

I manage to swallow it down and suddenly my mug is already refilled and I'm somehow holding two mugs.

"That one is for Brynla," Toombs says. "The girl has been awfully quiet these last two days. She might want something for the nerves. We'll be landing in the Banished Land tomorrow."

"Ask her if she'll play cards," Feet adds.

I nod and head up the stairs to the top deck, two mugs filled with grog rum.

It's quiet up here, the winds steady but the seas calm, and the sky is peppered with bright stars. The first few days at sail after leaving the Midlands we had the same rough waves as we had going into it, but as we get closer to Esland and the Banished Land of the south, the more things have turned. I wonder if it's an omen, a warning that things might not be so calm ahead.

Kirney is at the helm for the evening, which is just as well when Toombs has broken out the homemade rum. I nod at him at the wheel and then look down the deck to see Brynla at the bow, Lemi lying dutifully by her side. She's staring right at the moonlit waters, the reflection slightly pink in the faint glow of the cycle's pink moon, and though her face is turned away from me, I can picture the serious, wistful expression on her face.

Ever since we got off the Midlands with our lives barely intact, she's become a little distant. Sometimes I wonder if her pain is back and she's been trying to hide it. Other times I wonder if perhaps I said too much. Maybe I acted too strongly. I thought I was keeping myself in check; I thought I was doing the noble thing, the right thing, by offering to let her go. To free her from the bargain she never wanted to make in the first place.

Perhaps she regretted not taking me up on it.

Perhaps the moment we step foot in the Dark City, a place I've never been but one she would know like the back of her hand, she plans to leave me for good.

Or lead me into a trap.

Moon didn't say anything about her aunt except that she was waiting for us.

So she'll be waiting for us . . .

I push the thought out of my head. Brynla saved my life the other day. I have no reason not to trust her. It's especially fair when I keep asking her to trust me.

Lemi's head comes up and his tail thumps a couple of times

against the deck when he sees me. Honestly, the idea of Brynla not being by my side pains me, but I'd miss the dog almost as much.

Her head turns slightly and she eyes me from the side, but she doesn't move from where she's leaning on the bow, the waves slicing below in a rhythmic manner, music to my ears. Her hair is in a loose braid and she's wearing her leather breeches and a navy shirt she borrowed from me, made more fitted by tying it with rope at the waist. I've never seen a woman wearing my clothes before, and I have to admit, it does something for me, like it's a visual sign that she's *mine*.

But I'd be a fool to start thinking that way, especially when so much hangs in the balance.

"I have something for you," I say, holding out the mug. "You're under no pressure to drink it. It's Toombs's rum. Well, grog. Rum grog."

She takes it and gives it a sniff, her nose wrinkling. "Ah, Toombs's infamous grog. I was wondering when he would finally break it open."

Then to my surprise she puts the mug to her lips and gulps it back with ease.

"Whoa," I say, reaching out to stop her. "Careful now, this is very strong."

She winces, making a face. "I know."

Then she drinks the rest of it in a few more gulps until the mug is empty, and she hands it back to me.

"Gods of the realm, I can't tell if I should be impressed or turned on," I admit.

She bursts out laughing.

"I think that's the first time I've heard you laugh in days," I add quietly.

She composes herself quickly and I feel bad that I mentioned it at all. I love her laugh. It sounds like joy and music.

"Sorry if I've been keeping to myself," she says, looking back at the sea. "I haven't been feeling right."

"Does it hurt?" I ask warily. "Is the pain back?"

She shrugs. "A little, barely noticeable."

I can't help but feel deflated. Now it's my time to drink. I slam back a few gulps before I have to quit. Gods, it's awful.

She quickly looks at me with an apologetic expression. "You gave me relief for days, Andor. That's more than anyone has given me. If the pain comes back, you know I'll come calling. This is the closest thing to a miracle that I've ever witnessed."

At least I'm useful for something, I think, though I wish it weren't wrapped around her pain.

Then she reaches out and takes my mug from me. "May I?"

Before I can say anything she finishes the rest of the grog. I take it from her fingers before she drops it, studying her as if she'll give me any sort of hint as to why she's drinking like a fish.

"Are you all right?" I ask. "Because you're drinking rum grog like you're not all right. Even Toombs wouldn't drink that much, that fast, and he has that for his breakfast."

"I'm just a little anxious," she says, rubbing her hands together as she looks up at the moon. "I don't know what's going to happen when I get there. I don't know if Ellestra will leave with us, if she'll put up a fuss if I leave, if she'll try to kill you. If Lemi will decide he doesn't want to leave. I don't know. That city has always felt like my home—whether I wanted to claim it or not—and the idea of saying goodbye scares me. In a good way, maybe, but . . . I know once I leave, I won't ever go back. And though the people there can seem dejected and hardened, they are kind in a rough sort of way and loyal, and I fit in there. I don't fit in when it comes to Norland, and especially not the Kolbecks."

"I don't want you to fit in," I tell her. "I want you to stay the way you are. Let everyone else adapt."

"Easy for you to say," she says, glancing at me with a caustic smile.

REALM of THIEVES

My chest flares with indignation. "It's not easy for me to say. I don't adapt. I struggle with it."

She takes in the tone of my voice. "Nothing ever seems like a struggle to you, Andor."

I shake my head. "I'm the black sheep of the family. The outcast. Everyone has their place in the family business except for me. Because I refuse to do it their way . . ." I trail off, knowing that's not quite true. "Or should I say, it's not because I won't do it, but because I can't. I've tried, time and time again, to do the role like my uncle has. I've tried to be the master of the coins, to run the numbers, to stay organized on the raids, keep track of the substances Steiner produces and how much money the armies need, but I couldn't do it. I just can't. My brain doesn't work that way, it's as if it physically won't let me. It's like a slab of stone falls in front of my thoughts and I can't get through. I fuck things up left and right, I forget things, I'm a disaster. And no matter how hard I try to be the person my father wants me to be, I just can't."

I let out a shaking breath and look out to the waves. "So I adapt but in the only way I can. I find something else, something that no one else will do, because no one else is foolish enough to do it."

"I steal eggs too," she says.

"Yes, and you got paid for it. I don't get paid for it. I do it because it's the only way to feel like I'm contributing, to feel like I'm some use. I know my father could hire out thieves—I bet he'd love to keep you onboard and lose me in the process. But as long as I do the job and I'm good enough at it, I'm doing my part. And yet . . . I'm still on the fringes of the family. I don't belong. I'm just Andor, the son my father wishes he'd never had." I peer inside the glass. "Fuck. Now I'm the one who could drink a whole one of these."

She reaches out and puts her hand over mine. "Your father is an idiot, Andor. Your uncle too. You make them feel small because you are out here risking your life and slaying dragons and getting the very

190   KARINA HALLE

product that keeps your house in business. They're jealous and they'll always be jealous of you, because you know who you are and you don't give a fuck if someone has a problem with it. Now, where do we get more grog? Apparently we both need it tonight."

We start walking down the deck and she's starting to wobble a little, the drinks finally hitting her. Once we're downstairs, the card game is already underway.

"I thought you wanted Brynla to join in," I say to Feet while gesturing at Toombs to get me us two more things of rum grog.

"I couldn't wait," Feet says, shuffling his cards. "I'm itching to earn some goddess gold before we get to the Dark City. I want to buy one of those fabled lava teas that make women horny when they drink it." He looks at Brynla. "Do those teas really exist?"

"No one is buying any horny tea," I tell them, looking them all in the eye before they get carried away. "None of you are even going inside the Dark City."

"What?" Toombs says as he comes over with the jug of rum grog. "We're not letting you go on your own."

"I'm not on my own. I've got Brynla. The less people we have, the better. Believe me, you don't want to attract attention when you're there. You can help us get to the entrance of the city in case we're attacked in a raid from the Black Guard or nomads from elsewhere, but after that we'll be on our own."

I look to Brynla for her to back me up on this, but she's sipping her drink and already looking pretty drunk.

"I don't like this," Toombs says. "And when I tell Kirney, he won't like this either."

He eyes Brynla with trepidation, and I know that he doesn't trust her alone with me, not in the Dark City. But I have to trust her if I want to get any of this done. The whole reason we took this side trip to south Esland is to get Brynla's aunt, a promise I wouldn't dare break. There's no use in worrying about it now.

REALM of THIEVES   191

Toombs pulls out chairs for Brynla and me and we sit down at the card table. I slow down with my drinking and wish Brynla would do the same, but maybe she needs to do this. She's been through a lot and after everything she admitted, I know that much.

The boys seem to be in good spirits regardless. I'm starting to think that most of them were probably relieved to not have to go to the Dark City. Brynla may look fondly upon it, but it's a place with a harsh reputation for a reason and one that would probably eat my crew alive.

The card game continues, with Brynla being roped in for some of it before she loses all the money she doesn't have and has enough sense to bow out.

And the ship sails on.

The drinking continues.

The card games come to an end.

And eventually the crew disperses, leaving just Brynla and me sitting side by side at the empty table, our chairs pressed next to each other.

My hand on her thigh.

Her head on my shoulder.

Closer than we should be.

But I'm not moving an inch.

"Well, what do you think?" I ask her, my lips moving against the top of her head. "Time for bed?"

She giggles. She's been giggling all night.

"Only if we're sharing one," she says in a breathy voice.

I gulp, my body stiffening at the totality of her words, the implications in her tone.

"I'm afraid that's not possible," I tell her, trying to keep things light. "Cabins are too small for those shenanigans."

"The floor will do," she says, tilting up her head to meet my eyes. "Even standing up."

I bite my lip, hard. Fuck. I don't think I'll survive this.

"I think we're both a little drunk," I tell her.

She frowns, pouting slightly. "Don't you want me?"

Is she seriously asking me this?

"What do you think?" I manage to say.

"I think you should kiss me," she whispers, her inebriated gaze flicking over my features. "I think you should show me."

I swallow the brick in my throat. "I think it would be ungentlemanly of me to take advantage of a rum-drunk woman."

She smiles and it's so fucking beautiful I can barely breathe. The carnality in her eyes, the playfulness of her lips. A side of her I'd only dreamed of late in the night, one I imagined over and over again.

"Who says I need a gentleman?" she says in a sultry tone. "Maybe I'm the kind of rum-drunk woman who appreciates an animal."

My nostrils flare at that, hunger panging through me, my cock painfully hard and straining against the fly of my trousers. "Don't tempt me."

"Or what?" she asks, reaching up and lightly running her fingers over the half-healed cuts on my cheekbone. "What happens if I succeed? What will you do to me?"

I close my eyes, needing a break from the lust in her gaze. "A good spanking, for one," I say, my voice coming out in a growl. "Maybe a good choking while I'm at it."

She goes silent, her fingers pausing on my skin.

I open my eyes, expecting to see her look horrified at my answer.

Instead there's something like curiosity. And want. Her mouth is open slightly as she breathes hard, showing the pink of her tongue beyond the soft swell of her lips, and I know if I don't do something soon, I'm going to end up doing something I regret.

It's not always easy to be a man of honor.

"Am I interrupting something?" Toombs says as he enters the

cabin, the mug of ale spilling over onto his hand, his eyes bouncing between the two of us.

"Just bringing Brynla to her quarters," I tell him, carefully getting up so that she doesn't slump over.

She grins and looks at Toombs, sticking her tongue out at him. "You are interrupting something," she says, slurring her words slightly. "I'm trying to corrupt him."

Toombs glances at me, a merry look on his face. "Corrupt him? I would like to see you try. The only honest Kolbeck left, if you don't mind my saying. He can afford to have his morals dragged under for a bit."

I sigh and reach down under Brynla's arms, pulling her unsteadily to her feet. "No one is corrupting anyone tonight. We have a big day tomorrow."

"You taking me to bed?" she asks. If I weren't holding her up she'd be flat on the floor.

"I am," I tell her, half making her walk, half dragging her past Toombs and toward her cabin. Lemi gets up and follows us, looking at his master in concern. From what I've learned about Brynla over the last month, she rarely lets her guard down, rarely lets herself be loose and vulnerable. And with that in mind, it only strengthens my resolve to do right by her so that she isn't regretful tomorrow. "You need your sleep," I tell her. "We all do."

"Bye, Toombs," she says, waving at him lazily and blowing him a kiss.

"My goodness," I hear Toombs mutter as we leave the galley behind, and I can't help but chuckle.

"What's so funny?" she says as I kick open the door to her cabin.

"Oh, nothing much, just that Toombs is probably in love with you now."

"At least someone is," she says, giving me a crooked smile.

My skin immediately feels flushed, like the ship has gotten too

194 KARINA HALLE

stuffy and hot suddenly. I need fresh air. I need to dunk my head in the sea. And I need Brynla to go to bed lest she lead me down a path I'll regret.

Oh, but what a beautiful path it would be.

It doesn't help that her cabin feels unbearably small. Lemi goes and sits patiently by her berth, his body taking up half the floor. I lead her over to the edge of her bed and sit her down. She wavers slightly, rocking back and forth for a moment as I crouch down at her feet and attempt to pull off her boots. But just before I can do so, she starts pitching backward.

I act fast, grabbing her shoulders and the back of her head before it crashes into the wall.

She giggles and leans forward, her forehead pressed against mine, her fingers looped around my neck.

"Goddesses," I can't help but whisper, our mouths too close together.

"They can't help you now," she says softly.

Then she leans up, just enough to place her lips on mine.

My eyes fall closed, my decorum slipping, the wait finally over.

This is what I want.

This is all I've wanted since I laid eyes on her.

And she's drugging me with her wiles, she's making me slip into the undertow.

I can't breathe, I can't speak, all I can do is open my mouth wider, my tongue sliding out to meet hers, to kiss her deeply, completely.

"Fuck," I grunt against her mouth, my hand making a fist in her hair, holding her tight until she gasps, a sound that shoots straight to my cock. Gods, I don't think I can hold back, I don't think I can stop myself from kissing her, touching her, fucking her raw.

Then Lemi lets out a snuff of air.

REALM of THIEVES

Brings a kernel of strength back to my resolve.

I pull back, my jaw clenching, *everything* clenching as I try to breathe in deep.

"I think it's time we say good night," I say hoarsely, my forehead pressing against hers, my breathing labored.

"You don't want me," she says, so quietly, with a wash of shame that feels like it's removing one of my ribs.

I take her hand in mine and place it on my cock, stiff, hot and pulsing against the material.

"Does this feel like I don't want you?" I manage to say, pressing her hand there, fighting the urge to thrust against her palm. It wouldn't take much for me to come, not now, not after all of this.

Lemi lets out another snuff, another sign to move on.

I give him a sharp look. "You can be a cockblocker this time, doggo," I say gruffly. "One time is all you get."

He stares at me with wild, loyal intensity, not budging. If I didn't know any better I'd think he was close to growling at me.

I look back at Brynla, wondering what she's going to say. But her hand drops away and her eyes are falling closed. I'm moments from telling her that this is the second time she's fallen asleep after giving me an immeasurable hard-on, but I don't want to rile up the spirit inside her. This is for the best, for everyone's sake.

"Okay," I say quietly, gently placing her on the bed. I go to the end of it, pull off her boots, thinking twice about taking off the rest of her clothes, and then pull the quilt over her, tucking it under her chin.

I place my hand on her head, staring at her with this overwhelming tenderness that's taking me like a storm, tearing my heart to pieces, and I lean over, placing a soft kiss on her forehead.

"Good night, Brynla," I whisper against her skin before pulling back. "Please don't hate me tomorrow."

The Banished Land appears on the horizon like something out of a barren dream. A white haze barely visible beyond the shimmering heat lines and the sea. The closer we get, the more the haze takes shape into a dune-colored land that slopes up gently from the shore. A line of sharp cliffs and canyons runs along the north, a natural divider between the Banished Land and the rest of Esland, while the land slopes to the south. Far in the distance are chalklike mountains that lead to a giant volcano. I believe it's dormant since there's no smoke rising from the crater, but it's a formidable beast all the same.

And somewhere, in the empty lava tubes left behind by that volcano's last eruption, is the Dark City.

"It looks so pretty from a distance, doesn't it?" Brynla says as she sidles up to me.

I glance down at her, surprised to see her up already. Most of the crew is sleeping still.

"I thought you'd sleep in," I tell her, noting the dark circles under her eyes and her uneasy pallor, though she still looks absolutely stunning, even under this harsh desert light.

"I woke up to a racing heart and the urge to vomit," she admits. "Thought fresh air would be the best thing for me."

"You're probably right. Though Toombs should start passing out the hair of the dog soon."

She grimaces and squints into the sunlight. "I guess I owe you an apology."

"For what?"

"For acting like an utter fool last night."

"You weren't a fool," I tell her. "You were just drunk."

"Same difference."

"Nah," I tell her, tapping her elbow with mine. "Believe me, I

REALM of THIEVES

know. You were fine. In fact, you were better than fine. It was nice to see you with your hair down, so to speak."

At that her eyes go wide. She swallows.

"Did I . . . ?" she begins.

"Did you what?" I ask, enjoying this too much already.

She licks her lips, her brows furrowed uneasily as she looks away. "Did I . . . Did we . . . I have a memory, a feeling . . ."

"Ah," I say, giving her a reassuring smile. "You were drunk, that's for certain, but you were fine. You didn't do anything stupid."

Relief floods her features and her shoulders lower. "Oh, thank the gods," she says, giving me a nervous smile.

I nod and look back at the land. "You did kiss me, though." She gasps. "Sorry it wasn't very memorable," I add.

I glance at her with a grin and she blinks, her face paling even more, holding her hand at her chest. "I'm so sorry," she says, glancing at me only briefly. "I don't know what came over me."

I chuckle. "I do. You were drunk on grog rum or rum grog and your inhibitions were tossed overboard. Don't worry, I found it mostly amusing."

She breathes out shakily. "We didn't . . ."

I shake my head and lean sideways against the rail, facing her. "No. We didn't do anything else. Your dog would have never let that happen."

She looks chagrined. "I guess that's good to know. Wait. You found it *mostly* amusing?"

I give her a pointed look. "I enjoyed seeing that side of you, lavender girl," I say, my voice lowering. "And I encourage you to let her out more often. But perhaps stay sober next time. So that I can take you up on it and not let my stupid morals get in the way. Though I have to say, if it weren't for your dog, perhaps I'd be one moral less this morning."

Her dark eyes widen slightly and I reach out, grabbing her hand and squeezing it. "Saying no to you was one of the hardest things I've had to do."

She gulps audibly and I run my thumb over her knuckles, knowing I might be overstepping my bounds, but after last night perhaps anything goes now. "It was the best kiss I've ever had," I add. "I hope you decide to do it again one day."

Her cheeks flush pink and she shakes her head, looking down at the deck. "Now I think I'm going to be sick."

I laugh and let go of her hand. "Just what a man wants to hear. Not only is he an unmemorable kiss, but that same kiss has the ability to make a woman sick."

She looks up and gives me a pained look, unsure of what to say.

"I'm just giving you a hard time," I tell her, smacking her on the side of the arm. I lean in. "And I'm pretty good at giving it hard."

Then I walk off down the deck to discuss our landing operations with Toombs, knowing that Brynla is watching me go.

"Not much longer, is there?" I say to Toombs as I take my place beside him at the helm.

"Not much," he agrees. "You should get the rest of the crew up soon. I'm surprised the lady is standing up on her two legs."

"She's tougher than she looks," I tell him.

"That's what worries me," he says, his voice lowering.

"I know," I tell him, meeting his kindly eyes. "But it's a risk I'm willing to take."

"Because you're smitten with her," he says gruffly.

"Yes," I agree with a long sigh. "I am."

"This won't end well, Andor," he says.

I ignore the pinch in my ribs. "No. It probably won't. But I'm used to that by now."

Now he sighs and places his meaty palm on my shoulder. "I just don't want to see you get hurt, my boy. I want to trust her and I want

REALM of THIEVES

her to be good for you. Maybe she can be, what do I know? I'm a grumpy old sea captain. But I still worry. You deserve a good woman and an equal match . . ."

"She is a good woman and she is an equal match," I say to him, my tone coming out sharper than I intended.

He blinks. "Perhaps," he allows. "But even if you do bring her back onboard with her aunt, even if she keeps working for House Kolbeck . . . what are you going to do about the woman you're betrothed to?"

I close my eyes, resentment bubbling up inside me like acid.

"I am not betrothed to anyone," I tell him adamantly. "That is just a dream of my father's. I haven't agreed to it."

"That's because you don't need to," he says. "Because it's the only thing your father has ever asked of you that you're able to give."

Fuck.

"The princess and I don't even know each other," I tell him. "We've never met."

"You know that doesn't matter when it comes to the houses. That's why I'm grateful as the blazes that I'm not rich. I can marry whomever I please and turn down as many ladies as I like," he adds with a chuckle.

"Vidar is the true heir," I say. "He's the one who will be married off. My father thinks an alliance between us and Altus Dugrell is the way forward, but let the royal houses figure this one out. We're not royals; why should the pressure fall on us?"

He just gives me a steady look. We've discussed this many times. The thing is, even though my father has some idea that I'll get married to Princess Frida of Altus Dugrell, there's never been any commitment on either side. I don't think about her, I don't think about the marriage. It's not going to happen no matter how much pressure my father puts on me.

Though I guess at one point I might have been more likely to follow through.

All of that has changed since I met Brynla.

I stare at her as she stands at the bow, her lavender hair blowing in the breeze of her homeland, Lemi at her side. I don't want a princess. I want a thief.

"Your happiness is my happiness, boy," Toombs says, putting his hand back on the wheel. "I hope beyond hope you get exactly what you want. You deserve it."

I give him a grateful smile, though it's hard to ignore the tension in my chest now. So much at fucking stake.

"I'll go wake up the crew," I tell him.

Chapter 19

Brynla

 I DON'T GET EMBARRASSED VERY OFTEN, BUT THE TWO MOST mortifying times have both involved Andor—him seeing me naked after the bath, and learning that I kissed him while I was drunk.

I could crawl under a rock. The moment he told me what I did last night, some memories came back. I remember the strange pull I felt toward him, the urge to be incredibly shameless, to use the alcohol as fuel to test the waters. I didn't even know those were waters I truly wanted tested, and yet I was pulling out all my cards and he was doing his best to hold back.

He acted like a gentleman when that wasn't what I wanted from him at all. I can't be all that upset about it—perhaps I would have felt used and vulnerable otherwise.

I do remember the kiss, though.

I remember the low moan he gave, the slight tremble of his lips against mine, the easy yet hungry slide of his tongue. I believe he was joking when he told me it was the best kiss of his life, but even half-remembered, it was the best kiss of mine.

And then I remember the very hard, thick, and daunting feel of his cock when he pressed my palm against it, the fire that burned in his eyes when he asked if this felt like he didn't want me, and I immediately feel my pulse quicken, the heat flashing between my legs.

Fuck.

I splash cold water over my face again and lean over the washbasin for a moment, trying to compose myself. My physical wants and desires are going to have to go ignored for now. I have to stay focused on the task at hand. We're going to the Dark City today. We're going home. And I have no idea what's going to happen. I'll need to prepare for each and every scenario.

There's a knock at the latrine's door. "Brynla?"

It's Andor.

I give myself one last look in the rusted, cloudy mirror hanging above the washbasin, glad that I can't see my face all that well, and then take in a deep breath, opening the door.

His brows are furrowed, wrinkling his forehead and giving him a puppy-dog look. What a rotten time to start being so sexually attracted to him. "Are you all right?"

I nod. "Just getting nervous."

His mouth twists in sympathy and I notice that the dragon-tooth necklace is on the outside of his shirt, which means he's been fidgeting with it.

"We're just about to drop anchor," he says. "Toombs thought you might know of a good spot."

I nod and step out of the cabin. "It's all sand on this coast, he shouldn't have a—"

Before I can finish my sentence, Andor lets out a little grunt and reaches out with both hands and cups my face in his palms before pulling me toward him. He swiftly leans down and envelops my lips with his. At first I press my hands against his chest in shock, prepared to push him away, but then I feel the hard muscles of his chest and the heat that's flaring inside me, the sudden rush of desire taking flight, and I decide I don't want to pretend anymore. There's no pretending for me after last night, anyway.

His kiss is possessive. It's controlling and deep, a slow, hard melding of our lips, mouths parting in hunger, giving way to our tongues, stoking more and more heat, and I feel like I'm melting in his hands, as though if he didn't have such a strong grip I'd be a puddle on the floor. I feel him all the way to my toes, making them curl inside my boots, the rest of my body burning beautifully alive.

I want to do this forever.

I want this and so much more.

I dig my nails into his shirt and he presses me up against the wall until I feel every hard inch of him and suddenly the desire feels like it's choking me, panicked and wild, and all I can think about is the feel of his tongue inside my mouth, as if he's thoroughly fucking me, and that panting need that—

"All right," he breathes as he breaks away, resting his damp forehead against mine, his eyes lazily focused on my lips. "Maybe *that's* the best kiss I've ever had. It counts for more when you're sober."

I can't even speak. It's like he stole the air from my lungs and my words from my mind. I'm rendered brainless, boneless, unable to do anything but stare at his gorgeous face, feel the ghost of his lips on mine, and wish that he would do it again.

I want it more than anything.

"Andor!" Kirney shouts from above.

Andor lets out a low, impatient growl that matches the carnal intensity in his eyes, and my stomach twists giddily. He turns his head. "On my way!" he yells, and then he looks back to me. "I realize this may have not been the perfect time to do this," he says. "But I don't know what lies ahead for us. And, above all . . . I really fucking wanted to."

He turns, grabbing my hand, and leads me along to the stairs and up to the top deck and now all my unmet desires have been buried by total fear. There was finality in that kiss, the idea that it was now or never because we don't know what will happen next. The kiss of someone who doesn't know if they'll come back alive.

"Maybe I should go on my own to the Dark City," I tell him. "You stay on the ship. I'll get my aunt and bring her back."

He looks down at me as we step out on the top deck, the sun baking us in an instant now that we're no longer out at sea. "I'm not letting you out of my sight for a minute," he says gravely, giving my hand a firm squeeze.

"Because you don't trust me," I say. "You think I won't return."

"Because it doesn't matter how well you know your city," he says, his gaze hard. "This time you're returning as someone who has worked for the Kolbecks. I don't trust anyone around you."

"You can trust my aunt."

"I'm going to have to."

"Brynla," Toombs says, calling me over to the helm. I lock eyes with Andor for a moment and join the captain at his side. "I'm afraid I've never taken any ship this far south," Toombs admits, rubbing at his chin. "Do you know of any reefs in the area? The charts aren't very helpful . . . or trustworthy."

I give him a reassuring smile. "Watch out for shoals when you get closer to shore, the tide can be drastic and unpredictable, but if you anchor here you should be fine. Are you staying on the ship?"

"Aye," he says. "Tromson and I will stay behind and guard her. We can't get very far without a ship and, no offense, but I don't trust a Freelander as far as I can throw them."

"None taken," I tell him with a raise of my chin. "Trust here is earned and rarely given. If you were closer to the borderland canyons I would be more wary of raiders, but rarely does anyone come down this far unless they're heading to the Midlands or Sorland."

He leans in close and fixes me with a sharp eye. "And let me ask you, when it comes to Andor, has he earned your trust?"

His question throws me off guard. "I trust him," I admit.

"And have you earned his?"

Ah. This is what he really wanted to ask me. Not about anchoring a ship.

"I know you care about him," I say, "but I care about him too."

"I can see you do, my lady, but that doesn't mean he can trust you. Doesn't mean I can trust you either. I need that boy to return in one piece, preferably with you along with him. But if for some reason you have a change of heart and wish to stay in the Dark City with your aunt, please just let Andor go. Don't get him involved. Make it easy for him to leave. Sometimes he acts without thinking, and the last thing I want is for him to lose his life doing something silly to protect you or bring you back."

I'm touched at how much affection the grizzled captain has for Andor. In some ways it seems like the way a proper father-and-son relationship should be, much more sincere and honest than the one Andor has with his own father.

"I'm sure you won't hold my promises to a high regard if you don't hold my trust," I say, "but I promise you that I will cut him loose if he at any point seems in danger."

He stares at me for a moment, then nods and slaps me on the back. "Good. Now we just have to hope and pray he has the sense to listen."

I let out a small laugh. "That might take more than a hope and a prayer."

Lemi barks for my attention, and I look to the side of the ship where they are loading up the rowboat.

"Anchors down!" Toombs yells, and clanking and clattering sounds begin as Rolph and Tromson start lowering the anchor. I make my way over to Andor, Kirney, Feet, and Lemi at the boat.

"Are you ready?" Andor asks.

I nod, feeling strangely shy around him suddenly. It doesn't seem real that moments earlier he had me pressed against the wall below-decks and was kissing me.

Kissing me as if he doesn't expect to return.

After talking to Toombs, I'm going to assume the whole crew thinks he's heading on some sort of suicide mission. I understand why they're so paranoid too. All the stories they must have been told about Freelanders and what goes on in the Banished Land, thanks to Soffers propaganda, has them thinking any outsider won't survive. But that's not the case at all. Freelanders are outsiders by nature; that's the whole reason we were banished to begin with. We're naturally suspicious of newcomers because the Black Guard will often infiltrate our networks, gathering information about some of Esland's most wanted who are in hiding. But even so, they're usually easy to spot. Andor, like the rest of us, is an outsider too. I think he'll fit right in.

It's my aunt I'm more worried about. And the fact that Andor mentioned that it might be known that I'm working for the Kolbecks. But other than House Dalgaard, I don't think anyone will care, and it's not as if anyone from that syndikat can just waltz into the underground unnoticed.

I take in a steadying breath, trying to stay positive, though that's never been an easy feat, and I get in the boat, Lemi taking the easy route and shifting beside me.

As soon as the anchor is set, Kirney, Feet, and Andor climb inside the boat while Toombs and Tromson lower it down to the sea. We're about a hundred feet from the coast, the water startlingly clear and the lightest of aqua blues as it gets closer to the shore. I peer over the side and see the shadow of the boat on the bottom, and a few fish darting about.

But despite the coolness of the water, the air is desert dry and the temperature is climbing with each second. I'm wearing a long gauzy skirt that I know the seamstress created to be an undergarment for me, but it's not see-through and anything else would be too hot. On top I just have my support garment and one of Andor's white shirts that I knotted at the waist. All the men are dressed in white or tan tunics and loose pants, a few with linen scarves around their necks, ready to be wrapped around their heads.

"Do you have any salve?" I ask Andor as Feet starts to row us to shore and we wave our goodbyes to Toombs on the ship. "The sun is only going to get brighter from here on in."

He nods and takes it out of his pack, wiping the black substance around his eyes before passing it to me. I do the same and then give it to Kirney and Feet. They hesitate at first but I let them know that it not only protects against the volcanic air found in the Midlands but also cuts the glare from the sun in the Banished Land. We have to cross an expansive desert called the Burning Sands once we leave the coast, with near-white sand dunes that will blind us otherwise.

By the time we reach the shore it's like we've passed through a wall of shimmering heat, and Feet is sweating from the exertion, though it doesn't take long to evaporate from his skin. I'm used to it to some degree, but it's cooler where I grew up in Lerick and there's a reason why the Freelanders moved into the Dark City.

We get out onto the sand, hauling the boat up onto the shore, and Lemi immediately starts shifting from spot to spot, disappearing and reappearing just a foot or two farther away.

"What's he doing?" Andor asks, his gaze bouncing along with Lemi's movements.

"It's hot on his paws," I tell him. "He shifts continuously so that they don't have time to burn. Even with his thick skin he won't be able to stand for more than thirty seconds before the sand does damage. We wouldn't last five. Hopefully the bottoms of your boots won't melt off."

The men exchange a worried look.

"Best to copy Lemi and just keep moving," I tell them, leading the way through the sand. I glance over my shoulder at the ship, anchored in the glistening harbor, then survey the land around us. The border-land canyons are far off to the north, camouflaged by the shimmering heat, and to the south of us there's nothing but the coast and sloping sands. In front of us the dunes rise, and I know from experience they will seem endless until we finally see the volcano that presides over the underground city.

"So far so good," I say, looking back at Andor. "I'm sure Lemi will be the first to let us know if there are any hostiles."

"So who usually are the hostiles in these parts? Did you deal with them when you had to take your boat to the Midlands?"

I shake my head. "Not really. There's a small harbor of sorts to the north of here that the Freelanders use to go fishing. We bypassed it for a good reason—any outsider ship will most likely be attacked and raided. That's where I usually hire a boat to the Midlands, but the Black Guard rarely patrols the area and I doubt they'd be this far south in the middle of the Burning Sands. I doubt we'll come across anyone."

I look over my shoulder at Kirney and Feet. "Sorry, you might be making this horrible journey for nothing."

"Eh, it's good to get off the ship," Feet says, trying to sound non-chalant even though he's red-faced and panting already. Kirney seems to be handling the heat better, and of course Andor is barely breaking a sweat. I know that all the crew have taken suen at some point, but I'm pretty sure Feet's powers aren't helping him at the moment.

"How long is the walk to the city?" Andor asks.

"The dunes will take us a few hours," I tell him. "Perhaps on the way out of the city we can borrow some free-roaming camels to make the trek back easier."

He looks intrigued. "I've never ridden a camel before," he says.

"Don't get too excited," I warn him. "They either move too slow or too fast. Oh, and they spit."

"Nothing venomous, I hope," Kirney says.

REALM of THIEVES

"No, but it's gross," I say, making face. "Though not as gross as the slug webs."

Andor's eyes widen. "The what?"

I just smile. "You'll find out soon enough."

No point in letting them know before we get to the city itself. They'll have enough to worry about on the journey there.

Still, the walk across the Burning Sands is uneventful, if not exhausting. Our water doesn't last long, the heat is relentless, and even a grain of sand blown upon our skin is hot enough to burn. I end up having to tuck my skirt into the tops of my boots so that my thighs stop getting burned. Everyone has their scarves wrapped around their heads, and even Lemi looks taxed from having to shift so often. The dunes in this area are even taller than I thought, making the trip longer than I had estimated.

Finally, as we crest the last dune, we stop and find ourselves looking down over the entrance to the Dark City.

"There she is," I say, gasping for breath. At least Andor looks equally tired as I do. Everyone's salve has melted away from their eyes, gathering in their scarves in messy black pools.

"Not as I pictured it," Andor admits. "But it's nice to see these bloody dunes come to an end."

He's right in that it doesn't look like much. Below us the dunes peter out into steppes of dirt and low shrubs with severe swatches of cooled black lava cutting through every now and then like a river delta, all of them running from the slopes of the volcano in the distance. Halfway between us is a series of black caves that are barely visible between the shrubs. If you didn't know what to look for, you wouldn't be able to see it.

"Where is it?" Feet says, leaning over with his hand on his knees, slipping slightly in the sand.

"See those camels?" I point to a small herd of them grazing among the spiny bushes. "The entrance is the cave just beyond them. People feed the camels and provide water occasionally to keep them around so that they're easier to catch when we want to go somewhere."

"Thank the goddesses," Feet says. "There is no blazing way I am walking that distance back again."

"Well, that's where you'll be waiting too," Andor points out. "Hopefully you'll have enough time to become best friends with them."

We run down the slope, careful not to trip on our loose clothes, sand flying everywhere, until we reach the bottom. Then it's a short distance to the camels and the entrance to the city. Lemi stops shifting and pants the whole way back, the ground no longer painful to walk on, and I wish I had some extra water to give him.

But he knows what to do. When we're close enough to the entrance, he shifts and I have no doubt he's appearing by the water trough, hopefully finding it full and probably fighting some ornery camels for it.

We hurry the rest of the way, and when we finally arrive we see Lemi lying down in the shade of the trough, some water still left. The camels are a few yards away, half-hidden by the shrubs and eyeing us suspiciously.

"Normally I wouldn't suggest you have the water here, but if you can get past the fact that it's full of dog and camel slobber, it's all yours," I say to Feet and Kirney. "It's otherwise safe."

"Are you boys going to be all right?" Andor asks, adjusting the pack on his back.

Kirney takes out both his knives from his boots, twirls them, and slides them back in. They look to be made from the same water crystals as Andor's dagger. "We'll be fine," he says. "Just come back quick." He seems to give Andor a look that says for him to come back in general.

"Will do," he says with a grave nod.

We part ways, Feet and Kirney watching us go like they might come running after us at the last minute.

REALM of THIEVES 211

"You sure you don't want to stay with them?" I ask Andor as we march toward the cave, Lemi lagging behind lazily. "They won't have to worry so much."

"Not a chance," he says, flashing me a smile. "I'd rather them worry about me than me worry about you." We stop before the cave entrance. "Now is there anything I should know when we are in there? You say you can't see as well in the dark; do we need to light a torch? Do we not talk? Stay close?" His eyes sparkle at that last bit.

"There is light in the city's passageways," I tell him, realizing that he really doesn't know what to expect. "Just stay by my side, stay quiet, and let me do all of the talking." He opens his mouth to say something, but I press my fingers into his chest. "I mean it. All of the talking."

He presses his lips together firmly and nods, enough gravity coming over his expression that I think he knows to take this seriously. But that's the thing about Andor—he'll let you believe that nothing really matters when it turns out that so much does. It's what makes him so disarming—and dangerous.

I glance behind me at Lemi. "If at any point you want to shift home to see Auntie Ellestra and let her know I'm coming, that would be fine with me."

But Lemi only wags his tail. Perhaps he'll disappear when we get closer, but I don't expect him to leave my side until we're safe.

I just hope I can expect the same from Andor.

I take in a deep breath. "Let's go."

The entrance to the cave is only about twenty feet across, and the only sign that anything could be in there is the grooves left in the dirt at the entrance from carts and footprints.

I walk in front of Andor and step inside, following the curve to the right. The way is fairly level at first, going past various checkpoints that most people won't even notice. About twenty feet inside, just as the light from the outside starts to fade, the first torch appears.

KARINA HALLE

These torches burn all hours of the day, lit by a crew within the city known as the City Watch. They're in charge of the lighting, as well as providing the safety within the walls.

In the dark shadows that occur between the torches, you can always be sure that someone is watching you even if you can't see them. Many crevices in the lava rock run deep into the sides of the tunnels and men are often stationed in there, ready to rush you with their swords out if needed.

But they recognize me, and I assume that they aren't too worried about Andor either since no one comes out to stop and question us.

"Watch your step," Andor says. "I just stepped in something sticky."

I glance at the ground to see faint streaks of something white that glistens in the torchlight, then reach up and grab Andor's shoulder, pulling him down.

"I suggest ducking for the next few feet," I say, going into a stooped walk beside him.

"Why?" he asks as he bends over, staying closer to me now.

"Remember I mentioned slug webs? I suggest you don't look above you for the next bit."

Naturally Andor does what I've told him not to do.

"What the fuck are those?" he says in disgust.

I don't have to look up to know what's above us. There are cave spiders and many other types of insects in the lava tubes, but it's the slugs that are the worst. They build giant sticky webs across the tunnels, with some of the slugs growing up to several feet long.

"They aren't dangerous but the webs can leave a nasty rash," I tell him. "And I'm sure Feet would be delighted to know that the aphrodisiac tea he's coveting is made from the webslime."

Andor grimaces. "Thankfully I don't need any of that."

I can't help but give him a wry smile. Based on his actions (or lack thereof) from last night I would have thought he could use a bucketful.

When I'm sure it's safe, we straighten up again and keep walking down the torchlit tunnel. We've been walking for at least twenty minutes and are about to head down the grand staircase to the first part of the city, when suddenly two figures step out in front of us, each coming from either side of the tunnel walls. Andor instinctively goes to the short sword at his waist, but other than that he doesn't seem all that surprised. Knowing his heightened senses, he probably knew they were there.

"Halt," one of the guards says in the Freelander accent, making it sound like another language from the Common Tongue of Dragemor. "Who goes there?"

"Brynla Aihr," I tell him, doing the Freelanders sign across my forehead. "Niece of Ellestra Doon, fourth quarter, lower tenth."

"Ah yes, the thief and her dog," the guard says. He's wearing a mask made of blackened bones, and though I've probably encountered him many times before, it's hard to tell who he is. "And who is he?" He eyes Andor.

Andor opens his mouth, but I am quick to speak.

"This is my cousin, Lothare. I just got him out of Lerick."

"Is that so?" the guard says, peering closely at Andor as the other guard starts circling us from behind, eyeing his clothes. Luckily Andor is dressed as most Eslanders might be, and there's nothing marking him as a Norlander.

"Your name is Lothare?" the other guard asks, sidling up close. I wait with bated breath, expecting Andor to stiffen, to make a move for his sword, but to his credit he remains still.

"Lothare Doon," Andor says, his Lerick accent flawless. Still, I won't breathe a sigh of relief yet.

"And you're willing to give up the good life and live one of darkness?" guard number one says, testing him, his face right up in Andor's.

"I would rather live a life of darkness if it means my freedom,"

Andor says, his voice like steel. "What good is light if your soul is in the dark?"

That answer seems to satisfy them because the guards nod in unison.

"All right," the second says. "Welcome to the Dark City, the land of the free."

They both move to the sides to let us pass and do the sign of the Freelander on their foreheads.

I don't dare relax until we're past them and are heading down the grand staircase. If the guards had at all suspected that Andor was a spy from Esland, there would have been a grisly fight. One that I'm sure both Andor and I could handle, but where there are two guards, there are always more hiding in the cracks.

"Having a backstory would have been helpful *before* we went into the lava tube," Andor whispers in my ear as we walk side by side down the stairs, the darkness punctuated by the occasional torch.

I shrug. "Sometimes having something rehearsed can backfire. Improv often seems more realistic. You should know that."

He gives me a wry look, the torch flames catching in his eyes as we head down.

"So where are we now?" he says in a low voice. "Any more guards that Lothare Doon should worry about?"

"We'll see them here and there once we start the descent, but we've passed the official checkpoints."

"We haven't started the descent?" he asks.

I nod ahead at where dim light appears at the end of the blackened tunnel. "That's the descent. It's the official entrance into the city."

I can tell he wants to ask me more questions, but he keeps his pretty mouth shut. It's better he just sees it.

We continue down the steps until the white light gets closer and the tunnel roof appears to curve upward for a moment.

REALM of THIEVES   215

Then everything opens up below us, both of us wincing at the light and the sight below us.

The Dark City's name comes from the fact that most of it, especially the lower quarters where my aunt and I live, is in pitch-blackness. But sometimes there are tubes that go straight to the surface, and with the use of mirrors, the Freelanders have been able to project that light into the darkest reaches of the cave system.

And then there's the descent, which is right below a hole in the surface, hundreds of feet high. The hole is about two hundred feet across, letting the world below have light and access to the sun and sky. The grand staircase cuts down the middle, leading to the green-houses and farmed patches of the first quarter, where farmers take advantage of the natural sunlight. On either side of the staircase, greenery spreads, and on the fringes, where the light continues thanks to cleverly placed mirrors, the real city starts and thrives with various shops, cafés, and business establishments.

"Bloody blazes," Andor says under his breath as we pause on the staircase halfway down. I try to hide the prideful smile on my face, not wanting him to see how much I'm enjoying his appreciation of the place. I know he underestimated the Dark City—everyone always does.

"This is the cultural hub for the Freelanders," I explain, letting him stand and take it all in. "Using the natural light, we grow our fruits, vegetables, and plants that don't require much water. This is also where the Freelanders come to be social. You don't get to survive as a culture if you don't have a place to meet and exchange thoughts and ideas. Much like Menheimr, I suppose, except on a smaller scale."

By now a few people below are glancing up at us with interest, since it isn't that often that someone comes in or goes out, and fisher-men and raiders tend to take the loop way, which curves around the natural atrium on a flat path, making it easier for carts to get down to the city levels.

"Come on," I tell him. "I don't want people to have too long to no-tice you. Last thing we need is for someone to double-check with my aunt and have her tell them she doesn't have a son."

"So how dangerous is your aunt?" he asks as we continue our de-scent down the stairs.

"It's not so much that she's dangerous," I tell him. "It's more that she's fearless. And has a short temper. Much like me. And you, I sup-pose. You'll find you have more in common with her than you think."

"She was the one who helped you escape from the Daughters of Silence," he notes. "That couldn't have been an easy feat."

There's a curious tone to his voice. I glance at him, his eyes glow-ing against the black smudges of his salve. "No. It wasn't."

"I should like to talk to her about how she did it," he says as we continue walking down the staircase.

"Why?"

He shrugs. "Perhaps there's a lesson in it for me."

"The lesson is lots of planning. It helps that Ellestra was in the convent herself when she was a child. She knows the ins and outs. But if you think she's going to open herself up to a stranger, you're wrong. She's just as cagey as I am."

He snorts at that. "I think I'm slowly winning you over."

"Very slowly," I tell him, but I'm smiling.

We finally step off onto the main level, Lemi ahead of us and sniff-ing each storefront that we pass. I recognize almost everyone, even if I don't know their names, and while they generally nod or regard me with mild interest, they all eye Andor with suspicion. It's estimated that there are several thousand people living in the Dark City, which is a lot of people, but because everything here is confined to a rela-tively small area, we get used to seeing each other. Anyone new stands out.

"This way," I tell Andor, following Lemi down a tunnel that heads

REALM of THIEVES

off to the right, passing through a candlemaker's shop and a café that has tasty but expensive desserts crafted from cave bee honey.

"To get to my quarter we have to travel a ways down. You might find that the air pressure in your ears changes," I say, rounding a bend until we're faced with total darkness.

I come to a stop.

"What's wrong?" Andor asks.

Unease prickles my scalp. "It's too dark. This passage is usually lit."

"I can see well enough," he says.

I shake my head. "I don't like this. We should go back and try another route."

But when I turn around to face him, he's gone.

Chapter 20

Andor

 I watch as Brynla stops in the darkness, voicing her concerns about taking another route. But before she can turn around to face me, there's a blade at my throat.

Every instinct tells me to twist backward, away from the sharp edge, and flip over the attacker behind me, but then another blade is poised at my spine, the point hard enough to break the skin.

Then the attacker moves sideways, using their legs to trip up mine, spinning me around all while keeping both blades in the exact same position, showcasing a skill in motion that I've rarely seen, and then I'm thrown against the wall. The blade now moves to the side of my throat, right under the jaw, a piercing pain.

"Andor!" Brynla cries out, and I find it curious that Lemi hasn't tried to jump to my defense. Perhaps the hound isn't as loyal to me as I thought.

"I've got him," says a woman's voice at my ear, cool and confident.

"Ellestra?" Brynla croaks. Of course this is her fucking aunt. I suppose I was expecting our meet to start violently. "Stop! Let him go. He's with me."

"I know he's with you," Ellestra says, still not taking her knives

REALM of THIEVES

away. "That's why he's not dead yet. After that bloody magicked raven came to deliver the message, I wasn't about to take my chances. Figured this was a trap of some sort."

"It's not a trap," I tell her, speaking my words carefully so that she doesn't puncture my throat.

She grunts at my ear. "Now is the time to tell me the truth, Bryn. Say the word and I'll put him down easy."

Brynla sighs and I hear her stomp over to us, and then suddenly the knives are gone.

"I said stop it," Brynla says. "He's with me."

"And you're with him," her aunt says bitterly. But she steps away from me, leaving me to properly exhale and turn around, facing both women.

Brynla's aunt looks nothing like I expected. From the way she handled me I assumed she'd be a tall woman with as much muscle as I have, but instead she's thin and wiry, not much taller than Brynla, and looks much older than I thought. Her eyes are sharp and light, though their exact color is hard to tell in the dark, and her hair is dark and cut short to her ears. Her clothes are black and tight, making her look like a shadow, and her knives are swiftly put back in secret compartments.

Her face is a scowl as she looks me up and down, but when she looks at Brynla her expression doesn't change. I can already see where Brynla gets her demeanor from.

"Not exactly the welcome I was hoping for," Brynla says, giving me a brief, vaguely apologetic look.

"What did you expect?" Ellestra says. "For the red carpet to be rolled out and trumpeters to descend from the heavens?" But there's a wryness to her tone and just a fleeting glimpse of a smile.

Then the tension seems to break as Ellestra pulls Brynla into a tight embrace. I'm watching Brynla's face closely. The wariness and anxiety seem to disappear, melting into something like security and comfort. Love. Her brows soften, her face becoming innocent and younger somehow, causing a pang between my ribs.

All at once I feel both envious and deeply ashamed. I'm the one who blackmailed Brynla into leaving her one remaining family member, her friend, her blood. I pulled her away from this city and this life. I never once thought that Brynla might have missed her aunt, or yearned for this life, a life I now see I knew nothing about. I never considered her own feelings in what I was doing—I was too focused on what she could do for me. At most I thought I was taking her away from something awful, as if I were doing her a favor. I needed to think that in order to justify what I was doing.

I was wrong, plain and simple. And though I've already given Brynla a way out of this mess—which she declined—part of me hopes she takes me up on it.

And part of me dreads the idea of her staying here for good.

Finally, they pull apart, Brynla's eyes meeting mine for a moment. In the darkness of the tunnel I'm not sure that she can see me but I can clearly see her, the way her eyes glisten with tears, the furrows in her brow. She looks away, squaring her shoulders as she steps back, that firm set to her jaw coming back again. I know she has to be tough, how it's been demanded of her, probably since she was born. But seeing those glimpses of softness inside her—whether it be in her aunt's embrace, in a cave while I healed her pain, or when she leaned against my shoulder last night and gazed at me with larger, adoring brown eyes, asking if I wanted her—makes me want her more. Like she's letting me in on a secret, a part of her no one else sees.

"Come on," Ellestra says, giving Lemi a thorough pat and a scratch behind the ears. "We better get going before we attract attention. I imagine you've had quite the journey."

She's addressing Brynla more than me, so I let her do the talking. "We've fared well so far," Brynla says to her as they start walking down the tunnel in the direction we were originally going, with Lemi

REALM of THIEVES

behind them and then me. "The guards were touch and go, but other than that we had a smooth journey over the Burning Sands."

I hold back a laugh. As if our crossing could have been described as anything but arduous. I might have enhanced physical prowess, but I struggled to keep up with Brynla in the dunes. I'm unused to the sensation of wayward sand burning my legs, and even now I wonder how long it will take for my eyesight to go back to normal after being exposed to all that glare.

I follow them down the tunnel, lit again by intermittent torches, and listen to their conversation while taking in what I can. The Dark City is nothing like I imagined. I envisioned a pit of the uncivilized filled with miserable cretins, those who were deemed too unsavory for Esland—a place that already had a bad reputation.

But I had been wrong, at least from what I can see with my own eyes. Walking down the grand staircase that descends into the city is like stepping into another world, one with color and light and life inside all the darkness. There were patches of farmed greenery beneath the beating sun that shone from the cavernous hole in the ceiling, butterflies and hummingbirds in the air, people who were more refined than I imagined. Sure, they cast a wary eye toward me and their clothes were by no means new, but they were cleanly attired, wrapped in layers of linen, and their faces didn't harbor any malevolence. There were smells that wouldn't seem out of place in the markets of Menheimr: spices, fried meats, sweet wine, and the sounds of laughter and chatter in beguiling accents.

I wouldn't trade my life at Stormglen for one underground, but I can see why Brynla wasn't jumping at the chance to escape. And no matter what, a life of relative freedom here in the Dark City offers more than one under the fanatical tyrants of Esland.

Ellestra and Brynla's conversation stays light, talking about their neighbors and whatever else Brynla has missed while she's been away. I have a feeling the deeper questions will be brought to me later.

We walk for another fifteen minutes or so, through winding tunnels and down narrow clay stairs, occasionally passing by other people. Most of them nod politely at us, me included, though the ones who seem to know Brynla and her aunt personally are more apt to give me a disparaging look.

Finally we come to a wide passageway that's lit by torches with a few makeshift doors on either side. Outside each door is something to sit on, like a dilapidated chair or a tree-stump stool or a rock affixed with a sheepskin rug on top. One even has an orange cat sleeping in a wooden box, which takes a lazy look at Lemi before going back to sleep.

"Here we are," Ellestra says, stopping outside a door with two tree stumps outside it, a chipped cup and saucer on one of them. The door is flimsy and seems to be made from some combination of frayed wood and dried palm fronds. She pushes it open and we step inside into a dark cavern.

"Give me a moment to light things," she says, taking a torch off the wall outside and walking around the room, lighting sconces and lamps at different intervals. In glowing orange flame, their house reveals itself.

It's larger than I thought, the furnishings nice enough if not sparse—faded rugs overlapping on the cave floor, a low dresser along the wall with candles and a small stack of books, a small couch and a rocking chair piled with blankets facing a hearth that Ellestra is currently lighting with her torch. At the other end is a round table with a couple of chairs and a stool; a small nook for a kitchen with a cistern and woodstove, the pipes leading somewhere out of the cave ceiling; and what looks to be a mound of hay covered with a blanket on the ground. I'm curious about it for a moment until Lemi goes straight to it and flops down—his dog bed.

"I'm sure we live like peasants compared to you," Ellestra says to me as she replaces her torch outside and shuts the door. "But it's home."

"It looks lovely," I say to her, trying to come across as genuine as possible. I have a feeling she'll be quick to hold a dagger to my throat if given the slightest provocation.

Ellestra rolls her eyes and looks over at Brynla. "I can't tell if he's being sarcastic or not. That Norlander slang."

"Does 'lovely' not mean the same here?" I ask, but both of them seem to ignore me as they go to the kitchen. Brynla takes a torch off the wall and lights the woodstove while Ellestra fills up a kettle from the basin. They maneuver past each other with ease, movements matching each other, and I feel like I'm getting a glimpse into Brynla's everyday life, a peek at her past.

"Tell your boy to sit down," Ellestra says to her.

"He's not my boy," Brynla says, looking slightly embarrassed. Good to know I still bring a flush to her cheeks.

"He's your something, that's for sure," Ellestra mumbles under her breath.

I take a dutiful seat at the table, unable to take my eyes off Brynla as she rummages through a threadbare pantry, wondering what's to come and wishing we were alone.

"Do we have any of that mint tea?" Brynla asks her aunt.

"Right there." She nods at a small linen bag.

Brynla sniffs it. "This isn't the good stuff. I'm talking about the one from Farmer Vale. The one for guests."

Ellestra sighs as if Brynla's asked for the moon. She stands beside her and pulls out a small paper bag, shoving it in Brynla's hands.

"I don't need anything fancy," I say, splaying my hands. "Don't waste the good tea on me."

Ellestra gives me a tired look while Brynla sprinkles the tea leaves into the kettle's sieve.

224 KARINA HALLE

"It's customary for Freelanders to offer water in two forms when a guest comes to stay or visit," Ellestra says to me. "In a tea, and in a bath or basin."

"I don't need a bath," I tell her, though I quickly smell myself to make sure that I'm right. So far so good. "I took one in the ocean yesterday. Brynla did too." At least I assume she did—she went off the bow and out of sight while the rest of the crew had a dip off the stern. Salt water doesn't clean as well as fresh, but with the right soap it works in a pinch.

"As I said, it's customary," Ellestra says sternly. "Water is in short supply in the Banished Land. This offering is the highest honor. And one you shouldn't refuse, unless you want to be cast into a slug web. I'll get a bath going for you."

At that she grabs a torch and walks off down the hallway that leads out from the room.

"You saw me take a bath yesterday," I tell Brynla. "At least, I saw you avert your eyes once I took my pants off."

"Take the bath," she advises me, that flush still on her skin. "You never know when it could be your last. Take whatever my aunt is giving you, to be honest."

"She doesn't like me much," I tell her. "She might have poisoned the water."

She laughs, causing the dried black salve to crack on her cheeks. She still looks impossibly beautiful. "If she wanted you dead, you'd be dead already."

She puts a small teacup on the table in front of me and I impulsively reach out, placing my hand on top of hers, holding it down as I stare into her eyes. I don't even know what to say. I don't know what I'm doing. I just know I want to touch her, feel her, and I want her to know that I want that.

I want *her*.

REALM of THIEVES   225

Brynla holds my gaze, her dark eyes swimming with emotions I find hard to read—lust, shame, sadness, affection? All of the above?

It doesn't matter. I'm about to get to my feet to march over there and kiss her, the need becoming unbearable, when Ellestra comes bustling back into the room. Brynla swipes her hand away and turns to the stove, but her aunt stops and looks between the two of us with a cocked brow.

"It will take time for it to heat up," Ellestra says coolly, pulling out the seat across from me and sitting down. "That will give me time to decide whether you're even worthy of our water."

I lean back in the chair and try to look as unimposing as possible by flashing her a smile. That only makes her narrow her eyes. "Ask me anything," I tell her. "I'm an open book."

"We shall see about that," Ellestra says, slowly tapping her nails on the table. "Now, imagine, the both of you, that Brynla and Lemi go away to the Midlands on an egg-stealing mission. And they don't come back when they should. I figure, all right, so perhaps she had to stay a little longer. Maybe she needed more time to get the eggs. After all, it wouldn't be the first time that Brynla's taken her time. But then another day passes. And another. And I am worried sick. I think that Brynla has died, or if not, she's been injured, or stranded. There's no way for me to find the boatman that she used for the journey because she used someone I didn't know and her old boatman is dead. So I'm wondering . . . what happens when Brynla doesn't return with the suen? When will House Dalgaard show up at my door and demand payment?"

"Did they show up?" Brynla asks warily as she brings the kettle off the stove and fills our cups.

"No," Ellestra says. "But that doesn't mean I didn't spend this last moon waiting for them. Waiting to hear if you died or were captured. Every moment I was waiting until I saw that white raven. And even then, I knew better than to believe it."

226   KARINA HALLE

"Knew better?" I ask, taking a deep sniff of the drink, the mint scent enticing. "We're right here."

"I see that," she says. "That doesn't mean I trust you or what's happening." She glances at Brynla as she takes a seat at the table. "What happened to you? Why did you go with House Kolbeck?"

Brynla meets my eyes and I press my lips together to show that I'm not going to speak for her.

"Andor made me an offer I couldn't refuse," she says dryly. "Work for House Kolbeck instead of House Dalgaard."

Ellestra frowns. "And what was in it for you?"

Brynla looks down at her tea, moving the cup around in her hands. "A better tomorrow."

Her aunt swings her wary eye back on me, her lips pursed together. "What kind of snake oil are you selling? There is no better tomorrow for the Freelanders. *This* is our tomorrow." She gestures to her house. "This is as good as it gets for us, but at least it's a place we know, a place we can control."

"There are an infinite number of tomorrows," I tell her. "And some of them are better than others. I offered Brynla a chance to have a life in Norland, a life of freedom in a world where she doesn't have to hide underground, where she won't be persecuted. And you are part of that offer too."

"In exchange for what?" Ellestra asks. "For her skill? For Lemi? Tell me how she has any freedom if she has to be used in exchange for this so-called better tomorrow."

I stare at her for a moment, struck again by how unyielding she is. I admire her, I do. I would probably be just as stubborn in her situation.

"Nothing is free," Brynla says quietly. "In the end, I trust Andor and would rather work for House Kolbeck than House Dalgaard."

Ellestra narrows her eyes. "Trust, huh? Is that what the two of you have?" She glances at me. "Why don't you take your tea to the bathroom, Andor of House Kolbeck? Water in the tub should be hot enough now. Brynla and I have a lot to discuss."

I get to my feet and pick up the cup of tea. "Does that mean I'm officially worthy of your water?"

She grunts. "For now. Enjoy it while it lasts." Then she jerks her chin to the hallway.

I know when I'm not wanted.

Chapter 21

Brynla

"You could have been a little nicer," I whisper to my aunt as Andor disappears around the corner and down the hall. The sound of the bathroom door sliding shut follows.

"Nicer?" she says, her tone icy. "You should be thankful he's still alive. And that you are too, for that matter. What the blazes happened to you, Bryn? Do you know how damn worried I was?" Her eyes are fire, her voice rising with each word. She'd been playing it fairly cool so far, which worried me. This was more the aunt I knew, the one with the temperament of an active volcano.

"I'm sorry," I say. "I had no choice."

She shakes her head, her lips twisting as she seems to wrestle with it. "That's not like you. You always have a choice. You always *make* a choice."

"Sometimes you don't," I tell her. "I was kidnapped *and* blackmailed."

Her eyes widen before her mouth flattens out into a smug smile. "And yet here you are, vouching for this man. Let me guess, you're sleeping with him too."

REALM of THIEVES

"I am not," I say quickly, wishing my cheeks didn't automatically burn at the assumption.

She studies me for a moment, her fingernails clicking against the teacup. "Fine. But you wish you were. That's somehow worse. What do the Kolbecks have over you, Bryn?"

"They don't have anything over me," I tell her, unable to keep from glaring.

"And yet he started off blackmailing you. So they just changed their mind from the goodness of their hearts?"

"Andor did. The rest of them didn't care for me to be part of their operation anyway. But Andor saw my potential."

She lets out a derisive snort. "Your potential. They want your skills, and what Lemi is, and to take it for themselves. They want to use you, Bryn. And you're acting as if it flatters you."

I press my lips together, growing silent. My aunt and I argue often—our tempers come from my father's side—but I can tell there's nothing I can say right now that will make her see things any differently.

And she's not wrong, either. I feel like the Brynla Aihr of a moon cycle ago would have cut ties with Andor already, perhaps violently, and never looked over her shoulder. I would have found some way to escape and made my way back here.

But I'm not that girl. In the month that I've been with Andor I've developed . . . feelings. Unwelcome feelings, feelings I know I should run from, feelings I could do a better job of ignoring. Yet still, they remain.

I like Andor.

I think I *really* like Andor.

More than that, I *want* Andor.

And my aunt can see that on my face, clear as day.

And with the way I behaved last night, Andor can see it too.

Ellestra sighs. "Bryn," she says, the hard edge to her voice fading.

"I was worried sick about you. And to be honest, I was worried for me as well. I'm so relieved that you are here in front of me, alive and well, but I fear that you are only bringing greater danger into your life. Into our life. You know that we can't trust anyone other than ourselves, and especially not a member of a syndikat. They're all in the pockets and on the payrolls of the government. Esland might be awful, but don't think the other realms are any better. No one is truly free under the thumb of their kings and queens."

"I'm worried too," I admit. Then I give her a placating smile. "There. Does that make you feel any better?"

She chuckles dryly. "A little. Just as long as you know what's at stake."

"What's at stake?" I repeat. "Everything is at stake. It always is. It was since the day I was born."

Both of us fall silent at that. Eventually my aunt starts talking about what I've missed while I've been gone, what the neighbors have been complaining about, who the new family down the tunnel is, whether the café we always go to should be charging more for their cactus-blossom pastries. While she talks, Lemi naps on his bed, and my mind is lulled elsewhere. There's only so much gossip I can take, and frankly, after being in Norland, the lives of the people here no longer interest me. It's not that they themselves are boring, but when you've finally been exposed to the world outside, you start to crave more from the people around you.

And I'm starting to crave Andor above all else.

As much as that scares me, tonight I just want . . .

I just want him.

I finish the cup of tea my aunt makes me and then I excuse myself to go check on Andor. My aunt's brow is raised so high, you'd think it was making a go for the ceiling. I know exactly what she's thinking at this point, and I don't care. She already thought I was sleeping with him anyway.

Might as well make that a reality.

"I'm, uh, going to go for a walk," my aunt says, clearing her throat awkwardly. "Give you two some privacy." She walks to the door muttering under her breath, "I'm sure you'll need it."

I can't help but smile to myself as I walk down the hall to the bathroom. I'm no virgin. I've had my fun with men, though at this point I'm realizing they were really just boys. But this feels different already. I feel both emboldened in going after what I want—Andor—and nervous, because . . . well, it's Andor. I know he won't reject me, he's made that clear, but it's still him. It's *us* when there wasn't really an us before. Lines have already been crossed, but I feel this is the line you don't get to return from. After this, everything changes.

And I want everything to change.

I think that's all I ever wanted.

I slowly push open the sliding palm door to the bathroom and poke my head in.

"Are you decent?"

A pause and I hear him clear his throat. "Not even a little."

The bathroom is spacious compared to the rest of the house, chosen because of the natural drainage holes in the corners in which all the water flows out and into the depths of the bedrock below. A couple of torches are lit, shadows dancing on the black lava rock walls, and Andor is in the tub, his back to me so that all I see is the back of his head, his hair wet and sticking to the nape of his neck.

A shiver rolls through me as I step inside the room and shut the door behind me.

"Is everything all right?" he asks, turning his head slightly so that I see his profile, his strong nose and jaw illuminated from the glow of the torches. His voice is rough, enough to send another tickle down my spine.

"It could be," I say softly, and begin to take off my clothing as I slowly walk around the bathtub, discarding my boots, then Andor's shirt I had borrowed, then ripping out the laces of my stays, leaving them in my wake. When I appear before him, I'm only in the gauzy skirt and am completely bare from the waist up.

His gaze goes to my breasts, a heated look that makes his eyes look like tarnished gold, breathing in sharply through his nose.

"Your aunt, she's . . ." he stammers, licking his lips.

"She went out," I tell him, my gaze dropping to his dick, already half-hard in the bathwater. I swallow at the sight, warmth pulsing through me. He's impressive, that's a given, but I never expected anything less from a man of his stature, or his nature.

We don't say anything to each other. There's nothing to say. Our eyes, our bodies, already express the pent-up sexual frustration that we've both been feeling over the last month. Somehow, though I'm shaking from nerves on the inside, I manage to loosen my skirt until it falls around my ankles and now there is nothing left to hide.

I was once his captive, then his thief, and now I am only his.

His stare turns to smoldering as it rests between my thighs, and I hold my head high, ignoring any shame I might feel about being completely nude in front of him. I focus on the carnal tug of his lips, the unabashed way that he devours me with his eyes as I slowly come forward. If I usually have insecurities with being seen this way, I don't with him. He makes me feel wanted, he makes me feel *needed*.

I step into the tub. Perhaps not my most graceful moment, but I manage to do so without falling over.

"Goddesses help me," Andor says softly, roughly, his voice catching. He inches back in the tub to make room for me but there's not a lot of room to be had.

"Help you with what?" I ask, lowering myself into the warm water so that I'm straddling him, his cock hard, thick and pushed down against his stomach.

He looks at me like he's pleading for mercy, his brow furrowed with lines. His jaw clenched as if he's barely holding himself together.

I feel the same, like I'm about to come apart at the seams, and when he raises his arms out of the water, placing his large, strong hands on either side of my hips, I'm unsure if he's holding me together or pulling me further apart.

"Help me to never let go of you," he says, his voice hoarse as his fingertips dig into my skin, hard enough to bruise, and I start moving back and forth over him. Even in the water, I'm slick with desire for him, sliding easily over the stiff length of his shaft, making his eyes flutter and roll back in his head.

I bite my lip and grind down on him, one hand on the edge of the tub bracing me, the other on his shoulder. My breasts swing near his face, full and heavy, and his gaze goes molten as he takes them in, then turns into an outright volcano as it drops down to where I'm spread over his length.

"Fuck," he growls. "I want to come inside you."

"You will," I say playfully, my breath starting to hitch, not just from the delicious friction of my body sliding over his cock, getting me wetter by the second, but the fact that I'm doing *this* with Andor. I feel decadent, allowing myself to take pleasure from him so brazenly, and at the same time I feel like my heart is exposed, like he's pried my ribs open and is staring at everything I've tried so hard to protect.

"Oh," I cry out, feeling the pressure inside me build, and my eyes fall closed to the feeling. The water in the tub begins to slosh back and forth, the sound competing with my soft noises, his hard grunts. I let go of his shoulder and grip the edge of the tub harder, my head dropping. He leans up, giving me a quick kiss, his tongue licking the inside of my mouth, one hand still in a viselike grip as he moves my hips back and forth on top of him. The other cups my breast, thumb running over the hardened peak of my nipple until I'm moaning loudly.

"Are you going to come just like this?" he murmurs before briefly

234   KARINA HALLE

kissing my neck. "Riding my cock like you can't even wait long enough for me to be inside you?"

"I suppose I take what I can get," I tell him. He pinches my nipple hard, enough for me to whimper in pain.

"Sorry," he says, his expression chagrined as he takes his hand away.

"No," I tell him quickly, the pain making the need between my legs pulse intensely, pushing my desire to the next level. "Do it again. I like a bit of pain. Don't you?"

He gives me a salacious grin and grabs my breast harder, pinching my nipple until I'm squirming, the hurt turning into pleasure. "I don't think you have any idea how much pain I'm in right now. I need to be inside you so badly it's killing me."

I can't help but smile. I could come and keep riding him until he releases, but I don't think that's what he has in mind.

I pick up the pace, grinding harder, and his hand drops from my hip, fingers splayed against my thigh while he presses his thumb at my clit. I'm already so hot and swollen that it doesn't take long for the tight thread inside me to snap, and like a storm unleashed, I'm coming.

"Andor," I moan out his name, barely able to keep moving as I lose control of my limbs, my back arching sharply. He grunts, both hands at my waist as he grinds me down on him and I lose myself to the waves of bliss that crash over me, again and again. I feel weightless and free, all the tension inside me that has kept me wound up for weeks finally coming loose.

I slump forward, nearly collapsing on him, still holding on to the rim of the tub as my breasts are flattened against his firm, warm chest. He reaches up and grabs my face, staring up at me like he's about to devour me whole.

"You said you like a little pain," he rasps, running his thumb over my lower lip. "Then you'll forgive me if I'm a little rough."

REALM of THIEVES

I give him a lopsided smile that turns into a gasp as he reaches down for my waist. With the same strength and agility I saw him use out in the Midlands, he somehow gets out of the tub while simultaneously hoisting me up until I'm placed on the floor, bending forward for balance. He's behind me now, wet hand between my shoulder blades as he pushes me down until I'm on all fours, my knees digging into the hard cave floor.

He hesitates a little and I know he's wondering if he was perhaps too rough, so I glance at him over my shoulder, through my damp strands of hair to encourage him.

His eyes are filled with shock, glued to the scars I have on my back, reminders of the constant punishment at the hands of the convent.

"What happened?" he grinds out. "Who did this to you?"

"The price for breaking silence," I tell him. "The cost of being at the hands of the Soffers." I soften my gaze, to let him know that I don't want either of us to be distracted about it right now. "It's in the past, Andor. What I have with you, right now, that's far more important."

He meets my eyes, his expression unsure.

"Please," I tell him, spreading my legs apart a couple of inches. "Fuck me like you mean it."

That's enough to snap some sense back into him.

His nostrils flare and I let my eyes flick over his body, a sight to behold. I can't help but stare as he kneels behind me, the ridged planes of his abs stretching up to his chest, his large, rounded shoulders, the thick muscles of his arms snaked with veins, his strong hands that slide over my rear. His eyes practically burn, the gold catching the flicker of the torches, simmering with desire that I'm desperate for him to unleash.

He brings one hand to my hip, the fingers pressing in hard and

236 KARINA HALLE

mean, and then with other he positions his cock behind me, the heat of him flaring at me from behind, making flames race up my spine.

With a carnal curl of his upper lip he pushes the head of his cock in.

I let out a gasp, my eyes pinching shut as I face forward, head hanging above the floor. I knew he was big, but even as wet and ready as I am from the aftereffects of my orgasm, he still doesn't feel like he'll fit.

"Fuck, you're tight," he hisses, his grip tightening. "Breathe, lavender girl. Breathe."

I inhale deeply through my nose, willing my body to relax.

"That's it," he rasps, "you can take a little more."

I want to tell him that it's easy for him to say, but I can't speak, can only concentrate on my breath coming in and out, my body finally letting him slide, slowly, all the way in until he's all I can feel.

"You can take it. Good girl."

His encouragement unfurls something inside me, a need to be praised, to be told that I am, in fact, good. Even if it's because I can handle the size of his cock in this position.

"How does that feel?" he asks, his voice throaty and raw, and I let out a soft whimper as my body adjusts, as he slowly slides his cock in and out, pausing for a moment before pushing it back in, deeper than ever.

I gasp, my fingers trying to grip the rug. "Good," I manage to say, trying to catch my breath.

He lets out a rough grunt. "Good isn't good enough. Not when it comes to you."

Then he leans down, his damp chest pressed against my back, his cock pressing against every sensitive nerve inside me. Then he reaches forward and wraps his hand around my throat, pulling me back into him so that I'm on my knees. He squeezes my throat lightly, just enough to hold me, and slips a hand down between my thighs.

His fingers slide over my clit and I moan, the vibrations flowing up my neck and reverberating against his palm.

"How about now?" Andor asks, his mouth at my ear, biting my earlobe before licking up the rim and making me shiver.

I swallow against his hand, his grip strong, possessive, enough to hamper my breathing a little but not take it away. He holds me there in place and starts to rut into me, pumping his hips against my rear, making my body tremble and shake from the impact.

All the while his fingers make the knot inside me grow tighter and tighter, gliding around where I'm so very wet and slippery. He keeps his mouth at my ear, his breath raspy as he tells me how good I feel, how he wants to do this forever, how I belong to him, how badly he's wanted me.

And I can't even reply. I'm lost to the sensation of him inside me, of giving myself over to him so completely. At this moment my body belongs to him and I am so thoroughly his that it's as if his heart beating hard against my back has joined with my own. And maybe after this moment I'll go back to belonging to myself, I'll be able to be whole, but right now . . .

I'm his, I'm his, I'm his.

Not just my body but my soul.

"Oh fuck!" I cry out, suddenly taken over by my orgasm, a crashing wave that makes me feel obliterated, inside out, and trembling on my knees as I lose control. If he didn't hold my throat just so, I would collapse straight to the ground.

He comes shortly after, with a hiss and a deep groan, spilling deep inside me as he whispers my name.

"I needed this," he says through a shaking breath as he finally pulls back, letting me go. "I've needed you. Just like this."

I make a sated noise of agreement and collapse on all fours, my head hanging down as I catch my breath and my body comes back to normal.

"I needed you too," I say, quietly, because the admission feels so raw right now, so vulnerable.

But from the way he plants kisses along my shoulders and down my spine, I know I'm still safe with him.

The question is, how long will that safety last?

Chapter 22

<u>Andor</u>

THE WORLD HAS CHANGED WHEN THE MORNING ROLLS AROUND. My senses have always been heightened because of the suen, but I'm starting to think that Brynla is her own kind of drug. The air smells fresher, feels warm like a midsummer morning, the straw mattress softer; the sound of her steady breathing is like hearing the fairest music. I feel as if I've been elevated to a higher state of being and it's all because of her.

You're in over your head, I chide myself as I carefully adjust my position on the narrow bed, not wanting to wake Brynla up. Her body is naked, her back against mine, and in the dim light of her room, lit only by a flickering torch that is running out of fuel, her lavender hair spills around her like a sunset turning to dusk. The sight of those scars from all the pain she endured at the convent mixing with her beauty makes a violence rise up inside me so tightly that I can barely breathe.

Fuck. Definitely in over my head. That's not unusual for me—I always leap before I look—but I've never felt so infatuated with anyone before. While I've garnered a reputation for loving them and leaving them, I've always wanted to feel that heady rush of obsession. I

240   KARINA HALLE

wanted something more. I just never found it with anyone before Brynla came into my life. It's like I have tunnel vision and all my focus is sharp and narrowed precisely on her. The rest of the world, the rest of my problems, the very problems that brought her into my life, have faded away. If I could spend the remainder of my days in bed with her, than I would die a happy man.

But nature calls.

I shift beside her and she stirs, letting out a low moan that goes straight to my half-hard cock. Damn, she makes it hard to leave.

"What time is it?" she murmurs in a sleepy voice, her eyes half-closed as she raises her head enough to look at me over her shoulder. I meet her gaze and my heart jolts in my chest.

Calm down, Andor.

I place a kiss on that bare, tempting shoulder, my lips lingering on her soft skin, relishing the taste. "I have no idea," I admit softly, my eyes closing briefly.

"I think I got used to all the daylight in Norland," she says with a yawn. "I could sleep for days."

"Go back to bed, no need to get up," I tell her, pulling away slowly.

She gives me a sleepy smile before her eyes flutter closed and she lays her head back down. Somehow this makes it harder to leave her.

I get up and survey the dim bedroom, wondering what the time is. We were fucking like there was no end for what felt like the whole night and my body seems to think it's morning, but without any natural light this far underground, it's hard to tell.

The rest of the abode is quiet as I make my way to the latrine, though by the time I'm finishing up, I hear the snuffle of Lemi's muzzle on the other side of the door.

I open it to find the giant dog crouched down, wanting to play. Before I can pet him he bounds off down the hall and disappears into thin air. I then hear Ellestra laugh from the kitchen where he's obviously reappeared.

The smile fades from my face and I let out a long breath. I suppose this morning is as good a time as any to try to win over Brynla's aunt. If we're going to stick to our plan, then she has to understand that we're *all* leaving today and heading back to the ship. Not just for Brynla's own good, but for Ellestra's as well.

I make my way to the kitchen, pausing in the doorway to assess the scene. Ellestra is over the stove, stirring something in a pot, as the kettle beside her whistles gently. She takes it off the fire and without looking up says, "Are you just going to stand there and stare, or do you have something to say?"

I offer her a smile she doesn't notice. "I'm known to blurt out the first thing on my mind. I don't think I'd get very far with you if I didn't take my time and choose the right words to say."

She chuckles lightly at that, which I take as a prize. "That's where you're wrong. I don't want carefully selected platitudes. I want the truth. So give me the truth, Andor Kolbeck, as blunt as you'll throw it." She looks up at me, her gaze intense as she meets mine. "What are your plans for my niece? Other than what you were doing throughout the night."

I ignore that last part. Should have figured that sound travels well down here.

"We need Brynla," I inform her as I take a seat. "And she needs to work for someone better than House Dalgaard."

She gives me a twisted smile and leans back against the counter, her arms folded over her long beige linen robe. "Remind me again why House Kolbeck is so special?"

"Because we're not monsters, despite your view of the houses and the other realms. Because she can really thrive in Norland. As can you."

She shakes her head, breaking eye contact. "All I have to go on is your word. I can't take your word for it or I would be a fool. And I can't take Brynla's because she's been compromised by you . . . in more ways than one."

I don't need to infer her meaning.

"Then you at least have to understand that she can't stay here. For her own safety. If Sjef Ruunon finds out that she's been with me . . ."

"And whose fault would that be?" she snaps at me, eyes blazing. "You put Brynla in this position by taking her and using her for the gains of your house. If she's leaving, it's all because of you!"

"You're right," I tell her as she stomps over to the pot on the stove and starts angrily stirring again. "It *is* my fault. Which means Brynla is my full responsibility now, as is everything she cares about, which means you and Lemi."

At the mention of his name, Lemi thumps his tail from the dog bed.

Ellestra doesn't say anything, just keeps the scowl on her face as she fusses about the stove.

"Listen," I say gravely, letting out a heavy sigh as I press my palms together in a plea. "We have reason to believe that Sjef Ruunon is building an army for an invasion north." This finally seems to get her attention, and she puts the wooden spoon down. "I know that war was before both our lifetimes, but the Dalgaards' bloodlines are thick and Ruunon is no different than his forefathers. If I had to guess, he wants Altus Dugrell in its entirety. He succeeded in fracturing it once before."

"Why should that concern us? We're the Freelanders. We mind our own business. We don't concern ourselves with wars in other realms."

"But it will become your war in your realm. They will come north by ship and by land. They'll spread out to Vesland and Esland, taking both sides of the world. The southern tip of the Banished Land will be their landing point. Do you really think they'll march straight to the capital without stopping by the Dark City? Without taking the people here for their own army?"

"Then we will fight!" she says, brandishing her spoon. "We can fight against the Soffers, we can fight against House Dalgaard."

"Not this army," I tell her. I pause, knowing I haven't shared this with Brynla yet. "There's a reason that Sjef Ruunon has doubled his interest in procuring suen. It's not just that he has an army to power. He's looking for something in particular. And whether he finds it on the Midlands or in the guarded galleries of Esland's infamous convent, once he gets it there will be no stopping him."

She frowns at me and puts the spoon down, her stance cagey. "What is this thing in particular?"

From the way she's asking the question, I feel like she might already know the answer.

"To be honest with you, I thought it was just a rumor. We always thought it was just a rumor. But we have gotten more credible intelligence over the years. Have you heard of the slangedrage? The two-headed dragon that was thought once to exist?"

Her stony expression doesn't change. "The dragon no one has seen in centuries?" she asks carefully. "A legend, like other things."

"So it would seem. After all, the only proof we have of their existence are the paintings people left behind on the Midlands. I've seen one of these paintings myself, a blue two-headed dragon sketched into a cliffside. They say once upon a time there were more paintings, perhaps left by Magni himself when he lived there with the dragons, but they no longer exist. As if someone was trying to erase their existence, or perhaps the rocks they were painted on have been squirreled away somewhere, so that people forget and turn it into legend."

"Where are you going with this?" she asks pointedly.

"The very same people who may have stolen the paintings, who have created tapestries and sculptures honoring these fabled dragons, may have something else in their possession. Something that all the realms would be fighting for, if only they knew it was real. A slangedrage's egg. An egg that only provides one type of magic. The one of immortality. Everyone who consumes it will become immortal." I pause to let it sink in. "In the wrong hands, immortality is disastrous. In a war, it is the key to winning, the key to taking over the world."

"You think suen can grant you immortality?"

"This suen can. I know it exists. And Sjef Ruunon knows this too. It's just a matter of who finds it first."

"So you think you can beat them to it."

"I know I can. Now that I have Brynla."

A knowing look comes over her face and she nods. "Ah. The real reason why you want her."

I give her a stiff smile. "One of many. Yes, Brynla and Lemi are adept at finding eggs. There's more to her, though, than meets the eye. There's a reason why Ruunon wanted her specifically to work for Dalgaard. Two reasons, actually. One is her skill. And two . . . if you know that the egg of immortality is being kept under lock and key at the fabled convent of the Daughters of Silence, then you would want someone who has experience with that place, who knows it in and out. Brynla does."

"So do I," Ellestra says quietly. "I had to spend most of my life there. If that was truly part of his plan, why not ask me to steal the egg?"

"Because you're not the whole package, and I don't mean the dog. It's not just that Brynla could break into the convent and take the egg. It's that there is something special about her. Isn't there? Ruunon got wind of this somehow. And I know you're aware of it too."

She swallows hard and looks back to the stove. The water boils over from the pot, making the flames dance, but she doesn't flinch. She slowly takes it off the flames and puts it aside. "I don't know what you mean," she finally says. Lying, of course.

"I've seen it with my own eyes. I've watched dragons swoop down, ready to attack, but Brynla escapes without a scratch. It's as if the dragons don't want to hurt her, not if they don't have to. Why is that?"

REALM of THIEVES   245

"I don't know," she says, finally meeting my eyes. She looks worn, like this whole conversation is exhausting her. "When I went to the Midlands with her back in the day, it sure seemed like the dragons would have eaten both of us. I fought like hell to keep them back."

I believe what she's saying and yet she's omitting something. I just don't know what.

"What does Brynla think about your plan?" she asks, changing the subject.

I let it go. For now. There will be plenty of time to badger her about it after. I might even bring it up with Brynla myself. She might know and if she doesn't, perhaps she can ask her aunt all the right questions.

I clear my throat. "I haven't told her yet."

Her brows rise. "You haven't told her yet?"

"I didn't want to bring it up until I knew it was something she could do, that she would be willing to do it."

Ellestra shakes her head and grabs a few mugs from the cupboard, throwing tea into them. "You didn't know that until now? Brynla's been dreaming of revenge against the Daughters ever since she left them. You give her a sword and order her to march in there and she'll do it without hesitation. To her own detriment."

"Look, I know you feel protective over her."

"I would harm myself before I let any harm come to her," she says, pouring water into the mugs. "Her life is dangerous enough as it is." She places the mugs on the table and then sits down, her head in her hands, and lets out a heavy sigh. "But you're also not wrong about the egg. We Freelanders have our own knowledge that gets passed down."

"So you know about the slangedrage?"

She lifts her head and gives me a weary look. "It might be extinct. It might not be. But that egg could change the world. Look at Magni. That sorcerer is still alive because of that particular suen, I know it. The Soffers just don't want that secret out. They want to believe he truly is immortal because not only does he possess magic but he *is* magic. It keeps up the façade."

"We could use your help, then. You already know a lot more than we do."

She gives me a faint smile. "I'll help you, only because I want to make sure Brynla is okay and that the egg goes into the right hands. That doesn't mean yours. It means I want that egg destroyed completely so that no one has it."

"That's fair," I say, though I know I won't promise her that. I need the egg for the Kolbecks. I need the egg for myself.

"Though I doubt there's only one egg at the convent. I'm sure there are more. Maybe in the capitol buildings. Maybe all the Soffers have ingested it already."

"You think they would share it among their followers?"

"You said that Dalgaard is building an army the same way. The Soffers have as much interest in immortality as anyone else. When those wards come down, which they are prophesized to do, which country will survive? The one that can't die. And when the prophecy ends up coming true, not because it was fated to be that way, but because it was engineered, then they'll have the advantage over everyone. All the realms, all the kingdoms, all the houses."

I frown as I take the tea from her. "Engineered?"

She gives me a look of surprise. "Don't tell me you believe the prophecy isn't something they're controlling. They—"

Suddenly a knock at the door.

Both of us stiffen.

Lemi's head goes up and he lets out a low growl.

"Stay here," Ellestra whispers to me, carefully getting to her feet and motioning me not to move. "You're a liability."

I watch as she walks out of the kitchen and into the parlor, disappearing just out of my sight as she goes to the door.

"Who is it?" I hear her ask.

REALM of THIEVES 247

Despite her telling me to stay put, I silently stand up and start moving past the table.

"Zolar," a man's voice says faintly from outside. I don't know who Zolar is or what he normally sounds like, but there's something off about it.

Warning bells go off in my head, my chest tightening.

No. Don't open it.

"It's early, Zolar," Ellestra says with a sigh.

"Wait!" I yell, running into the room just to see her slide open the door.

A man dressed completely in black, including a face mask, is on the other side.

A sword in his hand.

Ellestra looks from me back to the man.

Just as he raises the sword and slams it right into Ellestra's chest.

Lemi barks and Ellestra screams, trying to rip the sword out of her heart, the blood spilling everywhere, and I'm running at the man, looking for the closest object to use as a weapon.

The man at the door is joined by three more, weapons drawn and advancing toward me.

Chapter 23

BRYNLA

I WAKE UP TO MY AUNT'S SCREAM, THE RAZOR-SHARP SOUND slicing through my dreams and right into the marrow of me. I hurl myself out of bed, no time to think, only time to act. In the fading light of a flickering torch I throw on a gauzy tunic to cover my nudity, grab my closest ash-glass sword, and then I'm racing out of the room.

And into complete chaos.

Lemi's barks fill the air, but he's nowhere to be seen. Instead I see my aunt on the ground, a sword sticking straight out of her chest, her screams dying to a gurgling sound that I know will haunt my nightmares for the rest of my life. I run to her in a panic, to the foreign man in black trying to pull the sword out of her chest. Andor has picked up a stool and is racing toward three other men who are bursting in through the door. In a blur of movement, Andor snaps the legs off the stool with his bare hands, then grasps them like jagged spears, ducking as the assailants lunge at him.

Lemi appears suddenly behind one of the men, jumping up at his back and knocking him to the ground, his jaws snapping at the man's head. I look back down at my aunt, at the blood pouring out of her chest as the man grasps the sword. Hysteria overwhelms me, and before I can think, I quickly raise my sword, stabbing it through the back of the man's neck just as he looks up. The blade pierces through the skin and bone with a sickening stab that vibrates up my arms, and the man falls down dead next to me.

The first man I've ever killed.

There is no time to feel anything.

"Brynla!" Andor yells, and I look to see him stab someone with the stool leg while one of the other men comes at me, two knives drawn and glinting in the torchlight.

Lemi disappears and then reappears right in front of me, his heavy body between me and my attacker. I scream for Lemi to move as the knives slash toward him and he disappears, the action creating enough of a distraction for the man to lose his focus. I take the opportunity to brandish my sword and with a scream I swing it through the air with all my might until it slices across the man's throat, nearly severing his head clean off.

He slumps to the ground beside the other dead man and then Lemi reappears beside Andor, helping him take down the last remaining assailant. I should get up and help him, but I feel like I'm moving through water now. At least Andor now has the upper hand as Lemi causes the man to drop his weapon and Andor has him pressed against the wall, blade at the man's temple.

"Who do you work for?" Andor growls, a vein throbbing at his temple. "Who sent you?"

He pulls the man's mask down and the man grins at him. Pale skin, yellow hair. I've never seen him before and I don't have time to care.

I look back to my aunt and feel my world start to fall apart, like the thin threads of reality that were holding me together are starting to disintegrate. I collapse on the ground beside her and pull her into my arms, taking the edge of my tunic and pressing it against the wound where blood rushes out like a crimson river.

"You're going to be okay," I tell her, my voice shaking. She stares up at me with glassy eyes, an emptiness inside them that seems to be spreading. "We're going to make sure you're okay."

I look over at Andor, who is still threatening the man, hoping he can save my aunt.

He has to.

I saw him bring Lemi back to life; I know that's what happened. He took my pain away. He was young when he couldn't save his own mother, and maybe her illness was too much, but my aunt is strong and it's just a wound, it can heal, she can be saved.

"Andor," I whisper, holding my aunt tighter. "Andor, you can save her."

He pauses briefly, finding me from the corner of his eye, but then he growls at the man. "Tell me who sent you or I'll drive this dagger right into your tiny little brain."

The man smiles at him like he knows Andor will kill him.

Like he wants that.

We will get no answers.

And it doesn't matter anyway.

"Andor!" I say again, louder now. "Please! Save her!"

Andor sneers at the man, his face going red, the knife's tip starting to shake against the man's temple. "Tell me!"

"Andor!" I call out again. "He's never going to tell. Just kill him and help me! Please, she's dying!" I'm yelling now, the sound coming out of me like some awful rabid beast.

Andor relents for a moment, looking down at the ground with a small shake of his head, and I fear he's about to let the man go. But then he lets out an anguished roar, pulling back enough to drive the rest of the dagger into the man's head.

I look back down at my aunt to see that her eyes are no longer just glassy.

They are still.

REALM of THIEVES 251

They are blank.

She's staring at the ceiling, at nothing.

There is nothing.

"No!" I scream, squeezing her shoulders so hard that I know it must hurt.

But she doesn't react.

She is stillness.

She is death.

Lemi walks over slowly, sniffing my aunt's feet, then lies down beside her, ears back, letting out a mournful whimper that nearly shakes the whole house.

This can't be it.

"Ellestra," I whisper to her, giving her a shake. "Auntie. Please. Come back. We can save you."

But the tears fall from my eyes and splash onto her face and she is so, so still.

"I'm sorry," Andor says. He sounds like he's in another world, but he's standing behind me. I feel his presence and I'm angry. Angry he wasn't quicker. He should have killed that man right away and maybe he would have had time to save her.

But the anger sparks and flames and burns inside me, and it morphs into hatred for myself.

Because this is my fault.

This is all my fault.

"Brynla," Andor says gently. He places his hand on my shoulder as he crouches down beside me, but I barely feel it, barely hear him. "Brynla, I am so sorry. It happened so quickly. There was a knock at the door and she told me to stay where I was in the kitchen. I heard the voice, she seemed to know the man but there was something off and by the time I got to the parlor . . ."

"She's gone," I whisper, brushing my aunt's hair off her face. I've never seen her still before, not even in sleep. She was always scowling, always moving, always busy with something. She didn't suffer fools and at times she was tough to love, but I loved her all the same. She saved me from the Daughters of Silence, she saved me from ending my own life when I realized nothing would bring my father or my mother back. I wouldn't be here without her and now . . . now she's gone.

It's not fair at all.

She brought me into her life and I brought death into it.

"I know, I'm sorry," he says again. but all the apologies and words and platitudes in the world won't bring her back.

Fuck. *Fuck.*

This can't be real. It can't be.

His grip on my shoulder tightens. "But whoever sent those people after her meant for them to get to us. To you. We have to leave."

I shake my head and press my lips against my aunt's forehead. She already feels cold. She shouldn't, she should still feel warm, and yet it feels like everything that made her fiery has faded away.

"We have to leave, Brynla. Now. You, me, and Lemi. They are coming for us."

"You don't even know who," I whisper. I stare into her open eyes, willing her to come back to life. My aunt had ingested suen at some point; she was strong and fast, wasn't it possible that the substance and power could fight through death and bring her back to life?

"It doesn't matter," he says. "It's either House Dalgaard or it's Esland. Whoever they are, they want you dead. There will be more in their wake. We have to go. Now."

I shake my head. "And I'm not leaving. I'm not leaving her."

"Brynla," he says, his voice hard as he gets to his feet.

"I'm not leaving her!" I scream, whipping my head around to stare up at him. He's staring down at me, brows furrowed, eyes sad, and the memory of us together last night visits me like a butterfly, a gentle-

REALM of THIEVES 253

ness that drifts away, buried by anger and grief. None of that matters now. Nothing matters now.

He grows blurry in my vision as the tears fall.

But I'm not going anywhere.

"I'm staying with her," I manage to say, my mouth thick. "I'm not leaving her. She might come back to life at any moment. You might still be able to save her."

I look back down at her, hoping that maybe she's moved, showed some sign of life.

But her body just feels heavier now.

"I'm not leaving her," I say again. "You go. Go back to your ship, back to your land and your family. She was the only family I had. I must stay with her."

"You'll die if you do," he says imploringly. "They'll kill you. They'll kill Lemi too."

"I'd like to see them try," I say, though that last part hits deep inside. I don't care if they do kill me, whoever they are, but I don't want Lemi to die.

"Take him with you," I say. "Take Lemi with you, please."

"He'll never leave your side," he says. "Just like you'll never leave your aunt's."

I nod, trying to swallow.

This can't be real. This must be a bad dream. I must still be asleep.

"But you know that I won't leave you either," he continues. He walks across the room and I look up, watching him disappear around the corner.

He can stay if he wants. Part of me wants to be that selfish, to ask him to. Maybe we can fight off the next wave of attackers. After all, there are four dead men here, four assassins that we managed to take down. We could stay and fight and I could give my aunt the proper burial and respect she deserves. She doesn't deserve to be left behind, even in death.

Time doesn't seem to pass the way it should. Everything seems to dwindle down to just me and my aunt and I know I can't let go of her, not now, maybe not ever. I can just sit here with her and be and as long as I can do that, then she's never really dead, never really gone.

"Brynla," Andor says, and I realize he's come back into the room. He stands beside me and I tear my gaze off my aunt and glance up at him.

Sorrow furrows his brow, his eyes wet at the corners.

"Stay with me," I tell him. "Don't leave me. Promise you won't leave me."

"I promise I won't leave you," he says, his voice rough with determination.

Then he crouches low beside me and before I know what's happening, he's stabbed a needle into my arm.

The shock of his action registers before the pain does.

I yelp, the sound strangled, and try to move away from him but my aunt's body is suddenly too heavy.

"What did you do?" I cry out, twisting futilely, while Lemi gets up and delivers a low, threatening bark aimed at Andor.

"I had to," Andor says, holding the needle out as if he might do it again. "It's the only way I'll be able to get you out of here." He glances at Lemi warily. "I know you're just a dog, but you have to let me do this, for her own good. Don't make me use this on you too. I don't know how I'll be able to smuggle a girl *and* a dog out of here."

I blink at him slowly and try to speak, but no words come out. The room starts to spin.

No, I think. He can't have drugged me. He wouldn't do that. He wouldn't take me away from here, from my aunt.

But from the apologetic look on his brow, watching as I slump to the floor, I know that's exactly what he plans to do.

REALM of THIEVES   255

"You'll wake up on the boat, safe and sound," he says to me, his voice echoing and becoming farther away as my eyes close. "I'm not about to lose you and I promised I wouldn't leave."

Then all sound ceases.

And everything is black.

Chapter 24

ANDOR

"ABOUT TIME THE SUN CAME OUT," I SAY AS I EXIT THE BACK OF the castle and walk toward Solla, Vidar, and Steiner, who are sitting at the oak table situated among the vines and fruit trees, the last of the cherry blossoms scattered on the ground in mounds of white and pink.

My siblings are in deep discussion about something, but all talking abruptly stops when I sit down at the table and take a sip of the cold beer in my hand.

"Didn't bring any for the rest of us?" Vidar asks, raising his empty mug and tipping it against the edge of the table in show.

"Another? When I asked the cook it seems the keg has nearly been drained dry," I tell him. "Next time I go inside, I'll get you a refill."

"Nah," Steiner says. "Next time you go inside we won't see you again for a day or two."

"How is she?" Solla asks me, meaning Brynla. She's the reason I've been so preoccupied over the last few days. "I keep bringing her food but she barely touches it. She won't say a word. Even her dog won't bark."

REALM of THIEVES 257

"Is this why you called this family meeting?" I ask. "Are you legitimately worried about her?"

"Yes." Vidar nods. "I also think we all need to have a frank discussion about what happened out there in the Banished Land."

I take a long sip of my beer, preparing to get the third degree from my older brother. "I told you what happened. We were ambushed."

"But by whom?" he asks.

"Again, I don't know."

"Well, Brynla must have some idea. Have you asked her?"

I give him a steady look. "What do you think? Of course I've asked her. But she's inconsolable. She's lost the last person close to her. Her whole family is now gone. She wasn't even paying attention while the attack was happening, she was trying to prevent her aunt from dying."

Although that's not completely true. Brynla was paying attention. She helped kill two of the attackers. But she doesn't know if they were sent by the Black Guard or House Dalgaard. It could be either. The Black Guard might have been tipped off that Brynla was stealing eggs for us, perhaps by Dalgaard themselves. Or maybe the assassins were hired by Dalgaard to take her—and me—out of the picture.

It doesn't help that Brynla refuses to talk to me about it. My siblings think I've been spending a lot of time with her, but the truth is more that I've been *trying* to spend time with her. She's giving me the cold shoulder, pissed off at me for drugging her the way I did and bringing her and Lemi back on the ship.

I don't blame her; I know I violated her trust by doing that, but I didn't have a choice. I wasn't about to wait in the Dark City for the next ambush, one that we probably wouldn't survive.

I had to make some quick decisions since I hadn't planned on needing to drag her out unconscious. Luckily there was a cart parked a little way down the alley, filled with water.

Unluckily, the cart belonged to her neighbors, an elderly man and woman, who had gathered in their doorway having heard all the commotion with the assassins. They didn't do or say anything when I dumped out the water, but when I reemerged from Ellestra's house with Brynla in the cart, buried underneath a mound of blankets, they grew suspicious. Thankfully Lemi seemed to understand that I was trying to help Brynla, and he barked at the neighbors to stay back while I quickly wheeled Brynla away.

Getting out of the Dark City itself was another story. I took lower passageways back, finding my way on instinct and assuming that goods had to be constantly carted in and out of the tunnels instead of the stairs. There weren't as many guards that way, but when I did run across them I had to dispatch them quickly or risk discovery. Thankfully, I'd had enough forethought to prepare the syringe with more drugs. It meant I didn't have to kill more people than I already had that morning. Not that I would have hesitated.

"I assume whoever the assassins were, they knew the social system of the Dark City well enough to get through," I tell Vidar, bringing my focus back to my brother's intense gaze.

"Do you think they knew you were with her?" Steiner asks. "Strange coincidence for them to attack the moment you get there."

"No question they knew Brynla was on her way back and waited for that moment." Dalgaard has spies everywhere. "I can't say if they were after me—perhaps they would have sent more men if they knew."

Vidar snorts at that and I stare at him steadily until he seems to retract his derision. He clears his throat. "So then someone intercepted Moon—"

"Not possible. Moon would have told me," Steiner says.

"*Or*," Vidar continues, not wanting to get into an old debate of whether his raven really understands him or is capable of lying, "Brynla's aunt got careless."

I appreciate him not bringing up the accusation that Ellestra was behind all of it, which was what he'd been saying when we first arrived back.

"Careless or confided in the wrong person," I point out.

"That's the same thing," Vidar says.

"So what does this mean?" Solla asks, tucking her hair behind her ears. "Are we in danger?"

"We're always in danger," I tell her. "It's just that we've always had an enemy we knew—House Dalgaard. If they killed Ellestra, then that changes nothing for us. But it if was the Black Guard, and we're now enemies of the state of Esland, well, that might change a few things."

"Everyone is their enemy," Steiner says. "They know how the syndikats deal and what they deal with. I wouldn't worry about Esland coming to Norland and trying anything."

"Even if they did, we would be ready. They wouldn't get far," Vidar says sternly.

"And Dalgaard is already our enemy anyway," I say, finishing the rest of my beer. I set it down and stare at my siblings with as much gravity as I can convey. "What I mean is that this changes our plans a little. If we're being looked at more closely by Esland's Black Guard, we'll need to make an adjustment."

Vidar straightens and eyes me sharply. I hadn't mentioned anything of this nature yet, and I know he hates surprises. "An adjustment to what?"

"To the plan," I tell him.

"What plan?" Solla asks.

"To steal the egg of immortality from the Daughters of Silence."

Everyone goes silent. Solla looks puzzled, Steiner seems thoughtful, and Vidar's eyes showcase puzzle pieces sliding into place. I had told them what happened with Ellestra and the assassins in the Dark City. I *didn't* tell them about my conversations with Ellestra or what my plans have been for Brynla all along.

260 KARINA HALLE

I still haven't told Brynla either.

Suddenly all my siblings erupt at once.

"The egg of immortality? You know that's just a myth," Steiner scoffs.

"You couldn't set foot on Esland proper without being killed," Vidar says with a raise of his brow.

"What in the world is the egg of immortality?" Solla asks.

I suppose a better man wouldn't revel in the fact that he knows something that his siblings don't. But I am not a better man.

I grin at them, savoring their confusion and enjoying the secrecy for a drawn-out moment before I plunge into everything I know. Though the egg is news to Solla, it had been of some interest to Steiner for a while before he declared it just a legend, and Vidar and my father were the first to bring it to my attention, also speculating on its existence.

But I took that one step further. If there were such a thing, it would change the fate of our family and syndikats forever. And if it were to get into the wrong hands, well . . .

"Brynla's aunt doesn't know of its existence for sure, though," Steiner says when I've finished, his eyes excited yet cautious.

"Only what others have said," I say. "So I'd wager no one knows much of anything. That's why it's a risk. But what isn't a risk?"

I'd also wager that Dalgaard wanted to use Brynla for this exact thing. He chose her because of where she came from, his plans no different than mine. But *I* also know that there really is something special about Brynla, something I'm certain her aunt was about to confirm before that unfortunate turn of events. I'm not about to voice that to my siblings, though. Not until I talk to Brynla about it.

"Well, obviously Brynla must want her revenge on the convent," Solla says.

"She does," I say cautiously.

REALM of THIEVES   261

Vidar stares at me for a moment before he shakes his head. "Oh, for fuck's sake, Andor. She doesn't know, does she?"

"I've been a little preoccupied."

Solla gasps.

"She's been here for a month," Vidar points out, jabbing his finger into the whorls on the table.

"I wanted to make sure that it was true before I roped her into it."

"You're going to have to tell her soon," Steiner says. "Otherwise she's going to feel even further betrayed."

"Further betrayed?" I repeat, getting to my feet. "I haven't betrayed her."

"You drugged her," he says. "You took her back to the ship against her will and left the body of her aunt behind. You should have at least taken her aunt's body with you. You're strong enough to have handled the both of them."

Guilt stabs me through the ribs.

"I wasn't thinking," I admit quietly, sitting back down in my seat. "All I could do was get Brynla out of there. She was my priority, not her aunt."

"That might be one reason why she's not coming out of her room," Solla mutters.

"Or it could be that she's grieving," I tell her sharply.

"You need to get her to see Sae Balek," Vidar says. "Take some of the resin, have the visions. It's the only way she'll be able to channel her grief."

"Maybe she doesn't need to channel her grief," I say, feeling annoyed at his suggestion, as if grief is something to use. "Maybe she needs to just deal with it as it comes, day by day."

"We don't have time to deal with it day by day," Vidar says sternly. "You said it yourself: if the Black Guard is behind Ellestra's assassination, then they're going to be on the lookout for you. Perhaps they don't know your plans to steal the egg, but they're going to expect you stepping foot on their shores." He pauses. "Which is why I'm going to come with you."

I balk at that. The last thing I want—and need—is my brother's help.

"You're not," I tell him, though my protest is feeble.

"Give me one reason," he says with a patient look.

I glance at Solla and Steiner but they seem to be waiting for an answer, same as he is.

Because this is my thing, I want to say. *I'm the only one who can do this and I can't risk anything happening to you.*

Instead I say, "You're needed here. And this doesn't involve you."

"If you it involves you, dear brother, it involves me," he says, a small, slightly smug smile tugging at his lips. "And I'm sure Father will see things the same way. If you're going to Esland to perform a robbery, you might as well turn it into a heist."

Chapter 25

<u>Brynla</u>

THE MOON IS KEEPING ME AWAKE. ROTUND AND TINGED WITH blue, it sits in the dark sky just above the castle spires, slicing through the half-closed curtain. The light illuminates Lemi as he sleeps curled up beside the bed, turning his black coat into shades of indigo. I would get up and close the curtain but I couldn't move, even if I wanted to. My body feels depleted, my soul outside myself. The longer I stare at the moon, the more hollow I feel, as if it's shining a light on my loss.

My loss.

This morning Andor told me it had been a week since I lost my aunt, a fact that still seems less of a fact and more of a notion. An awful, terrible, impossible notion, about two things that couldn't be true. One is that my aunt is dead. Two, that time has passed. Because how can time just . . . pass? How can it move on past her death? How come the world didn't stop when she died? Because *my* world stopped when she died.

Though, looking back on our conversation, I should have told him I didn't *lose* her. To lose someone is to admit fault on your behalf. To lose someone is to imagine that one day they'll return, back in the place you last left them.

I didn't lose my aunt in that sense. She wasn't misplaced, she didn't wander off. She won't someday come back and we'll be happily reunited. She was instead brutally murdered and died in front of my eyes.

And *loss* is too pithy of a word; it doesn't reflect at all the magnitude of having someone you love more than anything, the only solid, real family you have left in the world, ripped from your life. It doesn't even begin to describe the hole gouged in you with tainted claws, creating a wound that not only won't heal but will fester and infect the rest of you, spreading right into your very soul.

But perhaps it was my fault. I may not have lost her like I've lost my coin purse before, but it was my responsibility. It all happened because I came back to the Dark City and put her life in danger. I had Steiner send the message via raven. I am the one who put all these events in motion. Yes, I could blame Andor. I do blame Andor, since he was the one who put me in this horrible position. But in the end I'm still the one who decided getting my aunt out of the Banished Land was more important than anything else. And that was selfish of me, there's no getting around it. I wanted her out because I wanted her with me, because I thought I knew what was best for her.

How naïve and foolish I was. I don't know what's best for anyone, let alone myself. My ego, my need to save my aunt when she didn't need saving, is what cost her her life.

And I don't know how I will ever recover from this.

I wish Andor had left me behind in the city to grieve.

I wish he had left me behind to die.

In the background, there's a faint knock at the door. I don't even lift my head to look. Usually it's either Solla, bringing food I won't eat but which Lemi happily laps up, or it's Andor. Given that the moon is high, I'm guessing it's Andor.

I hear the door creak open. Flickering candlelight spills across the room, competing with the moon. Lemi's tail thumps against the floor and for a moment I feel betrayed by my hound. Why did Lemi let Andor leave with my unconscious body? Why didn't he stop him? Even now he seems happy to have Andor around, oblivious to my feelings.

Then again, I think I'm oblivious to them.

"Are you awake?" Andor asks softly.

I clear my throat. "Yes," I whisper.

"Can I come in?"

I usually tell him to go. Or I let him stay for a few moments as he tries to talk to me, tries to reach me through my grief, searches for the person I was before this all happened. He can't find her. Neither can I.

But tonight, with that cold, cold moon peering into the room, making the shadows darker while illuminating my pain, I don't think I want to send Andor away. For once, I don't want to be alone. I want to forget.

"Yes," I tell him again, and he's closing the door softly behind him. I reposition myself on the bed to make room for him, watching as he moves across the room, his tall, muscled body moving with such grace that it makes my heart trip. Funny how my body still has the capacity for lust, for desire, for physical need, even when it's absolutely breaking inside.

Lemi lifts his head and Andor crouches down to stroke the dog, scratching behind the ears. "Be a good boy and give us some privacy," he says.

Lemi understands. In a flash he disappears and reappears on the balcony, sitting with his back to us.

Andor lets out a quiet chuckle. "He's awfully considerate, isn't he?"

I smile, just a little, but it's enough that he notices. His expression softens as he sits on the edge of the bed, staring down at me with liquid eyes. "That's the first smile I've seen in a long time."

Instinctively I turn it into a frown. He reaches down and runs his thumb over my lip. "It's all right," he says. "You're allowed to feel some light. It doesn't erase the rest of it." He brings his fingers across my cheek, brushing my messy hair off my forehead. "I know what it's like, you know. What you're going through."

"Our families are nothing alike," I manage to say.

"That might be true, but death still comes for us all. You have lost so much more than I have, Brynla, more than I can even begin to imagine. I have had a life of privilege, a life that you never had. You have had a life of pain, in more ways than one." He pauses, letting out a shaky breath. "But I know what it's like to be so enveloped by your sorrow and grief, the way it consumes you like a ravenous beast. It becomes something physical, something real, something you feel you have to battle because if you give up, if you give in . . . you wonder how you'll ever find yourself again. But you will find yourself again, lavender girl. I promise you that. You will find yourself and you'll pull through and it starts with a smile. It starts with allowing yourself to see the light on the other side, even when you can't imagine anything but darkness."

The gravity in his words has a way of sinking in, of anchoring me in this place. I have been in the very darkness he speaks of before. My father, then my mother. Being in the Daughters of Silence didn't give you much space for grief. I had been so focused on just surviving the convent that I didn't have a lot of time to deal with what I had lost, and yet I was still stumbling in the dark.

In fact, I think I was stumbling until the moment I met him.

For a brief while, despite my fear of the Kolbecks and the circumstances of my being here, I actually had hope for a better life. I had hope for the first time ever.

Andor brought me that light and he's also brought me this darkness, the very one consuming me with gnashing teeth.

And right now I need him, in all his shades.

REALM of THIEVES

267

"You're allowed to feel good," he murmurs, his fingers trailing down my neck, over my collarbones, so gentle that it takes my breath away. "Can I make you feel good?"

I nod, my heart beating faster. I want him to make me feel good, to bring me relief even if it just stays between the sheets, even if just for the night.

He gives me a deliciously wanton grin, golden heat flaring in his eyes. "Good."

Then he reaches down and grabs me by the hips, yanking me to the side and to the edge of the bed. I gasp and he drops to his knees on the floor, kneeling as he spreads my legs roughly with one hand and pushes up the hem of my nightgown with the other.

Oh.

My cheeks go hot, my breath hitching as I raise my head to watch him. He's staring between my legs with such hungry intensity that my pulse leaps in my throat. I've never been so vulnerable and bare before.

"This is all right?" he asks, his fingers scorching as they push into the soft flesh of my inner thighs as he spreads them wider.

I nod, swallowing hard. "I, uh, have never done . . . this before."

He raises a brow. "You've never had a man feast on you like he was starved for a meal?"

I shake my head slightly, my fingers curling into the sheets in anticipation. Though I've been with my fair share of partners, none of them have done what he's about to do. Thank the gods I had enough strength today to take a long bath and make sure I was thoroughly clean.

My answer brings a wide grin to his face, a look of absolute pride.

"I'll try to be gentle, then," he says, lowering his face until I feel his hot breath tickling, making me squirm. "No promises, though."

His voice is so dark and raw, his desire for me so apparent that a wave of nerves and anticipation crashes over me, making my stomach flutter.

Andor moves closer, still kneeling between my legs, then presses his mouth against the sensitive skin of my thigh, leaving a warm, damp kiss there. Close, so close. I find myself arching toward him, my nerves screaming for contact.

His hands grip my thighs, pulling me closer, and I can feel the gentle brush of his stubble as he moves toward me, teasingly slow. I'm not sure what to expect, but I know I want whatever he has to give, so I simply let myself fall into his touch, letting him take control.

His tongue flicks out, wet and slick, touching me in places I've never been touched by a mouth before. It's an entirely new sensation, electric and intense, as if every cell in my body is singing with pleasure. I moan softly, my hands gripping the sheets beneath me, clutching them so hard my fingers hurt.

He licks me again, this time more forcefully, his tongue plunging into me as if he's claiming me, his mouth moving with hunger. And then, as suddenly as he started, he stops, pulling away from me and looking up at me with an intensity that makes my heart leap.

"You have no idea how good you taste," he murmurs, his mouth glistening with my desire. "How badly I want to drown myself in you."

I can't breathe, can't think. All I can feel is the heat of his body, the way his fingers grip my thighs, and the starvation in his eyes. He parts me with his fingers and watches me closely as he works them in and out of me, trying to savor me in every way.

And, fuck, do I need to be savored. Every bit of me taken and held and enjoyed. A respite from the sorrow, a soul lost to pleasure instead of pain.

He looks at me again, his eyes dark with lust, and then he lowers his face and plunges back in, his tongue darting and licking at my most intimate place. I gasp, my hips bucking upward, urging him to continue. He obliges, his tongue delving deeper. He's not teasing anymore.

I feel myself start to unravel, the waves of pleasure building higher and higher. My body responds to his touch, my hips bucking wildly, my breaths ragged. I feel as if I'm about to explode, and then, suddenly, I do.

In that moment, everything around me fades away. The only thing that exists is Andor's tongue, his mouth, his lips, his hands. I feel as if I'm soaring, as if I've left my body behind entirely and am floating on some celestial plane. I cry out, my voice a guttural, primal sound that fills the room.

Andor doesn't stop. He continues to pleasure me, his face buried between my legs, his tongue working its magic until I come again, blindsided. This time it's impossible to stay quiet and my cry fills the room, his name on my lips like a desperate prayer that's currently being fulfilled.

"Fuck," I whimper, the word ragged and choked as my body still bucks against his face, writhing wildly with the overwhelming sensations.

"I could do this all night," he murmurs against me, his lips brushing my cunt until I can't bear it anymore. "Eating you, tasting you, until I can't move my mouth. But I also want to fuck you senseless. Let my cock feel how wet I've made you. You don't mind, do you?"

I barely manage to shake my head, my brain addled by the sheer intensity of the sensations that have taken me over. Andor takes this as consent and wastes no time, rising from between my legs, his eyes aglow with possession as he looks at me.

"Look how fucking pretty you are," he growls, his voice low and gravelly. He makes a low, satisfied sound and quickly takes his shirt off, yanking down his pants.

I can't look away. I'm entranced, hypnotized by the pure animal lust that's taking him over, and as he stands before me, naked and imposing, I can't help but shiver. The sight of his muscular body, taut and glistening with a sheen of sweat, is almost too much for me to bear. Andor prowls over me and leans down, his mouth capturing mine in a searing kiss, his tongue delving deep into my mouth, and the salt of my own desire hits my tongue.

My hands grip his shoulders, my fingers digging into his skin as our tongues dance together. He reaches down for his cock and my legs spread wide for him. I can feel the warmth of his erection against my thigh, and the thought of what he's about to do to me sends a bolt of pleasure straight to my core.

He positions himself between my legs, his cock poised at my entrance. I look up at him, knowing I must look a little wild and desperate myself. We lock eyes, and for a moment, everything between us seems to shift. It's as if all the walls we've put up are crumbling, the barriers between our hearts and souls dissolving in the face of this primal connection.

I've needed this, I think, running my fingers up over the taut muscles of his arms, to his shoulders. *I've needed this terribly.*

Andor leans down, his mouth capturing mine once more as he pushes into me slowly, inch by inch. I gasp, my back arching off the bed as the sinful mix of pleasure and pain courses through me, igniting my nerves, almost too much to bear. His cock fills me, stretching me wide, and I can feel myself being claimed by him in a way that I never thought possible.

He pulls away from the kiss, our eye contact intense as he begins to move. Any gentleness is now gone. His thrusts are rough and hard, each one sending shock waves of pleasure through me. My fingers are digging into his shoulders now, and I can feel my own desire swelling, becoming even more wet than before.

"Harder, Andor," I gasp, my voice thick with lust. "Fuck me harder."

My command causes heat to flash in his eyes and he complies, his thrusts becoming more frenzied, more intense. His cock slides in and out of me, each push driving me closer and closer to the edge. I can feel my orgasm building, a fierce tempest within me that I know will consume me in no time at all.

Andor's eyes never leave mine, adding to the intensity of our connection, his face twisted with lust and pure possession. He reaches down, his hand finding my clit, and begins to rub it in circular motions. The sensation is overwhelming, and I can feel myself spiraling toward the edge.

"I . . . going to come," I gasp, my voice trembling.

Andor continues his assault on my body, his thrusts becoming even more powerful. His fingers find my clit again, and I can feel my orgasm building even faster until it becomes too much to bear.

"Now, Andor," I beg, my voice hoarse with desire. "Please, I need it now."

He responds with a savage growl, his cock thrusting into me with renewed vigor. His fingers continue their relentless pace on my clit, and I can feel myself shaking, on the brink of shattering into a million pieces.

I toss my head back, my entire body convulsing as an orgasm like nothing I've ever experienced before washes over me, my whole body arching. The rush that washes over me is so intense that my cries of pleasure echo around the room, mingling with Andor's own hurried grunts.

As the waves of my climax crash over me, Andor's own release follows close behind and with just as much power, his cock spasming deep within me as he comes with a ferocity that takes my breath away. He shudders above me, hard muscles straining as it rolls through him, our bodies still joined, our breaths ragged and uneven.

Slowly, we disentangle ourselves from one another, Andor carefully pulling out until I feel a strange hollowness inside from where he just was. Then he lies beside me on the bed, his face reflecting the same mixture of awe and emotion that I feel coursing through me.

"That was—" I stammer, my voice still thick with lust and emotion. I'm near tears, having a hard time processing everything.

He looks at me with a mixture of tenderness and fierce protectiveness. "I know. I felt it too. That was something we both needed." He pauses, letting out a deep breath. "The last time we . . . I've been giving you space and had only hoped I hadn't lost you. But I've needed you, Brynla. I've needed you like nothing else in this world. We both went through something traumatizing, and I've been so afraid we couldn't find our way back to each other."

I look into his eyes, still wide with wonder, and nod.

"I feared the same thing," I admit quietly. "But I'm still here, somehow. And you're still here."

In the midst of our grief and loss, we've found something that both connects and comforts us. It may not replace what we've lost but at least he's shown me some light. Light that might fade when he leaves this room, the darkness always ready to swoop back in, but something good—something *real*—all the same.

Chapter 26

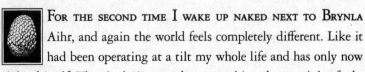

Andor

For the second time I wake up naked next to Brynla Aihr, and again the world feels completely different. Like it had been operating at a tilt my whole life and has only now righted itself. There's clarity, yes, but something deeper. A lot fucking deeper, something I can't even put into words but I believe it. Because I *feel* it.

Last night was intense. It was dark and wild and raw, and very much needed. A chance for us to reconnect, a chance for Brynla to heal, however long that may take her. Losing a family member, losing someone you love, produces a wound so deep that it will never scar over. My mother's death never resulted in scar tissue; it's just been this cut that's barely stitched together, the threads ready to pull loose at any moment. Brynla had already lost her mother and her father, and now she's lost the last person she had left. The wound is carved so deep I can see straight through her to the other side.

Yet somehow, last night, I was able to mend her, if only for a moment.

"Good morning," I whisper to her, my lips at her ear. I'm already hard and wondering if she'd like a repeat.

She lets out a soft moan as I run the tip of my nose through her hair, the lavender strands shining in threads of pink and silver from the early sun that's peeking in through the window. Lemi, bless his hound heart, is still on the balcony, his silhouette visible through the curtains.

I slowly slide my hand over the smooth skin of her shoulder and down her arm, appreciating the firm muscle underneath, the slight flexing at my touch, such a testament to her power. Then I let my fingers trail over her hips and she squirms slightly, letting out a breathy giggle that works like a bolt of lightning through my veins.

I grin against her skin, pressing more kisses behind her ear. I found a ticklish spot. I found a weakness, a tender spot surrounded by so much armor.

I temper the feel of my fingers even more, letting them trail over her skin like butterfly wings. She moves her hips back against my cock, grinding in hard, then pulling away, writhing against me like her body wants to escape but she doesn't.

"This good?" I murmur as my hand slips down, down, sliding between her thighs to where she's bare and warm and a little wet.

She nods, emitting another sweet sound that causes my cock to swell painfully against her. I work my fingers deeper into her slick space, her thighs parting slightly for me. My thumb finds her clit and I press the pad down, rubbing in slow circles in the way I've learned she likes.

"Oh," she says, almost in surprise, and I reach back with my other hand, making a tight ring around my girth and pushing it in between her legs. She opens them wider for me and I press the head of my cock tentatively between her cheeks, enough to startle her and make her stiffen.

"Don't worry," I say, chuckling. "We can save that for another day."

She relaxes slightly and I drag the tip down until it finds her wet and warm and I grit my teeth as I push myself inside her. From this

REALM of THIEVES 275

angle, her back to me, lying on our sides, I can't help but hiss. "Fuck," I swear. "You're so fucking tight. Let me know if I'm hurting you."

But she only pushes her hips back against mine, driving me in deeper. We both gasp at the same time, as if our lungs are forcing the air out before we become each other's oxygen. That raw connection from the throes of last night, unwavering, open and shared, is back, tethering us together.

My eyes fall shut and I lose myself to her, rocking into her body, my hand at her breast, rolling her nipple between my fingers, my other stroking her clit. I bite her shoulder, I pinch at her until she gives that wanton cry of pleasure-pain. I groan into her ear, asking if I feel good, if she feels good, telling her she's an elixir, stronger and sweeter than any magic. I give myself to her, in the hurried pumps of my hips, the sweat breaking between my chest and her back, the smell of sex in the room.

She comes, squeezing and pulsing around me, while her head arches back, a throaty, wild cry falling from her lips. I reach up and make a fist at the top of her head, pulling her head back farther, and then while she's bucking against me, the tension inside me comes to a crescendo. My balls rise up until heat explodes from the center of me and I'm unleashing myself, coming hard inside her.

"Fuck, fuck, fuck," I bite out through a low groan, the bed shaking beneath us as I slam myself deeper and deeper into her, as if I can be embedded inside her if I try hard enough.

By the time I'm finished—spent, my body limp against hers, our chests aching for breath—I feel like I'm in too deep with her in every which way.

I slowly pull out and she gives me a satisfied smile before she adjusts her head on the pillow again and lets out a deep, contented sigh.

"I'll be right back," I whisper to her, kissing the top of her head, taking a second to revel in her honey scent before I climb out of bed.

276   KARINA HALLE

I drape the sheets over her, a show of modesty that seems to amuse her, and then pull on my pants. I open the door slowly, quietly, looking up and down the hallway. It feels completely still this hour of the morning, not a sound to be heard.

I walk across the hall to the bathroom. When I've done my business and freshened up, I step back in the hall.

And right into my uncle.

"Shit," I swear, backing up. "You scared me."

My uncle's face twists venomously. That look of hatred mixed with self-satisfaction, like he's ensnared me. I immediately feel uneasy.

"Spent the night with the prisoner, did we?" he says with a sneer.

"Jealous?" I counter. Probably the wrong thing to say.

He comes at me fast and I duck just in time, spinning around as he tries to grab me, bludgeoning the wall with his shoulder. A painting down the hall crashes to the floor.

"You're jeopardizing your relationship with the princess!" he yells.

I eye the door to Brynla's room and want to tell him to shut the fuck up, because she doesn't need to hear any of this, but that will only provoke him. If I say anything at all he'll probably open the door and drag her out of bed, and if he dared to lay a hand on her there's no telling what I would do.

"What's going on?" My father's voice comes from down the hall.

Fuck.

I look over at him as my father slowly approaches, still in his plush morning robe, a cup of coffee in hand.

"Nothing, Father," I tell him, straightening up. "Just having a discussion with your brother."

"I caught him sneaking out of the bitch's room," my uncle says, jerking his thumb toward Brynla's door. He can barely put his thumb away before I'm at him, hand around his throat and pressing him back against the wall.

"Andor!" my father hisses, but I barely hear him. All I can think about is staring into my uncle's beady eyes as I squeeze the life out of him.

"Call her that one more time and it will be the last garbage to come from your mealy little mouth," I growl at him as he sputters under my grasp.

"Andor!" my father says, and he lunges for me. With a burst of strength he rarely displays, he grabs my arms and yanks me away from my uncle. "What in the goddesses has gotten into you?"

"She's polluting his mind with her Eslander ways," my uncle says, rubbing his throat and coughing with watering eyes.

"Is this true?" my father says, his expression surprised and ashamed. "After all we talked about?"

He expects me to look at the floor and apologize, as I have often done. But I refuse to cower this time.

"After all *you* talked about," I say to him, raising my chin. "This has never been my idea. None of this has ever been my idea."

I walk off down the hall, wanting to lead them away from Brynla. I'm sure she's already awake, already heard our fighting, but I don't want things to get worse.

My uncle and father hesitate and I'm terrified that they'll go into Brynla's room instead. But then I hear their footsteps follow me, echoing down the hall. I take the moment of relief to try to bolster myself against whatever they're about to throw at me. One would think that he would have interrogated me about what happened in the Midlands, but aside from small talk at the dinner table, inquiring about the suen I harvested, he hasn't asked me much. I expected him to call me into his office at some point and grill me about Brynla's performance, but that never happened either.

However, there's no time like the present.

I go straight to my father's office and lean back near the window, arms folded across my bare chest as I wait for them to step into the room. My father barges in and gestures wildly for me to sit down as

278   KARINA HALLE

he makes his way around his desk, but I shake my head. My uncle takes the spot instead.

"I'm calling a meeting," I say before they can get a word in first.

It angers my father like I knew it would, his nostrils flaring.

"Meeting?" my father practically spits. "There is no meeting! Tell me what you're—"

"I have no intention of marrying the princess," I say, raising my chin.

"I told you!" my uncle says to my father. "I told you that woman has gotten under his skin."

"She has," I say quickly. "She's gotten very much under my skin. And sure, it certainly complicates your plans for Princess Frida. But that's not all of it. That's not the only reason why I won't do it."

My father gets out of his chair and storms over to me, stepping just a foot away, close enough to jab his finger at my chest. "You can't betray me, Andor. You made a promise."

"*You* made a promise," I counter. "One I can't keep." I take in a deep breath and yet I'm shaking inside for finally saying no. "One that I won't keep."

"You are marrying Princess Frida!" He's practically spitting at me with rage, his eyes blazing, and for the first time I see the fear inside him. It's like I'm viewing my father from outside the room, a stranger peering through the window, and it's clear as day that this news, this *betrayal* at my behest, is terrifying him. He's truly afraid of losing Altus Dugrell, which makes me think everything is a lot more dire than he's ever let on.

"This is your one and only duty in your life, Andor," my father says through grinding teeth. "Don't you dare think you have agency. Don't you dare think you can fuck this up for me, for your family."

"I'm not fucking up anything," I say. I ignore the derisive snort that my uncle lets out. "Not this time. I have something we can offer the royal family that's even greater than my hand in marriage."

REALM of THIEVES 279

"You have nothing, nephew," my uncle says with a tired sigh. "Nothing to offer at all. Even your gifts, well, they never amounted to much, did they?"

I could fucking *kill* him. For the second time this morning I wonder how much trouble I'd get in for murdering my uncle. Death sentence? Or a prison I could one day escape from? Maybe the latter could be worth it.

My father gives him an icy look, but that's as far as he'll go to reprimand him. I know he often thinks the same thing, about how I'd fallen so short when it counted.

He faces me and frowns. "What in dragon's fire could we offer them if not you?"

"I wasn't aware you thought so highly of me," I say bitterly.

"Don't let it go to your head. You know your betrothal to the princess has been in the works for a long time. That is your contribution to the family."

"But what if I could contribute more? What if you could contribute more, to ensure the kingdom is united? What if this family not only strengthened the realm but strengthened us against Dalgaard and everyone else out there who wants a piece of the pie?"

My father blinks at me, slowly shaking his head as if he can't believe he's still talking to me. "Out with it, then."

"We steal the egg of immortality," I say simply.

His blinking continues.

My uncle laughs. "Ridiculous. The thing doesn't exist."

"So people say," I tell them. "But I have it on good authority that it does exist and there's one being kept at the convent of the Daughters of Silence."

"Is that right?" my father says, brow raised as he walks back to his desk. "And whose good opinion is that? The purple-haired girl?"

I shake my head. "No. Her aunt."

"The one you left to die?" my father says.

For fuck's sake. I grind my teeth together, hating that he knows exactly how to get to me. "I didn't leave her to die. She was already dead. And both Brynla and I would be dead too if I hadn't acted fast."

"So her aunt is the one who says this egg exists?" he asks. "And what does Brynla say?"

I gnaw on my lip for a moment, trying to ignore the growing shame. "Brynla doesn't know," I say carefully. "The aunt told me in confidence. She was quite certain the egg exists, that it's being held there, and that it's possible for Brynla to steal it, given her inside knowledge of the convent."

"Quite certain isn't good enough."

"Well, it fucking should be," I say. "When it comes to suen with the power to make you immortal, to have you live forever, then it should be. Just listen to yourself. You're waving this off when you should be jumping at this opportunity. Send us to Esland and we'll bring it back. If we don't . . ."

"If you don't, it will be because it doesn't exist," he says stiffly. "You need to stick to what you're good at. What about getting the fertilized dragon eggs? You know that Steiner thinks we could have some success breeding our own dragons here."

I shake my head. "Steiner doesn't think that, you do. He has his doubts."

"We won't know unless he tries."

"Well, either way, we're getting the egg of immortality. The dragon breeding experiment can come later."

"And if you go to Esland you'll only end up caught and imprisoned by the Black Guard."

"And if you think we're going to pull strings to have you pulled out, you have another think coming," my uncle adds.

"Fine," I say. "Though I'm sure you'll do it for Vidar."

My father's frame tenses. "What about Vidar?"

REALM of THIEVES

"He's coming with me," I tell him. "Along with our best men. It's a heist, Father, one that he was adamant about joining."

"No," he says with a violent shake of his head. "I will not risk my heir."

"But you will risk me?"

He clamps his mouth together for a moment, that fear still present in his eyes. "Vidar is the heir."

"And I'm disposable. Got it."

"You are being purposefully obtuse."

"I'm just calling it as it is," I say. "And it doesn't matter, because Vidar is coming with me. But just remember whose idea it was when we come back with the egg of immortality in hand. Remember who orchestrated the whole thing when you realize you'll never die. Remember this conversation when Altus Dugrell and Norland are bound together, bolstered by a large, undying army."

For once both my father and uncle grow silent.

For once they seem to hear me.

And for the first time, I realize the weight of what I just said.

Immortality for us all.

And an army that cannot die.

"Very well," my father eventually says, clearing his throat as he exchanges a nod with his brother. "But I need you to promise me something, Andor."

I know better than to promise anything before I've heard what it is. I raise my brow in response.

"Once you get the egg—if you do—you are to be done with the purple-haired girl. I want her disposed of."

I had a feeling it would come to this.

I open my mouth to protest, to tell him I'm not promising him that of all things, but he goes on quickly. "By being with her, you have disrespected the princess of Altus Dugrell, the girl you were supposed to marry. I should toss the Eslander and her damned dog out of

Stormglen right now," he says. "The only reason I won't throw her to the wolves is because you need her for your little heist. But when that need is over, Andor, whether you've had your fill of her or not, I won't let her step foot on our lands. If you plan to come back with her, then you won't be welcome either. Perhaps you should make it easier on yourself and conveniently leave her with the Black Guard in Esland. You'll need a scapegoat, after all."

The pulse in my throat pounds as I narrow my eyes at my father. "You know I can't promise that," I say, my voice going low.

The corner of his mouth lifts, liking this challenge. "Perhaps not." He pauses. "But then I'll just find someone who will."

Chapter 27

BRYNLA

I'M HALF-ASLEEP WHEN A SHOUTING MATCH MAKES ME JOLT. When the walls shake, as if someone is being thrown around in the hall outside my room, I leap out of bed, tangled in the sheets. Lemi comes in from the balcony and lets out a low growl, but I quickly motion for him to be quiet as I scurry toward the door. I rest my ear against it, wishing I could lock it without someone noticing from the other side.

I hear Andor's voice.

Then his uncle's.

Something about . . .

A princess?

He's jeopardizing his relationship with the princess?

I swallow hard, a sinking feeling in my stomach, almost afraid to keep listening. But I have to.

I hear his father's voice now, yelling at Andor.

Lemi lets out another growl, coming toward the door.

I motion for him to be quiet again, straining to hear the rest of the conversation. They're arguing about something . . . me, I think. Then there's another thud against the wall, enough that I leap back from the door, terrified that they're going to come in here. I look around the room for my swords but they're nowhere in sight. The room is a mess since I've done nothing but cry and stay in bed since we got off the ship. I can't even remember the last time I saw my weapons.

I rub my hands over my face, panic surging through me as I struggle to think, to feel even remotely competent. I can't stay in a stupor of grief like this forever, as tempting as it is to drown in it. I'm still in the Kolbecks' keep, and though I have Andor on my side, this is a hostile place and I need to keep my eyes open and my defenses up.

I hear someone, maybe his uncle, grumble something, and then footsteps fading away.

I rest my head against the door, willing my heart to calm down and waiting a full minute before I dare open it and glance outside.

The knob turns with a loud click that makes me wince, but when I poke my head out, the hallway is empty. The only sign anyone was here is a painting on the floor, having been knocked off the wall.

I know I should close the door and go back to bed. Forget the whole thing.

But I can't. Because his uncle had mentioned Andor's relationship with a princess and this is the first I've heard about this.

Could it be possible that he's had someone else this whole time? A princess, at that?

That sinking feeling grows deeper now, a gash inside me that makes me feel sick and weak. But I can't let my insecurities run away on me; I can't assume anything from only hearing a snippet of an argument.

Against my better judgment I slip on my nightgown plus a pair of slippers and head out into the hall. Lemi tries to follow but I motion for him to go back inside the room. I know he'll shift if I get into trouble, but I don't want him giving my whereabouts away, or getting protective before he should.

My dog gives me a wary look but resigns himself to sitting by the door as I gently close it and pad down the hall, listening for voices. I may not have hearing as good as someone with suen magic, but it's still pretty good. I think I hear them downstairs.

I hurry down the staircase, looking over my shoulder in case a servant or one of the siblings spots me, then head over to the door to Torsten's office. I place my cheek against the door like I did earlier.

"You are marrying Princess Frida!" Torsten bellows, so loud that I have to step away from the door.

Princess Frida? Who the fuck is Princess Frida? Could there be someone else in the room, Vidar maybe? That would make sense, that the heir would have to marry a princess. But not Andor.

Please, not Andor, I think hopelessly.

"This is your one and only duty in your life, Andor," his father grinds out, and the reveal is a dagger to the heart. "Don't you dare think you have agency. Don't you dare think you can fuck this up for me, for your family."

I feel like I'm bleeding out as I stand here, my hand at my stomach.

"I'm not fucking up anything," I hear Andor finally reply.

Oh gods.

"Brynla?"

I jump and whirl around to see Steiner standing at the end of the hall, his cat perched on his shoulder.

Damn it. Just caught snooping.

But Steiner doesn't approach me, nor does he say anything else. He just walks away, heading in the direction of his lab.

I stare at the office door, knowing it's only a matter of time before they discover I'm eavesdropping. Now I have to make sure Steiner doesn't say anything.

I decide to hurry down the hall after him now, moving as quickly and quietly as possible past the dining hall and the kitchen, coming into his lab just as he's about to close the door.

"Wait," I say, wedging my shoulder in. "I need to talk to you."

"I assume it's about whatever you were just spying on my father for," he says, but he steps back from the door and lets me in.

His cat hisses at me and then jumps off his shoulder, running down the shelves that surround the room. "Don't mind Woo-woo; he can smell Lemi on you."

"I can explain what just happened," I say to him, trying to catch my breath.

"Can you explain why you're in just your nightshift?" he asks idly, glancing briefly at my chest. "You must be cold because your nipples are showing."

I gasp, quickly folding my arms over my chest, my cheeks flaming at how casually direct Steiner is. "I overheard a fight outside my room," I tell him. "I was curious to hear what it was about."

He tilts his head. "And what was it about? I assume you thought it was your business?"

I give a half shrug, weighing that. "Well, more that it involved Andor . . ."

"And Andor is your business?"

I swallow. "I want him to be," I admit.

Steiner gives me a tiny smile just as the door opens and Solla pokes her head into the room. Her eyes go round when she sees me.

"Sorry. I didn't expect you to be here. Do you need privacy?" she asks, noticing the way I'm dressed.

"No," Steiner answers. "I just caught Brynla eavesdropping outside our father's office."

Ah, shit. Thanks a lot, I think.

But Solla only looks curious. "Oh really?" she asks brightly, closing the door behind her as she comes into the room. "Why? What were they talking about?"

"Andor," Steiner says.

"What about him?" Solla asks.

REALM of THIEVES 287

"We didn't get that far," Steiner says.

I sigh. "I heard them arguing outside my door. I heard them mention something about a princess and so I had to learn more."

Steiner and Solla exchange a wary glance.

"So you know, then," I say slowly, my heart feeling crushed. "Who is she? Who is Princess Frida?"

"The woman Andor is going to marry," Steiner says.

"Steiner," Solla chides him. She gestures to me with her eyes. "You don't have to be so blunt," she says under her breath. She turns and gives me an apologetic smile. "I'm sorry. I thought maybe Andor would have filled you in."

I give my head a rough shake, as if I can shake this all away. "He never told me about her."

"Because he doesn't want to marry her," she says. "Just as Vidar doesn't want to marry whoever it is he'll have to marry. There are things expected of us as Kolbecks. Even I will have to marry someone else and not the person I want."

"Heda?" Steiner says to his sister in surprise. "You would marry her?"

"If I could," Solla says.

Ah. Solla is in love with another woman?

"Are you not allowed to marry the same gender here?" I ask. Back in Esland it's common for people to marry whoever they feel like, regardless of gender or sexuality. Even polyamorous marriages are legal in the Banished Land.

"It's allowed . . ." she says carefully. "But not really accepted. Not yet. There is more tolerance in Altus Dugrell. In Vesland it's legal. Here it's a gray area."

"But it doesn't really matter since Solla is bound by our father to do as she's told or be rejected from the family," Steiner says. He sighs, looking completely despondent. "I'm sure I'll be handed off to some strange woman, too."

"This isn't about us, though," Solla quickly says, turning her attention back to me. "It's about you and Andor. I can guarantee Andor doesn't want to marry Frida. He's been scheming to get out of it since the day my father promised him to the royals of Altus Dugrell. It's a way to create unity between the lands. A bridge of sorts. We need the countries to be united as one, especially these days. If he marries her, then the royals can't turn against each other."

"So if he doesn't marry her, then he's making things worse for the lands," I say, hating that I even have to say those words.

"It's a sacrifice," Steiner says. "One that none of us are happy about, especially not Andor."

And yet he didn't say a thing. This whole time I've been sleeping with him, fighting with him, risking my life alongside him, falling for him, and he's been betrothed to someone else?

I feel flattened. Reduced. Into nothing. Like we now have nothing between us when it started to feel like we had everything.

And that's when I really feel the weight in my stomach.

I'd begun to think about Andor as if he was always going to be around. As if what we were doing together, this relationship or whatever it is, was not only just getting started but that it was leading somewhere. Maybe not here in the Stormglen, but somewhere else, together. I had hope for us, more than I let my silly brain know, that we were going in the same direction.

But he was heading in another direction all along.

"He's coming," Solla suddenly says, a strange white flash coming over her eyes.

"Who is?" I manage to ask.

"Andor. He's in the hall, heading here," she says. I suppose she has some kind of precognition along with her telekinesis. She nods at Steiner. "We should go, give them privacy."

"It's my lab," Steiner protests.

"And she's probably going to murder Andor for keeping the princess a secret," she says. "Do you want that to happen in the hall where everyone can see?"

He gives her a begrudging nod just as the door to the lab opens.

"Steiner, we need to talk about those fertilized dragon eggs," Andor says as he steps in. He comes to a halt when he sees me. "What's going on? Brynla, are you all right?"

He strides over to me while Solla and Steiner quickly exit the lab, shutting us inside, and Andor puts his hands on my shoulders. "Why are you out of bed? What happened?" His eyes search mine, completely oblivious.

For a moment I can barely speak. The hurt is too much; my emotions have already been at such a high level that I'm having a hard time pulling myself together.

Finally I say, "I overheard you and your father arguing."

His expression falls slightly. He knows what I'm about to say.

"I heard what was said about the princess," I go on. "About the woman you're going to marry. The woman that . . . isn't me." It pains me even more to say that last bit, to even admit that I think it should be me.

Fuck, how did I fall for this man so hard and so fast?

"Brynla," he says, his grip tightening on my shoulders. "I'm not marrying her."

"I heard your father. That this is your one and only duty. I heard your uncle tell you that you're jeopardizing your relationship with her. Relationship, Andor. You never even told me . . ."

I look away, the anger I felt earlier turning into something more pliable, into a hurt that sinks in deep and makes my chest feel hollow.

"I'm not marrying her," he says again. "Yes, I was promised to her but it was a promise I never made. I never agreed to it. It was decided for me by my father, by my uncle, and by the king of Norland. I've never had any intention in following through."

"And yet they still think you did."

"Because they don't know how to take no for an answer."

A coal of anger begins to simmer inside. "You never told me. At any point that we've known each other, you could have told me. You could have said you were betrothed to someone else. Instead you kept it a secret."

"Which I know was wrong of me," he says imploringly. "But you have to believe me when I say that I didn't spend any time thinking about the betrothal. Not even a little. The idea of their stupid bargain disappeared the moment I laid eyes on you."

I want to believe him. I think I believe him. But it doesn't stop me from feeling betrayed, from feeling sick that this was going on, something huge that was kept from me. Even if Andor had forgotten, his family sure hadn't. His father sounded livid. They certainly believed that Andor will follow through, or they did until today.

And all this time I really was just a pawn for their syndikat, a toy to be used and tossed away while he marries into royalty. How could I have thought anything else? As he told me last night, his life has been one of privilege and mine has been of pain. He's part of one of the most powerful and prestigious families in Norland, if not the world, and I am a poor Eslander who's been scraping by for most of her life.

"Brynla," he says again, his hands cupping my face now, his palms warm. He stares deeply into my eyes, forcing me to look into their amber depths, to take in his sincerity. "I care about you. A great deal. More than I've ever cared about anyone. And that might not seem like much coming from someone like me, but believe me . . . I didn't think I had it in me. I didn't think I could . . ."

He trails off, licking his lips. "Please, just know that this whole marriage isn't happening. I don't want it, and I'm pretty sure the princess doesn't want it either. It's just a thing our families do here, but today I made it clear that I won't be a part of it. No matter what. Didn't you hear that part of the conversation?"

REALM of THIEVES

I shake my head, though his hands still grip me in place. "I left."

He nods, taking that in. Then he kisses me, hard and quick, enough to put my emotions back into a spin.

He breaks away and rests his forehead against mine. "They know where I stand," he says. "But I don't think you do."

I stare at his lips, feeling too many things bubbling up inside me. Grief, fear, desire, comfort, need—and hope. It always comes down to hope with him.

"So tell me," I whisper, knowing I'm putting my heart on the line by asking for it. "Tell me where you stand."

He takes in a deep breath and runs his thumb over my lips. "I stand where you stand. And you stand at the forefront of my life. Everything else falls to the wayside. Every thought, every feeling, it revolves around you, like you've embedded yourself under my skin, deep enough that I couldn't get you out even if I tried. And it has been killing me this last week that I can't reach you, can't push away your pain, can't make it all go away, make it better. I know it's selfish of me to think like that, but it's true."

"I know," I say softly. "I'm sorry that—"

"No. You have nothing to be sorry for. Never with me. You are grieving and I will continue to do what I can to make you feel that you're not alone. I just wish . . . I just want . . ."

"What?"

"What I really want more than anything is to matter to you. To be something to you, to be *everything* to you." He pauses, swallowing hard. "I want to be your better tomorrow."

My eyes fall closed, my heart tumbling in my chest at his words.

"I want that too," I whisper.

Which is why this whole thing has caught me off guard. Hope can be such a dangerous thing when it's all you have left.

"Then let me," he says, running his hands through my hair. "Let me be your better tomorrow. Let me be whatever it is that you need me to be. Please."

I find myself nodding. I should be making him grovel for keeping secrets, but I'm so emotionally wiped that I can't seem to find the strength to keep being angry.

"There are no other secrets you're hiding from me?" I ask. "No secret children you have somewhere?"

He laughs. "Goddesses, no." Then he pauses and looks me over. "We need to get you something warm to wear."

"I'm fine," I say.

"Not where I'm taking you," he says. "Stay here."

He lets go of me and walks to the door, shutting it behind him. I have no idea what he's talking about or where he's taking me, but when he returns he's got my pants, boots, socks, and a large heavy coat in his arms.

"Put these on," he says.

"Why? I'm not that cold." I take the pants and pull them on, then kick off my slippers and put on the socks, which are made of thick wool and a little too big. I have to hike them up to my knees.

"Those are mine," Andor says. "Don't worry, freshly laundered."

I slip on my boots next while he puts the coat on me, and then he grabs my hand and leads me out the back door of Steiner's lab, into the garden.

"Where are you taking me?" I ask, but he doesn't say anything. The morning air is warm, though the breeze carries a hint of crispness, as if hinting at a change in seasons, but the coat is already too warm.

"You'll see," he says as we walk through the rows of plants and greenhouses, then through the chicken yard, where the birds scatter in all directions. When we get to the cook's vegetable garden at the end of the east wing, vines growing up the dark stone sides of the castle, Steiner suddenly appears holding on to the reins of a very large

REALM of THIEVES 293

black horse with a long flowing mane and tail. Probably the biggest horse I've ever seen and standing with such poise, it immediately reminds me of the ones bred for the Black Guard of Esland.

"We're going riding?" I ask, surprised.

"Hope you're all right with sharing a horse," Andor says as we step over the low veggie garden fence. "Unless you know how to ride."

"I've never ridden one before," I admit. "We had a donkey when I was young, but he was too ornery to mount."

"I bet you still tried, though," he says with a smile.

"Of course. I spent the whole first month we had that donkey getting bucked off into the sand. Finally, he took a big chunk out of my arm and my father pulled me aside to tell me it was one challenge I should probably let go."

"That doesn't surprise me," he comments as he takes the reins from Steiner. "Thanks," he says to him. "I doubt Father will notice I'm missing, but if he does just tell him I went to check the fences or something."

"Are you checking the fences?" Steiner asks.

Andor gives him a steady look. "You can lie, just this once."

Steiner sighs and then steps into the cook's garden and back to his lab.

"What fences?" I ask Andor as he softly strokes the horse's muzzle.

"Whenever I need to clear my head I say I'm checking the fences. We have some fields to the south where we let the cows loose in the summer months. I rarely make my way down there; I just want a chance to be alone."

"So we're not going to check the fences?" To be honest, that sounds thrilling enough. Not only have I never been on horseback, but the idea of roaming the fields among the cows seems like something out of a dream.

"We're going somewhere much better," he says. "My way of making things up to you. Now come, I'll hoist you into the saddle. Don't worry about Onyx, he can take our weight. He was raised to be a battle horse, though it's been a while since we saw war. He's certainly never seen it."

He leans over and puts his hands down and together like a step. Gingerly I place my boot on them and he hoists me up. I scramble, grabbing the horse's generous mane while trying to gracelessly flip my legs over his back and sit upright in the saddle, feeling chagrined that I'm not automatically a natural at riding.

"There you go," Andor says. "Wrap the reins around your three middle fingers and weave them between your thumb and pinky." I do so, holding the soft leather in each hand while he somehow swings himself up behind me, as effortlessly as if he were sliding into bed.

"Show-off," I comment under my breath. Then I gasp as he moves so that I'm pushed up by his thighs and I'm practically in his lap.

The horse begins to shift to the side and Andor puts his arms around me to keep my balance, curling his fingers over mine as he holds the reins too. "Comfortable?" he asks. "It's a long ride."

I nod. "You're still not going to tell me where we're going?"

"You wouldn't know anyway. Just trust me. Let me do all the work."

I can't help but smirk at that. He definitely did all the work this morning and last night.

He clucks his tongue and Onyx starts to walk forward. We're only a few strides away from the front of the castle when suddenly Lemi shifts beside us.

The horse rears and I cry out, Andor leaning forward to keep me bracketed in between the horse's neck and himself until we're level.

"At least you stayed on that time," Andor remarks.

Lemi wags his tail, somehow knowing I was about to embark somewhere without him, and seems to treat the horse like a large dog, sniffing at the horse's fetlocks as Onyx moves sideways.

"Lemi," I scold him. "You're being too forward."

Lemi's ears twitch as he eyes me and then the horse before he sits down next to us, waiting patiently.

"All right, let's go," Andor says, and the horse starts at a brisk walk, Lemi trotting beside us, as we head away from Stormglen.

Chapter 28

Brynla

I'm not sure how long we've been riding for, hours maybe, but I've enjoyed every single second of it. With each breath I'm relishing the fresh scent of the pine trees that line our path, mingling with the cold creek that runs by our side, the air that tastes damp and sweet and wonderful. I'm savoring the journey like I would a fine wine, aware that everything is so fleeting and that I might not get to experience this again. Even Lemi is running around with his muzzle raised high in the air, seeking out his own adventures, tail wagging happily. I have no idea where we're going but at this point it doesn't matter. It's just somewhere. Somewhere beautiful, somewhere new, and I'm with Andor.

We climb higher and higher into the mountains, the path snaking around towering trees that seem to stretch into the sky, along meadows filled with moss and tiny pink flowers, leading us through the occasional stream that Onyx plods through, fish darting away from our shadow.

After a while I start to feel the chill on my cheeks and neck. With Andor holding me so tightly from behind, I'm still warm, his body and the coat doing a good job of protecting me, while clouds start to gather above the treetops, obscuring the sun and the sharp mountain peaks.

I can't help but think about my aunt, and it hurts. The grief cuts too deeply to feel any other way.

I think about what it would have been like if I had pulled her out of the Dark City and put her in Norland like I was trying to do. I'm finding the change in climate to be a marvel, a novelty to relish, but would my aunt have truly enjoyed this? I projected my unhappiness onto her: how stifled I felt, how stagnant I was, how utterly unsatisfied with my life. I wanted to leave to become someone, but Ellestra was probably happy being the someone that she was, staying in her home, drinking her tea. She had a community there, a home, a couple of close friends. I tried to take that from her.

I did take that from her. Along with her life.

"Hey," Andor says in my ear, his breath hot. "I've got you."

He holds me tighter and my body relaxes into him, and the tightness in my chest, the way my heart is perpetually squeezed, loosens. Just enough to let me feel a moment of relief from the heavy spiral of my thoughts. Somehow he knows what I'm thinking and feeling, making sure I know he's there. As if he wants to shoulder the burden so I don't have to.

Because grief does feel like a burden, but one that you're scared to no longer carry. You're afraid that if you hand it off to someone for a second, if you forget even if for a brief instant that you've lost someone and that your heart has splintered into pieces, it will hit you harder when you do remember. It's like that blissful moment when you first wake up and your brain is a clean slate and all is well with the world, before the cold, deadly knife of reality cuts you to the bone.

So I lean back into the strength of Andor's body and his heart and take the leap. I will myself to stop focusing on the pain and the guilt and start being more present in what's happening now. I know it will hurt when the grief comes back, because it will always come back, for the rest of my life, but I know I still need to just . . . live.

I breathe in the fresh, bracing air, colder now, and Onyx walks through a stand of sparse trees until we reach a cavernous hole in the mountain face.

"Are we going through that?" I ask, my heart picking up the pace. Everything had been so nice and uneventful so far.

"We are," Andor says, kissing the back of my head. "But it's worth it."

One would think that I would be used to going through caves and tunnels, but here where the mountainside rises up so sharply, the darkness seems extra suffocating when I don't know where we are and where we are going.

I suck in my breath as Onyx enters the tunnel, the air damp, the hoofbeats sounding dull. I sniff at a peculiar smell that seems familiar but I can't quite place.

"That's the glowferns," Andor says. "Our version of your slugs, except they don't fall on you and they taste like aniseed if you cook them up. Just wait for your eyes to adjust."

For a moment I have no idea what he's talking about as we plod along in the darkness, the aniseed smell getting stronger, but then I start to see tiny pinpricks of blue-green light that begin to glow brighter, like stars in an ink-black sky.

"What?" I whisper, looking all around. The glowing dots shine, making Onyx's and Lemi's coats shine blue in their glimmering light. "What is this?"

"Those are the glowferns," Andor chuckles. "Small plants that grow in dark places here, especially up in this area."

"It's . . . magical," I say in awe. It's like moving through the night sky. "I can see why you wanted to bring me here," I add quietly, feeling as if I should keep my voice down or I'll disturb the plants.

"This isn't the only reason. See that light at the end of the tunnel?"

REALM of THIEVES 299

I look over Onyx's head and see a small white spot at the end of the darkness, getting larger and larger as we move toward it. It's also getting brighter, not from the sun, but as if the white is expanding until the glowferns fade away and the walls of the cave recede.

I put a hand in front of my face and wince at the harsh light, just as the coldest wind I've ever felt hits us like a hurricane. I close my eyes to the sting of it, Andor wrapping his arms around me tightly. "You'll get used to the cold," he whispers in my ear. "Take your time and open your eyes."

Onyx walks for a few more feet, a strange yet familiar shuffling sound coming from his movement that reminds me a little of a camel in the desert, then comes to a stop, snorting loudly.

Lemi barks and I hear the galumphing of his run.

I pry my eyes open.

Like before, I can barely see, having to squint through my eyelashes at the glare.

Then my eyes start to get used to it.

And I realize that white is everywhere around us, blanketing the ground beneath us in waves of ivory, glittering like tiny gemstones, frosting the boughs of the tallest trees, and falling in flakes onto my arms and nose and hair.

"Is this . . . is this . . . ?" I can't even form the words properly, watching as Lemi's black form speeds through it, white fluff kicked up in his wake and clearly having the time of his life. I look down at my own hand as a flake lands on it, a cold kiss that takes a few moments before it melts away, leaving a faint trace of glitter.

"Snow," Andor says. "I know how excited you were to see rain. I thought perhaps this might be the first time you've ever seen snow."

"It is," I say, my breath making a frosted cloud in the air. I'm cold but it seems worth it to experience this. Everywhere I look, snow covers the land, from where we stand at the mountainside, across the tall trees that flank a wide expanse that undulates gently to the shore of a bright blue lake that has steam rising from it and the tall icy mountains on the other side. All of it shimmers like crushed crystals.

"I didn't think snow was so glimmering, though," I say, looking at where the melted snow has left shiny patches on my hands and in Onyx's mane.

"It's normally not," Andor explains. "Lake Efst has always had an unusual weather system. It snows here year-round, even in the middle of summer. But you'll notice the lake is not frozen over. There are volcanic vents at the bottom, deep, deep down, that keep the lake comfortably warm at all times, and those vents shoot out crushed firestones into the water. The material floats to the surface and from there the wind seems to pick it up, take it into the clouds, and there you go. Comes down as glittery snow."

I can't help but laugh. "Figures you wouldn't show me normal snow."

"Only the best for you. Now, I'm curious. How well do you think you'd do in a snowball fight?"

I glance at him over my shoulder. The snow gathered in his black hair makes it look like it's adorned with rhinestones, a delightful contrast to his scruffy beard. "Considering I've never had a snowball fight before . . . I'll probably beat you."

He grins, all cocky, boyish charm, and pushes himself back until he's sliding off the rump of the horse. He's then at my side, arms out to help me dismount from Onyx. Thankfully I do that a little more gracefully than I did trying to mount him.

Lemi comes galloping over to me, tail wagging, and Andor quickly scoops up snow in his palm, rounding it into a ball before throwing it. Lemi barks and runs after the ball even though it sinks into the snow and disappears.

I waste no time and do what Andor did, the snow ice-cold against my skin. It's a little grittier than I thought it would be, making it easier to quickly form into a ball. Before Andor even has a chance to face me, I ping the ball at the back of his head—hard. It explodes and he gives a playful yelp as he whirls around.

"Does that count as a point?" I say. Then before he can come at me I duck under Onyx's neck and start running for the nearest rock that's jutting out of the snow, trying to take shelter behind it.

"You're dead," he says, staying behind Onyx and using him as a shield. His horse is patient, letting Andor crouch down and scoop up snowballs, not even flinching when I lob my own icy projectiles at him, even when my aim is off and they accidentally hit the horse, leaving pops of glitter like shooting stars.

"You're not playing fair!" I yell at him, ducking just in time as his snowball blasts the side of the rock, showering icy pellets over me. "Using your horse as a hostage!"

"How would you know what's fair? You haven't played this game before!" he shouts, and I pelt him with another ball. This time it soars over Onyx's back and I know it hits Andor right on the head.

We keep at this for a while until finally I've had enough. I take the risk and suddenly stand up, exposing myself to Andor's assault as I start waving my arms at Onyx. "Go on, get!" I yell.

Onyx's ears flicker back and forth for a moment; he doesn't seem too threatened by me, until Lemi suddenly shifts right beside him, letting out a loud bark.

Onyx rears and takes off at a trot, heading right down to the lake.

"That's our ride back!" Andor yells, wildly gesturing to the runaway.

But it doesn't matter because now I've got him.

I start lobbing as many snowballs as possible at him while he tries to do the same, staggering through the snow toward me. I get him square in the face more than once and by the time he's at the rock, his face is caked in shimmering white.

"Yield!" I yell at him.

"Never!"

Before I can move out of the way he leaps over the rock like a jack-rabbit and tackles me to the ground, snow flying everywhere. I screech, laughing as he puts his body over mine, pressing me into the cold. "I will never yield," he says, running his cold fingertips over my face. "Unless you beg me for mercy."

I'm about to tell him off but he kisses me instead. I should be freezing, should be trying to playfully fight him off, we should probably make sure Onyx isn't running away, but I can't help but feel the heat spreading through me. How is it that he's the one making *me* yield?

"This also isn't fair," I say as he pulls back, his golden eyes still gazing into mine. "You have me under some strange spell half the time."

"I can't help it if I'm charming," he says, brushing my hair off my face. Then his brows lower, his expression growing serious. "Though I wonder how far my charm extends. Is it enough to convince you to do anything?"

I frown. "What do you mean?"

He clears his throat. "How do you feel about partaking in a little revenge?"

Chapter 29

Brynla

A HEIST.

The moon has already waxed and waned since that time we lay in the glitter-snowed field by Lake Efst, and Andor asked if I would be willing to do a heist in order to exact revenge on the Daughters of Silence. We had just been joking about his charm, so I couldn't tell if he was serious or not, but the moment those words left his lips, the moment he said *revenge*, I knew I was already all in.

Of course I was furious with him, for the second time that day, for keeping yet another secret from me. He had clearly been thinking about this for some time, stealing the rumored egg of immortality—enough so that he talked to my aunt about it the morning of her death. But everything went to shit after that and he said he was waiting for the right time to fill me in.

That moment in the snow was a good a time as any. I think I managed to get out the majority of my anger at his betrayal through another onslaught of snowballs, even though I'm still a bit cranky about it.

Afterward we recovered Onyx and rode back through the tunnel and down the mountain to Stormglen, and we started discussing the heist in earnest. I wanted to stay mad at Andor, but the more he talked about the supposed egg of immortality—which is mind-blowing in itself—the more I focused my feelings on the idea of getting revenge on the convent and Esland as a whole. Even if the whole thing turns out to be a wild-goose chase, it at least makes me feel like vengeance is in my grasp for the first time in my life. Even if the egg isn't there, or it doesn't have any special powers, just fucking up the convent will be good enough for me.

By the time the evening rolled around—Andor and I conveniently skipped dinner to avoid his father and uncle—we had gathered in Steiner's lab with the rest of his siblings, tossing around ideas.

After that, the five of us would meet in Steiner's lab every evening to strategize. The following week we started going down to Menheimr, where we would involve the rest of the crew, the same men who joined us on our journey to the Banished Land.

I have to say, these last few weeks have saved my sanity. It's given me something to focus on, an action to take. Andor was worried I wouldn't want to go back to Esland; he thought I would think he was using me to get the precious egg. That hasn't been the case at all. I've thrown myself into the planning of this heist because without me, there is no heist. I'm the only one who has been to Esland, who has lived in Lerick, who knows how to deal with the Black Guards. I'm the only one who knows the convent inside and out, including where the egg would be kept.

None of this happens without me, which has made me crucial to every single meeting we've had, and in turn given me a sense of control.

But with the weeks of distraction, my grief has been shoved to the side. It's been buried, compartmentalized, something horrible and dark that hovers just beneath my surface like a hole in the ground. It's been waiting to swallow me alive.

REALM of THIEVES

And last night, as I lay in Andor's arms in my bed, the ground opened up.

I cried and screamed and thrashed as the pain and sorrow ripped through me. Every moment of grief that I tucked away was unleashed on me at once. I should have known better. I knew I couldn't escape it, I knew I had to make peace and look it in the eye every single day or it would try to destroy me.

Andor, bless his soul, held me. He simply held me when it felt like my body might shatter and I'd never be able to pick up all the pieces. He helped me stay intact and whole while the grief tried to eat me alive and spit me out.

Which is why he asked me this morning if I would have a session with Sae Balek, the Kolbecks' Truthmaster. To be honest, the idea scares me. I'd only seen the holy man a few times while I've been here, and he's always stared into me with those unseeing yet all-knowing eyes. I know that Torsten and Vidar have sessions with him several times a week, finding comfort or perhaps prophecy in the man's chapel, but I have wanted to stay far away from anyone who had anything to do with the Daughters of Silence and the Esland government at any point, even if his spiritual guidance is benign.

But Vidar promised that the Truthmaster was good at helping people move through grief instead of burying it, and while Andor wasn't a hundred percent sold on that idea, he did think the gold-eyed man could be an asset when it came to the heist. He might give us deeper info about the egg, about the details of the guard and government that I wouldn't know, and more than that, I might be granted a vision that could help us with our goal.

"Are you ready?" Vidar asks me as we stand in the hallway with Andor, just outside the chapel. The sweet, heady smell of incense is already permeating the air through the closed door.

"I guess?" I say. "I don't really know what to expect."

"Maybe that's a good thing," Andor says.

Truth is, I'm nervous. I would never admit that, especially not in front of Vidar, who has always been a bit of a grumpy enigma to me, enough so that I keep wanting his respect. Andor can tell, however, from the way he keeps reaching out for my hand and squeezing my fingers.

"It's a very good thing," Vidar says, briefly eyeing our hands before facing the door. "You need to keep your mind as open as possible."

"Andor," Torsten's stern voice says from down the hall.

I look to see him by Steiner's lab, beckoning for him to come over.

Andor sighs and straightens his shoulders before giving my hand another squeeze and walking off. He wasn't planning on being in the room with me and Vidar anyway—Sae Belak is adamant about it only being open to earnest believers—but even so I hate to see him go.

I catch Torsten's eye for a moment and he gives me the slightest nod. It's a lot more recognition than I've gotten over the last few weeks and I'll take it, only because his complete avoidance of me has been awkward to navigate. Like I'm a ghost in the room. Andor had told me that his father was somewhat impressed that I was going to see the Truthmaster, since it's something that only he and Vidar do and the rest of the family abstains. I thought maybe he would think I wasn't good enough for it, but that doesn't seem to be the case.

Perhaps yet another reason that Andor suggested I do this: to build up goodwill with his father.

Not that I care. I abhor his father, and his uncle even more so. But I can't live in a castle where the man in charge wants me dead and gone, especially when that man is my lover's father. I hate having to look over my shoulder every time I walk down the halls. It makes me feel so small when he addresses everyone at the dinner table except for me, and even though I have Andor's protection (as well as Lemi's, and my own skills), I know it weighs on Andor to have such strain between his father and me, even if it's all his father's doing.

REALM of THIEVES

So I nod back at his father. He holds my eye for a moment and there is no kindness in his stare. But it's enough for now.

A soft gong sounds from inside the room and I turn to face it just as the door opens, gray smoke wafting out. Sae Belak emerges as if he had been standing in front of us this whole time.

"I am so glad you finally accepted your truth," the Truthmaster says, pressing his fingertips together, not like prayer, however, since his long, skinny fingers remain bent. His eyes made of gold spheres stare right into me and I can feel myself being observed from the inside out. Can't say it's a good feeling. "Sometimes death makes us realize what we've always known. Come in."

He steps aside and gestures for us to come into the room, his long gray robe flowing from his arm like a sheet of water.

Vidar motions for me to go in first, gentlemanly in his manners, but I give him a subtle shake of my head. I don't care if he knows I'm scared now. He's going in first.

He gives me a reassuring look, which with him just means less of a frown, and steps into the smoke-filled room. I hesitate for a moment, comforted by the safety of the hallway, which is something I never thought I'd feel, before I square my shoulders and step inside.

"No need to hold your breath," Sae Belak says as he closes the door behind me. The smoke in here is thick; I can barely see Vidar's statuesque form, his dark clothes a moving shadow on the other side of the room near red velvet tapestries. "The smoke is what will help you. Breathe it in."

My jaw is set, my body fighting against the idea of inhaling smoke, until my lungs feel gripped with panic and I can't take it anymore.

I inhale, greedily, surprised to find the smoke to be cooling and fragrant, like I'm drinking water scented with various herbs and flowers.

"That's it," Sae Balek says as he walks across the room, his wavy red hair almost blending in with the tapestry. "Come, take a seat."

I watch as he sits down on one of three gold-tasseled cushions circled around a firepit, the source of the smoke. Except it's not quite a pit per se, but rather a large, wide dish made of gold, with a hunk of something waxy and brown in the middle where flames dance and flicker.

Two of the cushions are across from the Truthmaster, and Vidar takes a seat crosslegged on one of them, motioning with his chin for me to do the same.

I'm wearing a dress so I bundle it to the side, sitting on the pillow with my legs tucked under me. I'm a sorry attempt for a lady, but being here at Stormglen has instilled in me that I should at least try. "What is that?" I ask, staring at the burning brown stuff. "Incense?"

"A special resin that's collected from some of the trees in the area," Vidar says. "Steiner takes it and formulates it so it can burn for hours. It's a drug."

"And I'm just inhaling this drug?" I ask, suddenly feeling claustrophobic in the dim, smoky room.

"It does no harm but open your eyes," Sae Balek says. "It also takes a little while to work. Please relax, Lady Aihr. I can hear your heartbeat from here."

The fact that he can hear my galloping heart makes it worse, but I will myself to calm down. The last thing I want is to run out of the room because I can't handle a little mind-altering substance, though I suppose that would be very valid.

"Lady Aihr, please tell the goddesses why you are here," Sae Belak says, and he must see the consternation on my face because he quickly adds, "and if you have no such beliefs, then tell me and I will relay the message."

I take in a deep breath. The cool smoke fills my lungs and as it does so, it seems to clear my head, as if it's blowing away the cobwebs.

REALM of THIEVES 309

It strips away the lies, uncovers all I want to keep buried. I feel it pushing out the truth.

"I am . . . grieving," I say simply, though it isn't simple enough. I want to elaborate, but I can't. My chin starts to tremble, words becoming thick and choked in my throat.

"That much is visible for the whole world to see," Sae Balek says. "I am sorry about the passing of your aunt. I will not ply you with platitudes about her spirit and better worlds, because I know you are not here for that. You are only here to learn, as Vidar has, to move past your grief."

"But I don't want to move past it," I say, almost snarling, the anger inside me quick and vicious.

"You have the fear of forgetting," the Truthmaster says. "You are afraid that if you don't grieve, you will forget your aunt, your father, your mother."

I suppose there's no point in asking how he knew about them. "Grief is love," I tell him. "I don't want to not feel it, as painful as it is. My grief keeps them alive."

"It can keep them alive but at the cost of living," he says. "You need to find a balance or you won't have much of a life."

I go silent at that, pressing my lips together. I'm so terrified that if I don't keep my aunt in my thoughts, I'll lose my connection to her, just as I fear I've lost my connection to my mother and father.

"You are a vessel for all your untapped grief, and that is only fuel for rage, rage that will always burn out in the end, taking you into the ashes with it," Vidar says blankly.

I look at him in surprise. He hasn't said anything for some time, his cool eyes studying me from across the fire, gazing through the smoke.

"Very true, Vidar," Sae Balek says before he turns his metallic gaze back to me. "These sessions aren't for wiping the people from your life but for honoring them. It gives them space to exist still, while you can connect to them with time."

"I just . . ." I begin. "The last two weeks I've been busy, so busy that I haven't had time to grieve, and then it hit me all at once. I don't want that to keep happening; the blows, they're relentless, like they're trying to pummel me into submission."

"And that's why this here"—he gestures with his arms, his robe swinging and moving the smoke—"is a place for you to let it out. So that you may go on with your life and keep living like your family wants you to, knowing that you will pay respect to them and their energy and memory in a holy space, with the goddesses watching. You won't be alone, but it is wrong for us to grieve alone. We are social creatures at our base, and grieving with others sharing and making space for your pain is something that society has long forgotten. Perhaps all the wars and all the death have taken their toll on us, have made us forget what it is to share collective sorrow."

I stare at his face, his pale skin, his low brows, and the dark shadows under his eyes and cheeks, the wavy red hair that frames his face, and of course the eyes made from metal. I wonder who he is really and where he came from, what grief he may have encountered over the years, and how long ago he was born. The things he might have seen. The people he might have known.

"A good magician never reveals everything at once," he says in a low voice, giving me a lopsided smile. "In time, you will see things. You will know things. When you are ready to. For now, let's start with looking into the fire."

I look at the flames. Before they were small orange, red, and blue flickers that enveloped the chunk of resin. But now the flames are large and dancing. They move in unison, like each flame is its own entity and entirely sentient. I get the impression that they are moving for me, trying to show me something with each flicker.

I don't know how long I stare at them, my brain is feeling sticky, like it's been condensed into a mushy paste inside my head, and I'm thoroughly hypnotized by the fire.

And then I see it. The flames come together to form an image. Shapes at first, as if the shadows in the flames are attempting to look like something. Then it turns into something utterly, terribly real. I see color and texture and it's like looking through a portal into another world, another time.

I gasp. "I see . . . I see something. I really see something."

The others are silent as I try to grapple with and convey what I'm looking at.

"It's a cave, I think. A cave with black walls, and in the middle of the cave is a pool of lava. Bubbling lava that slowly streams out of the cave through a narrow channel, maybe a foot wide. The pool . . . I have a feeling this is the Midlands. Yes, someplace in the Midlands." It looks like many caves I've been to before, including the one I stayed in overnight with Andor, but none of those caves had lava inside them, obviously, or we would have never ventured there.

Then the lava pool starts to move; it no longer just pops and crackles in molten bubbles, but it's waving like there's something inside.

Suddenly, a head pops up out of the middle of the pool. A woman's head that seems both vaguely familiar and horrific and beautiful all at the same time.

"There's a woman," I cry out softly, afraid to take my eyes off the scene.

"What kind of woman?" the Truthmaster asks sharply.

"She's made of lava," I say excitedly, and I watch as she steps out of the pool: full breasts, small waist, thin hips, long legs. Her body cools slightly in places, holding her shape while turning black, and the rest of her burns molten-hot. "She's a woman made of lava."

"And what else do you see?" he asks. "Is she saying anything to you?"

"Why would she be saying anything to me?" I ask, but he doesn't answer. It doesn't seem like I'm part of this scene with the lava lady, especially since her attention is at the back of the cave where . . .

"She's not alone," I tell them. "There's a dragon there, I think I see a clawed foot, I . . ." I pause, blinking at the sight. "The dragon has two heads. It's blue, metallic blue, and it has two heads. She's talking to it and it's listening to her like it . . ."

"Slangedrage," Vidar whispers. "The dragon that lays the egg of immortality. This means we're on the right track."

I watch as she continues to say something to the dragon and then the dragon reaches down with its head and picks up something in its mouth.

A body.

I gasp again, hand to my mouth, but before I can see whose body it is, if it's human or not, the image suddenly fades until I'm staring at a hunk of resin again.

"It's gone," I whisper, feeling lightheaded. "It's gone."

I look across at Sae Balek. "How do I make it come back?"

"You can't," he says calmly. "It showed you what you needed to know for now. You can come back another time and try again, as the Kolbecks do, but—"

I shake my head. "I wish I knew about this sooner. We leave for Esland tomorrow."

"Then this is all that the goddesses decided you should see," Sae Balek says. "Including Voldansa, the goddess that you saw. The un-worshipped goddess of the Midlands."

"That was Voldansa?" I ask.

"The very one that the people of Esland choose to ignore and put their faith in the dragons instead. It will be their biggest mistake."

Well, that is ominous.

"What you saw is the future," Vidar says quietly. "And I have never seen any goddess in my future. We must take this seriously. We must take this as a sign."

"But you said the resin is a drug," I protest, looking between the both of them. "That this is a hallucination."

REALM of THIEVES   313

"Hallucinations aren't real," Sae Balek says. "Prophecy, telepathy, those are real. The drug merely opens your mind to what your higher self has already seen. What your higher self has already gone through. You are existing on a plane of reality right now, but there are other versions of yourself on other planes, and the drug opens the passage through them, like a tunnel into all timelines of your soul. Your future self is sending you something you need to examine deeply, perhaps even take heed." He pauses, his mouth crooked as he smiles faintly. "Time is a circle, Lady Aihr. You are everywhere all at once."

I blink, trying to take that in. Maybe I'm too stupid to understand it, but time being a circle instead of something linear is something that I just can't accept.

"Tell Lady Aihr what you saw," Sae Balek says to Vidar. "Tell her what you saw in the flames. Tell her you saw her . . . last year."

I stare at Vidar. "Last year?"

He slowly nods. "I was having a session. I saw the Midlands, a long shoreline of lava rock and black sand. And I saw you, and your dog. And Andor. I saw the three of you running before the image faded out."

"Did you tell Andor?" I ask, feeling incredulous. He knew about me before I even showed up?

"I didn't," he says carefully, in such a way that makes me wonder how many secrets the brothers keep from each other. "Andor never believes any of the resin visions at any rate. But once I had heard about you, I knew my vision had come true. And so the same will happen for you."

"But this still doesn't help us," I tell him. "We aren't even supposed to go to the Midlands tomorrow."

"No, but we will be heading there after the heist," Vidar points out. "That's the whole reason we're bringing Steiner with us. He needs to stay on the ship in the event we're successful with stealing the fertilized dragon eggs that my father has asked for."

"How is a lava lady going to help us with our heist?" I mutter, mainly to myself.

"You never know until you get there and beyond," the Truthmaster says. "We never know how one thing impacts another until we're past it and have the privilege of looking back. Keep faith that the goddesses showed you Voldansa and the dragon for a reason."

Doesn't he know how little faith I have?

The rest of the session was uneventful, with it being Vidar's turn to stare into the fire, but his vision was hazy and unclear, or so he said. I couldn't help but get the feeling that he was keeping something from us, mainly me, but I couldn't quite call him a liar.

Because I'd left something out of my vision, too.

I never told them about the body.

Chapter 30

Brynla

"Remember, if any of you are going to be seasick, you best be hanging your heads off the side of this ship. Get one drop of your vomit on my deck and you'll be strapped to the keel," Toombs says from the helm, the wind whipping back his thin hair, grinning like he's having the time of his life.

He is, of course. That's plain to see. We've been sailing toward Esland for two days straight, on nothing but the open, glasslike seas. It's been great for everyone to get used to being around each other as a crew, now that our heist is actually underway, and to go over the plan again and again. But I'd heard Toombs complain a few times that the voyage was boring somehow, and now that the waves and wind have picked up as we've neared Drage Passage, on the north end of Esland, he's finally in his element.

Luckily, I'm used to taking small boats from the Banished Land to the Midlands, so I've had a lot of experience with rough seas. Vidar, on the other hand, looks more than a little green, hanging out by the railing of the ship, even when the rain whips up and everyone retreats downstairs. He doesn't seem to have inherited Andor's constitution for adventure.

KARINA HALLE

"We should go over the plan one more time," Andor says as he rolls out the map of Esland on the galley table. Everyone groans in response. It's a different crew than I'm used to: Toombs, Feet, Belfaust, Kirney, Andor, me, Vidar and Vidar's guardsman Raine, and Steiner. And Lemi, but when we were deciding who was going to do what role, it was unanimously decided that Lemi must stay onboard with Toombs, Feet, and Steiner. There's no way we won't be discovered with a magic dog.

"Andor, please," I tell him. "We need to go to bed instead and get a good night's sleep. If we're going to be climbing up the cliffs before dawn, we need as much rest as possible."

"I'll be quick," Andor says with a nod.

I sigh while a few others snort. If he's not kept in check, he'll literally ramble on for days with all sorts of tangents and contingencies.

"How about I go over the plan," I tell him.

"Yes, please," Kirney says with a tired sigh.

Andor stares at me and I can see his stubbornness wanting to fight me on it. Another example of him not wanting to yield.

But he knows his faults.

"Have at it," he says, slumping down in his seat.

I stand up and look at the crew, clearing my throat. "An hour before dawn, at first light, Toombs will bring the ship here." I point at a place on the map just off a rocky peninsula. "This is the most northern point of Esland and the least patrolled, from what we have gathered from the Kolbecks' intelligence agents and what I know from my own birthland's history. We won't even anchor, for fear of the noise of the chain attracting attention. The two skiffs will be lowered and we will quietly row ashore. While there may be civilians about, there shouldn't be any of the Black Guard—but that doesn't mean we can relax. The six of us, armed with rope, will climb up the sand cliffs that line the shore. Once we're up, we split into two groups. One group, consisting of me, Andor, and Kirney, will take this road here that leads to the underground spring. This spring isn't mapped, but I

REALM of THIEVES

know people do go down there and it should lead all the way to the cistern under the Daughters of Silence. With any luck, we will be able to come up through the bottom of the convent."

"You keep saying 'with any luck,'" Steiner says. "You do realize that luck is something we can't depend on."

I roll my eyes. Always so literal. "Yes, Steiner, I realize that. But most everything in life is luck."

He purses his lips and frowns, and I know he doesn't agree with that at all. "And you used the word 'should,'" he adds. "As in it 'should' lead to the cistern. But you don't know that for a fact."

"Steiner, give it a rest," Andor says, palming his mug of ale. "I think we all know that every second of this heist is based on nothing but sheer chance and foolish hope."

"How reassuring," Steiner comments quietly, looking at his nails.

"But if luck is on our side, then we have a lot to hope for," Andor says. "This will change our lives."

And then everyone starts breaking out into chatter of what they would do with the gift of immortality. I have to admit, it's hard not to get swept up in the dreams, but I haven't yet decided if I would even want to be immortal. I may not have a faith, but I do feel in my heart that when death comes I will be reunited with my family again. I would hate for immortality to take that away from me.

I clear my throat to get everyone's attention, but they're just yapping louder, clinking their glasses together. "Fellas!" I yell.

All at once they stop and Lemi punctuates the silence with a well-timed bark.

"Meanwhile," I say loudly, "the other group of Vidar, Raine, and Belfaust will go along the main road to here"—I point at an X on the map beneath a crudely drawn picture of the convent—"to the fortress at the eastern gate of Lerick. It's a station for the Black Guard but one of the smaller ones. They'll take out the Black Guard, disguise themselves, and steal their horses so that when we make our way to the gate from the convent, we'll have safe passage through the city streets, all the way to the docks where the boat will be, with Toombs, Steiner, and Feet acting as merchants from Altus Dugrell. If this is timed right, through some magic, then the ship should be just pulling up and we'll look like customs agents out to meet it. Then we set sail for the Midlands, looking as if we were turned away. With any luck, we will be long gone before they discover what happened at the convent and the east gate."

"How much self-defense do the women in the convent know?" Kirney asks. "What about weapons?"

I give him a wry grin. "A good question. Don't let their cloaked, benign appearances fool you. Everyone in Esland, every gender, must serve in the military for two years. They have the training, though I am unsure about the weapons. Perhaps a couple of swords for self-defense. Or punishment," I add, shivering internally, remembering how Sister Marit would whip us repeatedly if we would even so much as coughed. She was always veiled, one of the Sisters of the Highest Order, just below the Harbringer, so I never saw her face as she made us bleed for daring to cry, but I know she would have been smiling. Not to mention the fact that many Daughters often went missing and we were never allowed to inquire about what happened to them. But we knew. Death was in the walls.

"Any other questions?" Andor asks, stifling a yawn as he looks around the galley. "I don't know, Brynla, I think you're trying to keep us up past our bedtime."

I give him my most frightening killer look, which makes everyone else go "Ooooh."

Meeting adjourned.

———

I barely slept. The seas seemed to get even rougher, tossing me and Andor around in our bunk like rag dolls. Even Lemi looked a little queasy. But had it been smooth sailing, I don't think I would have

REALM of THIEVES

slept anyway. There's too much on my mind and so many things that can go wrong.

We lowered our little boat and rowed in through the pounding surf to the shore, everything in muted shades in that gray dawn before the sun appears. I didn't let myself feel tired. I couldn't afford it.

We pull the boat ashore, quickly hiding it behind some sandstone rocks. All six of us have been silent so far, communicating with hand signals. In the distance the dark ship continues heading around the west side of the land, where they should meet us in Lerick in eighteen hours. I feel bad having to leave Lemi behind, but I know he'd only endanger us and possibly himself. But Steiner will take good care of him in the interim.

Andor pulls the rope from the boat and puts it on his shoulder. It's a heavy, giant spool of thick fibers, but to him it barely weighs anything. He goes to the cliff edge and starts climbing up the near-vertical face, his fingers and toes wedging into the smallest cracks as he scales it like a spider.

"Pfff," Belfaust mutters. "I could do that with my eyes closed."

"Well, you're going to have to," I remind him just as Vidar puts his finger to his lips to remind me to be quiet. I immediately bite my tongue. As I had told the others, this part of the land is scarcely populated, and there are no towns between here and the convent aside from rockdeer grazing lands, but even so, we could easily be spotted by a straggler before we have a chance to spot them.

Once Andor gets to the top, about forty feet up, he secures the line somewhere and then beckons for us to ascend the rope, one by one. I go after Kirney, and it takes every ounce of muscle to pull myself up. By the time I get to the top, scrambling over the edge on hands and knees, my palms are bleeding, rubbed raw from the rope, and my arms are shaking.

Kirney stares down at me while Andor helps me to my feet. "So suen really doesn't work on you," he muses, noticing my weakness.

I can't help but glare at him. At this point it's a touchy subject. "Suen doesn't give strength to everyone," I whisper harshly. "Maybe I got one of the hundreds of other magic traits that don't involve scaling a cliff with ease."

"Besides, she can still beat you up without it," Andor says, giving me a proud glance.

We stand by the edge, waiting as the rest of our crew scales the cliff, while Andor keeps scanning the horizon with his enhanced eyesight to make sure we're not being watched. Then when everyone else is up, we hurry as a group along a scrubby path of sagebrush and pricklepalms, doing our best not to kick up the dust. The sun is now starting to rise over the low eastern mountains, and soon all of us will be easy to spot.

"Time to split up," I tell them, pointing at the sandy stone path that gradually gets wider as it fades over the mesas and plateaus. "This will eventually turn into the northern road. Follow it east and as soon as you see the cover of those rocks over there, keep to them as much as possible. You should be camouflaged."

Everyone is dressed similarly to how they were when we trekked through the dunes to the Dark City, except here the fabrics are in shades of tan and clay to match the surroundings. Once my group gets to the spring we'll switch out for our black armor underneath to keep us incognito.

Vidar, Raine, and Belfaust head down the sandy path, their swords hidden under their beige flowing robes. I feel a hit of trepidation in my chest, hoping it goes smoothly for them. The Black Guard stationed at the east gate has always been a small band since there isn't anything beyond that gate except rockdeer and the convent, but that doesn't mean the three of them will have an easy fight taking the guard down. The only thing they truly have going for them is the element of surprise and the fact that the Black Guard doesn't ingest suen, nor does anyone else in the land.

REALM of THIEVES

"Come on, we don't want to be caught in the open," Andor says, and Kirney and I follow him, dodging to the left among cacti and rocky outcrops. I don't know exactly where the spring begins since I'd never made it to this area, so we're going by all the different maps Andor has collected. But luckily we have more cover from the chasms in the sand and various rock formations, and just as the sun gets too hot, Kirney stops and motions with his head.

I don't hear anything but it's apparent that Andor and Kirney do because they pick up the pace, and it's not long before the chasms in the rock start spreading wider, wide enough for a person to fit through.

"In there," Andor says. "It must be the spring. I can hear the running water."

He drops to the ground and sticks his head over the side, peering down into the cavern. "There's water all right. This must be it. There's maybe ten feet between us and the water and it doesn't look very deep." He glances up at us, wincing at the sun. "I'll go and report back."

"We're all going in there," I tell him, even though it's really the last thing I want to do. Out of the whole plan I think navigating an underground spring and cave system is my least favorite. I'm all right with caverns but once you add water to the mix, that's when I get nervous.

Andor slips down into the chasm feetfirst, his fingers holding on to the edge of the ground for a moment.

"It might be a farther drop than I thought," he says before he lets go. There's a moment of silence before a big splash.

"Andor!" I yell as Kirney and I drop to our knees and peer down the hole. "Are you okay?

I hear another splash, then him spitting out water and gasping for air. "Fucking deeper than I thought! Water is nice, though, cold. Current is strong enough to take up the brunt of the work." A pause, more splashing. I see a glimpse of him passing underneath as the sun hits his wet hair. "There might be places down the way to walk or crawl alongside the stream but I think we'll be swimming for most of it."

I exchange a glance with Kirney. "Well, it beats walking in the sun," he says just before he slips in through the crack and drops into the water below.

I take in a deep breath, bringing my legs over the side and lowering myself down, my muscles shaking from all the exertion of earlier, so much so that they give out and I fall the rest of the way.

My yelp echoes a second before I hit the water, my robes trying to pull me under. I quickly kick to the surface, taking in air while trying to get the robes off me. Andor and Kirney pull at them until I'm free and we let them carry on downstream.

"You all right?" Andor asks, treading water beside me. The current is already pushing us along at a gentle pace.

"I'm fine," I say. "Just lost my upper-body strength for a moment."

He gives me a sympathetic look. "I'm not sure if you remember what that's like," I add.

He grins. "Sorry, I don't."

Then he turns around and starts swimming.

We spend the next several hours floating in the spring water and letting the current usher us toward the convent. The longer we swim, the less the rock ceiling opens to the sky, and the darker it gets. If it weren't for Andor having the foresight to have Steiner create a light cube out of crushed glowferns, we wouldn't be able to see anything. Somehow the light makes it even worse, the water blacker in contrast, the walls of the cavern stretching into oblivion.

Suddenly the sound of a splash comes from behind us. I gasp and the three of us whirl around to stare into the darkness.

"What was that?" whispers Kirney.

REALM of THIEVES

"Could someone be following us?" Andor asks me, the whites of his eyes glinting blue. "Are there people that could live down here?"

I shake my head, dread creeping up my spine. "Not people . . ."

Another splash, closer now, and in the dim glow I see the shiny length of scaled skin before it slithers beneath the black water.

"What the fuck," Kirney says, his voice going high.

"Get out your swords," I tell them, reaching down through the water and grabbing my ash-glass swords from my belt. "I think it's a freshwater dredger."

"Are they . . . dangerous?" Andor asks, brandishing his sword, the tip only visible above the surface.

"If they weren't I wouldn't be about to tell you to kill the thing before it uses its—"

A strong tentacle wraps itself around my ankle and yanks me under the water before I even have a chance to finish my sentence. I scream, water filling my mouth, thrashing as I try to pull away, doing all I can not to let go of my swords. The snake tries to take me even deeper and I have no idea how far the water reaches here, but unless I free myself I'll drown.

I try in vain to slash and slice at the snake, but it keeps contorting itself out of my reach.

Oh damnation.

This is how I'm going to die.

Dragged to my death beneath the Daughters of Silence before I even had a chance to get my revenge.

The egg of immortality doesn't sound so frivolous now. I'd almost laugh but I don't even have the strength to fight back anymore. The only thing I can do is hold on to my swords as I'm dragged to the deep, and even then my fingers are starting to let go.

I'm going to let go.

Of everything.

It's already black so it's hard to tell if my vision is going fuzzy, but then I see a faint glow.

The light cube around Andor's neck.

Hope.

Suddenly the water fills with bubbles and blood and the serpent lets go of my leg.

Arms wrap around me, hauling me to the surface, where I burst through, spitting out water and gasping for air.

"We've got you," Andor says from one side, Kirney on the other.

"Snake thing is dead," Kirney says. "Andor sliced its head off. What were you going to say about them?"

I spit out more water and give him a steady look. "Just that it can kill you." Then I give them both a sheepish look. "Thanks for saving my life."

"Are there any other monsters you'd like to fill us in on?" Andor asks.

"No," I say, my breath coming back to me as we tread water. "Though we better pick up the pace in case there's another lurking." I pause, a flicker of a memory in the back of my head. "Except, perhaps, the one about the dungeon."

We start swimming faster now, helped by the current. We can't be too far from the cistern now, and yet I'm starting to lose faith that we'll get there.

"I'm sorry," Andor scoffs, "there's a dungeon here?"

"It's an old convent," I tell him. "What do you think happens in convents to those who stray from the path? Especially in the old days, when the Saints of Fire first settled in Esland. Punishment was a way of life."

"And so what was the rumor?" Kirney asks as we start swimming faster downstream.

"Just that they kept something, some creature, in the dungeon that no one was allowed to look at."

REALM of THIEVES

"You sure it wasn't a dredger that got loose?"

"I have no idea. I never saw anything."

"Tell me, how did rumors spread when you all had taken a vow of silence?" Andor asks.

"I didn't learn it here. Very few people have been inside the convent, and people like to gossip about what's hidden from them. We talk about what we don't understand, we invent things to make us feel important."

We fall silent at that and keep swimming, and I know that the moment I step inside the convent, most of the legwork is going to rely on me, the only one who knows the building, the culture, the rituals, and the only woman of the group. I'll have to do a lot of it alone. They may have been able to save me just now from the snake, but if anything goes wrong while I'm up on the administrative levels of the convent, there's a chance they won't get to me in time.

I take a deep, shaking breath to calm myself. This place fucked with my head when I was a child and there's no doubt it will do it again.

Stay focused on getting the revenge, I tell myself. *Stay focused on the egg.*

"I see something," Andor says, and I squint ahead. Instead of the incessant darkness, there's a light up ahead.

Not daylight, but . . . fire.

Chapter 31

Brynla

The fire flickers in the distance, reflecting on the black surface.

"The cistern," I whisper, keeping my chin above water as the dread in my gut grows larger. "They keep torches lit so we can check on the water. There's usually no one there, though, only in the mornings to light the torch. There will be a door to the side right next to it."

The stream collects in the cistern while a small channel of it runs off into the caverns, continuing the journey into Lerick. For a moment I wonder if we should have focused our revenge on the Saints of Fire and the Esland government. We could have so easily poisoned the water supply.

But then I remember that there are families just like the one I had, and though I am prepared to kill in self-defense, I'm not about to take the lives of innocent civilians.

We swim across the round opening and haul ourselves up the metal steps. Buckets and other collection materials line the cistern, some on rails that dip into the water, others hanging from pulleys.

The three of us sit on the rocky side, catching our breath, relieved

REALM of THIEVES

327

that we're no longer in the water. All my exposed skin is absolutely wrinkled like a prune and I would love nothing more than to take off the wet leather armor, which is a hundred times heavier now. But we have a schedule to keep and I feel that the journey took us longer already than it should have.

"Are you ready?" I ask the guys after a moment.

Andor puts his hand on my shoulder. "Brynla, we don't need to rush into this. You almost drowned back there. And I know how close this whole situation is to you. It's all right if you want to take a bit of time to—"

"No," I say quickly. "We have to get moving. You know we do. And more than that, if I spend another minute here, I might lose my nerve." I don't want to admit how close I am to just throwing myself back in the springs and letting them take me all the way to the ocean.

He stares at me for a moment with a rumpled look on his face, then leans forward and grabs the back of my head, giving me a quick kiss on the forehead. "You're so very fucking brave. I hope you know that. I hope you know how impressed I am by you, how we all are. We couldn't do this without you, lavender girl. None of us could."

My throat feels thick at his words. I don't even know what to say.

"Wow," he says quietly, flashing me a smile. "She's speechless. I can count on one hand how many times I've made you at a loss for words."

"Don't push your luck," I tell him, getting to my feet. I cringe at the water squishing at the bottom of my boots. But if everything goes as planned, I won't be in these wet clothes for long.

I walk to the door, stepping aside for Andor as he puts his ear against it to listen.

"I don't hear anything," he whispers. "You sure this is a safe place to enter?"

I nod and look at Kirney. "Are you dry enough to check the map?"

Kirney reaches for the small satchel at his side and unsnaps it, pulling out a small cylinder made of reeds found in the marshes around Stormglen that Steiner had discovered act as a waterproofer. Kirney takes the leather cork off and pulls out the map. We've looked at it a lot already, this cruddy map of the convent I drew from memory, but it doesn't hurt to have a refresher now that we're here.

I point to an X at the bottom. "This is where we are. It opens into the cellar and cold storage. Only the cooks would be here in the morning and then before supper. They don't linger here, though; they get the food and then they head back up to the kitchen."

"But we don't know what time it is," Andor points out. "It might be just before suppertime."

"If it's quiet, then I think we're fine." I turn my attention back to the map. "After we leave the cold storage, we head up the servants' stairs back here. These are Daughters of Silence, working for the convent. Even if we come upon them, they won't scream. The punishment for making a sound is worse than what we'll do to them, and they know it. It goes without saying, please refrain from killing anyone unless you absolutely have to."

"That's where I come in," Kirney says as he pushes his thumb into his chest, reminding me of his gift, which isn't just strength and fantastic aim but the ability to disarm people temporarily by pressing his thumb into their exposed skin. Apparently it doesn't work on dredgers, though.

"Right," I say. "Let's always let Kirney disarm people when he can. These Daughters are just like me, stuck in something with no escape. I don't want any harm to come to them."

"But the Harbringer . . ." Andor says with a wicked gleam in his eye.

"The Harbringer is all mine, if I even get the chance," I tell him. "The priority is the egg." I point at the map again. "The servants' stairs will get us to this level, where one of the chapels is and where the Sisters of the Highest Order, the fully veiled ones, pray most of the day. With any luck I'll get one and will be able to disguise myself in the veil and get myself to the Harbringer's chambers, where I know she keeps rare artifacts for herself. I know the egg is there, it has to be." I point at them. "By the chapel is where I'll say goodbye to you. There are many statues of dragons in those halls to sneak behind, and it's barely lit, always dark and shadowy. You'll have no problem hiding out there, but I'm afraid if you try to venture any further, you will be found. Kirney's thumb can't sedate them all."

"I can try," Kirney says good-naturedly.

"It will turn into a bloodbath and you know it," Andor tells him before leaning his ear against the door again. "Still nothing. I think we should move."

I nod and put my hand on the metal handle, slowly turning it.

I poke my head out into a dark room with an oil lamp in the corner, illuminating the stores of vegetables, fruits, and other food. The smell of the convent, those damned fermented herbs that permeated my life for years, immediately hits my nostrils and I almost choke on it. The scent probably isn't that strong, but my body wants nothing to do with it.

"Easy now," Andor whispers, briefly touching my hand. Then he reaches down and slides a sword from my sheath and places it in my palm. "You can't expect not to use this."

I grip the hilt. He's right. I have to be prepared.

We walk across the cellar, following the map, which Kirney keeps in his other hand, stopping every now and then to peer into a dark corner and to listen for footsteps or voices of the superiors. So far it's as quiet as a mouse, though once we reach the staircase, that changes. Because the staircase is carved in stone and goes up several levels, every noise echoes. Doors bang as servants come and go, and the occasional hush of the Sisters gossiping flows down the stairwell toward us.

We stop every time, waiting for the right moment to continue, and we're only a floor away from where we'll exit when suddenly the door bangs shut right beneath us and the sound of footsteps gets closer, closing the gap.

I stare down at Andor and Kirney on the steps beneath me, wide-eyed, swords clenched, then start running up the steps to the next floor as quickly as I can.

I reach it, Andor and Kirney behind me, quick and light on their feet, and just as I'm reaching for the handle the door swings inward, almost hitting me.

One the servants steps out, her robe black to signify her servitude, her hood back showcasing close-cropped hair, which means she hasn't been a servant very long.

She opens her mouth to scream but I quickly put my finger to my mouth to warn her and yank her inside the stairwell, shutting the door behind her. I push her up against the wall, my sword automatically pressed against her throat like a reflex.

"Don't say a word, Daughter," I whisper. "You know what they'll do to you."

I glance behind me at Andor and Kirney just in time to see a servant on the landing below carrying a stack of books. She drops them when she sees the men, and Kirney has to act fast, jumping down the flight of stairs and jamming his thumb against her throat before she can scream. Her eyes roll back in her head and she collapses into his arms. He swiftly lowers her to the floor in a heap.

The woman I'm holding whimpers.

I give her a warning look. "She's not dead and you won't be either as long as you comply," I tell her, but the fear in her eyes says she might act without thinking. When Daughters graduate they still have to take a vow of silence, but they're allowed to grow their hair and eyebrows back, which makes me think this girl is still new to the order.

She lets out another pitiful whine and when I press the blade against her throat, she opens her mouth and shows me . . .

REALM of THIEVES

Nothing.

Her tongue has been cut out.

I swallow hard, feeling nauseated.

"Brynla, we have to keep moving, let Kirney handle her," Andor whispers to me. Then he glances at the girl's open mouth. "Fucking drages, she has no tongue."

"Is this what they do when you become a servant?" I ask her frantically. "Is this what they do now to the Daughters of Silence? Do they cut out your tongue?"

She nods, tears streaming down her face, her lips quivering as they close.

"Fuck," I swear. I feel stretched too thin, my whole body starting to shake. They had threatened a few times that perhaps harsher discipline would be needed one day for all the Daughters, a way to guarantee their servitude to the convent after graduation.

"Brynla," Andor says again, moving to the side as Kirney comes up to my left and quickly reaches over and presses his thumb against the girl's forehead. She immediately slumps against me and I let her sink down against the wall.

"Time to go. Stick to the plan," Andor says, grabbing my hand with one hand as he grips the door handle with the other. "They'll wake up in a bit completely fine. But someone else will discover them any minute and we need to be out of here."

I can barely take in what he's saying as he opens the door and we're staring at the long, wide expanse of the chapel of the Sisters of the Highest Order. It's nearly all dark, except for a few sconces flickering here and there, and the dragon statues that flank the obsidian-tiled hall reach up to ten feet in the air, some nearly brushing the ceiling beams. At the end is the entrance to the chapel, where the fermented herbs smoke from hanging spheres.

The doors to the chapel are open. The hall is silent and empty.

Andor pulls me inside and Kirney quietly shuts the stairwell door behind us before we hurry to the shadows beneath a lumbering elder-drage statue, hidden from sight of anyone who might pass.

"Are you all right?" Andor whispers to me.

I shake my head. "No. I'm not."

"They'll recover with only a headache," Kirney assures me.

"It's not that," I say in a hush, aware of how silent this place really is. "It's that her tongue was cut out. Can you imagine?"

"But it didn't happen to you," he says quietly. "And what's one way to get back at this institution? Steal the prized possession that will give us the upper hand. Now come on, lavender girl. Let that anger fuel you. That's what it does best."

He's right. I need to hold myself together. I give them a determined nod. "All right. Eyes on the prize, then."

Unfortunately that means waiting in the shadows for the right opportunity to come along. We wait for a while under the dragon, breathing in the herbaceous air, studying the other dragon statues across from us, our wet clothes still dripping onto the tiles in a slowing rhythm. I can't help but think about my time spent here, drowning in rage and grief, feeling so fucking lonely that I thought I would die. I suppose in some ways I'm proud of myself for actually surviving it and eternally grateful to my aunt for helping me escape.

She would have loved this, I think to myself, and for the first time since she died, my heart swells with gratitude for her, and the pain is kept at bay. *She would have loved to join this team. She would have led the charge.*

Footsteps break up my thoughts.

"Listen," I whisper to the guys, but obviously they've already heard it from a mile away. The footsteps keep coming, growing closer, originating from behind us and down another hall. They build and build, along with small chatter that reminds me of squeaking rats. The older Daughters are no longer bound by the vow of silence, and I think this makes them talk more to make up for it.

REALM of THIEVES   333

"Get ready," Andor says to me. "Pick off the easiest one. We'll be waiting here for you when you get back with the egg."

Then they enter our frame, the Sisters of the Highest Order, a dozen of them walking single file with large spaces between them, muttering a prayer over and over. I remember that prayer, the one that prayed for the wards to fall.

Their religion is based on the end of the world for everyone but them, I think bitterly. *As if they're that special.*

We watch as they head toward the chapel. I don't have much time to act.

I give the guys a knowing look and then we start running as quietly as possible along the backside of the dragons, between them and the obsidian walls.

I scurry along until I'm keeping pace with the last Sister in line, just before they're all swallowed up by the mouth of the chapel. Then I quickly run across the aisle and grab her by the mouth, sword at her throat, pulling her back into the shadows before she has a chance to scream.

The woman squirms beneath my grip, but she's weak, and I flip her over and press her to the cold floor, my hand still over her mouth, pressing the black veil into her lips as I straddle her. "I'm going to give you a choice," I tell her, knowing I could just drag her back to Kirney for him to work his magic. "You make a sound, you die. You stay quiet, you just might live."

The woman stops squirming and I take it as a sign that she wants to play nice. I remove the sword and my hand long enough to flip the veil up over her head.

And see Sister Marit staring back at me with cold beady eyes, her skin pale and sagging. Her eyes widen at the sight of me, but in pure fright. She wouldn't recognize me with my long lilac hair.

"You don't remember me, do you?" I sneer at her, holding the sword so the tip is pressed up under her chin. "But I remember you.

The scars on my back remember you. The sound of a whip makes me remember you. And after this, you'll certainly remember me."

"I see," she says, speaking slowly so that my sword doesn't puncture her. "One of our flock who has fallen to the wolves."

"I haven't fallen to the wolves," I sneer. "I *am* the wolf."

She blinks at me, finally afraid.

I press the blade in deeper, enough to draw blood.

"Tell me where they keep the egg of immortality. Tell me and I won't punish you in the way you deserve."

"I would rather die," Sister Marit says starkly, and in the coldness of her eyes, she means it.

She *wants* it. These lunatics have craved the superiority of death since the day they were born.

As much as I need—want—to slit her throat, I can't give in to her.

"Andor, Kirney," I whisper to the guys who have been hovering in the shadows. "Open her mouth."

They don't hesitate. They're on her in a flash, Kirney grabbing hold of her top teeth, careful not to use his thumbs yet, while Andor grips her jaw open at the bottom. The woman starts to thrash and scream but I work fast, lodging the blade of my sword sideways into her mouth to muffle the sound. I've never cut out anyone's tongue before and I know she'll die from this in the end, but at least I'm making a point, even if it's one that only has weight with me.

"This is for all of those you've silenced," I tell her, and start sawing the sword in her mouth. It cuts through the corners, making blood pour down, and I think I only get halfway through her tongue before she starts to gurgle and cough on her blood.

I remove the sword and nod at Kirney. "Now."

He places his thumb on the woman's cheek and she goes limp and I quickly roll her over on her side so that the blood pours out of her mouth. Then, with the help of Andor, I start pulling her clothes off until I've removed her black robe and veil, leaving her in her shift. I

REALM of THIEVES

335

try not to look at her frail, old body, try not to feel remorse for what I've just done, try to remember the monster that resides in this woman, the same monster that lives inside all the Sisters here.

But is it really her fault? Brainwashed by the cult, by the government? Did they not create the evil inside her?

I shake the thoughts out of my head. I can't take it back and I have no time for guilt or reflection, not now.

I slip on her robe and veil, wrinkling my nose at the smell, like something astringent mixed with rotted herbs, and look at the guys, trying my best not to stare at her unconscious body as it bleeds out onto the floor.

"I have to leave you now," I whisper.

"We'll be here when you get back," Andor says. We stare at each other for a moment, though I'm aware he can't actually see my eyes through the black veil. Then he flips the veil back over my head, grabs me by the face, and kisses me deeply. "Good luck, lavender girl," he whispers as he pulls away, his gaze feverish, mouth open like he wants to say something else. "I . . . I . . ."

"I'll be fine," I assure him, though my heart feels like it's in a vise. What if I don't see him again? There's a chance I won't come out of this alive. From now on, I'm by myself. No Lemi, no Andor, no El- lestra.

Just me.

And it's just as well. The score I have to settle is all my own.

I give them both a curt nod before I crumble under the weight of it all, and then I look both ways and step out into the black-tiled cor- ridor. Instinct tells me to run all the way to the Harbringer's quarters, but with the disguise I have to believe that I won't be found out. I just have to act the part, I have to blend in.

I walk away from the chapel, making sure my gait is slow and del- icate, just like Sister Marit, but hands clasped at my waist. I keep the robe material pulled over them, as my unlined olive skin will be the only thing that will give me away, and stride down the hall in the direction the Sisters had come from.

So far I see no one else, but that doesn't mean my heart isn't in my throat, that sweat isn't prickling the back of my neck. It isn't until I'm at the main staircase that winds up through nearly all levels of the convent that my disguise is put to the test, light coming in from the stained-glass windows that rise from the bottom, reaching several stories high. Here you can look up to the pointed ceiling where the mural of the end days is painted, dragons flying around the realm, their fire torching everyone except the Saints of Fire.

Absolutely ludicrous.

Then I look down at the main floor, at the Great Hall of Zoreth, where a group of the Daughters of Silence has gathered by the hearth, listening to one of the Sisters drone on about servitude. What I wouldn't give to set them all free, but I know that's not what I'm here to do. Perhaps some other day. Perhaps that will become my new purpose.

So I head up the stairs. On the way I pass a couple of Daughters of Silence, as well as a few Sisters. The Sisters I nod to, the Daughters I ignore, though under my veil I can see how they make the sign of respect across their heart, their eyes filled with so much fear.

I let that fear fuel me. I keep walking, taking careful steps in my robe, until I'm at the highest level, where the painted dragons seem to torch me with their fire. From here I walk down a hall where the Sisters have their rooms. I pass by a few more of them, coming toward me like a black mass, gliding like ghosts.

"Sister," one of them says to me as the group slows down, coming straight for me.

Oh fuck.

I slow my gait, not enough to stop, and make the sign of prayer, as if I am in the middle of one and can't speak.

Three veiled heads nod, understanding.

REALM of THIEVES

"Fiery blessings," the one Sister says as they continue past.

I feel like I'm going to throw up. I let out a shaky breath of relief, trying to remind myself that there is absolutely no reason for anyone to suspect who I really am.

Still, I glance over my shoulder and wait until the Sisters are gone before I go up the last narrow staircase that leads to the turret where the Harbringer's quarters are.

I can only hope that she's not there.

I hurry up the stairs and then down the narrow hall. I've never been up here before and assumed the whole space was her quarters, but there are several closed doors leading into different rooms, and I don't know which one is hers, or if they all are.

I try the first one. The door is locked, which I take as a good sign.

I reach under my robe and into the pocket sewn into my armor, pulling out the lock-picking device that Steiner created for me. I make quick work of the lock, having done a few practice sessions back at Stormglen.

The lock clicks, to my relief, and I slowly push the door open.

I'm in an office, plain looking yet a little disorganized with a large oak desk piled with loose papers, surrounded by rolls of maps and charts and prayer banners, and shelves and shelves of books, portraits of dragons, Cappus Zoreth, and Magni peppering the walls.

I work quickly, going through drawers and searching among the books, but everything in here is in the open with not a lot of spots to hide things. Besides, I don't think one of the most valuable commodities in the world would be here, especially when things seem a little unkempt. I wonder if this is her dirty little secret, the fact that her godly order isn't very orderly at all.

I pop my head back into the hall, making sure it's still empty before locking the door and going to the next one, all while feeling I'm running out of time and luck. Because the longer I'm up here, the more likely I'm going to be found out.

338 KARINA HALLE

The next door is also locked, and when I step inside I think I've hit the jackpot. It looks like a tiny museum, with tapestries and art on the walls and in the middle a row of glass cases showcasing different items inside.

But my excitement is short-lived. Each glass case displays one item: a knife with a jeweled hilt; a crown made of black lavaglass and diamonds; an aged leather book with the text worn off the cover; a couple of crystals carved into dragons; and a human skull. The last is disturbing, but there's no plaque to indicate who the skull belongs to.

There are no dragon eggs.

Now I'm really starting to get worried. If the egg of immortality was going to be anywhere, it would be here. What if the rumors were just that: rumors? What if Ellestra was wrong?

I try to ignore the sinking feeling in my chest, knowing I still have one more door left to try.

I lock the door to the gallery and then try the final one.

The lock puts up a fight. I try again and again, wondering if perhaps the door has been magicked by someone. Then again, magic is illegal here. Magic is the product of suen.

I take in a deep breath, not wanting to throw my weight against the door and attempt to break it down. Doing so would be the quickest route to being found out.

I try again and nothing.

I sigh, resting my forehead against the door, wondering what I should do. Give up? All of this for nothing?

Help me, I think, praying not to the goddesses but to my family. *Help me.*

It's a futile prayer, one anchored in wavering faith.

I try the lock again, wondering how quickly I can get out of here if my break-in attracts attention, if it's possible to scale down the side of the convent or would I fall to my death?

And then *click*.

REALM of THIEVES

I nearly cry.

"Thank you," I whisper.

The lock undoes itself and the door opens.

This is the Harbringer's bedchamber. I'm lucky that she doesn't happen to be in here or I'd have no excuse. While the Daughters of Silence, and perhaps the Sisters, all have sparse quarters with thin mattresses, I'm not surprised to see that the Harbringer's room is the opposite.

I step inside and stare at it in awe. It is as lavishly decorated as any room of the Kolbecks', but instead of gold, everything is in black, red, and silver. The chandelier; the ornate dragon statues carved from onyx, crimson agate, and fire quartz that flank the large windows that overlook the scrublands and desert and the low hills between here and Lerick; the four-poster bed with tasseled blankets; the velvet tapestries on the stone walls. It's both gorgeous and evil at the same time.

My focus goes to finding the egg. I hurry across the richly woven carpets, opening jeweled boxes, pulling open drawers, then finally narrowing in on the glass armoire where various stones and crystals are kept. My eyes quickly search each one, looking for something to stand out, when I finally see it.

On the top shelf, almost out of my reach, is a large carving of a two-headed dragon made out of a color-shifting stone that looks both gray and vibrant blue.

The same blue I saw in my vision.

And beneath the dragon is an egg perched on a silver stand. The egg doesn't look like anything special, a light gray color tinged with muted shades of violet and pink on the scales, about the size of my hand. At first glance it looks like it could be the same color-changing crystal as the dragon, which makes it perfectly disguised, hiding in plain sight.

But I immediately know it's no crystal.

It's almost singing to me, emitting an energy that makes me feel like electricity is traveling through my palms, up into my body.

This is the egg of immortality.

I open the cupboard, my hands shaking.

I stand on my tiptoes and reach up.

Clasp the egg between my fingers.

A jolt runs through me, making my blood feel like it's singing.

This is it.

This is it.

I almost cry tears of joy, though I'm not sure if it's because I found what we came here for, an egg with the power to change the world, or if it's something else, something calling to me that I don't quite understand, igniting a fire deep in my soul, like I've had something inside me that's been dormant since the day I was born.

I open my palm and stare at the egg, heavier than any dragon egg I've ever held. It pulses metallic pink for a moment before it goes back to being a muted shade of purple gray, the color of twilight.

"What are you doing?"

I gasp and whirl around while tucking the egg into one of my robed sleeves, sliding it into the pouch sewn into my armor.

"Sister Marit?" the Harbringer asks sharply, having identified something about my robe and veil that gives away who I'm trying to be.

I can't answer, not even if I wanted to. I'm so struck by the sight of the Harbringer's awful face, thrust back to my very first day here, grieving the deaths of my father and mother, that I'm speechless.

Her cataracted eyes sweep over me, her expression hardening. She's still so pale, so ancient looking that I'm starting to wonder if she'll live forever.

"You're not Sister Marit," she says stiffly, slowly reaching into her robe.

I have no time to weigh my options.

I reach into mine, pulling out my ash-glass sword just as she brings out something dark and small that fits into her palm. A miniature bolt-thrower with a button trigger, the arrowhead razor-sharp and shiny.

It's aimed right at me.

"Who are you?" the Harbringer says. "Reveal yourself before I shoot you."

"I'll just deflect it with my sword," I say through gritted teeth. "And I'll cut your throat a second after that."

"And if you can't?" she counters, raising her chin as she takes a step toward me. "If this arrow pierces your skin, you'll have five seconds before you succumb to an agonizing death. It is laced with the blood of a sandviper. Perhaps you're familiar with those."

I was. Many of my parents' livestock were bitten by them. A horrible, drawn-out way to die, but part of life in the plains outside Lerick.

I don't want to call this woman's bluff—I don't think she's bluffing.

But I need to kill her if I want to make it out of here with the egg.

I refuse to die.

"I'm familiar with everything," I tell her.

The corner of her wrinkled mouth curls, as potent as a viper's bite. "And you are familiar to me. Tell me, who are you? There are so many disgruntled youths whose backs I never had the pleasure of breaking."

How many? I think. *How many others are like me, who have escaped your torment?*

But that question is for another day.

Instead, I say nothing. With my eyes locked on her, my sword acting as a shield, I rip back my veil so that she can see my face.

She doesn't seem surprised.

"Daughter of Pain," she croaks to me. "I have been waiting for this moment."

"I bet you have," I tell her, brandishing my sword. "I'm flattered that I've been on your mind all this time."

"And I'm glad I've been on yours. How long has it been, Daughter of Pain, since I've been at the forefront of all your thoughts? Since I became the scapegoat for all your anger? How many years have you tried to start a new life in the Dark City, corrupted by your aunt?"

I swallow hard. She's just guessing now.

"Ah," she says with a knowing nod. "You really think we haven't kept tabs on you all this time? You thought you could escape into the Banished Land and we would be done with you? We never forget one of our own, my dear. You know that. We don't let our daughters become so easily corrupted, especially by Freelanders. It's taken time, of course, to build a case against you. For us to realize what you had become a bloody thief. Stealing dragon eggs, the most punishable, blasphemous offense that ever was, especially for you. You of all people should have known better. Spreading magic throughout the syndikats. It wasn't until our spies in the Dark City were able to home in on you that we were finally able to bring our case to the Black Guard and have you dealt with."

She pauses and I feel like I'm drowning under her words.

"It wasn't Sjef Ruunon or the Dalgaards who had your aunt killed." A smile. "It was me."

My knees are about to give out, shock rolling through my body.

I had suspected it could have been the Black Guard that came after us, but I never thought that the Harbringer was the one behind it.

Now, of course, it's all too obvious.

I let myself believe I was worth nothing to them, that once I was in the Banished Land they would forget me. There was always another daughter to take my place.

I swallow the dust in my throat. "You let Ellestra go when she escaped the convent," I say, my voice hoarse. "Why bother with me?"

"Because your aunt isn't you," she says. She tilts her head, though my gaze drops to the bolt-thrower in her hand, still aimed at me. Her grip seems more relaxed. Perhaps I have a chance to get her before she gets me. I start calculating how fast I can throw this sword and if it can wound her first.

"Your aunt doesn't have your blood," she adds, her words more measured now. She frowns. "You don't know, do you? She never told you."

This is a ruse! She's luring you into a sense of security! Don't play into it!

"Tell me what?" I can't help but ask, licking my lips. Curious until the day I die.

Which might just be today.

"You never thought you were different?" she says, raising a gray brow. "You never questioned things about yourself?"

I can't even form the words.

"We called you the Daughter of Pain because of your grief inside, your anger, and the monthly pains in your desolate womb," she says, her eyes piercing into me. "And for the truth inside you'd not yet realized. Oh, no wonder you're here, trying to exact some sort of revenge. You're lashing out because you want to blame someone for being lied to all your life. You want to blame someone for all the things your parents never told you. The truth about your mother. The truth about what you are."

"And what am I?" I whisper.

"A false idol," she says. "One that should have been struck down long ago."

At those words, everything goes into slow motion.

She pulls the trigger.

I throw my sword.

The arrow hits the sword in midair, halfway between us. The impact deflects the arrow to the side of my head; it redirects the sword to the bedpost, where it lodges into the wood with a crack.

I start running for the Harbringer, pulling my other sword out, coming at her like lightning as she reloads the bolt-thrower.

I leap into the air, robes flying, my sword poised and ready to plunge into the old crone's heart.

And then I hit something.

Hard.

Fly backward until I'm on the carpet.

Stare up at the Harbringer as she aims her bolt thrower at me, a crackle of shimmering light between us before it disappears.

A ward.

She has a magicked ward for protection, the very thing the rest of Esland would be killed for.

"You think Magni wouldn't protect his best disciples?" she says, the arrow aimed at my head.

Her finger twitches on the trigger.

I'm about to die.

It squeezes.

This.

Is.

It.

I love you, I can't help but think, projecting my thoughts at Andor. At Lemi. At my family.

But the room brightens from behind the Harbringer, the air changing, popping my ears.

There's a snarl.

And before the Harbringer can pull the trigger, she turns around to see a large black shape leaping up at her, knocking her to the ground.

"Lemi!" I cry out.

Lemi ignores me and bites the Harbringer's neck, tearing into the skin, tearing out her throat in a bloody mess before she has a chance to scream. He wolfs down her jugular, jaws snapping, and looks at me briefly, enough to wag his tail, before he goes back for another strike.

He bites the Harbringer's face and I finally look away. I stumble

REALM of THIEVES   345

to my feet, picking up the bolt-thrower that has slid across the room, the arrow still unfired. I carefully unhook the arrow, tuck it where the lock-picker is, then slide the device into my boot before I pull my sword from the bedpost.

I glance down at Lemi, who has left a bloody mess. The Harbringer's face is an unrecognizable pulp.

He notices me looking and stops, about to come over to lick me, but I hold his bloody mouth back. "How in damnation did you do that, Lemi?" I ask him, scratching him behind the ears. "I thought you couldn't shift where you hadn't been before?"

He just wags his tail in response. I guess I had only assumed that. I've never been so glad to be wrong.

"Good dog," I tell him, kissing the top of his head. "Now how are we going to get out of here?"

He looks up at me with liquid eyes and while I'm staring down at him, so grateful for my best friend, a movement catches the corner of my eye.

The Harbringer twitches.

Then sits upright.

Chapter 32

ANDOR

"DO YOU THINK SHE'S ALL RIGHT?" KIRNEY WHISPERS TO ME. We've been standing behind the creepy dragon statues for what feels like forever, waiting for Brynla to appear. With every veiled Sister who makes her way to their private chapel, I keep hoping one will stop before us—that Brynla will pull back a veil and reveal her beautiful face.

But that doesn't happen.

"I'm sure she's fine," I say to Kirney, but I have no idea at this point. I shouldn't have let her do this alone. I should have taken down another Sister and worn the veil. No one would have known. The three of us could have done this together, even though I know the more lives we take here, the riskier things get. But the biggest, most unbearable risk of all is that Brynla won't make it out of here alive.

Have faith, I remind myself, my palms starting to sweat. *You know Brynla can take care of herself. She might not have suen in her blood, but she's more than evenly matched against them.*

But part of me wonders how pure this cult really is and how much is for show. It may be against the law to ingest suen in Esland, but that doesn't mean the government isn't doing it behind closed doors.

REALM of THIEVES 347

It doesn't mean that the Sister in charge, hasn't ingested it. And it certainly doesn't mean the Black Guard isn't under the influence.

Fuck. I hope to the goddesses that Vidar hasn't discounted that.

"I don't think this lady is ever going to wake up," Kirney says wearily.

I glance at her body. She's very dead. If this woman had ingested suen, it certainly didn't help her fight back, or give her immortality.

"You did what you had to do," I tell him. "You didn't kill her. Brynla did."

"I helped."

I sigh. "Atonement is for another day. Today is about getting out of here alive."

"With the egg."

"With the egg," I repeat. But the truth is, I don't give a flying fuck about the egg right now. As much as the idea of immortality excites me, as much as we need the egg, Brynla is the only thing that matters.

And I'm the one who involved her in this. She might lose her life before the rest of us.

Before I even had the courage to tell her that I love her.

"Look," Kirney whispers, nudging me.

The doors to the chapel open and the Sisters file out in a line, like a row of giant black ants, two by two. They are chattering among themselves and I can only hear snippets of their conversation as they pass us unseen.

But near the back of the line, I hear something as clear as day.

One Sister says to the other, "I can't go with you, I have to go feed the dragon now."

I exchange a wide-eyed glance with Kirney.

"Ugly business," the other one says. "Perhaps we can meet later."

We poke our heads out from the shadows and watch as they disappear around the corner, but the one who just said she was going to feed the dragon goes to the servants' staircase we had previously come out of.

"You stay here and wait for Brynla," I tell Kirney. "I'm going to go check this out. I'll wait for you in the cistern."

Before Kirney can protest, I step out of the shadows and start running after the woman, managing to get back into the stairwell without anyone seeing me.

The bodies of the women that Kirney disarmed are now gone and I know we don't have a lot of time before the alarm is sounded. They might not be able to speak, but they can sure as fuck write.

I quietly hurry down the stairs after the woman, her footsteps going down, down, down until she goes into the cellar. I follow her, watching as she crosses the cold-storage room and then goes to a small wooden door on the opposite side of the room. She grabs a torch off the wall, then takes out a set of jangling keys from her robe and unlocks it and then steps inside.

I'm across the room in a flash, getting to the door just before I'm shut out, taking my glowfern cube out of my pocket, the light already burned out, and I use it to prop open the door an inch, just in case.

Then I hurry down the stairs, following the flame, though my eyes are already adjusted to the dark. Down and down we go, the air growing colder, smelling damp and metallic, like mildew and blood. It must be at least a hundred steps until I watch as she steps off the last stair and heads down a narrow, rock-lined passage. I follow along, the floor made of hard-packed dirt, keeping my distance and hugging the shadows. Even if she turns around with her torch, I don't think she'll see me.

As she walks along, though, her pace slows. Like she's reluctant.

And the corridor starts to fill with sound.

A shrill sound. Muffled crying. Pure fear vibrates around me, making my scalp prickle.

Is this the dungeon that Brynla was talking about? Could the convent be keeping an actual dragon on the premises, tended to by the Sisters of the Highest Order? Is this dragon worshipped like a god?

The corridor opens up and all at once my questions are answered.

We're in a massive underground keep, with stone buttresses that rise fifty feet in the air. Nearest to us are three cages.

There are people in the cages. Some dead, some alive, some women, some men, some robed like the Daughters of Silence, all blindfolded and gagged.

The veiled woman stands in the middle of the room, facing the dark shadows at the back, holding up her torch, which trembles slightly in her hand.

"Magni," she calls into the darkness. "For your wisdom and grace we give you your gift. May it sustain you, may it sustain us."

I stare in horror, her words sinking in, watching as something comes lumbering out of the shadows, the sounds of heavy chains clinking.

Its head appears.

Far larger than any deathdrage, with slick green skin that reflects the torch that seems so tiny in comparison, and protruding fangs that are as long as my body. Its tongue shoots out of its mouth, flickering in the air like a snake. It lets out a low hissing sound that rattles my bones.

It's unlike any dragon I have ever seen. An entirely new species.

And one named Magni. Whether it's named after the Grand Sorcerer or they think it is the Grand Sorcerer, I'm not sure. But it doesn't matter, because they have a fucking dragon chained in their dungeon.

The woman lets out a shaking breath and then quickly moves over to the cages. She unlocks one of them and reaches in, grabbing an old, naked man by the arm and hauling him out. Along with being blindfolded and gagged, the man is bound at the feet and ankles.

My stomach twists in disgust as she drags him across the dirt floor toward where she was standing before.

"I will bring him closer to you now," she says, projecting her voice at the dragon in warning. "This is your gift, not I."

I have to wonder how many Sisters lose their life doing this. What if the dragon decides it doesn't want to play nice? Are dragons even sentient enough to know that they are gods? Does this one?

I have to do something.

"Hey!" I cry out, raising my sword. I don't know what I expect to do from here because I certainly don't want to run into the dragon's line of fire.

But it's enough for the woman to turn around to look at me.

Enough for the dragon to be surprised, unsure if I'm friend or foe.

Enough for the dragon to lunge forward, its heavy claws smacking the ground and making the whole keep shake, dust falling from the rafters, the iron collar visible at its neck, the chains rattling, straining to keep the beast in place.

Enough for it to open its mouth and bite the woman in two, swallowing down her upper half before doing the same to her lower.

The muffled cries in the cages intensify. I wait for the dragon to breathe fire on me, but instead it retreats into the shadows, chewing as it goes. Perhaps it doesn't breathe fire at all.

I take my chance and run forward, picking up the old man and carrying him on my shoulders, removing him from the dragon's reach, just as I hear a scream coming from down the corridor in front of me.

Suddenly Lemi appears in front of me, having shifted.

"What the fuck," I exclaim.

Lemi just runs around in a circle as Kirney and Brynla run into view.

I almost break down at the sight of her.

But from the fear in their eyes, I know there is no time.

She looks around the room wildly while Kirney says, "What the drage is this place?"

"What's happening?" I ask her as she runs to me.

REALM of THIEVES
351

"She's immortal," she says through a gasping breath. "The Harbinger is immortal. She came back to life after Lemi ate her face, and now the rest of the convent is on our tail. We have the egg, though, so at least there's that. What's happening here?"

"They have a dragon and they've been feeding people to it," I explain, adjusting the old man on my back and nodding at the cages. I'm thrilled she has the egg but I don't have time to take it in.

She gasps and runs over to them, taking out her lock-picking device and hastily undoing each cage.

"We need to get out of here," Kirney says, reaching over and removing the man's blindfold and gag. "Excuse me, sir, how do we get out of here? Is there another way?"

The man sputters, clearly shocked.

"Down there," one of the women says after Brynla removes her gag and blindfold before untying the rest of her. She brushes her unruly mint-green hair from her face and points at the other side of the keep at another door. "Sometimes people come from that door," she says.

"Good, can you help me undo the others?" Brynla asks the woman.

The woman nods and Kirney runs over to them. In seconds, the remaining prisoners are free.

"Let's go!" I yell, and we start running for the door. I kick it down without bothering with the lock and we find ourselves in another passage, this one sloping on an incline to the surface.

"This is where they brought us through," the woman says. "I had been sentenced by the Black Guard for saying something blasphemous and instead of jail or a hanging, they brought me here."

"Did you know this would happen?" Brynla asks her, huffing behind me.

"No," she says. "There's already a monthly sacrifice to the Midlands. I never heard of this happening beneath the convent."

"They called the dragon Magni," I say. "Do you think it's the sorcerer?"

352   KARINA HALLE

"Yes," the woman says breathlessly. "They believe it's Magni in his true form."

"And you?" Brynla asks her.

"I think they're full of shit," she says.

Finally I see faint light up ahead, the outline of a door, and we burst through it into a space filled with filtered light, the air heavy with the smell of hay and manure. It's disorienting for a moment, until I realize we've come out into a stable, a row of stalls with horses, with a carriage parked outside, two horses attached and nibbling on hay scattered on the sandy ground. This wasn't something we were counting on—we thought Vidar, Raine, and Feet would be back here by now under the disguise of the Black Guard—but beggars can't be choosers.

"Everyone in the carriage!" I yell. Everyone runs forward out of the barn and I climb up onto the driver's seat with Kirney beside me, Brynla and Lemi staying in the coach with the rest of the freed prisoners.

I clack my tongue and snap the reins, and the horses rear in surprise before thundering across the desert. I keep coaxing them, glancing over my shoulder at the convent, the dark mass of a castle as it rises from the stark desert floor, like a blight on the land. So far no one has emerged in pursuit of us, giving us a head start.

It isn't until we've passed through a narrow gorge, the east gate of Lerick on the horizon, flanked by dragon statues, that a Black Guardsman bursts out from a row of sagebrush and comes galloping from around the corner, heading straight for us.

"Vidar!" I yell at the quickly approaching guard, his black steed, the same breed as Onyx, moving faster than any horse should. Even if the guardsmen aren't using suen, it's apparent their horses are.

"Vidar! Belfaust! Raine!" Kirney hollers at him. "Raise your hand if it's you!"

The guardsman raises his mace instead, swinging around the

REALM of THIEVES 353

spiked ball, about to aim it at our horses. With his other hand he raises the shield of his helmet, showcasing a pale man with red eyes underneath.

"Oh fuck, not them," I say, trying to maneuver the horses out of the way.

But the guardsman keeps coming, letting go of the reins, a sword in the other hand now, almost upon us.

He's about to let the mace go when suddenly he's hit with something, right between the eyes, like a tiny arrow, and he falls backward off the horse, left in a heap in the dust.

"What the fuck was that?" I yell, passing the reins to Kirney while I stare behind me, the guardsman writhing in the sand while his horse runs off in another direction.

Suddenly Brynla pops her head out of the carriage, grinning at me, her purple hair having come loose from her braids and flowing behind her.

I don't think she can get any more beautiful.

"I stole more than an egg from the Harbringer," she says proudly. "A miniature poisoned arrow."

I stand corrected. She's now the most beautiful sight in the world.

She blows me a kiss and then sticks her head back into the carriage.

I let out a little growl, my cock pulsing beneath my armor. If we make it out of here alive, I'm going to ravage the fuck out of her and I don't care if the entire ship hears it.

Kirney gives me an odd look.

"Just keep driving," I tell him. "We have to get through Lerick before we can relax."

And a carriage galloping at full speed is going to attract a lot of attention.

Luckily by the time we pass underneath the east gate, there isn't a Black Guard to be seen. Seems Vidar and the rest did their job.

I take the reins over from Kirney as the city appears and the streets get narrow, doing my best to dodge the civilians, even though we're taking out and knocking over every street cart we see, galloping through shop awnings, decimating the tents of a market, spices flying in the air until the horses are painted in shades of red, yellow, and white.

People are yelling, running around in a panic, and in the distance I see dark figures up on scaffolding and the roofs of buildings, arrows being drawn, and then three guardsmen galloping toward us.

"Friend or foe, friend or foe?" I yell, not daring to slow down as the carriage careens around another tight corner, everyone yelping from behind me.

It isn't until one of the guards gets close and flips up his shield that I see that it's Vidar.

"Head for the ship!" he yells, as he, Raine, and Feet come into formation behind us. "Watch for the arrows."

Just as he says that, arrows fly from the rooftops, hitting the sides of the carriage.

One of them hits Kirney in the arm.

"Fuck!" he yells, grabbing his biceps. "It pierced the armor!"

"Hold on," I tell him just as the lane opens up and we find ourselves at the waterfront. "Almost there."

Here the tiles are white, giving the whole area a clean appearance, fishing boats neatly tied along the docks, the horses' hoofbeats echoing loudly as we gallop through throngs of people.

Up ahead is the wharf and at the very end of it, my ship, with Steiner and Toombs on deck and Feet standing on the dock, holding on to the ship's lines, the sun setting over the horizon behind them.

"Almost there," I say under my breath. "Come on."

The wharf itself is wide enough for the carriage, but even so it's hard to maneuver around all the people fishing off it, most of them having to launch themselves into the water to get out of the way.

"Set sail!" I yell at Toombs.

REALM of THIEVES

355

He nods and he and Steiner run around the ship, attempting to get it underway. Any other time I would have been tickled pink at the idea of Steiner, the most unphysical person I know, lending a helping hand, but he's actually doing good quick work.

I pull the horses to a stop and jump off the carriage, giving them an appreciative pat as I run to the boat and take the line from Feet. "Get on board, everyone, go, go, go." The ship is already starting to pull away from the dock, Kirney running past me to leap onboard, along with Vidar, Raine, and Belfaust.

"What about us?" the mint-haired woman says, the other prisoners huddling behind her.

"You can come with us," I tell them. "Start a new life. Or you can go back to the one you have here."

"Remember there's always the Banished Land," Brynla tells them. "You can keep your freedoms in the Dark City. But if you come with us, you can't come back here."

"Brynla, hurry!" I yell at her. I appreciate her compassion but not at the cost of her life.

"All right," the woman says. "I'm coming." She looks at the rest of the group. "If you stay, you will die here. Or you'll find yourself back in that place."

That's enough to get the group moving. Brynla and the woman help the old man and the rest of the prisoners toward the ship, helping them onboard.

"What's your name?" I ask the woman as she hurries past.

"Eydis," she says, and for the first time I realize how young she must be. Around Steiner's age.

"Nice to have you on board, Eydis," I say to her.

Then, once everyone is clear, I let the line go slack and start pushing the ship away from the dock. When it's at the end of the rope, I leap into the air, rope in hand, splashing into the ocean before climbing up the rope and onto the boat.

Vidar grabs my arm and pulls me the rest of the way, helping me to my feet. "Good to see you, brother," I tell him.

"Were you successful?" he asks me.

I wipe the wet hair from my forehead and stare at the harbor, watching as the Black Guard starts galloping across the white tiles, like a spreading stain. With any luck the wind will be on our side, taking us straight to the Midlands, a place they wouldn't dare follow anyway.

Though after all I've seen today, I wouldn't put anything past them.

"Andor?" Vidar says again, until I meet his eyes. They have a feverish sheen to them, no longer as cool and collected as they usually are. "Were you successful? Did you get the egg?"

I nod slowly. "Brynla did, yes."

"Are you sure it's the right one?"

"I'm sure we'll find out," I tell him carefully.

As if he can tell I'm studying him, his features go blank. "Job well done, then," he says, before he turns and walks off.

Chapter 33

Brynla

We arrive at the Midlands a day later, the winds favoring us the whole way, anchoring on the other side of the wards. We're near the northwestern tip of the island, an area that Andor was familiar with but was too far to travel to by small boat from the Banished Land. The region is known for its large sycledrage breeding ground, which are the kind of eggs Steiner thinks will work best for raising dragons. Of all the dragons to attempt to raise, I wouldn't pick the sycledrage, with its cunning and those huge claws, but I don't really get a say with the Kolbecks. Part of me thought it was best that we head back to Menheimr first and deal with our stolen egg, but apparently Torsten was adamant on getting his breeding program underway in the event that we weren't successful, and since we already have a ship and a crew (albeit one that has nearly doubled in size), it was decided we'd still continue on to the Midlands.

At least the day at sea gave Andor a chance to heal Kirney's arm and help Belfaust, who had sustained a stab wound to his thigh when they overtook the Black Guard. It turns out that the Black Guard had also been ingesting suen, making it a bloody battle.

It also gave everyone a chance to get to know one another, since we suddenly had five new crewmates. There was Eydis, the girl with the pale green eyes and matching hair; Artemen, the old man; Syla, a former Daughter of Silence who had her tongue cut out and can only communicate in writing; Damiel, a rockdeer herder whose wife was chosen as a monthly sacrifice, just as my mother had been; and Tamber, a middle-aged woman with sky-blue hair in tiny braids, who was known to the government as a troublemaker, shipping supplies across the border to Freelanders.

I for one am just happy that the convent no longer has the egg. Steiner has examined it, saying it looks like there are no visible puncture holes to indicate suen extraction, but because of the way the scales lie, it's impossible to tell. There's always a chance that there are more eggs elsewhere. Shit, I mean, considering the convent has an undiscovered species of the realm's largest dragon chained up in its basement, who knows what else they've been hiding?

Still, there's something about the whole mission that has left me feeling uneasy. It's not just what the Harbinger said to me, that my parents had hidden the truth from me, that I was a false idol, that they had been watching me all this time and orchestrated the assassination of my aunt . . .

It's the fact that the Kolbecks have control of an egg with immense power. Torsten Kolbeck is not a good man, neither is his brother, and I'm not quite sold on Vidar either. I've seen the way he looks at the egg, like he's possessed by it.

But not in the same way I am. The egg calls to me, a soft murmuring sound that puts me at ease. It feels like it belongs to me, while Vidar acts as if he belongs to it.

Though Steiner's interest in the egg and its suen is intellectual, I'm not convinced such a prize wouldn't bring out the mad scientist in even the most rational of beings.

And then there's Andor, who has staked all his hopes and credibility on its magic.

REALM of THIEVES

Something to keep an eye on, at any rate.

"Are you ready?" Andor asks me, hoisting a collection bag over his shoulder.

"I am," I say, strapping on the last buckle of my boot. I wait until Andor's back is turned before I grab my pouch and fasten it around my waist, being extra careful with the contents. Then we exit our cabin and head up the stairs to the deck. We should already be on the Midlands by now, but we were feeling a little amorous this morning, which delayed our mission. Actually we've been going at it like rabbits ever since we returned from Esland. Something about an elevated heart rate and nearly escaping death really makes you want to jump a man. I feel bad for everyone else on the ship who has to listen to us, but not bad enough to stop. Hey, we wouldn't have the egg if it weren't for me—I deserve a little release.

"About time," Toombs comments under his breath as he steadies the rowboat on the side of the ship as Andor and I climb inside. Lemi galumphs down the deck and leaps into the boat, making it rock violently.

"Better late than never," Andor says. "Lower us down. If the goddesses are on our side we'll be back before nightfall. If not . . ."

"Then I'm coming after you," Vidar says, crossing his arms across his chest as he stands beside the pulley. "I still don't know why I can't come now and help."

"Let's leave this to the experts, eh?" Andor says, winking at him, which clearly irritates Vidar more. While his oldest brother is more than physically capable of retrieving dragon eggs—after all, he was able to take down a section of the Black Guard—he hasn't had any experience in it. All his training has been in defense of their holdings as heir. Though I'm starting to realize that Vidar might be a little bit jealous of Andor. While Vidar is usually kept at home and coddled by Torsten, Andor is the one sent off on adventures. I could see how that might be frustrating. It could be why Vidar has had that intense

360   KARINA HALLE

gleam in his eyes over the last day. I've been attributing it to some strange desire for the egg, but maybe it's that he finally feels useful and alive.

I know I certainly do.

I glance over at Andor as the boat is lowered into the waves and he starts rowing, the muscles under his armor flexing. He's the reason I feel a fluttering sensation in my chest, the feeling like something inside me slowly but fully awakening, unfurling like a desert bloom. He's put me on a path that has changed my life for better or worse, but a path I feel destined to have taken all the same. I still don't know what my purpose is, I still don't why the Harbringer said I was different, why I *am* different, but I know I'm one step closer to discovering it each day.

"What?" Andor asks with a quizzical frown as we slice through the water, its color turning from deep inky blue to azure as we get closer to the wards and the shore.

"Nothing," I tell him, because of course I can't tell him these things. I feel them, so deeply, but the moment I know I should share them with him, they die on my tongue. It's almost as if the moment I say them he'll find it laughable and silly, like he won't actually see how serious I am about it. I worry he'll think I'm lying or just trying to be nice, when that's not the case at all. As long as I keep my feelings inside, they'll stay real and true.

He studies my face for a moment and I fear he's going to push me, because he knows I'm hiding something even if he doesn't know what, but he just grins at me. "All that sex rattled your brain, did it?"

I laugh. "You could say that."

His focus goes behind me. "We're about to go through the wards."

I twist around as the shimmery light gets close, rainbows refracted in the shield. There's a familiar resistance as we push through, followed by a faint pop as we reach the other side.

I shake the feeling out of my ears and concentrate on our landing.

REALM of THIEVES

I suppose I should be more focused on what we're about to do than on Andor. After all, this mission is unlike any of the ones we've done before. We're not just stealing eggs, we're stealing fertilized eggs from sycledrages, which means there will be a lot of aggressive mamas to defend ourselves from, and those dragons *are* aggressive. Once we have the eggs, we have to keep them warm and close to our bodies and immediately head back to the ship, where Steiner will put them in an incubator.

At least this part of the Midlands isn't as volcanic as the rest. We still have our black salve around the eyes to protect them, but so far there's been no need for a mask. The air is tinged yellow and smells of sulfur but there is no real smoke.

We're near the shore when Lemi shifts and appears on top of a volcanic rock, poised like a statue and scouting in all directions for dragons or danger, though they're pretty much the same thing.

Once the boat scrapes along the rocky coral bottom, Andor jumps in, knee-deep in the water as he effortlessly pulls the vessel ashore with me in it. He grabs my hand and helps me off the bow, and then we grab our packs and a few extra weapons. Both of us are carrying a bow and arrows now, since I proved to be such a good shot with the Harbringer's miniature bolt-thrower. We also have our usual swords and the egg collection sack that has been insulated with goose feathers.

Lemi barks at us, his nose pointed inland.

"That way, I guess," I say as we scramble up a rough embankment of scree and lava rock, Andor helping me up as my boots try to find purchase. Once on top of the ridge we have a clear view of the land, nothing but undulating earth and rock all the way to the mountains in the distance, their sides blown off from explosions long ago.

"No active volcanoes," Andor says. "That's a win."

"Doesn't look like the type of terrain that gives way to fire tornadoes either," I point out. "Another win."

Lemi barks again, going into play pose and wagging his tail. "And I think he's found a scent. Lead the way, boy. But don't go too far."

My hound immediately disappears and reappears about half a mile away. "How is that not going too far?" I yell after him.

Andor and I break into a jog, knowing we need to be quick about this mission. If Lemi finds any sort of eggs at all, we're bringing them back, fertilized or not.

We run over the rock, jumping over fissures, heading toward a group of dark gray boulders that jut out from the blackened landscape like a city. Lemi slips between them and we follow, the dirt here the same gray as the rock.

"I'm unfamiliar with this kind of rock," I say. "Doesn't seem volcanic."

"Or perhaps it's so old and so volcanic, it doesn't resemble the rest of the island," Andor points out as we run around another boulder. "Maybe this is the birthplace of the islands."

Birthplace or not, there doesn't seem to be much of a path here, and I hope Lemi is actually running up ahead and checking it out and not shifting us to a dead end. The more we run, the narrower it gets, and the more the boulders start to melt into each other until finally we burst out of the chasm and into a large, circular area, the ground a mix of coarse gray sand and pebbles, towering rock walls all around us except for a slit in the side, which might be a cave.

It reminds me of an arena, and Lemi is standing in the middle of it, huffing his lips with his nose pointed at a giant nest of deathdrage eggs, the biggest ones to exist.

"Oh," I say, coming to a halt. "This isn't what I expected."

The eggs are three to four feet tall, all of them in shades of green and blue.

And if mama comes back, we're in a lot of trouble.

"What do you think?" I say to Andor, pulling an arrow from the quiver on my shoulder, the tips laced with the tranquilizer though I have no idea how many we need to take down a deathdrage. "Push our luck and move on, hoping we come across a sycledrage nest? Or

REALM of THIEVES   363

push our luck and try to take one of these? This isn't even the dragon your father wanted."

"Does it matter?" Andor asks. "I think this will keep him happy for now. What if we raise it from birth? What if we could tame it?"

"I think you're delusional if you think you can tame one of those," I admit. "Same goes for any dragon. They aren't horses, they aren't dogs. They aren't our friends. They are vicious, wild beasts that will probably kill you first chance they get. Ever seen someone with a snake as a pet? In the end they always get bitten. And these creatures happen to have a very large bite."

He sucks at his teeth, seeming to think it over. "I'm doing it."

Then he starts running toward Lemi.

"Fuck," I grumble, getting the arrow onto the notch and running after him, keeping my eye on the skies, even though there will be no missing a deathdrage's arrival.

"You cover me," he says, approaching the eggs. "I'll get this sorted."

He picks the smallest one, its scales tinged with metallic green, and pushes it back and forth. "I think it's fertilized." He does the same to the others, which move much more easily than the first one. "Yep. These aren't fertilized. That one is. If I'm quick enough I'll try to extract suen from the others."

"Just hurry," I tell him. "I don't want mama coming back."

He spreads out his satchel on the ground and rolls the egg on top of it before closing the bag back up. "Easy," he says. "Might as well get some suen while we're here."

A little too easy, I think, as the hair on the back of my neck stands up, my stomach sour.

Suddenly Lemi barks and shifts, making Andor stop just before he's plunged the extractor into the egg. Lemi then appears on top of the rock wall, staring into the distance and barking repeatedly.

"Andor, we have to go now," I tell him. "I don't want to wait to see what he's barking at."

KARINA HALLE

"Just a minute," he says, plunging it in.

"Andor!" I yell. "Just stop and—"

I'm cut off by a terrible screech that rattles my bones and a whumping sound that blows back my hair.

Lemi shifts just in time as a deathdrage flies over the wall, heading right to Andor. It's so big it nearly blots out the sky.

"Andor, run!" I scream, aiming the bow at the dragon and letting the arrow fly. It hits the neck but bounces right off, its hide too thick. I pull out another and another as Andor abandons the eggs and starts running toward me, Lemi nowhere in sight. This time the arrows hit the dragon but they don't slow it down.

It's coming right for us.

I don't know what to do.

Andor is running and it's catching up and in a few seconds it will be upon him. He's not on the defensive, he's trying to get away, and he's as vulnerable as he'll ever be.

So I start running toward him.

Toward the dragon as it swoops toward us, each powerful blast from the wings enough to almost knock me backward.

But I don't stop.

I throw the bow to the ground and pull out my ash-glass swords, wondering if I could somehow run up on Andor, if I could use him as leverage and leap up onto the dragon's head, stabbing my swords through its skull.

It has to work, I think. It has to.

But then Andor's boot slips on the loose pebbles underfoot and he stumbles for a moment.

I'm screaming, praying for him not to fall.

He doesn't.

He manages to right himself.

Staring at me with that cocky smile of his.

REALM of THIEVES

Right before the dragon lands behind him, making the earth shake.

Both of us fall to the ground, and I'm scrambling to my feet staring at Andor through the clearing dust, watching as he tries to get up.

Watching as the dragon lunges forward.

Andor is pushed forward as well, his face contorted in a scream.

Two large white teeth puncture his chest, the dragon having caught him with its lower jaw.

My scream rises as his fades, as he chokes on the red blood flowing from his mouth and down his chest.

I'm outside myself.

This can't be happening.

This can't be real.

After all we've gone through, this can't be it.

I see the light fade in his golden eyes, his body slump in the dragon's mouth.

I become something else entirely.

Chapter 34

Brynla

I am the wolf, I think to myself.

I keeping running at the dragon, my blades raised, but when the dragon notices me, it merely swipes at me, knocking me to the ground with its forefoot.

I roll and roll and for a moment I think perhaps I should just let it end me like it just ended Andor.

But something inside me makes me get to my feet.

And I use my rage to fuel me.

I scream, a battle cry, a warrior's creed, and run at the dragon again. It still has Andor's broken, bloody body in its mouth, seeming to pay me no attention. Perhaps I'm not of interest when it already has its meal.

The dragon shouldn't underestimate me.

I'm still screaming as I throw myself at its neck, using the arrows that are stuck there to help me climb up it until I'm situated right above its head.

It drops Andor in a heap and starts shaking itself back and forth but I hold on, inching forward until I'm in the right position. Then, with a final, terrible scream, a scream for all the people I've lost, a

REALM of THIEVES   367

scream that feels like an exorcism, I plunge the ash-glass swords into the dragon's skull.

The dragon roars and immediately slumps to the ground, throwing me. I land a few feet away, my side taking the brunt of the fall, cracking something in one of my pouches, and my ankle twists painfully. I yelp and try to sit up, grinding my teeth through the pain as I watch the beast carefully. It doesn't move, its yellow eyes unseeing, no breath to be had.

Lemi's whimper brings my attention over to my dog, the only thing I have left in this world.

Lemi is lying beside Andor's lifeless body and whining. He touches his arm with his paw and then sits back, eyes never leaving him. He does it again and again, followed by a bark, hoping in vain that Andor will get up.

But Andor won't. He said the ability to heal never worked on himself, and besides, I'm unsure anyone could be brought back from this. If he couldn't save his mother from a terminal illness, he couldn't save himself from his body being lacerated by dragon teeth. Every part of his torso has been punctured, and the blood pooling out from around him won't stop flowing.

And yet I find myself crawling toward him, my ankle useless.

I pull myself along the pebbles until I'm climbing through his blood. I manage to sit beside his body and pull it up into my lap. His head tilts back and I cradle it, pressing my fingers against his face.

"Hey," I whisper to him, tears falling from my eyes and splattering on his cheek and nose. "Hey, you can come back now. You can wake up now. You can try, can't you? Please? For me?" I brush my tears off his face. "Do it for your lavender girl?"

But Andor's eyes are like the dragon's. They see nothing. They stare at the sky above, empty golden pools that once were the window of the most beautiful soul I knew. If I keep staring at his face, though, maybe I can pretend a little longer.

"Hey," I say again, running my fingertips over his lips, slick with blood. "What if I tell you that I love you? Will that make you come back?" I swallow thickly; it's getting harder to speak. My jaw aches from trembling. "Would you have said it back? Would you forgive me for not saying it earlier?"

I sniff, cradling him harder, holding his head in my arms like a baby. I put my head up and stare at the sky, wanting to see what he could see. "I wanted to," I go on. "There were many times I wanted to but I felt stupid. Like it would ring false if I said it and you wouldn't believe me, and, fuck, it would have killed me if you didn't believe me, if you didn't take my heart when I gave it to you, but I've never been more honest in my life. I might be a thief, but I am not a liar. And I love you, Andor Kolbeck, and that's the fucking truth, no matter how ridiculous it might sound."

My chin quivers as I feel the grief bubble up. I'm already filled to the brim with it; I don't know where it's supposed to go.

"One person shouldn't have to take so much," I whisper, my chin dipping down, eyes pinched shut as the tears stream down my cheeks. I scream, I whimper, I cry. I keep holding on to him because I know that the moment I let go is the moment I let go of him.

And I never want to let go of him.

Lemi whines beside me, licking the back of my head, then leaning against me as if he knows that I'll collapse at any minute.

And my loyal friend stays there as the air grows cool and the sky grows dark, blending into twilight. In another world we would be back on the boat already. Instead I'm here. And I belong here on this forsaken land. More than I do on a ship, more than I do at Stormglen, more than I do in the Dark City.

The Midlands, a realm of fire and beasts, is where I should lay my head.

This is where I should stay.

This is where I should die.

Why didn't we take suen from the egg of immortality before we came here, just in case?

I kiss the top of Andor's head. "I'm not going anywhere," I whisper. "My love."

Suddenly Lemi growls.

I slowly raise my head, prepared for the end to come soon. You can't hang out by a dead deathdrage for long before you attract attention.

From the narrow cave to the side, something lurks, glowing green eyes in the dark.

Lemi's growl deepens and he steps away from me, the hair on his back raised, focused on the cave.

"Lemi," I manage to say. Whatever happens, I'll have to make sure he's not hurt. I'll give my life for him with ease. "Lemi, stay back."

The green eyes blink.

And then a dragon steps forward.

About twenty feet tall, half the size of a deathdrage.

Metallic blue.

Two heads with long, fine snouts.

"Oh my gods," I whisper, nearly choking on the words.

It's the slangedrage, the one that lays the eggs of immortality.

It walks toward us, an even gait, tail swinging back and forth.

Lemi barks wildly, putting himself between me and the dragon.

"Lemi, please!" I scream at him. "Lemi, stop! Go back, go back, let me be!"

But Lemi doesn't listen. He runs at the dragon and I know I'm about to lose my best friend.

The dragon keeps walking.

Completely ignores him.

It keeps coming straight for me.

Closer and closer until I can smell its hot breath, sulfur and the sea.

Both heads peer down at me.

"Go," I whisper. "Please."

The dragon lowers one head and grasps Andor's legs in them.

Oh no, please no.

"Stop," I say. "Let him be."

But the other head comes for me now, about to bite my own head off.

I close my eyes, refusing to let go of Andor's body.

Teeth pinch at my arm, grazing the skin without breaking it.

And suddenly a weight is lifted.

I open my eyes to see Andor's upper body in the dragon's mouth, the other half held by the other set of teeth.

I stare in awe, unsure what to do, what's happening.

Then the dragon carefully turns around, keeping its heads together so that Andor's body remains intact.

It turns, its tail whipping alongside me, and starts slowly walking back to the cave.

"Stop!" I yell. I try to get to my feet but my ankle gives out and I go tumbling into the scree. I start picking up the pebbles and pelting them at the dragon, each one bouncing off its blue hide, and still the dragon doesn't stop.

Meanwhile Lemi is trotting after it, barking as he goes.

"Lemi!" I scream but no to avail.

I try to get to my feet again, wincing as I have to put all my weight on the other leg. I start shuffling forward at an angle, grunting in pain as I try my best to hurry after Lemi and the dragon. Now the dragon has already reached the cave and has gone inside, and Lemi runs in after it, disappearing into the shadows.

"Fuck, fuck, fuck," I swear, moving faster now, ignoring the sharp stabbing pain that wants to bring me to my knees. My body is releasing some sort of chemical to keep me going and I let it run through my body, until the pain doesn't seem to matter anymore.

REALM of THIEVES

I limp into the cave, yelling and pleading for Lemi to come back.

Then I come to a stop.

And can't believe my eyes. Lemi is standing right in front of me, staring at the dragon, which lowers Andor's body to the ground, gently, as if with reverence.

Right in front of a bubbling pool of lava.

"No," I whisper. "This can't be."

But the lava pool, with its small channel that runs off it, is exactly the same as the one in my vision, the molten fire causing a faint glow that illuminates the cave.

I stare at the middle of the pool, daring it to come true, to be real.

And yet even when it starts to move, like waves in an ocean, I still can't believe it, not until the top of a head emerges.

Then a full head.

A woman's head.

Her hair, her shoulders, her arms, her breasts. Torso, hips, thighs, calves.

All of it made from swirling magma, shades of red and orange and blinding yellow, flowing in some places, like her stomach and down the middle of her thighs, hardened into cooled lava in others, like her breasts, hips, hands. Her face is like rock, most of her features obscured.

Lemi stops barking.

Instead he sits down and starts wagging his tail.

I'm too shocked to think, too confused to even be scared anymore.

"Who are you?" I whisper.

And why do I know you? I think.

Why do I *know* you?

"Brynla," the woman says.

And her voice turns me inside out.

Brings me to my knees.

I collapse to the ground, hand at my heart, afraid that if I let go it will burst from my chest.

"No," I whisper. "It can't be you."

Her face contorts for a second, the hardened rock crumbling away to reveal the flowing lava underneath, magma rising and falling to create a face. High cheekbones, low-set brow, a doll's nose. And if her eyes had any color other than red and orange, they would be a bright blue. The same as the dragon. The same eyes I never inherited because I got my father's brown ones.

"It's taken you so long to find me," she says, her voice sounding far away, like I'm hearing it from another room, but hers all the same. "I was starting to think maybe you never would."

"Mama," I say, my voice cracking. I try to say more but I can't, because how can I?

How is this my mother? A woman made of lava.

Voldansa, Sae Balek had said. *The unworshipped goddess of the Midlands.*

"You're a goddess?" I ask. "How?"

How? What does this mean?

No, I tell myself, closing my eyes and pressing the heel of my hand into my forehead. *No, none of this is real. You died, Brynla. You died out there and none of this is real.*

"It's real, my sweet dear," my mother says. "And I wish more than anything I could hold you and tell you that you'll be all right. I think then you would know. But I am real, darling, I promise you."

I shake my head, daring to look at her. "How? The goddesses aren't real."

"They are," she says.

"You're dead," I say simply, staring down at the pool. "I'm seeing ghosts."

"I never died, Bryn," she says to me, my old nickname jarring to

REALM of THIEVES

373

hear. "They sent me away on purpose because they were afraid of what I could do. They had theories about my blood. But that was their biggest mistake."

"I don't understand," I mutter. Everything hurts, including my head but especially my heart.

"You will. But right now, we don't have a lot of time, do we?" She looks over her shoulder at Andor's lifeless body. "Not if you want to save him."

My head snaps up. "What?"

"This man here," she says. "He is with you, isn't he?"

"Andor," I tell her, trying to tamp down the hope in my chest, flaring like a star. "His name is Andor. If you were a goddess you would know that."

Her lava face smiles. "It doesn't work like that. But I can still help you, in the way that a goddess can."

She waves her fingers at the dragon and steps back toward me. I stare at the back of her head for a moment, entranced by the lava, and at the same time, I know this really is her.

The dragon heads pick Andor up again.

"What are you doing?" I call out, panicking. "Leave him alone."

"I'm saving him," she says, glancing at me over her shoulder. "That is what you want me to do, isn't it?"

"Yes," I cry. "Can you?"

She nods. "But it will come at a cost."

"I don't care about the cost," I tell her truthfully. "Bring him back, please bring him back."

"You might not care," she says. "But he might. If I bring him back to life, that means draining the suen from his body. It means he'll no longer be able to heal anyone."

"I thought you didn't know everything," I say softly, my heart in my throat.

"I am Voldansa," she says. "Goddess of the dragons. Goddess of the Midlands. I know when suen is in someone's blood and I know what it does."

"Andor won't care if he can't heal," I say, even though I'm not sure I should be speaking for him. But at this point, I have no choice.

"It means he can't heal you," she says, her face turning grim. "I know your pains, child. I feel them when you do. I feel you in the blood and earth."

My brain still isn't able to catch up with what's happening. My mother is alive and a goddess? She can bring Andor back to life?

"I don't care about my pain," I tell her. "I'll deal with it as I always have. I never expected a miracle anyway."

"All right," she says. Then she waves her fingers at the dragon, embers flying from them, and the dragon drops Andor into the lava pool.

I cry out, putting my hands over my eyes, feeling like the rug has been pulled out from under me. As long as I saw his body I somehow believed that maybe he would come back, but now that he's been dropped into the lava pool, I can't . . . I can't . . .

I stay on my knees, praying to anyone, praying to her, that this works, that he'll come back, that I'll be all right, that I won't lose him, that I won't lose myself. I pray and I cry, hoping my words have the power to change things, begging for them to.

Then I hear my mother whisper my name.

I open my eyes to see her standing to the side of me, placing a hot hand made of hardened lava rock on my shoulder. It shouldn't feel like her but it does.

"Look," she says.

I follow her gaze to the pool, where ripples have formed in the middle.

One of the dragon's heads dunks into the ripples, fully submerged, and then comes back out. Its teeth are caught on one of the straps that runs across Andor's armor.

REALM of THIEVES

It pulls Andor out of the lava pool and backs up until Andor is a few feet away. The lava slides right off him, disappearing into puffs of smoke, and there don't seem to be any wounds on him.

I stare at him for a second, stunned, watching to see if he's alive.

Then he jerks, coughing, and I yelp, running toward him.

I drop to my knees beside him, grabbing his hand, putting my fingers to his cheek. He's not hurt at all, he's not even burned. It's like he's been purified, better than he was before.

And he opens his eyes and looks at me. Smiles softly.

"Why are you crying, lavender girl?"

Chapter 35

Andor

One minute I felt a horrible kind of pressure on my back, watching Brynla scream as she ran toward me. I was relieved; I thought maybe the dragon hit me with its snout, and I was mad at Brynla for running toward me instead of away to safety like she should have.

But then I couldn't breathe and all I could taste was blood.

And Brynla's face, still beautiful even when twisted in horror, was the last thing I saw before everything went white.

Blinding white. Pure white.

And then I felt nothing.

And there was nothing.

It was peaceful and it was wrong.

It felt like centuries passed while I was in this white, wrong place. I grew old, died, and was born again. And still it was wrong.

Until finally the light started to fade, shrinking into darkness.

The dark ceiling of a cave, illuminated by a faint orange glow that doesn't flicker like a torch but moves like liquid.

And now Brynla's face is peering over mine. She looks like a ghost.

Her skin pale, eyes puffy and red as tears stream down her dirty cheeks.

"Why are you crying, lavender girl?" I ask, my voice sounding hoarse.

She just shakes her head and says, "I love you."

I don't know where I am or what's happened but that doesn't even matter because she just told me that she loves me.

Brynla loves me.

Me.

"Even though I absolutely don't deserve your love?" I ask her, and though I'm trying to come across as joking, there's a bite in my tone. Because I've never believed it. Not since my mother died have I ever believed that anyone would willingly open their heart to someone who makes a mess of everything.

"You deserve the world, Andor." She leans in and kisses me softly.

I quickly reach up and grab her face, kissing her in return before I pull back. "And you deserve more," I murmur against her lips. "And while my love might not matter in the grand scheme of things, I love you too. I think I did from the moment I first laid eyes on you. Should have figured a thief would steal my heart from under me."

She laughs at that, which makes Lemi bark.

"Lemi," I say, slowly sitting up to look at him.

But he's not all I see.

"What the fuck?" I cry out.

Not only is there a blue, two-headed dragon in this cave with us, but there's also a pool of lava and a lady made of lava standing right beside Lemi, her hardened palm over Lemi's head.

Lemi wags his tail and bolts over to me, licking me up the side of the face, but I can't help but stare at the lava lady in horror. "What the fuck is going on? Who is that?" I glance again at the dragon. "Is that a slangedrage? Oh my goddesses, Brynla, this is just like the vision you had with the Truthmaster, isn't it?"

"There's a lot to explain," Brynla says, placing her hands on my chest to steady me. "You need to take it easy. You died."

"I what?" I yelp. "I died?"

She nods solemnly. "The deathdrage nearly bit you in half. You died almost instantly. I stayed with you, I couldn't let go, until this dragon showed up and took you from me. Took you in here, where my mother told me that she could bring you back to life."

I shake my head, trying to get my thoughts straight but it's fucking impossible. "Your mother? Your *mother*?" I look at the lava lady. "That lava lady is your mother?"

"Voldansa is what I go by now," the lava lady says in a faraway voice. "But now that you're alive and awake, I have time to explain."

"Now that I'm alive?" I repeat.

"It's a lot, I know," Brynla says to me, rubbing her hand down my back. "I'm still not sure of anything except that you're here and you're back and that's all that matters."

I look at the lava lady. She would be quite attractive if it weren't for the, you know, magma. I can even see the resemblance to Brynla in her upturned nose and small chin.

The lady smiles. "You will know the truth when you hear it."

"But I don't understand," I say. "How are you a goddess?" I look at Brynla. "Does this mean you're a goddess?"

"Not quite, though she certainly seems like one, doesn't she?" her mother says. "I have the blood of Magni in me. I am a direct descendant, which makes Brynla a descendant. I had been told this, a rumor in our family, kept close to the heart because of the risk of it being blasphemous. But I felt it was true. I think the government did too. Once they were able to try my husband for our crimes, they were more than happy to sacrifice me to the dragons in some twist of fate. But I never knew what I was; the only proof I had was when I arrived at the Midlands with that ship full of bleating rockdeer. I watched as all of them were eaten and yet the dragons wouldn't eat me. They would sniff me, circle me, but they'd always walk away."

I glance at Brynla. She's sucking it all in like oxygen, her eyes hungry.

Her mother continues. "So I lived among them for a few moon cycles. I ate seaweed and crab. When the next ship came, I was tempted to sneak on and go back to Esland. But at that point, I knew there was a chance I could really die. My husband was dead, and my daughter I knew would be taken to the convent, though I had hope that my sister-in-law would pull her out like we had discussed one day, had the worst-case scenario happened. And at that point, the dragons started to bring me meat."

"And so how did this happen?" I ask, gesturing to her body.

"A volcano exploded, burying me in lava. I thought I was dying an agonizing death, burned and smothered alive, but I didn't die. Instead I emerged from the lava, just like you did, except I didn't revert to normal. I stay as part of the islands. Part of the earth. Part of my home. I became Voldansa, the unworshipped goddess, known by no one else but the dragons. Even the dragons have to worship someone, you know."

"So I'm related to Magni," Brynla says in awe.

"Wait, I saw a dragon in the dungeon at the convent," I say. "The Sister called it Magni. She thought it was the sorcerer."

"The Sisters are wrong," Voldansa says. "Magni is still alive, fueled by suen, his own magic, it's hard to say. He's out there but he is not in any dragon form. They believe what they want to believe."

"But where did they get that dragon from? It was bigger than any I've ever seen."

She gives me a small smile. "Not all dragons are kept behind the wards. Some of them were out in the realms when the wards went up. Those dragons eventually died off, but there are pockets of them still remaining. The ice caves in Sorland, for one. The volcanic vents of Vesland. There might be dragons on every continent, keeping hidden until the end of days."

"So there is an end of days," Brynla whispers, wringing her hands together.

"Not all prophecies come true for the same reasons," she says. "The wards will fall but there's only one group of people who are interested in making that happen. If you can't get the world to follow your beliefs, then you can create something that will."

"And when is this happening?" I ask.

"I don't have the gift of sight, I'm sorry. But I'm sure someone out there does, thanks to suen."

"Well, it's not me, since suen has never worked on me," Brynla grumbles.

"And it never will," her mother says. "It doesn't work in your system because you have the blood of dragon in you."

"But Magni is a man," she says, though the truth seems to widen her eyes.

"Magni was a man at some point, but he was always a sorcerer. The Midlands changed him in ways I still don't understand."

"Wait, does that mean Brynla's blood might act like suen does?"

"Don't get any ideas," Brynla says, glaring at me. Then she clears her throat. "So the egg of immortality would never work on me, would it?"

Her mother stares at her for a moment before exchanging a look of some kind with the two-headed dragon. "The egg of immortality is something that should never fall into human hands, or the world will end a lot faster than the prophecy predicts." Her voice is grave, heavy, and she's staring right at me with burning white eyes. "That kind of power corrupts even the purest souls."

Brynla clears her throat. "I'm glad you've said that. Because something has been weighing on me. You see . . ."

"Brynla," I warn her.

"We just stole the egg of immortality from the Harbringer. We broke into the convent."

Her mother doesn't say anything for a moment, just stares at her. Then she nods. "I am grateful you did that, for the egg was part of their plan. Make their citizens, or at least their officials, immortal, so when the wards fall, no dragon can hurt them."

Brynla looks relieved.

"Of course, the egg must now be destroyed," her mother adds.

"The egg is with Steiner," I tell her. "With my brother, back on the ship. It's going to be hard to get it back from them at this point."

"No," Brynla says, a sheepish look on her face. "It's not." She reaches into one of the side pouches at her hips and pulls out the egg of immortality. The squashed, broken egg of immortality, yolk dripping from it.

I stare at it, stunned.

"I'm sorry," she says. "I couldn't let Steiner hold on to it. I stole it when he wasn't looking. I don't think anyone in your family is impartial enough for this."

"You were planning to get rid of it?" I ask, feeling a twinge of betrayal.

She shakes her head. "No. I just wanted to keep it safe. I felt like it was my responsibility; I couldn't even explain it . . ." She trails off and looks at her mother. "I guess now I can explain it, though." She glances back at me. "I was going to tell you," she says. "But things started happening right away. "I didn't trust it on that ship. Your brother . . ."

I swallow hard, not wanting to hear what she's saying, and yet I believe it too. I've been watching Vidar closely this whole trip because of something my father had said. How if I wasn't going to get rid of Brynla, he'd find someone else to do it. But I keep that thought to myself. It's bad enough that I suspect Vidar was going to steal the egg from us at some point.

"Plus we don't know the people we rescued from the Daughters of Silence," she says quickly. "It was too much of a risk and deep down I don't even think Steiner can be that impartial. His brain gets too excited." She pauses, licking her lips and looking downtrodden. "Do you forgive me?"

"Of course I forgive you," I tell her. "You acted on your instincts, which are a lot more complicated than you could have known. Plus, you know, once a thief, always a thief."

I reach out and cup her face.

"It's a blessing," Voldansa says, her voice loud. "That this egg was crushed. Now we don't have to worry about it getting into the wrong hands, at least not for now."

"But I heard that there might be more eggs out there," I say. "Surely someone else is going to come across this power. The Harbinger herself couldn't die even when Lemi ate her face. I would assume the government of Esland has also taken the same."

"Perhaps, perhaps not," her mother says. "All you can control is what you have control of. If something else happens, then it will be dealt with, but believe me, you don't want to be the ones responsible for this kind of magic. Not all magic is good, and immortality belongs to the goddesses, not to humans. Or else the world would be a very different place indeed."

I exhale heavily. Feels like everything is a bust. I'll be heading back home with no precious egg, no fertilized egg, and a cargo full of Eslanders.

"You won't be going back empty-handed," Brynla says. "We'll gather eggs on the way back to the ship." She shoots a wary glance at her mother. "I hope you're okay with that."

"As long as you are," her mother says, walking back over to the

REALM of THIEVES 383

pool, her footprints turning into steam. "Ever since the wards have gone up, all the dragons have longed for is to be free. If you can grant them their freedom by breeding them on the other side, I don't see anything wrong with that." She waits a beat. "So long as you know what the risks are. Brynla might be able to tame them with time, perhaps as well as she has dear Lemi. But that is not a guarantee. And dragons know deep in their blood, passed down through generations, what the humans have done to them. They remember the collective trauma. If you breed these creatures . . . you best sleep with one eye open."

Brynla gets to her feet and reaches down, pulling me up. At first I want to brush her off, because I don't need the help, but suddenly I feel heavy. Terribly heavy, like my legs don't work anymore and my muscles have atrophied.

"What the fuck?" I swear for the millionth time today, leaning into Brynla.

"You just died, take it easy," she says, pressing her hand against my chest.

"He's noticing the effects," her mother says, looking me over. "It will take some getting used to, not being limitless."

I frown. "What are you talking about?"

And it's then that I notice I don't have great night vision like I did before.

"Some of it will linger," she says. "You'll still be stronger than the average man, faster too, perhaps smarter. But it will be nothing like it was before. That was the risk Brynla was willing to take."

I stare at Brynla for an explanation.

She gives me a wan smile. "In order to bring you back to life, she had to drain your healing suen from your body. I guess the other suen went with it, mostly anyway." She pauses. "Suen won't work on you going forward. You're as normal as I am."

I blink at her, slowly shaking my head. "You have dragon blood. You're not normal." Then the realization hits me in the heart. "I'm not going to be able to heal you."

"We'll find another solution," she says. "It was either this or leave you for dead. And I'm sorry, but I can put up with my pains, especially with help from Steiner's medicine, as long as I have you in my life."

"I am sure you will find a healer in good time," her mother says. "And speaking of time, you should return to your ship. I have a feeling that they'll come looking for you soon."

She steps back into the pool and Brynla runs over to the edge. "But wait," she says tearfully. "I don't want you to go."

"I won't be gone," she says as she starts to lower herself into the lava. "I'll always be here. Anytime you want to see me, to talk, I will be here. I hear your prayers too, you know, even the ones you don't realize you're saying."

"But I love you!" Brynla sobs, dropping to her knees beside the pool. "Mama."

"I love you, my darling," her mother says sweetly before she's fully submerged and all that's left is an empty pool.

Brynla cries and I crouch beside her, putting my arm around her. "Come on, let's get you away from the edge. You might have dragon blood, but I'm not about to test your resistance to fire." I pull her up to her feet and for the first time I feel the full weight of her.

I have to say, I kind of like it.

She's packed with muscle, she's solid, she's curvy, she's strong.

She keeps me anchored to her, my rock.

I pull her to me and kiss the top of her head, enveloping her in my arms.

"I guess I'm going to have to start calling you dragon girl now," I tease her. "I'm telling you, if you end up taming the Kolbecks' drag-ons, there will officially be nothing that you can't do."

She glances up at me. "Your father is still going to hate us for not having that egg."

"My father can go fuck himself, quite frankly," I tell her. "Come on. Let's go home."

Chapter 36

Andor

I'm used to disappointing people, especially when it comes to my family.

But when Brynla and I ran into Vidar, Kirney, and Belfaust's search party on our walk back from the slangedrage's cave, and I saw the look on my brother's face once I told him we'd lost the egg of immortality, it was like a knife to the fucking heart.

It didn't seem like he cared much that I had died. Literally died. Nearly chomped in half by a deathdrage before being brought back to life by an actual goddess—one who happens to be Brynla's mother and is made entirely out of lava. No, none of that seemed to matter to Vidar. All that mattered is that Brynla stole the egg and it got destroyed in the process, therefore negating their entire operation.

I have no right to judge Brynla. After all, I'd kept Princess Frida a secret, as well as the plan for the heist, so I suppose this makes us even. And I know now that the fates twisted our path. The egg was never meant to be ours.

I'm glad my father won't be able to use it. Though it would have given the Kolbecks, and the army of the Elgins, the royal house, the upper hand in the long game, we'd be playing with something we don't fully understand. I can't help but think about the Harbringer, the way that Brynla described Lemi tearing out her throat and eating her face and how she still managed to live after that, to chase after them. Will the Harbringer be forced to remain like that for eternity? Is there truly no way out?

But that's something we don't have to worry about anymore. Yes, there could be more eggs. There probably are. But right now, we have to let go of that dangerous dream and concentrate on the actual dangerous dream that's in our hands.

Before we ran into the search party, Brynla and I found the deathdrage's fertilized egg stored safely in my pouch that I'd dropped when the dragon attacked. We took the egg and the remaining vials of suen back with us, unsure if Steiner would be able to save the egg since it had been without it's mother's heat for so long. But once we got back to the boat and set sail, Steiner put the egg in the incubator, and we could see the faint pulse of its heartbeat under a special light; the dragon inside is still alive and growing.

Like I said, another dangerous dream. The idea that we'll be raising a deathdrage is utterly insane. Voldansa's words still ring in my head, even after the multiday journey home. That dragons remember what has been done to them.

This might be the best thing that could ever happen to House Kolbeck.

Or it could be the worst.

"Good luck, brother," Vidar whispers to me as we exit the carriage.

I step onto the wide path outside Stormglen, my home looking especially imposing today. I suppose there's a chance it may not be my home after my father finds out what happened. After all, the only reason I was able to blow off my engagement to Princess Frida was that I promised to get the egg of immortality instead.

And there's my father now, flanked by my uncle, stepping out of the gates. My father's tall, lanky body looking extra intimidating in his long black garb. He claps his hands together with gleeful anticipation, which only makes my heart sink like a stone.

Oh, I am so fucked.

"It's going to be all right," Brynla says softly as my father approaches, giving my hand a brief squeeze. "I'll take the fall."

"You will not," I practically hiss at her. "You don't say a damned word. Promise me that. Promise me."

I can tell she wants to defy me, but she pinches her mouth shut and nods.

"So, tell me, were you successful?" my father says, stopping in front of me. "Did you find the egg of immortality?"

"Yes," Vidar says, and I've never seen my father's eyes light up like that. "And no."

My father frowns, a scowl already twisting his lips. That didn't last long. "What do you mean, no?" he asks, his voice sharp and commanding.

"The heist was successful, thanks to Brynla," I say to him. "We broke into the convent and she retrieved the egg. However, it was broken while Brynla was trying to save my life. She did save my life."

I can feel Steiner staring at the back of my neck, and I silently plead for him to remain silent. He has such a hard time with lying, but we all decided that it was the best course of action with my father. I would take the blame for everything, but it would be an accident. We would tell him that the egg was destroyed while we were trying to escape. All of my crewmates agreed to this, as did the Freelanders unwittingly roped up in our affairs. Those Freelanders are now in Menheimr, attempting a fresh start at life, with Toombs and Kirney serving as their guides.

Vidar and Steiner were harder to convince, but I made it seem like my father would find a way to blame them both if the truth came out—that they let Brynla steal it from under their noses. Vidar was first to acquiesce. Steiner took more convincing thanks to his moral code, but once I pointed out that our father would probably have Brynla killed, he finally agreed.

"Broken?" my uncle says with a sneer. "And you didn't save any of the yolk?"

"They did," Steiner speaks up. I look at my brother in surprise. "They saved the yolk and brought it back to me. But when I tried to extract and refine it on the ship, it had already turned. I'm guessing the egg was so old it lost its value the moment it was exposed to air. Even if we had saved the egg, there was nothing I could have done."

Sweet, sweet Steiner. I've never been so relieved, or proud of him.

"I see," my father says. "Well, that's just terrible luck, isn't it?" His hawk eyes fix on me as he starts to stroll forward, hands clasped behind his back. "Especially for you, Andor. Without the egg of immortality, we have nothing to bind Norland's favor with Altus Dugrell. Nothing except you marrying Princess Frida."

Brynla stiffens beside me, and I reach out and grab her hand, making it obvious for my father.

"Which I still refuse to do," I say, squaring my shoulders, not letting him intimidate me anymore. "I will not marry Princess Frida."

"Because of her." He jerks his head to Brynla with a sneer, even though he refuses to look at her.

"Because of her," I say. "Because I am not a puppet on a string. I am your son and I have my own life and dreams, dreams you have tried to shame me for ever since my mother died. We are your family, your children, your flesh and blood. Does none of that mean anything to you? Is there not a heart inside your chest, one that wants to be a father, not a ruler? Can you not see that your disdain for your own offspring is the very thing that will break this family apart instead of bringing us together?"

My father continues to stare at me, unblinking, so motionless that

I wonder how I could have come from him when my heart is racing, my palms are sweating, and I feel the ground is about to swallow me whole. Everything inside me is messy and chaotic and real and he's just a statue with ice in his veins.

"Seize her," he says coldly, and before I can register what's happening, two guards come from behind my uncle and grab Brynla. She cries out, Vidar yells, and there's chaos.

Lemi barks and shifts out of the carriage in front of Brynla, about to attack, but she quickly tells him with her intense gaze and flick of her wrist to stay put, not wanting him to get hurt.

He listens, sitting on his haunches but growling wildly, and the distraction provides me with an opportunity.

I grab my father from behind, my dagger already out and pressed against his neck.

"Let Brynla go or I will end him," I command.

"Andor!" my uncle yells as he stumbles toward me. "Unhand him!"

"Stay back," I say. "I'll do it."

"You don't have the guts," my father sneers.

"I have more guts than you'll ever have," I tell him, pressing the dagger in deeper, enough that he gasps and I know I'm drawing blood.

"Andor, please," Vidar says, approaching me slowly with a show of his hands, as if I'm a wild horse. Perhaps I usually am, but even though my blood is whooshing in my head, my heart a frantic drum, I'm in complete control and thinking clearly.

"I will let him go," I say. "I won't hurt him any further. All he has to do is let Brynla go and promise that she is safe in this house, promise that he will never come after her. That he accepts that she is with me, the woman that I love, and there is no threat or disappointed look or hateful comment that would ever make me change my mind. I am not marrying the princess. I am choosing Brynla as mine, just as I will choose every other path in my life. Not for you, not for the syndikat, but for me." I swallow hard, meeting Brynla's watery, fearful eyes. "For her."

My father grunts, not saying anything.

I press the dagger in farther until he starts to squirm.

Everyone else is silent. Everyone is waiting for my father to yield. "All right, all right," he says. "Guards, let the woman go."

The guards immediately release Brynla and step back. She brings her ash-glass sword out of her sheath, holding it at her side as a warning, just in case.

But I keep hold of my father. "Promise me that she is free to live in our house, that you will send no harm to her, whether from you or your brother, or so help me goddesses, I will kill the both of you in your sleep."

"Fine, fine," he says.

"Promise!"

"I promise." He's practically begging. I don't think any of us have ever seen him like this.

So I let him go.

He stumbles away from me toward his brother, grabbing his bloody throat, which has only produced a trickle. "But you are no son of mine," he says.

I shrug, sliding my knife back into its holder. "And I bet that won't change a damn thing between us."

We stare at each other for a moment, hatred and animosity flowing between us. Though there is something else now in the air, something to complicate things. I think I might see a flicker of respect. Best not to dwell on it.

Steiner clears his throat from behind me. I turn around to see him reaching for the carriage door. "I suppose this is a good time to tell you that there is a consolation prize, Father."

He steps inside and brings out the giant deathdrage egg, barely able to lift it but handling it well all the same.

"What is that?" my father asks tiredly, his voice hoarse.

"A fertilized deathdrage egg," Steiner says. "Just like you asked. Although technically, you did ask for sycledrage eggs, but we had to make do."

"You brought a fertilized deathdrage egg?" my uncle spits out. He throws his arms out. "Where the fuck are we supposed to raise that giant thing once it's hatched?"

Steiner shrugs. "I'm sure we can figure that out."

I look to my father. He stares at the egg, his expression changing from discomfort and disappointment to that elated look again. Not as happy as when he thought he was going to become immortal, but close enough. He's probably picturing a forty-foot dragon with him as its rider, laying waste to soldiers in some war that's yet to come. If I really wanted to rub it in, I'd tell him that there is no way he'll ever be able to train it and that Brynla will be the only one who can, or at least the only one the dragon won't eat.

But because my father looks happy, deviously so, it means that the pressure is off me. I'm no longer his concern, nor is Brynla.

Chapter 37

Brynla
Three months later

"**Snowball fight?**" **Andor says to me from atop Onyx,** the horse dancing back and forth in anticipation.

"Only if you feel like losing again," I say, gripping the reins of Juniper, the white mare I ride. She belongs to Steiner technically, but since the youngest Kolbeck has no interest in riding, she's become mine by default.

Which is great, because she's a lot faster than Andor's horse.

He grins at me, his eyes crinkling at the corners, and I feel that flutter in my heart. How much I love this man. It should be a crime.

He knows it too. He uses his looks to disarm me.

"Hee-yah!" he cries out to Onyx, flapping the reins, and his horse takes off, galloping down the lane away from Stormglen.

He leaves me in a trail of dust and fallen leaves, but I only have to cluck to Juniper before she takes off like a bolt of lightning, her white mane flowing in the wind.

Lemi barks, joining in the chase, and he gallops beside me as we catch up to Andor just before we hit the main road. Once we go faster than he can run, he starts to shift and will merrily shift all the way up to Lake Efst.

Not that we've come back here since the original visit, summer having faded into shades of gold and bronze, autumn at our doorstep. A change in seasons is a new thing for me, since the only thing that changes in Esland is the path of the sun, and I'm soaking it up every chance I get. The first falling leaf from the mighty oaks outside the castle filled me with such delight, even though Solla lamented that it was a sign of the long winter ahead.

But winter isn't here yet. Even though there will always be snowfall in the mountains, Andor says we won't get snow at Stormglen for a couple of months. Until then I'm soaking in the long shadows and shimmering wheat fields and chilled nights that lend themselves to talking with hot pear cider by the hearth.

I've been keeping busy too. Andor and I have gone back to the Midlands twice, both to collect more suen and to visit my mother. Our talks are short—and strange, if I'm being honest. She's my mother and yet she's not anymore. But even just those brief sessions with her are enough to heal the hole inside my heart, knowing that she's not quite gone from my life. She's also been helpful with tips on how to raise the deathdrage, which should be hatching in, oh, about sixteen months. It turns out that the egg has a very long gestation period due to the dragon's size. But that's fine with everyone since we need the time to prepare for it. Well, fine for everyone but Torsten, who wants his damned dragon *now*. For what purpose, we aren't really sure. One dragon that will want to kill everyone but me doesn't really help the Kolbecks or the people of Norland. It's not as if anyone can ride the thing into a coming war.

Speaking of the patriarch, ever since we returned from the heist, Torsten has begrudgingly welcomed me into the family. I know he doesn't like me, I know he thinks I'm beneath him (though he thinks that of everyone), and Andor's uncle still goes out of his way to make me feel uncomfortable, but at least I've been accepted. They know I'm here to stay. Andor waxed poetic about me while he held his knife to his father's throat, something that would have been romantic if I hadn't been so afraid for our lives at the time. But other than publicly declaring his feelings for me in a fascinating display of courage and vulnerability, things haven't really progressed.

And I'm not complaining. I don't actually expect Andor to want to marry me. I'm an Eslander, a Freelander, and I don't know of any Norlander that has married into my people. We're either fanatical dragon worshippers or rebels, and neither of those things is an asset to either the Kolbecks or the royal family of Norland.

But still. Some nights we lie in bed together and I wonder how long I have. I love Andor with all my heart and I know he loves me. I know he has declared me to be his, that he has chosen me over his family. And yet I've never been in a relationship before. They've seemed so trivial when so much of my life was about survival, and I'm not sure of how one should go.

I suppose I should keep taking each day as it comes. Be grateful for what I have with Andor and ignore the fear in my heart that perhaps this is only for now and not forever.

So I push that feeling away and I surrender to the moment, galloping beneath the tall pines, their smell extra fragrant as a few fallen boughs pepper the path, chasing after my dark prince and his black horse. When the woodland path opens up into a field of shimmering wheat and tall white flowers, I urge Juniper onward, galloping until we're neck and neck with Andor.

I give him a saucy grin, the one that tells him I'm about to win this race, and his eyes flare in determination as he kicks at Onyx.

But it's no use. Juniper is at her top speed now and we soar past the heavier horse until we're in the lead.

I whoop and holler, twisting in my saddle enough to stick my tongue out at Andor, and then guide Juniper back into the forest, following the trail up the mountain. After a while we both slow down to give the horses a chance to catch their breath, but Andor starts getting closer again as we approach the glowfern tunnel and soon both of us are galloping through the darkness. The glowferns whiz past us like blue shooting stars, and I'm breathless and giddy by the time we stampede out of the tunnel and into the white world of Lake Efst.

The cold is a shock to my lungs, enough that I pull Juniper to a stop. She throws her head up, steam rising from her nostrils as she snorts, and I stare at the beauty in front of me, the wide expanse of glittering white snow, the light fog that showers us with sparkling flakes, the bright blue lake that seems to glow like a crystal.

And then Onyx races past me, all the way to the lake, before galloping back.

"I won," he announces, head held high. "The race was to the lake."

"What?" I cry out. "We never agreed on that!"

He shrugs, giving me a smug smile. "Those are the rules."

"You just made that up! You'll do anything to win!"

"Won you over, didn't I?" he says as he dismounts, the snow just past his ankles. He pats Onyx on the flank. "Now, how do you want to do this? I feel using our horses as shields is a little unfair."

My mouth drops. "You're the one who used your horse as a shield last time."

"But we both have horses now. That's no fun."

With a wicked glint in his eyes, he reaches into his pocket.

Then he reaches down into the snow with that same hand and starts to make a snowball.

"No," I say, starting to panic as I get my boots out of the stirrups. "No, that's not fair, wait until I get down."

But my dress is caught over the tip of my boots, making it harder to pull them out of the stirrups and dismount, so instead I'm squirming in the saddle.

And Andor has already shaped the snowball perfectly and holds it back, ready to fire.

"Andor, don't you dare!" I yell.

REALM of THIEVES 397

Too late. I attempt to duck but he anticipated that and the snowball hits me square in the middle of my forehead, the cold blast showering me with snow. It's while I'm noticing that despite the lack of suen in his body, he still has incredible aim, something heavy falls right onto the base of Juniper's neck.

I stare down, blinking hard at the sight. Snow has scattered across Juniper's mane, but nestled right in front of the saddle's pommel is something even more glittering.

It's a silver ring.

My heart pounds in my throat as I dare to glance at Andor, so afraid of getting ahead of myself, of what this ring could be.

But he's walking toward me, a grave yet anxious look wrinkling his brow, his eyes imploring as he stops at the side of the horse and goes down on one knee.

"Oh," I cry out softly, my chest tight, my breath stolen.

He nods at the ring. "I hope you like it."

As if in slow motion I reach out and pick it up. The ring is silver but there's a hint of gold in it, reflective and bright. The band is simple until it gets toward the stone, where it forms wavering branches and ferns, wrapping around the stone like a nest. And the stone itself is a light blue crystal, fully transparent, with a glow that seems to come from within, bathing the air around it with an azure tinge.

It's the most beautiful piece of jewelry I have ever seen.

"What is this?" I ask, my fingers trembling.

"It's a proposal, lavender girl," he says. I glance down at him and he stares up at me with so much hope in his gaze that my eyes immediately burn, my chest constricting until it feels like my heart has outgrown it. "Will you do me the honor of becoming my wife?"

I stare at the ring, at the surreal glow, then back at him. "Are you serious?"

I expect him to crack a joke about how he's always serious, but his expression remains intense and entirely focused on me. "More serious than I've ever been in my life. I love you, Brynla. And I want to be with you for the rest of my life. Whether that means at Stormglen or wherever our adventures take us, I want to be your husband. I want us to be a family."

I try to swallow the knot in my throat. "Even though I might not be able to have children?" I whisper.

"We don't need children to make a family," he says gravely. "You are my family and we are all we need. Now, please, my knee is getting very wet and very cold."

I let out a laugh, joy rising up through my body like a flock of doves. "Yes. Then yes, I will be your wife. I will marry you."

He breaks into the most beautiful smile and gets to his feet. He comes over to the side of the horse and reaches for my hand. He holds it and slips the ring over my finger. "Thank the goddesses it fits," he comments in relief. "I was a little worried there."

I pull my hand back to admire it. "What is it made of?" I ask, turning it around, watching the blue glow of the sparkling crystal.

"Diamonds, from Esland," he says to me. I look at him in surprise. "I wanted to give you something that reminded you of where you came from. So it would be a part of you always."

I shake my head. "Our diamonds don't glow like this."

"Ah, well that's from the cave right there," he says, nodding past me. "I took the glowferns to Steiner and asked him to make another cube but one that would ensure that it would never lose its glow. He was able to melt them down and amalgamate them in with the diamond. Turns out his latest hit of suen turned him into an alchemist."

"What can't he do?" I mutter, still admiring the ring.

"Well, he doesn't get to marry you, that's for sure," Andor says, a wicked gleam in his eyes. "Now come here and kiss me."

He reaches up and grabs me by the waist and hauls me off the horse. I giggle and kick at him, and though I know I'm heavier to him now than I once was, he still does it with ease.

Until I lean on him and we both collapse back into the snow.

"Will you yield?" I say to him, grinding my body on top of him.

"You're the one who just yielded to me," he says, and with a grunt, he flips me back so I'm pressed into the snow. "My fiancée."

Then he kisses me.

Deep, sweet, and full of joy.

A kiss full of hope.

The first kiss of the next chapter of our lives.

Epilogue

Vidar
A year later

 "Your future bride is here," my father says as he stands next to me, speaking out of the side of his mouth.

Dread floods my veins. Pure, cold dread.

I crack my knuckles, which prompts a *tsk* from my father. "Terrible habit, Vidar. Best you get it out of your system before the marriage. House Haugen is a family of manners. Better yet, get everything out of your system while you can."

"Fuck every hole in sight over the next six moons is what you're saying," I say bitterly, taking a sip of my drink. It's not strong enough. It's Andor's wedding; he can drink anyone under the table, and yet his drinks aren't fucking strong enough.

"Language, boy," my father chides, though there is amusement in his tone.

I'm staring into the distance, at Brynla in her lavender wedding gown that matches her hair, which is piled on top of her head in loops of various braid, as is customary in Norland. She's pressing her bouquet of wildflowers and ferns into the hair of any guests who want to be blessed with luck, though the line is mostly of women hoping to marry well.

REALM of THIEVES   401

Andor is off to the side with his friends Kirney and Toombs, having a laugh about something while they pass around a bottle of wine. Every now and then he looks over at Brynla and the elated look on his face should make me happy. I should be happy that my brother is so in love, so joyous that he gets to marry Brynla.

But I'm not happy.

Because once again Andor is allowed to do what he wants. And I have to marry Princess Liva of House Haugen, a woman I don't know and haven't even met. Haven't even seen.

It shouldn't have been this way.

But thanks to Andor, it is.

Even though I'm staring at them, I know my father is looking at *me*. I can feel his eyes burning. His hatred for me. His disappointment in his heir.

I glance at him, acknowledging his look. He doesn't even blink.

I know I have a long game to play here. I have something that he doesn't, that no one else does. If I have to marry into House Haugen, so be it. My father will be happy but I'll be the one with the card up my sleeve.

"It's a lovely wedding," I tell him, raising my glass.

I walk off, staying to the back of the party where the lawn fades into brush, the wildflowers brushing against the legs of my suit. It's being held in the Blomfields beside Stormglen. For months it's been transformed into a venue for the wedding, complete with stone altar and a newly built barn that can hold the feast for hundreds of people. At the moment, everyone is outside, drinking the free-flowing booze under the warm summer sun, celebrating the first marriage of the Kolbecks. Soon, I will be expected to marry Princess Liva here. Then Solla will have to marry someone. Then Steiner. All of us little ducks being sent out into the world, doing our role for the family.

I pause near the back of the crowd, scanning for my future bride.

She must have come with her family when I was wrapped up in the ceremony. Or perhaps I've been brooding and drinking too much to pay any close attention to the guests. I'm surprised that my father allowed Andor's crewmates and friends to join the festivities—goddess forbid they leach class from the event—but he's been in a surprisingly good mood. I thought he would have put up a fuss and prevented Andor from marrying Brynla, but I can see now that this is once again part of my father's political strategy. A high figure from Norland marrying a commoner from Esland, and a Freelander at that? How noble of him to look past class, how cunning to extend a hand to the Freelanders in order to spite the Saints of Fire. After our heist at the convent, we now know that the Eslanders are as much of a danger to us as the Dalgaards are.

I pause by the table lined with honeycakes and spot the Haugens near the entrance to the barn, all dressed in white, as they are always said to be.

There is Princess Odelle, the heiress, her sparse white gown adorned with lush flowers, flax, and palm fronds, symbols of the volcanic, tropical landscape of Vesland. She's staring across the wedding venue at Andor with a curled lip, and I can't blame her. She's the one that Andor was supposed to marry years ago, but Andor was caught sleeping with her handmaiden instead. After that, we assumed our chance with the house of Vesland was over, until my father pulled his puppet strings and betrothed me to Liva, the second in line, instead.

Then there is Queen Anahera with a coral crown on her head, the matriarch of House Haugen, flanked by her knights. The women rule the families in Vesland, and the Haugens are no exception. Not only does Anahera rule the land but the suen syndikat as well. She's an example of what my father aspires to for us: not only having the syndikat but holding royal power as well, for ultimate status and control.

Something I aim to make happen.

But first, I must marry Liva.

REALM of THIEVES   403

And there she is, standing to the side, talking with one of the Freelanders we'd rescued from the convent. She's giggling with her hand to her mouth, her bright blue eyes sparkling.

Something in my chest burns at the sight of her, like she's a shot of potent alcohol when I was expecting to drink water.

She's of short stature, and isn't thin by any means, though her voluptuous curves are showcased by her flowing white pleated gown. Her wavy hair is long, and a muted pinkish orange, the color of the coral flowers that grow on the reefs of the Crystal Islands. Freckles adorn her olive-toned face, sweet and beautiful and sensual all at once.

When she moves to place her hand on the Freelander's shoulder, letting out a raucous laugh, she steps more into view, and that's when I see what I've been wondering about. She has a staff she leans on for support and a leg that's covered to the knee in a silver cast. I've been told that her leg is intact but she needs the brace to correct her foot and get around with more ease. Something that suen would possibly correct, but I also have heard that the Haugens are selective about using it.

"So you're to be my wife," I say under my breath, picking up a honeycake and nibbling on it, so as not to seem like I'm outright leering. "I hope you know what you're getting into."

The elderly woman beside me looks up from her cake in elated surprise, perhaps thinking I'm talking to her, but once she realizes who I am, she gives me a quick, frightened nod and scurries away.

I have that effect on people.

And in time, my reputation will only get worse.

I think back to my chambers, to the drawer beside my bed, to the locked metal box inside that drawer.

To the vial of pale blue suen that lies inside it.

They never saw me extract it. Steiner had his back turned.

Back on the ship, when Brynla first handed the egg of immortality to Steiner, he put it away. When it was just the two of us in the room and he was occupied by preparing his incubator, I quickly extracted the suen from the egg, inserting the needle just below a scale, a shallow prick that only resulted in a quarter of a syringe, but perhaps that's enough.

It must be enough. That egg is now gone, squandered, supposedly, by Andor and Brynla, though I have my doubt it was destroyed. Part of me thinks they're lying, that they've already taken it, but of course it would be foolish of me to test the theory.

It doesn't matter anyway. Whether they have it or not, I do.

And the future will belong to me.

Acknowledgments

I'm going to level with you. Growing up, I never thought dragons were that cool. Instead, it was dinosaurs that had my heart (enough that I was convinced I was going to become a paleontologist—until I realized I would need to do some advanced math to get my degree). Even in my other romantasy series, Underworld Gods, I went so far as to say there were no such things as dragons in the Finnish underworld, something I regretted since it would have been really cool at some points to have a dragon show up.

But last summer, with a rewatch of *Game of Thrones* fresh on my mind, I decided maybe it was time for me to tackle dragons after all. Of course, I didn't want them to become tame, or to be pets, or be able to communicate one way or another. I wanted them like my beloved dinosaurs. I wanted them vicious, wild animals. I wanted them to be like the *T. rexes* or the *Velociraptors* from *Jurassic Park*. I wanted them to be ferocious beasts that the world would fear, with no hope of taming them.

And then I started to get realistic. Because if such beasts existed, there's no way that people would be able to live beside them peacefully.

ACKNOWLEDGMENTS

It would be more like *How to Tame Your Dragon* but with more blood. So I had to think of a way they could be controlled—or confined.

Again *Jurassic Park*—my favorite movie and one of my favorite books—reared its head, demanding I be inspired by it, *finally*.

So *Realm of Thieves* was born from that, as well as my desire to write a romantasy that went back to my roots writing cartel romance. I wanted that mafia-esque vibe, but with dragons. Add in some *Dune* vibes (the "spice" . . . no, not that kind) that subconsciously found their way into my work, and the book was up and running. Suddenly I was seeing Brynla, Lemi, Andor, all the Kolbecks, and the tangled family dynamics of Dragemor. I can't wait to share the rest of the books with you—but buckle up, it will get wild.

There are many people to thank with this book, starting with my agent, Taylor, for believing in this story even when it was just a vague "drugs 'n' dragons" idea, and the whole team at Root Literary, including Jasmine, Stacy, Alyssa, and Holly. Heather Baror and Alice Lawson. My editor, Sarah, for being so excited and passionate about this book, (plus her endless patience with the deadlines), as well as the entire team at Berkley, including Liz, Cindy, and Vikki Chu, who did the gorgeous cover.

I would also like to thank the authors who were kind enough to give me an early blurb (and they're also supercool, immensely talented people): Demi Winters and Kate Golden. I owe the both of you drinks, in Victoria and Los Angeles respectively. I'd like to thank Alicia MB for her input, Kathleen Tucker for putting up with me while I wrote this book WHILE ON OUR VACATION, Lauren for her tireless work with this book (at the time I write this, you have no idea lol), Laura, Sandra, Anna, Ali, Gianna, Jay, Stephanie, Michelle, Kelly, Alexa, Lucy, the Lilleys, Renee, and all my friends and readers who have offered support and encouragement. I can't do this without you!

Last but not least, Scott and Perry. I was already behind on my deadline by a couple of months when Scott and I decided to adopt a

ACKNOWLEDGMENTS 407

puppy, and while Perry threw our lives into complete turmoil (*who would have thought a puppy would interfere with my writing schedule?*) she's turned out to be the sweetest, happiest dog. And Scott, for those days when you bravely took on puppy duty so I could finish this book, I owe you a million! I love the hell out of you!

Photo courtesy of the author

Karina Halle is a screenwriter, a former music and travel journalist, and the *New York Times* bestselling author of *Realm of Thieves*, *River of Shadows*, and *The Royals Next Door*, as well as eighty other romances across all sub-genres, ranging from spicy rom-coms to gothic horror and dark fantasy. Needless to say, whatever you're into, she's probably written an HEA for it. When she's not traveling, she, her husband, and their pup Perry, split their time between a possibly haunted 120 year-old house in Victoria, BC, and their not-haunted condo in sunny Los Angeles.

VISIT KARINA HALLE ONLINE

AuthorKarinaHalle.com
AuthorKarinaHalle
AuthorHalle
AuthorKarinaHalle.Bsky.Social

Ready to find
your next great read?

Let us help.

Visit prh.com/nextread

Penguin
Random
House